VOYAGE

OF THE

ECLIPSE

VOYAGE

OF THE

ECLIPSE

A novel by

Erik T. Hirschmann

〰️ Epicenter Press

Kenmore, WA

⌁⌁⌁Epicenter Press

6524 NE 181st St., Suite 2, Kenmore, WA 98028

Epicenter Press is a regional press publishing nonfiction
books about the arts, history, environment, and diverse cultures
and lifestyles of Alaska and the Pacific Northwest.
For more information, visit www.EpicenterPress.com

Cover and interior design by Scott Book & Melissa Vail Coffman

ISBN: 978-1-684920-51-8 (Trade Paperback)

ISBN: 978-1-684920-52-5 (Ebook)

Printed in the United States of America

To my daughter HollyDale,
Alaska girl and lover of good books.

ONE

NORTH ATLANTIC OCEAN,
EARLY NOVEMBER 1801

BOUND FOR DISTANT ALASKAN WATERS, the American fur trader *Eclipse* tacked south by southeast through veils of thick mists and snow flurries, pursued by H.M.S. *Leopard* and her twenty-two guns. Second Mate Joshua Hall descended the aft mast with his small spyglass. Captain Jonathan Fletcher, First Mate Micah Triplett and the other eight *Eclipse* sailors remained silent in anticipation of the eighteen-year-old's report.

"Sirs, I spotted her masts above the fogs. Full sails. She's within a thousand yards, her firing range in all likelihood."

Light snow fell on Hall's grey woolen cap and blue jacket. He compressed his spyglass and brushed long strands of yellow hair from his face. Small flocks of shearwaters cried out and darted along the starboard side, their white undersides visible under dark narrow wings. Twenty-year-old Micah kicked a small deck bench over.

"Just two days out of Boston and the damned British admiralty is impressing us into their war against Napoleon."

Captain Fletcher lit fresh tobacco in a black pipe. The twenty-five-year-old veteran officer knew hesitation and panic were lethal to a young crew.

"The bloody bastards haven't caught us yet, Mr. Triplett. Dusk's less than an hour, and the weather's our ally. Mr. Folger, Mr. Harper, Mr.

Woods, arm our starboard guns. Mr. Clark, Mr. Lynch, Mr. O'Leary, arm the port guns. Tom, Thaddeus, Mr. Triplett, stand by for orders to adjust sails if needed."

Zach Lynch smiled.

"That's the spirit cap! You won't see me at heaven's gate if they board us!"

Hall and Triplett could not believe their ears. Triplett stood dumb-founded, his mouth agape as Hall spoke.

"With all respect cap, we're a small double-masted brig. That warship is more than twice our size with at least three times our guns."

"Don't second guess me, Mr. Hall. Your order is to go below and gather the custom house and Perkins Company documents into the designated folder. I need them secured in case we're boarded."

"Captain, I wasn't trying to second guess—

"Go below! And return to the helm as soon as you finish! That's an order!"

Lynch laughed.

"You're in over your head Hall. Boss Perkins never should've made ya an officer."

The twenty-two-year-old Irishman Dermot O'Leary, red faced, shot back.

"Shut the feck up! Thank Jaysus he's the officer and not yer sorry arse! Joshua had every right to break yer nose back in town after ya shoved that woman and her boy. I woulda busted yer nose twice if it'd been me self."

Lynch spat on O'Leary, who in turn launched his fist into the stocky twenty-one-year-old's face. Blood dripped from Lynch's nose and mouth as he swung back wildly and landed a right hook on O'Leary's left cheek. Triplett threw a bear hug around Lynch, but in adrenaline-fueled fury he broke free and inadvertently smashed an elbow into the first mate's temple. Triplett fell to the deck in writhing pain as Hall ran over and managed to grab O'Leary's arm and fling him away from the charging Lynch, who tripped over a toolbox and fell flat on the cold deck. Captain Fletcher kicked the thin layer of snow.

"Zach, Dermot, one more move and I'll label you Royal Navy deserters and hand you over to that Brit captain myself!"

Hall assisted Triplett up off the deck. The first mate grimaced and held his hand on the side of his head as anger simmered in his veins. *Damn Thomas Perkins for giving Fletcher command again! I should've been captain. I'm the one with prudence and patience!*

"Cap, if we escape you have to let Zach go. He's given Mr. Hall and I nothing but lip since we left Boston."

"Aw fuck off Micah!" Lynch protested. "Come on cap, I was on the '97 and '99 voyages with ya! You *know* me!"

Fletcher held his pipe at his waist and scratched his dark, days old beard. Snowflakes accumulated on his shoulder-length brown hair.

"This nonsense ends now. All of you have your orders. Mr. Hall, go below and secure the documents."

Hall turned to climb down the port hatch ladder and caught sight of a brown skua soaring over the bow. The large gull-like bird dove and attacked a slow shearwater, vanishing behind a thick snow flurry with its prey.

Below deck, Joshua lit a small whale oil lamp and grabbed a waterproof leather folder. Scattered over his cabin desk were charts, instructions from *Eclipse* owner Thomas Perkins, and U.S. citizenship papers for all eleven crew members. Hall first counted the documents sharing the title *Great Seal of the United States*, followed by an eagle symbol, ages, physical descriptions, affidavits, signatures, and the stamp *U.S. Customs House, Boston*. As he counted the documents, he noted the sailors Tom and Thaddeus shared the same custom house paper.

Mr. Thomas Perkins hereby certifies these two 17-year-old cousins, native Indians of the northwest coast of the American continent, have adopted the names Thaddeus and Tom and accepted United States citizenship. The two resided with Mr. Perkins in Boston as his guests from 1797 to 1801, and are now in the employ of his company.

Joshua slid the papers into the folder and turned his eyes to charts of Patagonia, the Hawaiian Islands, Northwest Coast, and China. Painful questions burned through his thoughts like a wildfire.

Will I ever see these places? Can I prove myself as an officer on this voyage? Will I even get the chance?

A cannon shot boomed outside, followed by a tremendous splash not far behind the stern of *Eclipse*.

A warning shot!

Hall's eyes raced over the charts and Perkins Company documents as shouting intensified above deck. Fletcher's deep voice penetrated the thick oak planks.

"Mr. Triplett, Tom, Thaddeus, pull the aft main sheets, we must make the thick cloud ahead on the port bow!"

Hall folded charts with handwritten notes by Perkins and Fletcher, financial documents, and intelligence reports on foreign merchants and sea captains. He slipped them into the leather folder and walked over to his sea chest in the corner to try and retrieve small treasures from home. Nicknamed a "Captain's Box" by Joshua's nieces, the chest was a gift from Tom and Thaddeus and had a thick cedar top with a carved raven of lined blocks of black and red. Stars, moons, and suns adorned the sides of the rectangular box.

Another cannon shot roared outside, mere yards from *Eclipse*.

"Mr. Hall, get your ass up here now!"

There was no time to open the chest.

"Shit!" Hall said to himself as he took off his blue coat and flung the strapped leather folder over his neck and right shoulder. He snatched the coat and put it back on as he scampered up the ladder.

Hall saw the outline of *Leopard* behind thick snow flurries. The British frigate was now within seven hundred yards. First Mate Triplett approached Captain Fletcher.

"Cap, the next shots won't be warnings. I say we take our chances with the custom house papers. I know the odds are long, but that Brit captain may let us go."

Fletcher pulled the helm hard to port, ignoring Triplett. The light eight knot wind pushed *Eclipse* deeper into a thick low cloud and sporadic but heavy flurries. Two orange flashes burst in the distance, followed seconds later by thunderous booms. The shots screamed over *Eclipse*, just yards from the ship's two masts.

O'Leary crouched beside his small cannon and adjusted a skull cap over his fire-colored hair.

"Those banshees just missed our rigging, sers. Another few yards and our mizzen sails would've been shredded."

Fletcher exhaled tobacco smoke through his nostrils.

"Mr. Hall, take the helm. Everyone quiet from now on, no loud voices."

Joshua scanned the deck as he held the course. Dejected, anxious eyes drifted towards him and the captain as the snowfall intensified. The light faded into the oncoming dusk, but every minute was agony.

"Cap," Joshua whispered, "what about furling our aft sails? Let the Brits pass us. She had all her sails when I spotted her."

"Too risky," Triplett countered. *Damn it, how long must I nurture and mentor Mr. Hall?* "We can't put our men in the rigging."

Fletcher brushed snow off his woolen black cap. Pipe smoke blew over the three officers as the captain spoke in a low tone.

"Mr. Triplett, Mr. Hall, have Lynch and O'Leary ascend the aft mast. This will atone for their latest insolence."

"Cap, that's a job for at least three or four men, they'll—

Triplett's hushed voice was silenced by another set of orange booms lighting up the fog to the left rear of *Eclipse*. An ear-piercing crack shattered an upper spar on the aft mast. *Leopard* closed fast on *Eclipse*.

"I'll go up with Lynch and O'Leary, cap," Joshua volunteered, "we can get those sails furled in five minutes or less."

"That's insane Joshua!" Triplett countered. "You'll get blown to bits up there!"

Fletcher removed his jacket and looked at Hall with approval.

"Permission granted. The documents please."

Hall handed the leather folder to Fletcher and motioned for O'Leary and Lynch to join him on the mast. Triplett protested.

"Cap, with respect, what the hell are you doing with the guns? We'll be blasted to kingdom come if we dare fire upon them."

"Patience, Mr. Triplett. Options need to remain open."

"Options? I want it noted in the log that I'm following these latest orders under duress."

Fletcher exhaled pipe smoke towards Triplett, and spat on the deck.

"Is that all, Mr. Triplett?"

"Yes."

"Very well, hold the helm, maintain our course."

The captain looked over his anxious crew.

"Take heart gentlemen, the darkness will be our refuge."

Two more thunderous cannon shots from *Leopard* shattered the air, with one ball severing a top gallant sail sheet mere yards above Dermot O'Leary and Joshua Hall.

"Mother Mary, Jaysus and Joseph."

"Focus on these anchor hitches Dermot and we'll be off this mast in another minute or two. Can't let these sails unfurl again in case more sheets and spars are hit."

Zach Lynch fastened the last sheets on the furled mizzen ten feet below Hall and O'Leary, and retreated down the mast to the deck. Hall climbed the rigging to inspect Lynch's work while O'Leary finished the final two anchor hitches.

"Goddamnit Zach, these are half-assed rolling hitches."

Lynch looked up with a sinister smile. He took advantage of Captain Fletcher's order of quiet and walked away.

O'Leary reached Hall over the furled mizzen. Another cannon shot screamed by them, its trail visible through the dense mists and flurries mere yards away.

"Oh, fer feck's sake. I swear, ser, I'll get that dirty bastard Lynch somehow."

"I'm reporting him to the cap. Let's just replace these two rolling hitches with anchor hitches. Then we get the hell off of here."

Another frantic half minute passed as Hall fought numb fingers to secure the final knot.

"Dermot, go ahead and descend, I've got this."

"Not on yer life, Mr. Hall. Here."

O'Leary, a sailor since age twelve, finished the last anchor hitch over Hall's shoulder. The two men scurried like spiders down the port side rigging to the deck. The snowfall intensified as a huge volley of six shots rang out, their reddish glows less than a hundred yards away but now far to the side of *Eclipse*.

The shots missed, they're passing us!

Hall strained to hold his excitement.

"Sirs, it's working. She's passed us and it's nearly pitch dark."

First Mate Triplett handed the helm to Joshua.

"Well done on the aft mast, Mr. Hall. Maintain this course. We should slip away from these Brit bastards soon enough. Cap, should I order the men off the guns?"

Fletcher signaled to Triplett to wait, and stared into the mists and flurries in the direction of the last shots of *Leopard*. An English voice amplified by a speaking horn called out over the sea.

"Captain and crew of *Eclipse*, you are ordered to surrender your vessel for inspection by His Majesty's Royal Navy!"

Fletcher stood rigid, his eyes unblinking like a predator.

"Mr. Hall, bring her a few degrees to starboard."

"Sir?"

"Follow my order, Mr. Hall."

Triplett's chest rose and fell as his breath's water vapor mixed with the thick snowfall.

"Jesus Christ, cap. We can escape. What the hell?"

"Steady your nerves, Micah. Order the men to prepare to fire off our port side on my signal. I don't want these bastards pursuing us again. We aim for their aft mast and rigging."

Fletcher held his left hand in the air. With winds decreased to five knots, *Eclipse* crawled over the sea in the thickening snows and dark fogs.

The English voice called out mere dozens of yards away as Triplett took position with the men beside the guns.

"Men of *Eclipse*, surrender for inspection! This is your final warning!"

Fletcher dropped his hand. The crew fired all eight guns and within seconds flames erupted in the sails and rigging above the stern of *Leopard*. Half the warship's aft mast cracked, groaned and fell like a tree sawed in a forest. *Eclipse* turned into the darkness in the opposite direction.

Fletcher took the helm from Hall and turned to his crew.

"That'll keep 'em busy! Well done boys!"

A collective cheer went up as Joshua scampered along the port side for a better view of the burning mast of *Leopard* in the distance. Triplett dodged around several skin boxes and tool crates on deck to stand beside the second mate.

"A goddamned British warship, Micah. Sir, pardon. I'm not sure whether to call the cap a madman or a genius."

Triplett removed his woolen cap to brush off accumulated snow.

"A master of reasoned lunacy. That's Jonathan Fletcher."

Hall folded his arms and sighed.

"Aye, sir. Lord knows what great trials await us over the horizons."

The red glow from *Leopard* faded behind frigid snows and fogs, and *Eclipse* ventured deeper into the oceanic wilderness.

TWO

NEAR THE EQUATOR, ATLANTIC OCEAN, NOVEMBER 1801

*E*CLIPSE CRAWLED OVER THE QUIET SEA in a faint breeze with all her sails fully unfurled from jibs over the bow to mizzens on the aft mast. The entire crew of eight sailors and three officers rested in the sails' shade under oppressive heat and humidity. Wearing only cotton shorts and a straw sun hat, and drinking often from a water cask, Joshua penned a detailed log entry.

November 19, 1801

Should pass into southern hemisphere in another day or two if current weak winds persist in the doldrums. Vast silence surrounds us over the flat ocean and only infrequent thunderstorms in the far distance break the monotony. To be expected, but all are anxious to escape the bondage of this stifling heat. Tom and Thaddeus are miserable, not knowing temperatures such as these at their northern latitude. O'Leary maintained his composure these last two weeks since one last confrontation on deck. Lynch less bombastic as well, but questions most orders before performing them. Captain still thinks highly of Lynch's skills and is reluctant to criticize him due to their long acquaintance from past voyages, but I think the cap's coming around to see this shallow man's true character. Unsettling though, how could the cap not see Lynch for what he is after two long voyages? Perhaps Lynch was different in the '90s. O'Leary has my back. Rest of crew also pleasant and supportive, most notably Nate Folger and Ben Harper. Perhaps the cap will let Lynch go soon and all of us can breathe easier. Had a dream last night. Was back at sister Laura's New Hampshire farm playing with little nieces, Grace and Margaret. Miss them terribly.

Twenty-eight-year-old Nathaniel Folger sat on the port railing and held his spyglass steady over his left eye. Cool beads of sweat trickled down the Bostonian's back over an array of circular and triangular Polynesian tattoos.

"Hey, cap, sirs, I see sails in the distance, port bow!"

Joshua set his log down and raised his spyglass towards the approaching ship of three masts that appeared twice as large as *Eclipse*.

"Probably a slaver from the Gold Coast," Fletcher mentioned casually as he sat up from a nap under the foremast. "Maintain our current course, Mr. Woods, a slow pass by and a shout out to the vessel's captain can't hurt us."

Joshua continued to hold his spyglass as he spoke.

"*Kreios Zephyros*, the vessel's name, I can just make it out now, captain. Greek for 'Master of the West Wind.'"

"Ah, a Newport, Rhode Island ship," Fletcher spoke in surprise, "makes runs to Savannah and Charleston. Mr. Clark, wake up Zach there beside the aft mast, I would like a word with him."

"Aye sir."

Eighteen-year-old Lavelle Clark proceeded to tap Lynch on the shoulder.

"Zach, get up, the cap wants a word with you. A ship approaches from the east."

Naked aside from a small loincloth, his myriad of tattoos from around the world glistening under sweat and sun, Lynch rose and walked toward Captain Fletcher. Joshua noticed Lynch was nervous despite being awake for only a minute.

"Mr. Lynch," Fletcher began as he continued to peer through his spyglass, "your continued insolence and defiance towards my junior officers and some of our crew has left me no choice but to hand you over to this oncoming Newport slaver."

"Cap please, no! I need this job! You can't do this!"

Hall glanced at Triplett across the deck. The first mate grinned and discretely held up his thumb as hope surged through Joshua. *The captain has come to his senses!* Hall strained to temper his excitement.

"Too late, Zach. Made up my mind. Ya should've listened to what I said a few days out of Boston. I'll write you a note of credit from the Perkins Company so you can fetch a ride on a coaster up to Boston from Charleston or Savannah. Now go below and get your belongings."

Lynch brushed sweat off his brow with his forearm and bent over for a moment, stressed and upset. Standing straight again, he rolled his tongue around his lips and glanced at other crew members. He let out a deep sigh before turning to Fletcher once more.

"Cap, I'll apologize to Mr. Hall and Mr. Triplett, even O'Leary! Right now! Just give me a chance, cap, I swear I'll make it up to you!"

The slaver drew closer and the *Eclipse* crew saw dozens of African slaves, mostly women and children, moving about on deck under the watch of heavily armed sailors standing beside small cannons. Joshua was shocked at the sight. He had seen slave ships before in the Atlantic and Indian Oceans, but never so close. His enthusiasm for Lynch's imminent departure was crushed by the repulsive scene now unfolding before his eyes.

"Go below, Mr. Lynch, and gather your things," Fletcher reiterated calmly, "that slaver will be upon us within a minute or two."

Lynch frowned before turning to a nearby hatch to descend below deck.

Kreios Zephyros approached within a hundred feet of *Eclipse* as Joshua wiped stinging sweat from around his eyes. Slavery disgusted him, but there was nothing he could do in the situation before him. His eyes locked on a young African boy staring into the blue ocean. Hall walked over to the port railing as the boy looked up and made eye contact for a moment. Sadness and longing encompassed the boy's expression and Hall looked away in torment like he had seen a ghost.

"Ahoy, officers and crew of *Kreios Zephyros*!" Captain Fletcher shouted over the few dozen yards of ocean separating the two vessels. "I'm Captain Jonathan Fletcher of Boston, bound for the Northwest Coast and Canton! We have a sailor we wish to hand over to you! The Perkins Brothers of Boston will compensate you for your troubles!"

"Captain Jedediah Paddock, delivering a cargo of slaves to Savannah, Georgia! For what reason does your man need transport?!"

"Pleased to acquaint with you, Captain Paddock! Our sailor, Zachary Lynch, has fallen ill with stomach pain and needs to return home to

Boston! If you will ready yourself to receive our skiff it would be most appreciated!"

Lynch appeared from the hatch with his belongings, but left them to go plead his case with Fletcher one last time.

Fletcher shouted, "One moment, Captain Paddock! Mr. Lynch has something to tell me!"

"Cap, listen to me, I swear to you there will be no more trouble. I'll apologize to the men! Give me a chance!"

Fletcher looked at Lynch and relished his complete power over the sailor. Milking the moment, Fletcher casually unscrewed the top of his water flask and drank deeply. After several seconds he exhaled in refreshment and took his time screwing the cap back on. He glanced at the slave ship to savor another moment of unbridled power.

"Very well then, Zach, you will remain on board."

Lynch's jaw dropped and morphed into a euphoric smile of near disbelief.

"Thank you, cap!"

"Captain Paddock, my man just informed me of his recovery and he wishes to remain on our voyage. I thank you for listening and safe travels!"

"And to you, Captain Fletcher, farewell!"

Lynch ran over to his belongings and went below deck as Dermot O'Leary angrily whispered in Micah Triplett's ear. Within moments the first mate protested Fletcher's sudden reversal on Lynch.

"With all respect, captain, why allow Mr. Lynch to remain?!"

"Mr. Triplett," Fletcher responded in a low tone as he sipped water, "I never intended to hand Mr. Lynch over to that vessel. He needed a good scaring, that's all. He's too good of a mariner to give up."

Incensed, Triplett called over to Joshua.

"Mr. Hall? Anything to tell the cap on Mr. Lynch?"

Hall spoke as he caught one last glimpse of the slaver sailing away to the north in the light breeze.

"The captain's made his decision, sir, but we'll hold Mr. Lynch to his promises of apology and cooperation. Mark my words."

Fletcher nodded with a slight grin.

O'Leary rubbed sweat from his brow, adding, "Oh, Jaysus above, save and deliver us from that bastard lurking below."

THREE

LEEWARD SIDE OF DECEIT ISLAND,
OFF CAPE HORN, SOUTH AMERICA,
LATE DECEMBER 1801

JOSHUA HALL SAT ALONE IN THE mess below deck, eating an early breakfast of biscuits, beans, salted pork, and coffee. A strong frigid gale howled outside over the anchored *Eclipse,* reminding Joshua that he and his crew would soon gamble their lives in the most violent seas on earth to reach the Pacific Ocean. Powerful gusts shrieked like demons over the deck, masts, and rigging from time to time to remind sailors of the great trial awaiting them in Drake Passage.

Joshua found his mind occupied by the slaver and the haunting memory of the young boy. He poked his fork into beans as he scolded himself.

Focus on Cape Horn goddamnit!

Lavelle Clark called from his small kitchen hearth as he pulled out a new sheet of baked biscuits.

"That nasty bitch outside still won't give up, Mr. Hall! It's been over a week now, stuck behind Deceit Island!"

"Aye Mr. Clark, just have to keep our patience. The gale will break soon to give us an opening over Drake Passage. We're near the peak of the Antarctic summer."

"Yeah, just rotten luck I guess."

Joshua set his coffee down, bit his lower lip, and stared into the candlelight. He opened his brown leather logbook to a side pouch of letters from home, and pulled a few marked "Elias" on their folded sides, one from *Eclipse* owner Thomas Perkins, the others from his retired sea captain father Joseph Hall. Joshua opened the Perkins letter to read for the first time in weeks.

John & Thomas Perkins Trading Company, Boston
September 30, 1801

Second Mate Joshua Hall,
   Congratulations on your first duty as a sea officer. I will expect nothing less than your finest abilities and tactful support of Captain Jonathan Fletcher and First Mate Micah Triplett in your upcoming voyage. In addition to acquiring a high volume of fur pelts on the northwest coast of our continent for the China trade, Eclipse will inquire into the disappearance of the Perkins Company vessel Panther and her crew of six in 1800, which of course was captained by your older brother Elias, age twenty-one at the time. As we discussed in my office with Captain Fletcher, First Mate Triplett, Tom, and Thaddeus, any number of misfortunes may have befallen Elias and his crew on the northwest coast, to include enslavement at the hands of Tlingit or Haida clan houses. Your brother and his crew may have, God forbid, perished on that treacherous shore, but I am of the firm conviction they are alive. Elias is a scholar, a master engineer, and an exceptional mariner. I pray, as you do, that he and his crew may be brought home.

Thomas Perkins

Joshua sipped coffee, scratched his neck, and sighed as he placed the letter back into his log and opened his father's instructions on Elias.

Joseph Hall, Salem
October 2, 1801

Dearest Joshua,
   I trust in you to bring Elias home if he is still alive. He has not spoken to me since he was seventeen, and only you fully understand him now. You know his wild passions. I fear the worst, short of death,

that he has succumbed to the unsound shadows of his mind in that distant wilderness. You are his shepherd in the desert, Joshua. Lead him back to the oasis of our home, family, and God.

Safe journeys on the far side of the world my son.

Your loving father,
Joseph

A powerful gust unleashed its fury over Deceit Island and rocked *Eclipse*. Joshua shuffled through more letters to locate old "Apprentice Reports" on Elias from former mentors, and moved a candle closer to read the faded ink. Bits and pieces of information originally meant for his father's eyes caught his attention. A New Hampshire minister concluded the fifteen-year-old Elias was brilliant but filled with "spiritual disorientation," while a Connecticut lawyer recorded Elias at age sixteen as having "formidable" intellectual ability but with "vicious irregularities" in behavior. The last mentor, a professor in Boston, reported an "incorrigible" Elias who was attracted to "seditious" poetry and religious teachings. Joshua noted his father's scribbled notes in the margins next to the professor's signature: *Get Elias out to sea. Contact Perkins brothers. August 1796.*

Joshua sipped more coffee. His thoughts swirled with emotions like the winds outside.

Mother died when Elias was fourteen, and father indulged him. The oldest son, vested with all of father's hopes and expectations. I'm just a damned errand boy sent to get Elias back.

Grasping a moment of self-pity, he hoped Elias was gone, lost. Then he would be relieved of the burden of finding his brother and bringing him home.

Joshua rolled his lips inward and closed his eyes. The image of the African slave boy drifted into distant and blurred memories of Elias.

Elias and I were close as young children. If I find him, maybe we can go back in spirit to those years and stay awhile. Perhaps that will get him home.

Zach Lynch entered the mess for his meal and, to the mild surprise of Hall and Clark, sat directly across the small table from Joshua. Lynch spoke as Clark brought over a plate of food and a mug of black coffee for him.

"Good morning, sir."

"Good morning, Mr. Lynch. Able to sleep much under these savage gales?"

"Oh yes, sir, no problem. If you remember, Mr. Hall, this'll be my fifth time. The cap knows Drake like the back of his hand and I've no worries."

"Glad to hear it, Mr. Lynch. This'll be my first time as you know, but I'm ready and eager, nothing like a dance between life and death to focus one's mind."

"Agreed, well said, sir."

Lynch scooped food into his mouth and sipped his coffee, his demeanor relaxed and expressions plain. For Hall, the moment was like a casual game of cards over low wagers, and he sensed there wasn't much to lose in speaking with Lynch. Besides, he welcomed the diversion away from tormented thoughts over Elias. Hall leaned back and took a bite of a hot biscuit as Lynch continued.

"Sir, my regrets again for our unfortunate encounter in port and those first days out of Boston. Since we're headin' into Drake soon, well, ya know, just wanted to offer reassurances of my respect and cooperation. What I said in my apologies up on the equator hasn't gone away."

Joshua set the biscuit down and nodded.

"Well, I appreciate that, Mr. Lynch. And I've noticed your hard work and respect since the equator. So again, you have my thanks."

"Aye sir, thanks for listenin' to me."

Hall stood up, grabbed a woolen hat and jacket, and walked a few feet to hand his plate to Clark. He placed his log in an inside coat pocket and turned to Lynch to speak one last time.

"My gratitude again, Zachary, I'll need all the help I can get in the coming days to be sure. Drake's a long, long way from Boston!"

Lynch set his mug down and nodded as Hall exited the mess and headed for a starboard side hatch ladder to climb on deck. A moment later Clark dropped a boiling pot of water near his hearth that knocked prepared plates of food to the floor.

"Ahhh! For fuck's sake, come on!"

Underneath Clark's colorful rantings and a clattering of pots, pans, and utensils, Lynch whispered to himself, "Boston's not as far away as you think, Hall, ya son of a bitch."

FOUR

Drake Passage, off Cape Horn, South America, January 1802

DERMOT O'LEARY KNEW THE SOUTHERN OCEAN offered no forgiveness as he gripped his lifeline and harness beside the aft mast waiting for orders to adjust sails. Gale-force westerlies screamed like haunted souls through the rigging above him, while a few miles to the east giant waves smashed into barren Deceit Island with savage fury. Battling her way west *Eclipse* faced oncoming sets of thirty-foot waves and troughs, punctuated every so often by a forty-foot monster, each a portal into a frigid hell that voraciously consumed men's courage.

As the woolen hood of his foul weather gear snapped over his face, O'Leary looked to the foremast, dozens of feet away, where Zach Lynch waited in turn for orders to adjust sails. Soaked by spray darting over the deck as he held his lifeline, Lynch found himself in the ship's most unenviable job as punishment for earlier weeks of jealous insolence towards Triplett and Hall. O'Leary had relished confronting Lynch again days after *Leopard*, so much so that he now found himself drenched with icy seawater while most of the crew remained snug and dry below. The only others on deck were Nate Folger and the three officers to face the Horn's wrath.

Captain Jonathan Fletcher screamed with all his might to Joshua Hall and Micah Triplett from the helm, the only volume that could be heard in the cauldron of wind and wave around them.

"Horn Island is within our grasp up ahead! We push on past it to the Pacific! We've delayed long enough under this tormenting bitch! Have Lynch, O'Leary, and Folger adjust our mainsail reefs, we just need another two or three knots of speed on our present tack!"

Triplett's mouth dropped in disbelief as he grabbed his hood. Frigid sea spray blasted between the two men. Hall, dumbfounded, stared at Fletcher for a few moments before responding.

"With all respect cap, I strongly urge you to withdraw back to the lee-ward side of Deceit Island! The weather's just as bad, if not worse than yesterday, and this gale is only getting stronger! The masts and their spars cannot take any more strain!"

"Cap, Mr. Hall is right! We risk our men's lives! I recommend a shelter further north, perhaps Isla Nueva beside Tierra Del Fuego!"

Fletcher's hood blew off, releasing his long, thick brown hair to flutter wildly over his shoulders and angry hazel eyes.

"Mr. Triplett, Mr. Hall, this whole damn voyage is a risk! We are in the peak of the Antarctic summer and I will not tolerate another several days' delay! Now, pass my orders on to the men!"

Triplett and Hall reluctantly rechecked their lifelines and harnesses tied in secure bowline and anchor hitch knots and headed out over the deck. *Eclipse* rose and fell violently in the massive waves and troughs, her timbers creaking in distressed agony. Hall saw the fear in Triplett, and after clawing their way to the closer aft mast in several prolonged, harrowing moments, Joshua seized the initiative.

"Sir, you can pass on the cap's orders to Folger and O'Leary and assist them in securing the aft mainsail sheets once they are let out a few yards! I'll continue on to the foremast to work with Mr. Lynch!"

Micah glanced at the aft mast a few feet away and recognized he didn't have to unfasten his lifeline. In a touch of guilt he blurted, "Joshua, your lifeline may be too short to reach the foremast, are you sure you want to trust . . ."

Joshua placed his hand on Triplett's shoulder. Hall's deep blue eyes possessed faith and confidence, reassuring Triplett.

"It's alright, sir! I can handle Mr. Lynch!"

"Aye, Mr. Hall! Godspeed!"

Joshua fought his way forward over the soaked deck, grasping any secure handhold. Zach Lynch stared down in cold smugness, secure in his own harness and lifeline about ten feet up the foremast. Hall drew within a few feet of the mast before a distant burst of light caught his eye. Brilliant sun beams illuminated the western horizon beyond Horn Island. The Pacific! Encouraged, Hall crouched and continued forward a few more feet, but his lifeline reached its limit a few yards from the foremast. He knelt down for better leverage, hand-signaling to Lynch in the ear-piercing gale to secure a free line and throw it down to him. Lynch obliged, but tied only a weak rolling hitch on the opposite side of the mast. He wanted to kill Joshua Hall and now was his chance.

Hall waited for *Eclipse* to clear yet another giant forty-foot wave before undoing his old lifeline. Rather than assist Hall up the mast, Lynch moved on to a lower spar to loosen and let out a mainsail sheet, having seen Triplett do the same with Folger and O'Leary at the aft mast. Joshua reached for the new line thrown to him by Lynch as the ship freefell into a deep trough. A sailor since he was fourteen, Hall tied a secure bowline in seconds despite numb fingers, and crouched and scurried the last few yards to the foremast. After climbing several feet to adjust another mainsail sheet, Hall looked eastward and saw only blackness. To turn back now would risk the ship almost as much as continuing west to the Pacific. Within moments Horn Island appeared behind swirling, angry clouds a few miles due north. To the west, the light grew brighter. *Eclipse* was on the verge of surpassing the last major stretch of turbulent ocean and Hall could see Fletcher grow confident at the helm.

A violent downdraft gale struck *Eclipse* without mercy, followed by a freak wave that swept over the front end of the ship.

"Williwaw!" Lynch screamed.

Sails ripped and his spar cracked, severing Lynch's lifeline and knocking him down to the railing where his legs touched the angry sea. Hall's line came loose as well, although it held long enough to prevent him from being washed to the railing. Stunned, Hall still managed to reach for Lynch, who in a wild panic grabbed hold of Joshua's forearm as a cold watery grave snapped at his lower body. Hall looked to the stern for help.

Dermot O'Leary raced over the deck in a crouch without his lifeline. Fletcher and Triplett barked orders but the words were lost to the williwaw's roar. O'Leary stumbled as *Eclipse* shot upward from a deep trough, while the suction of the sea pulled without mercy on Lynch's cold-numbed grip on Joshua's arm. Joshua fought with all his might, but he couldn't hold Lynch, who fell into the swirling white caps and failed to surface. Joshua turned to see O'Leary at the foremast secure a new lifeline and frantically prepare to throw it to Hall. A towering fifty-foot wave lifted *Eclipse* toward the sky as its white, foamy crest hovered over the deck. O'Leary tossed the line to Hall at the railing, who fastened it into his harness with a secure square knot. Hall screamed at O'Leary and pointed to the wave just as it broke over the deck. O'Leary clawed at the foremast, but the wave's violence knocked him over the deck towards the railing under a wall of water. Hall desperately reached for O'Leary, who coughed up seawater as he fell overboard. A detached wooden skin box followed O'Leary into the ocean. The Irishman grabbed the box and remained afloat for a few moments as he slipped behind the stern of *Eclipse*. Micah Triplett frantically threw a line to O'Leary, which landed within a foot of the sailor, but O'Leary could not grasp it in time as he was carried eastward in the boiling tempest. Triplett screamed to Captain Fletcher.

"Cap! We must turn her around to save Dermot!"

Fletcher shouted back at the first mate, pained, but unyielding.

"Another tack would endanger the entire vessel! Look at the waves, Micah! This williwaw bitch's wrath would kill us all!"

Tears poured from Triplett's eyes, red from sea spray and exhaustion as much as grief.

"Please sir, turn her around! We can save O'Leary!"

Fletcher stared at Triplett with unshakeable resolve.

"He's in God's hands now Mr. Triplett! Your order is to go forward and assist Mr. Hall! Do it now before we lose him as well!"

Triplett labored his way forward to Hall as Fletcher looked to the east behind the ship. The angry blackness of wind, wave, and cloud pouring forth from Horn Island obliterated any trace of Dermot O'Leary. Glancing back westward towards the Pacific, Fletcher observed widening rays of light puncture the dark clouds.

As *Eclipse* fought her way into the Pacific, the losses of Lynch and O'Leary loosened their grip on Fletcher's mind as he knew there would be new sailors for his ship. The great ocean before him was too immense for memories to survive long. His actions, he reasoned, would drift away like ghosts in deep shadows lost to time and space, and he would sail away from this voyage having fulfilled his most zealous ambitions.

FIVE

Juan Fernandez Islands,
400 miles off the Chilean coast,
South America, February 1802

"THERE'S CRUSOE'S ISLAND! I SEE IT behind the clouds!" Thaddeus shouted as he peered through a spyglass. "Here, sir, have a look!"

Joshua held the glass to his eye and grinned as Micah and Tom joined them near the bow.

"Almost a century since the marooned Alexander Selkirk walked those shores," Joshua quipped. "Looks beautiful and inviting, about eight miles long. Must've served those privateers well in the old days after raiding mainland ports and Spanish treasure ships."

Joshua handed the spyglass to Tom, who spoke as he raised it to his left eye.

"I read *Robinson Crusoe* not long before we left Boston. Oh, sirs, please insist that the cap let me ashore."

"Nothing to worry over, Tom, I'll see to it you make landfall," Joshua replied as he pulled out his log to make a brief entry. "Now's a good time to go below and wake the cap."

"I'll do it, sir," Thaddeus volunteered. He nodded to Tom and proceeded to the port hatch to go below deck.

Joshua noted Micah's rigid posture and strained expression as he stood beside him. Hall was puzzled since Thomas Perkins and Captain Fletcher both had mentioned the Juan Fernandez Islands as an alternative if the mainland offered no cost-effective options in securing provisions.

Micah folded his arms against his chest and sighed.

"Should've prevailed on the cap to accept those prices back on the mainland, goddamnit. Now we gotta deal with the cutthroats of Mas a Tierra Island. Riffraff sealers and whalers, Spanish convicts no different than pirates, shit, I'm volunteering for watch duty on board."

"Valparaiso, Concepcion, and Valdivia were all busts, sir," Joshua countered, "and the cap was right to refuse the outrageous prices demanded by Spanish imperial authorities and instead take the extra days to sail here. And don't forget the anti-contraband rantings of that obnoxious officer, Tomas O'Higgins, and his threats to seize our vessel."

"Agreed, Mr. Hall." Fletcher announced as he approached with Thaddeus alongside him. "No Spanish warships out here, Mr. Triplett, and the governor, Don Francisco de Quesada, is very reasonable after one offers a well-timed bribe. The extra sail days will be well worth our time."

"With respect, cap, that was in '99," Triplett countered, "and the Spaniards are fickle. Just look at how they've cracked down on the coastal trade."

"These islanders live far from Imperial Chile and Peru, Mr. Triplett. Quesada is not much different from the privateer captains who made Mas a Tierra their abode long ago. Now, make orders for arrival at Cumberland Bay and San Juan Bautista village."

Eclipse passed through low-lying clouds and sighted two ships anchored in the small bay, a British fur trader, *Centurion*, and an American sealing ship, *Batchelor's Delight*.

Fletcher spoke as he lit tobacco in a pipe.

"Ah, we just might get lucky, gentlemen, perhaps the newest member or two of our crew is on this island. Sure damn quiet compared to '99. Use to be all sorts of seals and sea lions along the shores and cliffs. Millions of 'em. Sealers must've made quick work. Chinese pay well for the pelts in Canton, plus the sandalwood from the mountains."

San Juan Bautista village appeared, tucked between lush forested hills and misty interior mountains dominated by a peak over three thousand feet high, "El Yunque." About fifty homes, a church, and a few buildings with straw roofs lined the shorefront, with a small road going up a hill into the interior. Several cannon fortifications rested above the settlement and the hills overlooking the bay. Hall estimated a population of three hundred people based upon the number of buildings and the adults and children wandering about. Several dozen American and British sailors were easily identified apart from the islanders by their dress and mannerisms, with a few engaged in stacking bales of fur seal pelts and crates of sandalwood and provisions. As *Eclipse* furled sails and dropped anchor, Hall noticed well over a hundred islanders and sailors gathered around a cockfight, cheering and shouting.

"Look Joshua, several man-made caves near the Spanish gun emplacements of Fort Santa Barbara," Triplett remarked. "That's where a few dozen convicts reside. I remember they were sent here after agitating for Chilean independence, but others were thieves and murderers, so be careful."

"A little Spanish Australia," Joshua chuckled, "but with all the children running about it must be somewhat civilized. Seems like a peaceful place. No one's manning those cannons."

"Looks can be deceiving Mr. Hall, just remember."

GRANTING TRIPLETT HIS REQUEST TO REMAIN ON WATCH, Captain Fletcher allowed the rest of the crew to go ashore. A rough, choppy, and cold ocean greeted the two skiffs, and after minutes of arduous rowing, the crew reached the shore and pulled their small boats over smooth, fist-sized black and grey rocks. Waiting for the crew were two Spanish men of average height in grey and dark red army officer uniforms, accompanied by two shoeless mestizo soldiers holding antiquated muskets. Captain Fletcher spoke in Spanish as his crew made their way over the rocks.

"El gobernador Don Francisco de Quesada, permitame presentarle mis marineros de *Eclipse*."

Quesada replied, "Buenas dias, Captain Fletcher, y bienvenidos otra vez a Isla Mas a Tierra. Allow me now to use English, captain, so all your crew can understand, as I am fluent now thanks to all your visiting countrymen these last three years."

"You are too kind, Governor Quesada, but I'm happy to speak in your—

"You and your crew will address me henceforth as Captain-Commander. And your presence on this island or on Mas a Fuera a hundred miles west is illegal. It's within my right under His Imperial Spanish Majesty's government to arrest all of you and seize your vessel. I have fifty soldiers, many cannons, and dozens of convicts to enforce His Majesty's will."

Hall and other crew members grew nervous, but Fletcher kept his poise as he replied.

"Captain-Commander, your excellency, on behalf of The Perkins

Company of Boston, our vessel is prepared to arrange an agreement for the right to procure provisions on His Majesty's Juan Fernandez Islands."

"Very well captain, Sergeant Castro will explain our new licensing system. Please note all fees and taxes are to be paid in advance."

Castro plainly recited Quesada's rules as if he were bored.

"Capitan Fletcher, a two-day license for gathering provisions in the mountains costs two hundred dollars. A separate license of three hundred dollars to acquire provisions in San Juan Bautista is mandatory, to include pelts and sandalwood. All winnings in card games and cockfights are taxed twenty-five percent, and any recovered pirate treasure is taxed forty percent. Digs for pirate treasure require a permit. The Captain-Commander hires out soldiers and convicts for treasure digs and sandalwood harvesting after a negotiated fee is paid in advance."

Joshua rolled his eyes and sighed in extreme disappointment, adding, "Captain Fletcher, these prices are almost as much as the mainland."

"Mr. Hall, I know what I'm doing."

Fletcher pulled out two hundred dollars cash from a leather shoulder case and handed it to Sergeant Castro, who duly recorded the transaction.

"Captain-Commander, Sergeant," Fletcher pronounced, "the two hundred dollars is for the two-day mountains procurement license. For now, I'll refrain from purchasing a town license. Perhaps in the near future we'll discuss some alternative, mutually beneficial arrangements."

Quesada nodded with a grin.

"A most agreeable proposition, capitan. Welcome to San Juan Bautista."

Fletcher turned to his crew.

"Mr. Harper, Mr. Woods, you'll come with me into the village. Mr. Hall, you'll lead Tom, Thaddeus, Mr. Clark, and Mr. Folger into the mountains to secure provisions. Plenty of goats, hogs, fruits, and vegetables for the taking, so get our money's worth, gentlemen. That will be all."

"Aye sir."

Hall turned to address his newly formed shore party. His heart beat out of his chest.

I must prove myself to the cap.

"Nate, Lavelle, grab the water flasks, knives, hatchets, muskets and powder from the skiffs. Tom, Thaddeus, the three of us will organize the gear on the backpacks."

The shore party went about preparations for their trek into the interior and Hall watched Fletcher, Harper, and Woods accompany the Spaniards towards the cockfighting arena at the opposite end of the village. Nate

Folger rested two muskets and bags of shot next to the growing pile of equipment before glancing at Fletcher's group in the distance.

"I know why the cap took Harper and Woods with him, sir."

Hall nodded for Nate to continue.

"When Ben Harper was a slave in Maryland, he presided over lots of cockfights for his owner. He knows the birds. And young Mr. Woods, well, as you've learned, sir, he's probably the best card player aboard *Eclipse*."

"Fuck, I know," Hall replied before biting his lower lip. "Let's just pray the cap keeps common sense as a companion and is reasonable."

"Agreed sir, but this ain't a reasonable world we live in."

SIX

HALL AND HIS FOUR-MAN PARTY HIKED with heavy packs high above San Juan Bautista through large meadows filled with wildflowers and cool misty woods of tree ferns and cabbage palms, with some as high as ninety feet.

"These must be the *luma* and *chonta* trees mentioned by Triplett and the cap," Hall remarked as he stared up the slender straight trunk of a *chonta* tree, its branches about twelve feet in length at the very top with four-foot-long leaves at only an inch broad.

"Look," Clark pointed, "there's the white cabbage and red berry clusters at the branches' base."

"We've hiked for nearly two hours, gentlemen, time for a rest. Nate, Lavelle, cut this *chonta*, the fruit'll provide a good meal. I'll help Tom and Thaddeus fetch water at the stream."

Joshua, Tom and Thaddeus rambled in the shade to the stream a few dozen yards away as Nate and Lavelle made quick work of the tree's narrow trunk with hatchets. A large, four-inch cinnamon-colored hummingbird darted alongside the three men and hovered every few seconds to their delight, its plumage sparkling in the slender patches of sunlight. The scent of thyme saturated the air as the three filled water caskets and drank. A white petrel darted over them for an instant high above the trees.

"This is the most delicious water I've ever tasted," Thaddeus remarked.

"Agreed," Hall replied as the three ambled back to Clark and Folger, who were already eating *chonta* cabbage and berries. The fresh fruit seemed like heaven to Clark after long, difficult weeks at sea.

"These clusters of berries must be five or six pounds, and so delicious. No wonder Alex Selkirk and all those pirates over the centuries thrived here," Clark marveled.

"Indeed Lavelle," Hall added after a large bite of cabbage. "Boss Perkins told me. The English privateer George Anson seized the treasure ship *Monte Carmelo* back in '41 and used this island as a base for raiding. Anson's crew returned to England as wealthy men. Led the Spaniards to colonize this place a few years later."

Folger rested against his pack, sipping water.

"And don't forget Captain Bartholomew Sharp in 1680, that Englishman hoarded Incan gold after sacking the ports of Peru and Chile. Heard in grog shops back home that he buried some of it here or on Mas a Fuera."

Clark's eyes opened wide. "Oh please, Mr. Hall, sir, can we look around the place the Spaniards call Puerto Ingles tonight after we get our provisions? I brought my spade!"

Joshua chuckled as he adjusted items in his backpack. The long hike and pleasant surroundings had shed the heaviest cares and burdens of sea.

"You're chasing some fanciful rumors, Mr. Clark, but yes, we can camp at Puerto Ingles tonight. Fifteen minutes, gentlemen."

STRONG BREEZES FROM THREE-THOUSAND-FOOT EL YUNQUE pressed hard on Hall's party as they made their way over treeless terrain of red and black grasses and shrubs.

"Good shots, Tom, Nate!" Joshua bellowed. "The two goats will provision us for some time at sea on top of all the wild turnips, peas, and carrots we've collected. Gotta get down to the woods fast to build a smoker for the meat."

Thaddeus pulled a small hand-sketched map of the island he made from a shipboard chart as Tom, Clark, and Folger started to skin the goats.

"Sir, looks as if we've arrived at El Mirador, Selkirk's lookout. Magnificent scene about us."

Lavelle Clark looked at Nate while Thaddeus handed his map to Hall and began butchering one of the goats.

"It's alright, Nate. Tom, Thaddeus, and I have this covered, just go sip some water with Mr. Hall and soak in the view."

"Appreciate that, Lavelle."

Nate stood up and walked a few paces to sit with Hall. Before them, the late afternoon sun drew out a myriad of yellow and green hues across the island that seemed suspended in air over an infinite blue ocean. White shreds of cloud from the summit blew past the two men, only to vanish above the distant forest.

"All this beauty makes me think of my late lovely wife, Mr. Hall, and all that might have been."

Hall nodded in empathy and placed his hand on Nate's shoulder, remaining silent as the two listened to the wind.

"WE MADE IT GENTLEMEN, PUERTO INGLES." Hall remarked by the campfire. "My gratitude to each of you for a job well done in hauling heavy packs over difficult terrain and getting the meat smoker and hearth built. Mr. Clark, although it's sunset, you're welcome to look around a bit for your Incan gold. Just be mindful of where you are, and keep an ear out."

"Aye, sir, it'll just be an hour or so. My curiosity's a dreadful itch, but I just need a little scratch."

Clark headed into the forest.

Hall's party settled in to a meal of goat meat and berries as several minutes passed over various stories of home, but soon Clark's distant shouts stopped all conversation.

"Stay away, goddamnit! Mr. Hall!"

Hall, Folger, Tom, and Thaddeus grabbed knives and muskets and ran towards Clark past tree ferns.

"Mr. Hall, Nate, somebody help me! Shit!"

The party arrived to see four large dogs surround Clark in complete silence.

"Go away!" Hall shouted. One dog lunged at Clark, but Folger fired a musket ball over the heads of the feral pack causing them to run away into a nearby ravine. The men ran over to watch the last of the dogs disappear into the thick greenery.

"Where the fuck did those dogs come from?!" Clark blurted.

Hall replied between heavy breaths, "Descended from mastiffs introduced by the Spaniards over a century ago, to try and diminish the livestock introduced by the privateers as food sources, Triplett told me. That's why we had to travel to high ground to get our meat."

"Hey, look at this over here!" Thaddeus shouted a few yards away.

Astonished, the men saw a pit about twenty feet deep and ten feet wide carefully concealed by branches, dirt, rocks, and fern leaves.

"A treasure pit! We found Sharp's Incan gold!" Clark triumphantly proclaimed.

"Hold on Lavelle," Hall cautioned. "Looks like a recent dig, and nothing but dirt in there."

"Oh, sir, please, let me grab a torch and bring my spade over. It's dark and there's no one around."

"That's what concerns me," Hall retorted, "and don't forget the dogs may come back. No, too risky. At first light you can return, Mr. Clark, assuming we're still alone then, but keep in mind we're breaking camp early to get back to the village."

"Aye, sir. I volunteer for first watch so I'm rested to rise early."

"Very well, Mr. Clark."

JOSHUA AWOKE TO THE SENSATION OF COLD STEEL pressed against his neck. A bearded man of about forty with a scar across one cheek stared at him with a sinister grin.

"Hola cabron. Soy Ramon, el asesino."

Over the next minute five more men arrived with knives and muskets pointed at Hall's party, who all awoke to their precarious predicament. Hall noticed whoever had been on watch fell asleep from the previous day's rigor. A barefoot mestizo man armed with multiple knives turned and shouted back down the main trail, "Mierda! Ladrones!"

"Lo siento," Hall said to Ramon as he held his palms open to show he held no weapons.

Nate Folger, also knowing some Spanish from past voyages, added to Hall's apology as a musket was held point blank against his cheek.

"Senor, tenemos la licencia de Quesada."

Clark, panicked as a musket was held to his face as well, blurted, "Shit, I don't know any Spanish!"

The mestizo man guarding Clark shouted angrily, "Vete a la mierda! El tesoro de Sharp esta aqui!"

Thaddeus blurted, "No me jodas, pendejos!"

Ramon took his eyes off Hall for an instant to glance at Thaddeus, allowing Hall to push him off and pull his own knife. Within seconds Hall was upon him and Ramon cried in fear, "Mierda! Lo siento!"

"Stop! Parate!"

A man with an English accent screamed to the Spaniards as he emerged from the woods with a few men in sailors' clothing. He continued, "I'm Captain Charles Stradling of *Centurion*! You men are near my licensed dig! Identify yourselves!"

"I'm Second Officer Joshua Hall of the American fur trader *Eclipse*, Captain Jonathan Fletcher, now call off these men! We're not treasure hunters!"

Stradling told his men to stand down in Spanish, and after backing off Hall's party, a few seemed disappointed that no fight had materialized.

"And just who are these men, Captain Stradling?" Joshua asked.

"Most of 'em are soldiers, a few are convicts hired out to me by Quesada for digging," Stradling answered as he grew impatient with Hall's party.

"I see," Joshua replied, astonished.

Stradling wiped sweat from his brow.

"Any relation to an Elias Hall?"

Hall's eyes froze on the English captain.

"Yes! I'm his younger brother! Do you have any news of him?"

"Only rumors from captains back in England. They told me Elias and his crew were ambushed and enslaved on the northwest coast by the natives, but that now he's won over his captors somehow."

Joshua folded his hands over his head in astonishment.

"Do you have any more information? Has *Panther* been seen at all?"

"Just a few other little rumors. 'Tis a shameful circumstance regarding your brother, Mr. Hall. Perhaps we can speak again later in San Juan Bautista. If you'll excuse us now, Mr. Hall, we'll be on our way to our treasure dig. For easy provisions let me recommend Pangal Bay, just over a large hill from the village to the east. Plenty of children there of various ages to assist you in gathering vegetables and catching cod and lobster."

"Thank you captain," Hall replied, exhaling deeply. "Everyone, we break camp for Pangal Bay after breakfast. Thaddeus, how the hell did you learn those foul Spanish words?"

"Overheard some boys fighting in the village, about twelve or thirteen years old."

Joshua shook his head as he watched Stradling and his heavily armed men prepare to enter the woods towards the dig site.

"Give my regards to Captain Sharp's ghost, Mr. Stradling, and see you back in town. We need to speak again," Hall quipped.

Stradling chuckled as he turned to leave, adding, "The privateers never really left this place, Mr. Hall, remember that. This island ignores time."

JOSHUA HALL AND NATE FOLGER WALKED ALONGSIDE a dozen island children ranging in age from six to fourteen through a meadow overlooking a cliff separating tiny Pangal Bay from San Juan Bautista. Every few minutes, the entourage halted to pick carrots and turnips from wild vegetable patches.

A nine-year-old girl shouted, "Mira! La pardela!"

For an instant, Joshua saw a small solitary grey bird burrow into the ground like a rabbit a few yards away, vanishing before the girl could catch the creature. Joshua nodded in acknowledgement to the child before turning to Nate.

"Probably an hour or so before Lavelle, Tom, and Thaddeus meet us with the skiffs at the bay's edge. Two older boys mentioned it's easy to catch codfish and lobsters right off the rocks near the bottom of a freshwater stream."

"Aye, sir. Look at the sun shine on these kids. Must say they're the most beautiful, delightful children I've ever seen, and so happy. If I were ever to have children, I would bring them to a place like this one, away from the over-civilized parts of our world with all their feverish traffics and frivolities," Nate commented with longing and sadness in his voice.

"Aye, I know what you're feelin'."

"Ya know Joshua, sir, ever since my wife and father passed around the same time not long ago, I've been stranded on an island of my own making. Just can't get off it, know what I mean?"

"Aye, we're all Selkirks from time to time, including myself. Never forget there's other shores out there waiting for you, Nate."

The two men and their youthful entourage made their way to the ocean along a cascading crystal-clear stream lined with ferns, and arrived at a deep pool encased in solid rock that tumbled into the sea in a ten-foot waterfall. The children swam and laughed, enticing Folger to sit at the edge of the pool and dip his legs in the water to relish fleeting moments of sunshine and companionship with the children. Joshua and two older boys sat and tossed fishing lines in for cod, while another boy threw a small lobster trap into the sea. Pulling in several cod and lobster over the next half hour, Joshua enjoyed peaceful contentment and the simple pleasures of his surroundings.

Elias is alive, I feel it.

Two skiffs slowly made their way through choppy whitecaps between Cumberland and Pangal Bays to the small waterfall emptying into the sea. Hall instantly recognized Tom and Lavelle Clark in one boat and Thaddeus and David Woods in the other as the skiffs passed rocks covered with Magellanic penguins and other seabirds.

"Mr. Hall!" Lavelle Clark shouted. "Make haste! Captain Fletcher is betting almost half our cargo on a cockfight in the village!"

SEVEN

Joshua Hall raced over the smooth shore rocks before taking San
Juan Bautista's dirt road to the cockfighting arena. Frantically moving
through two hundred boisterous islanders and sailors, he spotted Captain
Fletcher examining a bird with Ben Harper and an islander in his for-
ties. Unlike most other villagers this mestizo man wore shoes, well-tai-
lored clothes and a large sun hat with various cock feathers of red, green
and gold. On one side of the arena rested twenty bales of fur seal pelts
and twenty crates of prime cut sandalwood, and, to Joshua's disbelief and
shock, on the opposite side were stacked forty crates of *Eclipse* trade cargo
meant for Hawai'i and the Northwest Coast. A few of Quesada's soldiers
stood guard over the massive volume of wagered merchandise.

"Captain Fletcher, I demand to know what the hell is going on here!"

Calm and composed, Fletcher replied, "Mr. Hall, we're about to win for
ourselves thousands of dollars' worth of seal pelts and sandalwood from
the overconfident *Centurion* first mate, Billy Lee of Charleston, South
Carolina. Mr. Lee brought his own Carolina gamecocks and thinks no one
can beat his champion bird, 'General Sumter', the one he's holding now."

Hall looked at Lee, who grinned confidently several yards away, holding his large gamecock with a golden-feathered head. Clean shaven with
short dark hair, Lee appeared to be in his early thirties and about the same
height as Joshua.

The southerner tipped his sun hat to Joshua and shouted in a mild
drawl, "Mr. Hall, a pleasure to meet you. Pleased you arrived in time to
witness our wager!"

Ignoring Lee, Hall continued his protest to Fletcher.

"He's only first mate! Captain Stradling's in the hills treasure digging, I saw him not long ago! He has information on Elias!"

"Good, you can tell me later. Lee has Stradling's permission. Both men have wild passions for their sport, that's what brought the two together to command their mixed English-Yankee crew."

"Please sir, this is beyond reckless! If you lose, what will—

"Calm down, Mr. Hall, steady your nerves. Senor Ayala here and Captain-Commander Quesada confirm our bird, 'Butcher Boy', is the best on the island and has won many high-wagered contests. Lee doesn't know this fact."

Ben Harper, confident like Fletcher, tried to reassure Joshua.

"Mr. Hall, sir, I once did cockfights every year in Maryland when I was in bondage. This cinnamon-feathered fella is top of the line. He jumps like no other bird I've ever seen, and his sharp reflexes—

"Madness!" Joshua shouted at Harper and Fletcher. "All madness! I want it noted to Perkins that I protested this goddamned bird fight!"

"Won't be necessary, Mr. Hall," Fletcher countered. "Ben, Senor Ayala, say whatever you have to say to Butcher Boy." The *Eclipse* captain turned to Lee and the crowd, shouting, "Everyone feel alive?! Es hora de hacerlo!"

A roar went up among the growing crowd of over two hundred men, women, and children, many of whom exchanged items and coins in private bets. Sergeant Castro stood at the cockfighting circle's edge to officiate the fight to the death. After Harper made a few whispers to Butcher Boy, Ayala held the bird high and chanted a few words in Spanish lost to the crowd noise. Lee's golden-feathered General Sumter struggled to break free from his owner's grasp, already eager to attack as Ayala held Butcher Boy mere inches away to build aggression between the cocks. Hall glanced at Quesada's residence, a block up the hill from the village where the Captain-Commander remained sitting in a chair to watch the unfolding scene below him. Joshua got the impression he was waiting to greet someone, although for the moment Quesada's eyes seemed glued to the high stakes gamble about to unfold.

Sergeant Castro dropped his arm to commence the fight. Lee and Ayala launched their birds high into the air, their long rear feathers shining in the sun as they collided in combat on the descent. Hall at first could not bear to watch, but as he turned around he noticed that all the *Eclipse* crew excepting Triplett were fixated on the birds.

Folger shouted to Hall amid the excited crowd, "Sir, Mr. Triplett's like you, he can't bear to watch! He remains on board!"

"Well, shit," Joshua muttered in resignation. He forced himself to turn and watch the birds tear each other apart.

HALL WATCHED FLETCHER DOWN SEVERAL SIPS OF WHISKEY as the two gamecocks battled past five minutes. Gasps filled the air as Lee's General Sumter sliced open a wound on Butcher Boy.

"Fuck!" Fletcher screamed as he slammed his whiskey flask on the ground.

Joshua looked at his nervous crew before glancing over at smiling Billy Lee and his dozen sailors holding gambling notes in the air in anticipation of victory. General Sumter leapt for the kill and sliced another wound on Butcher Boy.

Fletcher turned and kicked his whiskey flask into the street before returning to watch the almost unbearable. Hall shook his head as Lee jumped up and down, ecstatic, ready to celebrate what was almost assuredly a victory. Fletcher glared at Ayala and Harper with an angry scowl.

Another agonizing minute passed with wounded Butcher Boy crouched in desperate defense. General Sumter jumped over two feet in the air, his golden feathers shining in glory as he descended for the final attack. All locked their eyes on what appeared to be the end for Butcher Boy, but at the last moment, the wounded cinnamon-feathered bird evaded his opponent's dive and ripped a gash on General Sumter's neck. Blood poured over his golden feathers and in seconds Lee's bird collapsed in death.

"Yes! Yes!" Fletcher shouted to the sky as he held both fists in the air. Ayala and Harper raced to tend to Butcher Boy, battered but alive. Hall bent over and exhaled in relief, while Lee and his crew stood still in shock.

One *Centurion* sailor moaned, "An entire week's work gone, goddamnit!"

Gleeful, Fletcher embraced David Woods, who had won a few bales of fur seal pelts in card games the previous evening.

Ayala and Harper carried Butcher Boy to Fletcher, who remarked, "Butcher Boy's a hero, well done."

"Aye, sir, he should make it. Never seen a gamecock take such a beatin', my goodness." Harper replied as Ayala nodded.

Joshua shook his head in amazement and noticed Governor Quesada leaving his residence with Captain Stradling. The two men met Sergeant Castro at the bottom of the hill to chat briefly before walking towards the cockfighting arena.

Unable to resist the temptation to gloat, Fletcher taunted Billy Lee.

"Well Billy, looks like you're on your way to being Carolina backcountry trash again. No more gentleman's residence in Charleston, you arrogant prancing fuck."

"You'll pay for that remark, Jonathan, mark my words. You best watch your back on the Northwest Coast. Captain Stradling will—"

"Captain-Commander Quesada has nullified the previous wager involving the vessels *Centurion* and *Eclipse*," Sergeant Castro interrupted as several armed soldiers and convicts joined Stradling and the Spanish officers. "We apologize for the oversight, Capitan Fletcher, but you did not purchase the required license to do business in San Juan Bautista."

"What?! This is outrageous Captain-Commander, I demand my winnings! We had an understanding!"

"Your recent payment did not involve obtaining the proper license, Senor Fletcher. The Captain-Commander designated the cash as a gratuity towards His Imperial Spanish Majesty," Castro replied.

Red in the face, Fletcher unleashed his fury at Captain Stradling.

"How much did you pay the Captain-Commander for this intrigue, you English bastard?! Or did you compensate him with more intimate means?!"

"How dare you insult me, my first officer, and the Captain-Commander!" Stradling replied with venom. "As a former officer of the Royal Navy, I demand a full restoration of honor! Captain-Commander Quesada, I challenge this filthy Boston Yankee to a duel!"

Joshua grabbed his captain's arm. He'd heard enough. Any more news on Elias was now lost.

"This is insanity, Captain Fletcher! Forget the goddamn wager, we've secured ourselves adequate provisions! Let's all just get the bloody hell off this island! Nate, take the crew and prepare the skiffs for departure, we—"

"No, Mr. Hall! Disregard that order, Nate," Fletcher demanded as he stared at Stradling and Quesada and spat towards them.

"You're on, you cocksucking son of a bitch!" Fletcher taunted Stradling before turning to address Quesada and Castro. "And after I kill him, I receive all my winnings and the remainder of his vessel's pelts and sandalwood, with no taxes paid."

"And if you die, Capitan Fletcher?" Quesada asked.

"Two-thirds of my vessel's cargo goes to you two schemers, but that's not gonna happen," Fletcher replied.

Hall sat with his face in his hands, stunned and exhausted by his captain's wild gambles. After a minute, he looked up to see the entire village and scores of sailors gathered to witness the deadly contest. Joshua closed his eyes again and prayed as Sergeant Castro announced the rules in English followed by Spanish. Fletcher and Stradling would get up to three hand musket shots apiece at forty paces away, and if both men still lived, swords could be drawn for a fight to the death.

EIGHT

CHARLES STRADLING WON THE COIN TOSS for the right to fire the first shot, and the two men held their loaded sidearms and walked twenty paces each before turning to face each other.

"Come on captain," Billy Lee shouted. "Finish him with a head shot!"

Stradling fired, but the musket ball passed a few inches over Fletcher's head. Hall and *Eclipse* crew members let out a cheer.

Ben Harper shouted, "Aim for his chest sir, wound him at least!"

Stradling took a big sip of whiskey and threw the cask to the side. Fletcher held his gun out and fired.

Stradling shrieked in pain as the ball tore through his left hip. Blood started to soak his white linen shirt.

Desperate, Billy Lee shouted, "Aim for his chest cap! Come on!"

The English sea captain's hand shook as he tried to aim at Fletcher. He fired and grazed Fletcher's right shoulder, but drew no blood.

Fletcher pointed his gun high in the air and slowly lowered it into position to taunt Stradling. He fired and hit the Englishman in his shooting arm. Stradling cried out in agony and dropped his firearm. He pulled his sword awkwardly with his left hand, prompting Sergeant Castro to shout, "Swords!"

Fletcher drew his sword and rushed at Stradling, who only poorly deflected the first blow. Fletcher spat in his face and ran Stradling through, killing him, before turning to address Billy Lee and his sailors.

"Congratulations, crew of *Centurion*, you now have an inbred backwoods bumpkin for a captain."

Fletcher pulled the sword from Stradling's body and tossed it at Lee, staining the new captain's shirt with blood as over three hundred villagers and sailors looked on in silence.

ECLIPSE WEIGHED ANCHOR AFTER THE LAST LOAD of Fletcher's winnings were delivered by two skiffs of Quesada's convicts and soldiers in rough whitecaps. Increasingly strong northerly winds blew over Cumberland Bay prompting Captain Fletcher to issue a new navigation order.

"Gentlemen, set a course due west after we clear the island, perhaps we can escape this oncoming storm. After we pass Mas a Fuera, we can turn north for Hawai'i."

"Aye, sir," Hall and Triplett replied simultaneously.

Fletcher noticed Sergeant Castro commanding one of the skiffs as they started rowing back towards the village.

"Hey Castro, chingate! Quesada es un hijo de puta!"

The convicts cheered Fletcher's insults directed towards the island's Spanish officers. Building on the convicts' enthusiasm, Fletcher continued, "Viva independencia! Viva Chile y Los Chilenos!" which, despite the loud winds and choppy whitecaps, brought even louder cries of approval from the prisoners as *Eclipse* departed for the open sea.

"THE INNOCENTS," MICAH TRIPLETT REMARKED IN HUSHED TONES to Joshua Hall, "the name of that tall peak on Mas a Fuera Island above the clouds. Looks like we're just gonna outrun the storm, we should give the order to turn north soon, thank God. O'ahu can't appear soon enough on our horizon."

Joshua stared at the island as *Eclipse* passed by, miles away from its coast.

"I feel a strange connection with Mas a Fuera, sir, even though I've never set foot on the island. Last bit of land before thousands of miles of ocean. 'Farther Away,' the Spaniards chose an apt name for the place."

"Aye, a place of isolation and solitude. You're more like the young Crusoe though, Mr. Hall, despite wrecks and disasters Crusoe's lust for the sea remained vast. I see that in you."

Joshua took a deep breath and sipped tea as he absorbed one last view of mysterious, distant Mas a Fuera.

"Would like to think so, thank you sir. I'm more concerned with Captain Fletcher though. I fear he's turning into a prisoner on the island of himself."

NINE

O'AHU, HAWAIIAN ISLANDS, MARCH 1802

JOSHUA MARVELED AT THE GREEN MOUNTAINOUS ISLAND in the distance and its surrounding glories as he drank in perfumed air offered from short bursts of gentle rain. White terns circled and darted over *Eclipse* as pods of porpoises raced alongside the ship. Brown noddies and boobies flew low over the blue sea and dove after food, only to have large and aggressive black frigate birds pirate away some of the hard-won catches.

Joshua smiled under a sail's shade as he finished sketching the wondrous scene around him in his log. He closed the leather-bound book, but did not tie it off with its small strap. He sighed and tied his yellow hair in a small bun. A few long, sun bleached strands remained loose to blow over his face, tanned and slightly burnt in places by weeks of intense sun. He bit his lower lip, and, after a moment's hesitation, opened the log again, this time to its front inside pouch holding a few letters from *Eclipse* owner Thomas Perkins. He pulled one out dated October 27, 1801, titled *CONFIDENTIAL: Second Officer Joshua Hall, Instructions for the Hawaiian Islands*, and unfolded the letter to read for the first time in months.

As you well know Mr. Hall, all young men have strong desires requiring management on long voyages such as this one. Since you have not been to the eastern Pacific, Joshua, let me inform you that the common Hawaiian women, wahines in their native tongue, are particularly open and forthright in accepting relations with our sailors, being ignorant of the teachings of Our Lord. Your winter layover at O'ahu is a good time, of course, to tactfully accommodate the ways of men and women. However, I strongly advise you to persuade the men, including the officers, to not take Hawai'i women on board Eclipse to the far north of the American continent. The wahines are excellent sailors, like the Hawaiian men, whom we frequently hire, but their complete lack of inhibitions and frequent distractive qualities disrupts business and weakens precautions on such a dangerous voyage as yours. In the past Mr. Fletcher has ignored this advice, but perhaps you can mitigate the circumstances by setting an example for the men as second officer.

The common wahines are quite shrewd and clever mind you, many see English-speaking officers from trading vessels as a means to win membership to the ranks of the ali'i, the high-ranking families of the islands. The ali'i covet and seek out willing officers to serve as interpreters, diplomats, and business partners.

Barefoot, his blue linen shirt and thick, brown hair blowing in the smooth trade winds, Micah sat beside Hall on the shady starboard railing.

"*Leahi*, the mountain sailors call Diamond Head, Mr. Hall. On the other side is Waikiki beach and Honolulu village. We'll anchor just beyond the reef. Hard to believe there's only nine of us on board. I don't miss Lynch one bit, but poor O'Leary, God rest his soul. Cap's gonna have to hire some islanders."

"Men, I assume."

Micah nervously laughed. His green eyes betrayed mischief. A few paces away beside the helm Captain Fletcher shouted orders to his excited crew scampering about the deck and rigging.

"Gentlemen! Make sure all valuables are locked below, including every last bit of iron and copper! Every nail we can spare is needed for the provisions we must procure on the island! Mr. Woods, come take the helm! Mr. Clark, inspect our anchor and landing skiff again. Mr. Folger and Mr. Harper, assist Tom and Thaddeus on securing the main sheets! I'm off to speak with Mr. Triplett and Mr. Hall!"

Eclipse rounded Diamond Head and approached Honolulu as Fletcher sat with his junior officers to review expectations for the coming layover. Hall noticed two outrigger canoes in the distance leave the beach with some islanders and head straight for the ship.

"Mr. Hall, Mr. Triplett, as we've reminded the men, they're entitled to leisure here on O'ahu, but all *kapu* must be respected. No eating with women, and no official trade with the commoners. Card games and exchanges of personal trinkets are fine, but all transactions involving our cargo fall under the monopoly of King Kamehameha. The Welshman, Isaac Davis, is his Chief *Ali'i* on this island."

Hall tried to ask a question on recruiting island men for the Northwest Coast, but Fletcher continued as the canoes approached *Eclipse.*

"One final point. Our night watch must be vigilant. These islanders are skilled swimmers and are like amphibians. I don't need to remind you, Mr. Triplett, of the copper and iron nails stolen when we were here in '99."

Wide eyed and excited like the other sailors, Triplett simply replied, "Aye, sir!"

Hall was astonished at the scene unfolding before him. Dozens of naked *wahines* jumped into the sea from the canoes and swarmed aboard *Eclipse,* their swaying breasts and wet curvy bodies glistening in the sun as they grabbed gifts and headed below deck with the young sailors. Overwhelmed with several women, Tom shouted to Joshua before heading below, "The Boston girls never acted like this!"

Hall resisted the temptation to run below deck and instead distributed a few sailor's shirts and hats to three wahines who surrounded him. One woman of about eighteen pulled at Joshua's arm aggressively, to the point where Hall thought she was fighting him as she screamed in Hawaiian. Triplett intervened, telling the woman in her native language to leave Hall alone. Undeterred, the woman called aboard a man of her age from one of the canoes and presented him to Joshua. The man took Joshua's hand and motioned to go below. Hall stared at Triplett with outrage and disbelief.

Micah crossed his hands several times in the air and shouted, "No! Boston kapu! Boston kapu!"

The Hawaiians puzzled over Joshua momentarily before leaving for another area on deck.

Triplett spoke in Hawaiian with two men on a small outrigger canoe beside the ship, where Joshua heard the names "Aolani" and "Alamea" anxiously repeated several times. Hall concluded the first mate was asking where the two women were on the island. It was the first time Joshua had heard the names and he shook his head in exasperation, realizing Triplett and Fletcher had clearly withheld information from him in their discussions of the Hawaiian Islands. As Joshua had anticipated after his meetings with Thomas Perkins, the task of maintaining an all-male crew for the Northwest Coast appeared almost impossible, but the boss in Boston held his future as a possible captain in his hands.

Joshua looked over the mayhem on deck and caught a glimpse of Captain Fletcher swigging rum and heading below with a wahine under each arm. Fixing a sun hat over his head, he realized he had to learn more about these islanders, and fast.

TEN

SOFT EVENING TRADE WINDS, TORCHLIGHTS, and groves of majestic koa and kukui trees created an almost magical ambiance for Hall. *Eclipse* sailors, and a few itinerant beachcombers long deserted from other ships mingled freely with the common people and shared stories, songs, and laughter over card games. Enchanted, Joshua shared sips of a calming, mildly narcotic island drink, *awa*, with Micah and a middle-aged Hawaiian man who offered to tattoo birds and celestial constellations on Hall's upper back, and recite a recent history of O'ahu. Joshua agreed, noting the man's beautiful tattoos of suns, fish, dogs, and two western names, "Thomas Jefferson" and "Caleb Evans" on his back and arms. Utilizing a small wooden rod, the man proceeded to lightly tap Hall's skin with sharpened bird bones attached to a handle. A liquid from burned kukui nuts and sugarcane juice was then inserted in the punctures.

Triplett translated for Joshua as Aolani arrived and embraced Micah, her arms and neck tattooed with the names "Micah Triplett" and "Eclipse," which in turn were surrounded by ornate images of turtles, birds, moons, and stars.

"By the way Joshua, your artist here says Kamehameha's planned invasion of Kaua'i has been postponed indefinitely, thank goodness. The King's fleet is at Lahaina, on Mau'i, and there are no plans to bring it to O'ahu."

"Very well, good news. Now, my history lesson on the ali'i."

"Yes, he says O'ahu was conquered twenty years ago by the King of Mau'i, Kahekili, who killed all the ali'i of O'ahu who opposed him. He built a 'House of Bones' to secure their *mana*, or power. Kahekili died in

'94, and control of O'ahu passed to his son, Kalanikupule, while Mau'i passed to Kahekili's brother Ka'eo. Ka'eo got greedy and tried to invade O'ahu, but was defeated. With King Kalanikupule weakened after fighting his uncle, King Kamehameha of Hawai'i invaded Mau'i and O'ahu in '95. Kamehameha's warriors surrounded Kalanikupule in the mountains at a place called the Nu'uanu Pali, where over four hundred O'ahu warriors fell to their deaths."

"And what happened to Kalanikupule?"

"He was captured months later and taken to Hawai'i, where he was sacrificed at a place called the Hill of the Whale. King Kamehameha and his Hawai'i ali'i hold strong mana. They have since ruled supreme over all lower ali'i and commoners of Mau'i and O'ahu."

Joshua grimaced as the artist tapped a bit harder and broke into song about the shape shifter *Kamapua'a*, who once made himself into a clever black noddy seabird and tricked a shark into freeing a drowned boy's soul. This clever noddy, Micah explained, was now on Joshua's back.

His senses dulled by awa as he lay on his chest with his head resting on tapa cloth, Hall remained silent and surrendered to the artist's hypnotic melody and the surf breaking on the beach in the near distance.

THE SUN'S RAYS BROKE THROUGH THE GROVES as Jonathan Fletcher arrived to wake his two officers. A few embers still remained in the firepit beside Joshua and Micah who slept soundly near a large kukui tree.

"Mr. Hall, Mr. Triplett, wake up! We have important business!"

His head pounding in pain, Joshua awoke, sat up, and ran his hand through his tangled sand-encrusted hair. Fletcher shouted again.

"Micah, get your ass up now! An ali'i approaches to take us to Mr. Davis's warehouse and *ahupua'a* lands inland, and I need your Hawaiian skills! Mr. Woods and Mr. Clark neglected their watch duties last night as we're missing some copper sheathing from our hull!"

His back aching from the new tattoos, Hall stood up and assisted the hungover Triplett in standing. As the three men walked inland past groves of koas and palms, Hall was struck by the scenes around him. Hawaiian commoners intensively worked taro patches, fish ponds, hog pens, as well as gardens of breadfruit, melons, and sweet potato. Joshua also noted some commoners lumbering bark and wood for tapa cloth, outrigger canoes, and small western-styled sailing vessels.

Fletcher jibed Joshua sarcastically, impatient and annoyed with the night's theft.

"Mr. Hall, I see you have some pretty new pictures on your back and shoulders. Charming birds and turtles under bright constellations, congratulations."

Fatigued and trying to get his bearings, Joshua simply stared at him.

"Aye, sir, thank you."

In the distance, a tall Hawaiian man approached the three New Englanders. Dressed in lavish tapa cloth and a yellow feathered hat, the man wore *pahoa*, iron daggers fixed with shark teeth, attached to his waist. Any commoner within sight of the ali'i instantly fell to the ground and remained still until he passed. Joshua was shocked to see the man scold and throw rocks at commoners who failed to prostrate themselves in time. Under Fletcher's order, Triplett asked the man in Hawaiian about the missing copper sheathing. Evasive in his answers, the ali'i added in English, "Davis tell you. He is a shark that travels on land."

The four men arrived at a grass hut and a large wooden warehouse filled with food and materials produced by the commoners' labors. A middle-aged white man adorned in Hawaiian tapa cloth and shell necklaces emerged from the hut.

"Ah, Captain Jonathan Fletcher, a delight to set eyes upon you once again. And what does your latest fur trading adventure have to offer His Majesty King Kamehameha? As you can see, my warehouse is well stocked with firewood, food, and salt from *Aliapa 'akai*."

"Plenty, but I want a discount. A kanaka or two stole some of our vessel's copper sheathing from our hull last night under the noses of our watch, who were distracted with their wahines. We can still sail of course, but it makes a brush with a shoal or reef more dangerous, especially up on the Northwest Coast."

"I understand completely, captain, and will refer the copper matter to the King himself on Mau'i. Perhaps when you return from your journey in the wild north I'll have an answer for you. For now, I can offer you the standard trade volumes for your iron and muskets."

Incensed, Fletcher scowled at the Welshman turned Hawaiian and closed his eyes, moving his hand over the top of his head. Triplett, sensitive to the captain's nature, hastily intervened.

"Great Ali'i Davis, with the captain's permission, I propose our crew assist your commoners in completing the small sailing vessels in your yards. We'll even perform some blacksmithing. In exchange for our labor, expertise, and the standard trade volume of iron and muskets, you will provide our vessel *Eclipse* with additional firewood and food, to include three choice hogs. And, a guarantee that our copper will be waiting for us upon our return here in a few months."

Fletcher's frown transformed into a smug smile as he nodded in approval. Davis rubbed his chin and chuckled in his response.

"Ah, Mr. Triplett, the clever one! Gentlemen of *Eclipse,* you have an agreement. His Majesty Kamehameha will be pleased to receive his new boats ahead of schedule, which, when combined with your muskets and powder, will hasten the downfall of the treacherous Kaumuali'i, King of Kaua'i."

Fletcher and Davis shook hands. The white ali'i then turned to Micah.

"Mr. Triplett, my fine young man. Perhaps you and your captain will join me as advisors and translators someday. And maybe this gentleman as well."

Hall nodded, replying, "Second Officer Joshua Hall, *Eclipse.*"

Micah tried to respond to Davis's statement, but Fletcher intervened emphatically as Hall turned to walk back towards the beach a few miles away.

"Only if our wahines, Aolani and Alamea, are granted title to ahupua'a lands with ample sandalwood groves. Then we'll talk."

Joshua froze in his footsteps to listen.

"These islands are more complicated than you imagine, Jonathan. Do not assume anything, especially when it comes to our women," Davis retorted.

SWEAT POURED OFF JOSHUA'S FACE AS HE ASSISTED two veteran Hawaiian sailors recruited to *Eclipse,* Liko and Kekoa, in bending and nailing planks to a small ship frame. Set back in a large palm grove, the modest boatyard was near Waikiki beach. As Joshua hoisted lumber and nails up to Liko, he noticed three American sailors drinking alcohol and lounging in the shade of a large palm tree extended over the beach. Hall recognized one of the men as Peter Bradley of Newport, Rhode Island, a young drifter who had jumped his ship months earlier and had, as far as Joshua could tell, engaged only in drinking, fornicating, and fighting. Joshua recalled Bradley's earlier drunken stupor when he had blurted,

"You're Elias Hall's brother? He leads a following of maroons up on that godforsaken coast. Lives like the savages and rants like a preacher, like he's lost his mind, some sailors tell me."

Joshua had pressed for more information, but Bradley took more sips from his jug, slurring, *"I told you what I know. Best leave it at that."*

Disgusted with much of the behavior displayed by the American sailors, including his own captain, Hall had volunteered to assist the Hawaiian commoners in hauling supplies between ship and shore when he was not working in the boatyard. While Micah Triplett and other *Eclipse* crew members worked shifts in the boatyards as well, none of them matched Joshua's work ethic.

Joshua drank deeply of the island's water from his flask and wiped more sweat from his forehead. At the edge of the beach beside the surf, Micah Triplett and two women jumped in a skiff to row out to *Eclipse*, laughing and speaking loudly above the waves. Joshua recognized one of the women as Aolani, but not the other.

"Liko, Kekoa, who is the other wahine in the skiff beside Aolani?"

Liko took a nail from his teeth and set down his hammer to drink from his water flask. He smiled and looked down at Joshua from atop the boat frame.

"That's my sister, Alamea. Fletcher's wahine, she journeys north with us. Don't worry, she and Aolani are very good sailors. They work hard."

Joshua sighed and stared for a few moments at the grassy ground strewn with bits of lumber and iron. Kekoa spoke from the opposite end of the boat frame a dozen yards away, first in Hawaiian to Liko, followed by English to Joshua.

"Joshua, you work hard like us commoners. We told Alamea we believe you may be a Hawaiian whose spirit after death sailed to America and returned in a foreigner's body."

Joshua laughed and sipped more water.

"And what did this woman, who I've never met, say in response?"

"After watching you from a distance and hearing stories about you from the sailors and Aolani, Alamea knows you have strong mana. You have strength of character and wisdom, and yet you are humble. So, regardless of whether an old islander resides within you or not, Joshua, we all believe you to be a Hawaiian," Liko replied.

ELEVEN

Off the coast of the Prince of Wales Archipelago, Southeast Alaska, late April 1802

JOSHUA HALL WALKED THE STARBOARD SIDE of *Eclipse*, his posture betraying anxious anticipation of the ship's first trade encounter and all its precautions and protocols.

First Mate Triplett spoke, his voice soft, as he made notes on charts.

"We'll be there soon enough, Mr. Hall, amidst the wildest of the wild, so try to enjoy your peace while it lasts as there will be plenty of opportunities for worry."

Combating his nervousness, Hall nodded to Triplett with a slight smile and visited each sailor on deck to monitor the ceaseless tasks of ship maintenance and repairs.

"Excellent job of caulking on deck, Mr. Harper."

His hands covered in a mix of sawdust and sticky material, Benjamin Harper looked up in appreciation from under a gray, woolen sailor cap, loose fitting brown linens, and a necklace holding a Christian cross.

"Thank you, sir."

Hall remained impressed with the crew assembled by Thomas Perkins and Captain Fletcher. At age twenty-four, Benjamin Harper was a tall, slender runaway slave from Maryland, whom Hall noticed was sharp witted, yet quiet. Working beside Harper was Lavelle Clark, a black haired, blue eyed eighteen-year-old who busied himself repairing a sail, though he actually served as the ship's cook. Hall thought the Rhode Island native to be an adventurous young man, having most likely taken the position in the galley in order to go to sea since Hall noted the frequent interventions by the O'ahu sailors, Liko and Kekoa, to improve shipboard cuisine.

Hall looked up at the two Hawaiian men hovering high on the aft mast and its spars as they made minor repairs to the rigging. Near the crow's nest at the top of the mast, the agile, muscular twenty-one-year-old Liko shouted as he lifted his sailor cap and let his long black hair catch the wind and spill down his shirtless back. Oblivious to the chill in the air, his bronzed skin shined in the sunlight.

"Hello, Mr. Joshua, sir! A grand day to spend with the birds!"

"Indeed, gentlemen! Keep up the fine work!"

A few feet from the mast was the ship's lead carpenter, Nathaniel Folger, the oldest of the *Eclipse* crew. His graying hair and weathered face, courtesy of many voyages at sea, made him seem older than his twenty-eight years. He was making additional "skin boxes" for storing pelts as he squinted in the sunlight, making the creases around his eyes more prominent. Hall was concerned with Folger's recurring depression over the recent deaths of his wife and father in the months before the voyage. He did his utmost to bolster Folger's spirits, but was hesitant to even consider mentioning his own recent broken relations with his sweetheart Anne, given Folger's loss of a spouse and parent.

Just across from Folger at the stern of the ship were Thaddeus and Tom. Hall remained impressed with the two young men since their first meeting in Boston, and enjoyed their sharp wits and unrelenting intellectual hunger. Having completed their maintenance duties, the two sipped tea and sat on a small portable bench reading and exchanging ideas.

Thaddeus glanced up at Joshua.

"Why so serious, boss?"

"Just nervous I guess."

The second mate sat on the deck against the railing next to the two seventeen-year-old cousins with dark coal eyes, shoulder length black hair, and light copper brown skin. Hall pulled out his log to rest on his right thigh and thumbed through the pages.

"Ah, here it is," Joshua began. "*Lingit aani*, the name you call the Northwest Coast, your homeland, correct?"

Tom began in an exotic, deliberately paced accent slower than the hurried New England dialect.

"You're right, sir. And Thaddeus and I are descended from the Raven lineage, our mothers are Ravens and our fathers are from the Wolf lineage. My clan house totem is Sea Lion. The Great Bear Constellation, *Yachte* in our tongue, 'The Big Dipper' as you call that set of stars, is the totem for Thaddeus' clan house. We are both Tlingit *aayatx'i*, of noble birth, from the *Taant'a* villages, or *kwaan*. Our village is *T'angaash*."

Thaddeus sipped tea, and looked over the deck of *Eclipse* with a grin as he spoke.

"And don't forget the great eagle of *e pluribus unum*, my Sea Lion cousin, the totem we share with Mr. Hall here!"

Hall laughed along with Tom and Thaddeus as he jotted a few notes in his log.

"Ah, just realized I need some numbers from Mr. Woods at the helm. Excuse me gentlemen."

Joshua rose and walked the few yards to the helm, manned by seventeen-year-old David Woods, a short, gregarious fellow who frequently centered his conversations on New England and O'ahu women, especially their anatomy. Hall perused his ragged leather-bound log as he sat a few feet from the young sailor.

"So, Mr. Woods, any estimates of the number of otter pelts and other furs we'll procure during our visit on this coast? The closest receives a modest amount of coin from my profit share."

"Ah, coin from ya primage, sir? Don't bet against the cap, Mr. Hall."

Woods scanned the decks for Captain Fletcher, who was below in his cabin.

Smiling, the redheaded sailor continued in his exceptionally thick Boston accent.

"Captain Fletcha may be a crusty sea dawg sometimes, but he knows wheh to go in the maze of islands and channels up on the coast. If this is indeed his last voyage, he won't hold back to gain a huge fur hawl to sell at Canton. Put my number down at 3,500."

"Very well, Mr. Woods. I admire your optimism. Your prediction is the highest yet," Hall replied as he wrote the number in his log. "If you're right, I'll double my coin reward gladly. You can even have a small bit of my privilege space below for storing some Chinese goods after we conclude trading pelts at Canton."

"Thanks aplenty, sir."

For several moments, only the familiar sounds of creaking timbers, a gentle wake, and the steady breeze filled Hall's ears as he stared down and recorded notes for his refereed contest.

A slight gust forced Woods to strain in keeping *Eclipse* on course. Hall was startled by the teenager's thick Boston tongue as it suddenly sliced through the air.

"Jaysus Gawd Almighty, would ya look at that wunda of creation over deh, Mr. Hall. Sir, that is, apologies. Port side hatch."

Hall fixed his gaze on Alamea, the beautiful young Hawaiian woman emerging from below deck, her long, black hair flowing in the steady breeze from the north as she climbed topside in a wool grey sweater belonging to Captain Fletcher. Her striking, deep-set eyes and high cheek bones were accompanied by a necklace of shells with a small wooden turtle pendant.

"Ah, send my sinnin' soul to hell now. Deh's the cap's wahine companion once again. She's glanced ya way a few times, sir, in case you haven't noticed. I wish she did the same to me, although the captain's a jealous one. I wish my wahine friend back on O'ahu had come north with me. Damn! I can't say I blame her though, not many want to leave the sun and warmth for the miserable, iron-bound coast up here. I'm surprised the island men, the kanakas up deh in the rigging, agree to work for us. Liko and Kekoa are good sailors though, as are Alamea and Aolani."

Hall tried unsuccessfully to avoid staring at Alamea.

"We'll be back at O'ahu soon enough after our adventures up here, Mr. Woods. I must confess I've been seduced by those islands."

Woods held a devilish grin.

"Indeed, sir, as they have with awl of us."

Nineteen-year-old Alamea looked at Hall with a smile as she stretched on deck and called out to her brother, Liko, as he was repairing one of the mainsails. Her easy manner and graceful movements seemed almost poetic to Hall, and he was forced to draw upon all his fortitude to resist the temptation to speak with her.

Woods breathed deeply and sighed.

"Just be careful deh with that lovely one. No one wants to be on the cap's bad side. Gawd, what I would give to see her, well, you know. Sorry. Makes me want to jump in the wada and swim back to O'ahu for my wahine."

Rolling his eyes, Hall ignored the last part of the remark.

"Anticipatory prudence. Yes, I understand Mr. Woods. Thank you."

Despite Hall's numerous efforts to discourage them, Triplett and Fletcher dismissed concerns over allowing Alamea and her cousin Aolani to sail with them from O'ahu to the Northwest Coast. Captain Fletcher had remarked with a mix of sarcasm and respect toward Hall when he protested.

You would have made a fine Puritan associate of Jonathan Winthrop in 1630s Boston, Mr. Hall! Your disciplined stance, however, has captured my truest admiration and wonder, Joshua. You have my word on that.

Hall remembered Micah Triplett's words a few days before they sailed northward, *Come on now, why don't you get yourself a wahine, Joshua? She might help you get over that girl who broke things off with you a while back. Hell, bring two of them! My girl Aolani is a pearl of a woman.*

Hall shook his head, smiling, as he recalled Triplett's mischievous expression and last sentence, *And a good cabin companion!*

Hall cringed when he thought of the inevitable arguments, fights, and jealousies to report to the Perkins office upon the ship's return to Boston. Laboring to forget the matter, he moved on and sat at the extreme rear of the ship, where he could hear the bubbling wake moving under the stern, blocking out most verbal exchanges on deck. After seemingly endless conversations with Captain Fletcher, First Mate Triplett, and a few other veteran crew members over the last several weeks, Hall welcomed one more chance to write before making landfall on the coast. Opening up the log, he noted his entry from a few days earlier.

Honor upheld on O'ahu, but a Pyrrhic victory in retrospect. The greatest trial rests before me now. Utmost fortitude and vigilance required. Must center on responsibilities to crew and owner Perkins. And brother Elias.

Loud laughs between Liko and Alamea interrupted Hall's thoughts and he glanced up once again. For an instant, Alamea looked upon Hall, not with a smile, but a mysterious look of confident reflection. She continued her conversation with Liko, frequently punctuated with laughter.

Scanning the masts and mainsails towards the fathomless blue sky, Joshua Hall clashed fiercely with the desires swirling inside him. *Obligation and duty, sustained by reason and faith,* he penned. He had to uphold his responsibilities, no matter the cost. Or could he?

Fighting his self-doubt, Joshua took a deep breath and closed his eyes. To his surprise, a memory of his two young nieces appeared before him vividly like a dream. The older sister, eight-year-old Grace, held the younger Margaret's hand as Joshua knelt before them under brightly colored autumn woods. Joshua's sea chest, given to him by Tom and Thaddeus weeks before the voyage, rested beside the feet of the two sisters, its front side presenting an ornately carved ship below a moon and stars. Margaret giggled as her uncle looked up to them while older sister, Grace, smiled.

> *Uncle Joshua, inside this Captain's Box is our present to you. It was our father's. Margaret and I want you to open it. There's something precious beyond measure.*

Hall remembered Grace's words as he visualized the two little girls, watching him with anticipation. He grinned as he reached to lift the top of the "Captain's Box," but paused for one last moment to glance at his nieces as his heart filled with love. Margaret squealed with delight when Joshua slowly lifted the top.

The memory vanished as Hall heard loud laughter from Alamea, who had climbed the rigging to assist Liko. Her long black hair was pushed back by the wind to reveal her softly feminine facial features and sculpted curves. Surging desire washed over Joshua as inevitably as the waves and troughs embracing *Eclipse*.

This voyage, he realized, would be more dangerous than he ever imagined.

TWELVE

SOUTHERN PRINCE OF WALES ARCHIPELAGO, SOUTHEAST ALASKA, EARLY MAY 1802

"*T*AAN," TOM TOLD JOSHUA, "ISLANDS OF the Sea Lion as we Tlingits call this place."

Hall nodded in appreciation as Captain Fletcher paced the decks of *Eclipse* to overlook his crew's labors in preparation for the first trading encounter. The crew secured anti-boarding nets and positioned muskets and small brass cannons as precautions. Micah Triplett assisted Benjamin Harper in fastening a port-side boarding net while Hall advised Kekoa and Liko in inspecting the muskets.

David Woods, at the helm, spoke to Lavelle Clark as he sat nearby fixing some rigging equipment.

"It seems odd that we have to do awl this work just to prepare for the Haidas," he complained. "I don't understand. Deh hasn't been a ship that's had trouble on the south side of Prince of Wales in dese outer island waters in yeers. This kinda thing is only used for the Tlingits furtha north, near the inland straits and mainland river valleys. There must be a reason for awl this that we don't know about, perhaps—

"Shut your trap, Mr. Woods!"

Fletcher glared at the two teenage sailors, exceedingly annoyed and tense.

"And Mr. Clark, your full attention, not idle conversation, is required by that broken rigging beside you!"

Fletcher grabbed the broken items beside Woods and Clark, unleashing a contemptuous monologue like an angry father scolding naughty children.

At the other side of the ship, close to the bow, Triplett approached Hall as *Eclipse* moved smoothly over wide ocean swells in soft winds. Not wanting to attract attention from the crew, Triplett deliberately looked toward the heavy mist hovering over the island in the near distance. Speaking softly, Triplett reminded Hall of some of their earlier conversations on *Eclipse* history.

"You see that, Mr. Hall? The cap is wound tight, like I told you a week ago. All the more reason to keep our ship's secrets buried for now. Jonathan's uneasy about the Haidas around here, even though we know them well and had decent trade with them in the '90s. He's worried about their clan leaders somehow uncovering his unfortunate past with the English Captain Ian Coe and the deaths of some Haida men."

"Yes, Captain Ian Coe and his ship, *Jackal*. So apparently those young Haida men killed in '99 are from these very waters, sir?"

"Yes, as far as can be certain. One other thing, Mr. Hall, *Jackal* is most likely here on the northwest coast and Coe is notoriously unpredictable. I don't know how Jonathan will react if we come across that English dog again. Knowing the cap, he'll probably scheme up some wild concoction. A merciful grace would see to it that our vessels never sight each other."

Joshua nodded, and noticed Captain Fletcher still haranguing Clark and Woods. Hall turned to Micah.

"Bear in mind what Thomas Perkins said in his office, 'Mr. Fletcher is the horse pulling my wagon, Joshua, and you and Mr. Triplett are holding the reins.'"

Triplett tightened his upper body, his jaw tense. He looked at Joshua like a startled animal.

"Yes, I haven't forgotten, Mr. Hall. Don't ever mention that again, for both our sakes. Do you understand?"

"Yes, sir."

Fletcher approached his two junior officers with a half-smile, apparently having satiated his anger with Clark and Woods.

"Ah, Mr. Hall, Mr. Triplett. Welcome to our first trading session of the season. Just around the point, there's a sheltered cove, Tattiskey, and nearby is the Haida village of Kaigani. We'll fire one brass cannon in salute three times and distribute gifts to their canoes to initiate discussions. While trouble is unlikely, we must always be on our guard gentlemen. The vilest treachery is always lurking beneath the surface with these savages, however dormant or far removed it may seem."

Hall nodded and scratched his chin, proffering, "Captain, assuming all goes well with our trade here, will we sojourn for a few days or cruise further north or east? Mr. Perkins indicated furs in these more southerly areas are already being exhausted, perhaps cruising would be a more advantageous strategy?"

"That is the key question, exactly, Mr. Hall," Fletcher interjected. "We'll see how the situation here unfolds, but I fully intend to exploit our ship's speed and secure trading advantages ahead of our competition. I anticipate no fewer than fifteen ships in these waters this spring. And don't forget about the Russians with their massive flotillas of Aleutian hunters in the straits just to the north of us, stealing otters from the clans and thus our own pockets. Mr. Baranov over on Kodiak Island has proven himself to be a stubborn son of a bitch, with his pretentious Saint Michael colony on Sitka Island. Most of the clans, fortunately, are inclined to trade with our ships as we offer superior goods."

Triplett scratched the back of his neck.

"Sir, I would imagine the Tlingit clans are growing more impatient with the Russians as their Sitka Island colony has been there since '99. Tom and Thaddeus believe the clans will want to drive them out if they don't leave soon."

Fletcher nodded, and pulled out tobacco and lit his pipe.

"If there is excessive haggling from the Haidas over trade volumes I'll require your assistance in managing the details. Final agreements, however, will be subject to my authorization. Remember gentlemen, in these situations my orders must be obeyed instantly and without question. Our lives and the success of this voyage are in the balance."

Triplett and Hall nodded.

"And Mr. Hall," Fletcher added, "Mr. Perkins is in Boston, thousands of miles away. Please don't lose sight of that fact."

"Understood, sir."

Fletcher exhaled pipe smoke over his two junior officers and walked away.

THIRTEEN

*E*CLIPSE ROUNDED THE POINT AND ENTERED A SPACIOUS, well-protect-ed cove. Instantly, the large Haida village came into view in the distance with well-constructed communal longhouses, smoke lodges to process fish, and smaller wooden homes covered with red and black images of various marine animals. Men, women, and children moved about on shore amidst small dogs and campfires. Giant totem poles decorated the edge of the forest just above the main buildings, carved with imaginative interlocking faces blending the human and animal worlds in bright shades of green, red, and white.

His long black hair tied in a bundle, Kekoa wore a shark tooth necklace beneath an unbuttoned blue linen shirt. He noticed Hall awestruck by the scene on shore.

"Big totems there like our *ki'i* back home, sir. Tallest one reminds me of our god, *Lono*."

"Indeed Kekoa, I recall Liko pointing out several carved deities to me on O'ahu. Your priestly kahunas were quite strict in protecting them."

"Strong kapu, yes. Indians here also have kapu to guard their totems' honor."

Within moments, Benjamin Harper fired three cannon shots to indicate the desire to open negotiations for trade, while a small canoe with two teenage Haida boys reached the hawser line tossed by Liko, tying it to a large fir tree onshore. The *Eclipse* crew stood at attention along the port side, with many crew members holding gifts of copper bracelets and rings, Hawaiian tapa cloth, and mother-of-pearl buttons. Alamea and

Aolani rushed to finish dishes of sweetened rice for the Haida dignitaries expected to board the ship. Further down the deck, Lavelle Clark prepared his blacksmithing forge, ready to accommodate any villagers' requests to make or refashion copper and iron goods. Kekoa held two young white and orange cats high on his shoulders to catch the eyes of otter pelt-owning villagers desiring a pet.

Moving their long canoes off the beach, several tall Haida men with muscular upper bodies paddled in strokes synchronized to a drum beat from the rear of the longest canoe, which was almost half the length of *Eclipse*. Their long hair wrapped in bundles, the men and one woman were adorned with dyed red and black wool upper body cloaks, furs, necklaces, and copper nose and ear rings. Red ocher and vibrant interlocking animal tattoos on legs, arms, and faces added to their ornamentation. Coming to rest around *Eclipse*, the Haidas broke into song for several minutes. Several white eagle feathers were dropped into the sea from three of the canoes at the melody's conclusion.

Triplett watched the scene unfold as he stood beside Hall.

"That there, Joshua, is a sign of friendship. Perhaps Jonathan will breathe more easily."

"Magnificent," Hall replied in amazement. "Artistry and performance apparently govern their everyday lives."

Triplett smiled and shook his head.

"You may be reevaluating that statement somewhat, once the negotiations commence. Wait until you meet the Haida women, they drive the hardest bargains."

"I fully admit I have much to learn. You're probably right, sir."

A tall, highly ornamented Haida man of about fifty years of age rose from the canoe closest to the ship, and in slow, thickly-accented English spoke over the green water.

"Great Boston Captain, Jonathan Fletcher, we welcome you and your sailors to our land as the snows begin melting. You are the first of the Boston and King George ships to arrive. We have much to discuss."

After a brief pause, Fletcher projected a slow, booming voice, using large, deliberate arm and hand gestures.

"My crew and I greet you, Little Orca Father. We welcome you and a few guests to come aboard to receive our gifts for you, your clan, and Kaigani villages."

Liko, Kekoa, and Nathaniel Folger assisted Little Orca Father and his wife, Red Sea Star, through a small opening in the boarding nets to reach the deck, where the *Eclipse* crew presented sweetened rice dishes and the gifts. After several minutes, Fletcher invited two more Haidas on board to assist handing gifts and rice dishes to the canoes.

"Mr. Triplett, Mr. Hall, the deck is yours," Captain Fletcher ordered.

Little Orca Father and Red Sea Star accompanied Fletcher to his cabin below deck to discuss business. Proficient in Haida, Tom and Thaddeus followed the two leaders to serve as interpreters. Hall and Triplett ordered the rest of the crew members to assist with dispensing presents to the surrounding canoes.

After only forty minutes, Tom and Thaddeus emerged from below deck followed by Fletcher, Little Orca Father, and Red Sea Star, who were all smiling. Haidas and *Eclipse* crew members became silent, listening intently for the forthcoming pronouncements. Little Orca Father stood in the middle of the deck so he could be seen and heard by all six canoes. He shouted in Haida as Thaddeus translated for his crew.

"He says he welcomes Captain Fletcher and his crew to Kaigani, and that Captain Fletcher agrees to generous terms for the village's sea otter pelts. For each pelt, ten yards of blue and red cloth will be traded along with two copper daggers fashioned by our shipboard blacksmith, Mr. Clark. Captain Fletcher also agrees to trade five large copper pots, eight new muskets, and one flintlock blunderbuss to Little Orca Father once all the exchanges are completed tomorrow."

Joshua Hall's initial enthusiasm over the rapidity of agreement soon soured. He looked down at the deck and shook his head.

"I believe that's somewhat excessive," Hall told Triplett and Tom, his eyes clouded in frustration.

Tom glanced at Triplett with an unsettled look on his face, before continuing.

"Actually, there's more, sir. Mr. Clark will provide cold-smithing lessons to villagers tomorrow morning and our shipboard cats will be given to Little Orca Father's children. The village is to prepare a great feast tonight and open their homes to us. They also agree to provide us with fresh provisions."

A hint of unease filled Triplett as he looked at Joshua.

"Mr. Hall, this is very unusual, that is, the rapidity at which Little Orca Father answered to our goods and agreement was reached, as it's not unheard of for some negotiations to drag on for many days. I caution, however, that circumstances can change quickly. And don't forget what I said about the Haida women. They have more power over the men than you might imagine."

Hall, frowning, closed his eyes as he pushed his hand back through his hair.

"The volume of goods agreed to by the captain is overly generous, given the general instructions from Mr. Perkins."

"I agree, but I don't blame Captain Fletcher. He wants to maintain his trade partnership with this village, but he also recognizes it's wise to conclude our business soon and move on to the Tlingit villages up north."

Joshua looked at Tom and Thaddeus before glancing at Triplett.

"Why, then, stay the night here? Could we not conclude our trade within a few hours and depart?"

"Sir, to refuse the Haidas' invitation to feast with them would be a great insult to the honor of Little Orca Father and his clan. There would be, consequently, no trade at all," Tom volunteered.

Hall nodded and folded his arms as Triplett gave orders.

"Gentlemen, commence preparations for the shore party."

FOURTEEN

T HE NORTHERN SUN SET LATE OVER THE VILLAGE as spring pushed the darkness into further retreat. Enchanted by the Haida dwellings surrounding him, Joshua walked with Liko into the shadow of a forty-foot totem pole that bisected the twenty-foot high pitched roof of a large home. Carved in dazzling human and animal faces protruding outward in a collage of colorful hues, the poles distorted animal and human traits by the home entrance. Smaller poles, off to the sides of the home's entrance, held carved images of long, spidery yellow rays radiating out from several suns.

"Liko, this must be the entrance through this oval in the toad creature's green belly. I remember Little Orca Father's instructions."

"*Mana Nui*. Big power is here, sir, lots of light in this home of Haida ali'i. Feel it? Mana grows larger with every new land encountered. Strengthens one's heart against the fear of death."

"Well said, Liko. To all that is curious and beautiful."

The two men walked into the large rectangular home, where they were greeted by Little Orca Father's second wife, Clever Orca Mother, and her seven-year-old son. Interior totem poles, carved with images of moons and stars, reached to the pitched cedar plank ceiling and lined the house's central walkway every ten feet. On the walls appeared rectangular, interlocking carved images of orcas, ravens, wolves, and toads painted in vibrant collages.

Hall was shocked for a moment to see a large shell labret protruding two inches in Clever Orca Mother's lower lip. Decorated with colored beads and abalone shell acquired in trade with vessels in previous years, the labret demonstrated high social rank in clan houses holding the Orca totem crest. Her long, black hair rested on her right side to perfectly complement a red and black cloak with striking Orca designs sewn into the wool.

The boy wore a dark black woolen cloak and a frontal headdress decorated with abalone shell and red and green mother-of-pearl buttons. His face and hands tattooed with Orca imagery similar to the home's interior, the boy proceeded to hold out two argillite pipes carved in the shape of a human face surrounded by orcas swimming in the sea.

The two mariners accepted the gifts, nodding to the boy in gratitude. In return, Hall presented five yards of fine red cloth to Clever Orca Mother, while Liko pulled one of the *Eclipse* cats from his deerskin sack and handed it to the boy. The ambiance in the house felt warm and inviting from the boy's smile and his mother's dignified demeanor.

HALL STROLLED ALONG THE CALM WATERS OF THE COVE and marveled at the cathedral immensity of the island's glacier-shrouded mountains under a full moon. With the exception of Micah Triplett, David Woods, and Kekoa, who remained on board to keep watch, Fletcher had allowed the rest of the crew ashore for the evening celebration and feast. Hall, like the rest of the *Eclipse* crew, was exuberant to once again walk on land after several weeks at sea. Laughter and lively conversation filled the air as Tom translated the *Eclipse* sailors' stories into Haida.

At another camp near the large ceremonial longhouse, Little Orca Father launched incessant but polite questions to Thaddeus, asking with insatiable curiosity about life in Boston and the larger world. Little Orca Father's two wives sat nearby, adorned in fine red woolen shawls over their most ornate Orca cloaks and jewelry, along with the labrets indicating their high standing. Their appearance was intended to impress and evoke their power in trading. Listening intently beside the large crackling flames and holding a small brown dog in her lap, Clever Orca Mother questioned Thaddeus just as Hall arrived to sit next to him.

"So, young Thaddeus of the Great Bear totem . . ."

She paused for a moment, reveling in her question.

". . . It sounds like Boston is very wealthy and has plenty of things to trade for our otter pelts. Perhaps your officer here, Mr. Joshua, can explain why Captain Fletcher is not being more generous with my husband."

As Thaddeus translated for Hall, Little Orca Father shouted to the longhouse and ordered a young slave woman to bring a large flask of whiskey, given to him privately by Fletcher.

"Come now, my wife, Clever Orca Mother, Fletcher has been good to us in the past and offers us generous terms. We honor our Orca totem with this agreement. Let us share these spirits among us."

Clever Orca Mother scolded her husband.

"That fire water will make you into a fool! Do you not remember our village's young men to whom you gave permission to travel with that English sea captain Coe three years ago? Fletcher advised you to do so only after you consumed the fire water he gave you! The young men have not returned from the Stikine River and we do not know what has become of them. If they are not dead, they are probably fetching wood and water as wretched slaves!"

Red Sea Star laughed and accepted the whiskey, while Little Orca Father shrugged his shoulders. Clever Orca Mother picked up her dog and stormed off into the dark towards their home at the far side of the village. After a few moments of awkward silence, Little Orca Father motioned to Hall and Thaddeus to share in the whiskey. They accepted in small amounts, wanting to keep their wits about them after the angry woman's outburst. Hall was shocked by the way the Haida women held sway over their husband and even influenced the fur trade. Although Micah had tried to prepare him for the power of women in their culture, he still couldn't believe how defiant Clever Orca Mother had been.

Sensing their unease, Little Orca Father took several sips of whiskey.

"My wife back there worries too much. Young men like to go on adventures and prove themselves. They're most likely working as translators or guides, 'pilots' as you sailors call them, on other Boston and King George ships, or living with their clan members in other villages. She is anxious because one of her favorite nephews was among the young men who departed with the Englishman, Coe, three years ago. I fear she will—

Red Sea Star interrupted, furious at Clever Orca Mother's interference in her trade agreement.

"Your nephew probably has not come back because he wanted to get away from her ceaseless ranting! We all fear her damned loose tongue and endless gossip. She wrecked many agreements with some of the Boston and King George ships last year. Does she not understand that if we do not trade with the white men, if we do not acquire their best muskets and cannons, we will eventually become weak and succumb to foreign clans and tribes that resent us? The damned Russians with their Aleut slaves are also out there stealing our otters, plundering our food stores, and desecrating our graves. Our proud lineages and totems would be forever shamed."

"Enough!" Little Orca Father blurted, taking more sips of whiskey. "Let us enjoy ourselves, for tomorrow we bring honor and privilege to our village and Orca totem. We honor you, too, Mr. Thaddeus, child of the Tlingit Great Bear Totem, and Mr. Joshua, child of Boston."

Nodding in appreciation, the group stared into the fire as laughter and boisterous storytelling from other nearby bonfires echoed across the beach.

Narrow dark clouds crossed over the bright moon as laughter soon faded to quiet chatter. Barely visible against the grayish horizon, the dark outline of a ship appeared beyond the edge of the cove. A small Haida canoe, fishing under a lit torch, shouted to shore.

"Little Orca Father, come, come! A new ship is arriving over at Tattiskey!"

The entire *Eclipse* shore party, along with numerous villagers, ran over to the rocky shore at the end of the village, straining to make out the ship. Joshua Hall noticed Captain Fletcher standing motionless on a pair of large rocks, apparently riveted to the spot in a state of disbelief. On board *Eclipse* over a hundred yards off the beach, Triplett and Woods shouted, "It's the English ship, *Jackal*! Captain Coe is here!"

FIFTEEN

THE BEACH BONFIRES CAST DANCING ORANGE and red hues upon the two ships in the cove, like devilish creatures celebrating the dangerous turn of events for the *Eclipse* crew. Joshua observed crew members of the well-armed 85-foot schooner, *Jackal,* come ashore in their skiff holding gifts for Little Orca Father and other prominent residents. Micah Triplett landed on the beach as well, recognizing the delicate situation at hand for Captain Fletcher. Speaking in broken, English-accented Haida, twenty-seven-year-old Captain Ian Coe presented a noticeably higher volume and more luxurious set of gifts to Little Orca Father and his extended kin, including Clever Orca Mother who dashed from her house to join her husband.

Switching to English, Captain Coe addressed the entire gathering while occasionally glancing at Fletcher and the other *Eclipse* crew members.

"Greetings, my fellow brothers and friends, it's a pleasure to set eyes upon you once again. His Majesty, King George III, sends his best wishes to each and every one of you and rejoices in his partnership with Little Orca Father and the Kaigani Haida people. I also recognize the presence of our American cousins from the vessel *Eclipse*. A pleasure, gentlemen."

Captain Fletcher prepared to speak, but was interrupted by Clever Orca Mother.

"Tell us where our young men are first, you rotten scheming Englishman! My husband will not agree to trade with you until you tell us!"

Before Little Orca Father or Captain Fletcher could respond, Coe spoke with calm decisiveness.

"I do have information regarding the five young men from your Kaigani villages who accompanied me to the Stikine River three years ago, but that information will be provided only after an agreement is reached. Captain Fletcher can continue to conduct his own negotiations separately if he wishes."

Frustrated with the sudden appearance of *Jackal*, Captain Fletcher barely concealed his anger as he spoke.

"Little Orca Father, with fervent urgency, we wish you to honor our agreement made earlier today. My crew appreciates your hospitality and we sincerely hope you enjoy our gifts."

Clever Orca Mother and several other kin began shouting and arguing with each other, grabbing the arms of Little Orca Father repeatedly. The Haida leader seemed to reconsider his course of action in a disoriented gaze, fueled by the whiskey he'd consumed. Tom and Thaddeus strained to make sense of the furious pace of the ongoing arguments. Thaddeus struggled to translate for Captain Fletcher, Hall, and Triplett, who listened intently to every word.

"They mentioned something about the Englishman Coe has more to offer us. They also said that Fletcher will have to pay more for each pelt and Coe will tell us the fate of our missing clan brothers first, if we bargain hard," Thaddeus whispered in an effort to remain unheard by the others.

"It sounds like Clever Orca Mother is prevailing on her husband to demand the news of the young men, first, before agreeing to any trade," Tom muttered.

Upon hearing this, Fletcher walked away from his two junior officers to speak directly with Captain Coe in an effort to divert the direction of the Haida demands. Hall and Triplett followed.

"Damn it Ian, don't you realize you're inviting disaster if you tell them the fates of the young men? You know these people's devotion to their kin and their propensity for swift justice! For God's sake, man, remember we're on the far side of the world!"

Coe maintained his composure, which immediately drew Hall's suspicion.

"Captain Fletcher," Coe replied, "who said I'd be telling these bloody Indians the truth? Now, perhaps you'll consider a mutual trade volume that will be beneficial to both of us. I propose trading a minimum of twelve yards of cloth and two quality muskets to the Haidas for each pelt."

"That's insane! We should lower the volume of goods for each pelt and stand in solidarity with each other. It will be at least another week or two before any significant number of ships visits these waters. And, if we act boldly, we can . . .

Coe interrupted like a school master disciplining an unruly adolescent.

"This isn't the bloody '90s anymore when a few shells and trinkets purchased an otter pelt! The Haidas and Tlingits will be demanding more inflationary volumes of goods. Unlike you, I was here last winter at Nootka Sound by Vancouver's Isle where more than a few ships anchored. The prices demanded by the savages everywhere on the coast are triple and quadruple from previous years. And to add to the difficulty they're becoming more aggressive in many areas. Our novelty to them has long since worn off."

Fletcher shook his head with a sarcastic grin before defiantly snapping back at the veteran captain.

"You exaggerate, Ian! Do you think me a fool? I thought you'd still be open to continuing our business partnership."

"Sir," Triplett interrupted. "The Haidas are dispatching three men in a canoe on the far side of the beach. They're surely on their way to inform the other nearby Haida villages of Coe's generous gifts. Perhaps we should depart to trade with the Kasaan and Klinkwan villages before they unify in solidarity for higher prices? The Orca clan has the highest prestige among all these Prince of Wales Haida villages, and if they demand a higher volume of goods for each pelt, we'll be in—"

"Damn it! Damn this all to hell!" Fletcher moaned as he pushed the sand and pebbles with his feet. He knew the moment of decision had come, a moment filled with disadvantage, loss, and haste. Coe stared at Fletcher, Triplett, and Hall, calculating his next move.

"Gentlemen, excuse me for just a few moments as I consult with my first officer, Peter Lansing," Coe insisted.

The Englishman walked several dozen yards away and motioned for Lansing to join him immediately. Departing the loud, boisterous Haidas still arguing among themselves, Lansing trotted over to Coe and nodded as the captain spoke. It seemed as if they were reviewing arrangements already in place.

Hall remembered conversations with Thomas Perkins over avoiding entanglements with Captain Coe.

"Captain Fletcher, I recommend we leave at once to reach the other Kaigani villages before the canoe reaches them. We'll lose our trade here of course, but if we do not act resolutely now, our future prospects will be diminished."

Fletcher kicked at the small rocks in front of him, his lips tight and body tense. Looking at his captain's pained expression, Hall struggled to add a further point of argument before Coe could return, but he was too late as the English captain and Lansing approached to offer their plan.

"Captain Fletcher, I have a proposal for you that will more than make up for your inconvenient loss here. In exchange for giving up your trade with Little Orca Father and the other Haida villages, I'll make you an equal partner in reclaiming several hundred furs lost three years ago to the Tlingit men of the Raven's Bones totem. The information I possess will assure us the services of several Haida fighting men in our endeavor, guided by their passions to avenge the deaths of their clan kin. Mr. Lansing and I have confirmed information."

Skeptical, Triplett confronted Captain Coe.

"And where exactly did you obtain this information? What intrigue is this?"

Lansing stepped closer and responded in the unhurried melodic accent of southwest England.

"Gentlemen, we picked up three slaves who escaped from their village, and who, in desiring revenge against their former Raven's Bones captors, provided us with the location of the furs. Apparently, the Tlingit Raven's Bones men kept most of the pelts in anticipation of higher trade volumes and hid them at a small village just a few miles south of the Stikine River, where our crew was attacked and the Haida men with us met their fate."

"We want to speak to these slaves," Triplett demanded, "right now."

Lansing pulled a pipe and lit tobacco.

"I'm afraid Captain Coe and I already parted ways with them. We dropped them at a rogue colony of young vagabonds and thieves in the central straits upon their request."

Joshua threw nervous glances at Lansing and Coe.

"Wait. Do you know of an Elias Hall or a small schooner named *Panther* at this settlement? I'm his brother, Joshua Hall."

Peter Lansing started to reply, but Captain Coe held his hand up and took command of the conversation.

"Elias Hall. The Russians at Sitka Island mentioned that name to me last year. They blame him for some attacks on their hunting parties and small ships in the straits. 'Tis all I know. We did not see or hear of him at the small pirate colony, as we only remained a short time."

Coe turned to Captain Fletcher.

"Listen Jonathan, *Jackal* and *Eclipse* can coordinate an attack on the

Raven's Bones village in a week's time. If you agree, I'll entrust Mr. Lansing here to you as a sign of good faith in this endeavor and to act as a liaison between our vessels. Mr. Lansing can lead you to an island in the straits, where we'll rendezvous in three days to better plan our attack. After we seize the furs, we'll divide them equally between ourselves. And then we can take you to that den of misfits that interests Mr. Hall here."

Triplett didn't trust Coe.

"Captain Fletcher, I strongly condemn this plot! It's far too dangerous, with no guarantee the furs will still be in the location. We're merchant sea-men and *Eclipse* is not a man of war."

"Point taken, Mr. Triplett."

Fletcher's pained expression morphed into a crazed look as he stared at Captain Coe.

"Agreed."

"Sir! I must advise against this dangerous gamble!" Triplett protested.

Fletcher rubbed the back of his neck.

"Mr. Triplett, I am fully aware of the risks involved and we do not have time for lengthy discussions given the rapid turn of events here. You and Mr. Hall will order the crew to make sail."

Coe grinned in triumph as he gazed at the moonlit sea.

"The Raven's Bones men will wish they never committed their murder-ous thievery against the Haidas and the interests of our two vessels. I'll see you in three days, gentlemen. Fair winds to *Eclipse* in the straits."

SIXTEEN

As *ECLIPSE* SAILED OFF UNDER THE FULL MOON in a light breeze, Captain Coe and his crew faced a raucous crowd of Haidas. Coe motioned to his crew to bring several more gifts ashore to distribute to villagers. Little Orca Father, dismayed at the departure of *Eclipse* and the lost trading opportunity, scolded Clever Orca Mother.

"Look at what you've done, you've scared away Fletcher! Mr. Joshua must have informed him of your outrageous price demands and loose talk about the young Orca men. Now we only have the Englishman Coe! I hope you are happy now!"

Before Clever Orca Mother could respond, Coe immediately announced his price offer for each otter pelt in Haida.

"Eight yards of red cloth will be traded for each fur, and once trading has been concluded two new rifles and a large copper pot will be provided to you as well."

Red Sea Star angrily denounced Coe's offer, shouting before her husband could respond.

"What double-crossing is this? Your offer is outrageously low, and my husband does not accept it!"

A chorus of discontent rose as the English sea captain lifted his hand slowly to indicate he had something to add. Clever Orca Mother's shell necklaces clattered as she stepped forward to stand by a nearby bonfire, pulling her red and black wool cloak with Orca designs closely around her to ward off the chill. Her dark eyes held power and locked on Captain Coe with a condescending glare of moral righteousness that pierced the bonfire's crackling flames. All fell silent in deference to the powerful Orca clan woman.

"Captain Coe, my husband will not trade with you until you tell us what happened to our young clansmen three years ago. We have rumors from our clan brothers and sisters they may have been killed, but we do not know if this is true. You will tell us now, or you will receive no otter pelts from us or the other Haida villages, who will be informed to cease trade with you until a second canoe arrives with Little Orca Father's authorization. As you well know, captain, if our young men have been insulted or killed, our clan must devote ourselves to restoring their dignity and the honor of our Orca totem. Last fall we killed a Boston sailor when his captain murdered one of our clansmen after he refused a bad trade. The dishonorable captain also set fire to a clan house before departing on his *Panther* ship."

Raising both arms and mustering his best Haida, Coe envisioned the beach as the stage of the Bristol City Theatre. He conjured his favorite Shakespearean actors' lamentations to address the entire village.

"Little Orca Father, Clever Orca Mother, Red Sea Star, Orca men and women, and Kaigani villagers, I accept these terms with humility and respect to you all. It saddens me to hear of the insults directed at you by the *Panther* rabble. I know where their captain, Elias Hall, resides, and can capture him for a price. Now, with much regret, I'll tell you what happened to the young men who accompanied *Jackal* three years ago to the Stikine River."

A hush fell over the villagers and Coe commanded his audience as he continued.

"As you well know, the Tlingit clans of the coastal river valleys jealously guard the interior trading routes, believing it all belongs to them when it should be open to all. The tribes living over the mountains are not Tlingits and speak different tongues. Your five Haida men assisted my crew in leading us to the interior villages, and we successfully traded for over five hundred pelts. On our return down the Stikine River, we were ambushed without warning by Tlingit men of several Raven's Bones Houses. Your young Haida men fought with honor and killed several Tlingits, but three were killed in the fight, and another was badly wounded. This man later died from his wounds despite the attentions of our ship's medical officer. Three of the *Jackal* sailors were also shot by the Raven's Bones men, one of whom survived, but another later died on board ship while the remaining sailor was taken as a slave."

Gasps filled the air. Rigid and angry, Clever Orca Mother prepared to speak, but was cut off by Coe.

"And your nephew, Clever Orca Mother . . ."

Coe paused and looked down, thinking of Prospero in *The Tempest*. After a prolonged moment of silence, he slowly lifted his chin and stared into her eyes.

". . . was wounded in his lower leg and captured."

Indignation fell over Clever Orca Mother.

"He is a slave! The dishonor! We demand justice! Justice! To battle for our fallen Orca men!"

Several Haida men and women shouted support for Clever Orca Mother. Coe raised his arms to indicate he had additional information. Little Orca Father motioned for all to fall silent. The Englishman continued, this time in an even slower, more deliberate tone.

"As you may remember, it was Captain Fletcher and his *Eclipse* crew who recruited your young men to serve on my vessel. Unfortunately, Captain Fletcher was not at the mouth of the Stikine River at the agreed time and did not render any assistance to your wounded young man, nor mount a rescue of your nephew, Clever Orca Mother."

With feigned regret, Coe glanced at Little Orca Father and his two wives beside him.

"Sadly, I later learned the greedy Captain Fletcher instead decided to bargain with other Tlingit villages as we were returning from the mountains down the Stikine. He traded several new muskets to the Raven's Bones men mere days before their dishonor against your young men and my crew. And, it is quite possible that Fletcher told them about your men and our journey over the mountains, but this latter point is only a suspicion of mine. As you observed, my officer Lansing is on *Eclipse* to discretely acquire information for us."

Little Orca Father and the Haida leadership huddled together to resume their conversations, but in contrast to the previous arguing over trade volumes, Coe and his crew noticed a consensus building among them.

A *Jackal* crew member leaned toward Coe.

"Sir, if you will indulge me, why did you tell them *Eclipse* did not assist us? Fletcher was there at the river mouth to help us, and as far as we know, he didn't trade weapons to those Tlingits you mention."

"I told Captain Fletcher I would not be telling these bloody Indians the truth." Coe hissed as a sinister smile crept across his face. "And, I'm keeping my word to him."

Silence fell upon the beach as Little Orca Father stepped forward to speak. Only the sound of the crackling bonfires and a barking dog broke the stillness.

"Captain Coe, you have my permission to load our men and canoes onto your ship. Our clan will redeem our fallen men and the honor of our Orca totem. Bring us some captured Raven's Bones men, their guns, and Captains Jonathan Fletcher and Elias Hall. If you accomplish this, you'll have all the furs you wish from us for all time."

SEVENTEEN

OFF THE COAST OF PRINCE OF WALES ISLAND, MAY 1802

To take advantage of stronger and more reliable winds, *Eclipse* sailed off the northwestern shore of Prince of Wales, facing the open sea. Joshua Hall, who was waiting to descend below deck with the ship's officers and Peter Lansing, was shocked to see Liko and Kekoa passionately embrace and kiss several yards away beside the aft mast. Captain Fletcher, who caught a fleeting glance of the two Hawaiian men before dipping below deck, noted Hall's dismayed expression.

"No New England *kapu* out here, Mr. Hall. Liko and Kekoa are excellent sailors mind you, and as long as they perform their duties, they are free to do as they please. Now, your full attention is required for the task at hand."

Stunned, Hall remained silent. He summoned his best efforts to read Peter Lansing's true intentions. *Captain's orders.*

One by one, the group descended a small ladder into Captain Fletcher's cabin to discuss business. Candle light illuminated several ornate carvings of stars, moons, and suns on the walls as the men devoured a breakfast of rice and biscuits. After finishing, they sipped coffee and stood over charts spread before them, detailing the coast's intricate mazes of islands and straits. The charts also highlighted several deadly shoals, scourges of shallow underwater rocks, sandbars, and reefs that wrecked more than a few ships and their crews' ambitions in previous years. Tom and Thaddeus sat in chairs near the table, ready to provide information as requested. Peter Lansing weighed in first.

"Captain, I propose *Eclipse* sojourn here among one of the Tlingit villages of north Prince of Wales for trade and fresh provisions. This would allow us adequate time to cruise around the northern end of Prince of Wales to the straits and the designated island to rendezvous with *Jackal*."

Without answering, Fletcher leaned back in his chair and called Alamea and Aolani to bring more coffee before shifting his gaze to Triplett.

"Mr. Triplett, your opinion please."

Triplett pointed to the position of *Eclipse* on the map and then slid his finger toward the coastline.

"Captain, the Tlingit villages here on north Prince of Wales are mostly small and usually don't have much to offer in the way of furs. They also frequently charge vessels to acquire fresh water and provisions. It would probably be best to focus our energies on getting to the rendezvous island as swiftly as possible and gather new provisions and fresh water there without having to haggle and pay for them. This would also provide our crew an opportunity to rest and prepare for our attack on the Raven's Bones men. Of course, this depends on whether the rendezvous island Mr. Lansing refers to is indeed uninhabited."

Alamea and Aolani entered Fletcher's cabin with a freshly brewed kettle of coffee. Alamea brushed the hair from her face and rested her hand on Hall's shoulder before proceeding to fill his cup. Annoyed, Fletcher raised his eyebrows and glared at Alamea before shifting his gaze to Hall.

"And so, Mr. Hall, do you concur with Mr. Triplett or Mr. Lansing?"

Hall drew a deep breath and glanced at Triplett, who broke eye contact.

"Neither, sir." Hall replied in a decisive tone as he leaned forward to look over the charts. Sipping his coffee, Hall looked at the other officers before continuing.

"I'm of the firm opinion that an attack on the village Captain Coe spoke of is too risky. You yourself cap reminded me on several occasions of how the Tlingits are fierce and well-armed. The risk to life and limb, as well as damage to our vessel, is too severe."

Hall stood, reaching toward the map as he pointed to the islands just to the north of Prince of Wales, noting several villages marked on the chart.

"Additionally, captain, we have not had an opportunity to trade with the northern Tlingit kwaans and their distinct sets of villages scattered about these islands. Our focus should be on utilizing the talents of Tom and Thaddeus, and finding the 'rogue colony' Captain Coe mentioned. Elias may be there."

Lansing rose and tapped his index finger impatiently on the charts. He gestured to north Prince of Wales and the small rendezvous island eastward in the straits, anxious to challenge Hall.

"Captain Fletcher! With all due respect to Mr. Hall here, Captain Coe is committed to retrieving what are well over one thousand furs, half of which will go to your vessel. He will have an army of Haida men, who, along with our cannon and muskets, will provide more than enough firepower to defeat the Raven's Bones men at the village. Captain, I respectfully insist we proceed to the rendezvous island, which is nearly two full days' sail from here. I can assure you the island has no permanent villages. I would disagree with Mr. Triplett as well, since the island does not have adequate game for fresh provisions, thus my recommendation is we trade here with the local Tlingit Henya kwaan."

Hall knew any delay or diversion would buy opportunities to change Fletcher's mind.

"Captain Fletcher, I strongly urge you to reconsider this entire path, it's not too late. At the very least, let us delay the attack and visit one of the major villages where Tom and Thaddeus have several kin. Perhaps we can acquire a good volume of furs and the most recent intelligence on the Raven's Bones men and Elias. Tom, Thaddeus, would the two of you care to comment?"

Tom rose slowly, gesturing to previously unmentioned areas on one of the charts.

"Sirs, there are indeed clans in the Kake-Kuiu kwaan to the north who held past quarrels with men of the Raven's Bones totem. They may be able to advise us on Captain Coe's plan. Perhaps they could even fight with us and lead us to Elias Hall."

Thaddeus pointed toward Kuiu Island before turning to Fletcher.

"Sirs, Tom is correct. We have kin at the Kake-Kuiu kwaan villages to the north who share our Sea Lion and Big Dipper totems. We would most assuredly get the fresh provisions we need there without cost along with advantageous trade and intelligence."

Lansing, alarmed at the direction of the conversation, held out his arms in indignation as if to plead his case in a courtroom.

"Captain Fletcher, I must protest the idea of diverting north to the Kake-Kuiu Tlingit villages! We would risk missing our rendezvous with *Jackal* given the unpredictable winds and currents of the straits, and Captain Coe and I already confirmed the location of the stolen furs. His Haida recruits will provide more than enough strength to ensure our success against the Raven's Bones men."

Fletcher sipped his coffee, pausing to set his cup on the table. He locked his fingers together in contemplation as he pondered his options.

"Mr. Triplett, go above deck and order the crew to set course for the Tlingit village on the western shore of Kuiu Island. Set out the main sails in full to arrive with all deliberate speed."

"Aye sir."

Eager to escape the drama, Triplett pulled the hatch open letting in sunshine and salty air as he climbed above on deck.

Lansing's expression turned from anger to rage as he struggled to maintain control.

"Captain Fletcher, I must protest, this will endanger our agreement, and—

"Mr. Lansing, sit down please. Our rendezvous with Captain Coe will be fulfilled as was agreed. If our vessel is delayed by a day or two, your captain will know to wait, given the frequently difficult conditions in the straits. Our possible recruitment of some Tlingit fighting men to assist our cause will more than offset any potential inconvenience to your ship."

"Captain, this course of action will jeopardize our—

"Why the concern over bringing additional fighting men on our vessel and the insistence on pursuing limited and difficult trade with the small villages around these waters? Perhaps, Mr. Lansing, you would like to enlighten us on any details Captain Coe omitted in our conversation?"

Lansing took his seat, glancing at the four remaining men in the cabin.

"No, captain, we went over all the details back at the Haida village."

Without responding, Fletcher rose to his feet to close the hatch left open by Micah Triplett before returning to the charts. With two of the table's candles nearly burnt out, Fletcher motioned to Alamea to light new ones. The fresh candle light illuminated Alamea's face, the men unable to avoid admiring her natural beauty and alluring presence. With a conceited smile to reinforce his power over the wooden world around them, Fletcher turned to Lansing.

"I'm glad to hear your professions of innocence, Mr. Lansing, because if you or your captain commits the slightest deceit against my ship and crew, I personally guarantee you will never see the shores of England again."

EIGHTEEN

KUIU ISLAND, MAY 1802

JOSHUA HALL AND MICAH TRIPLETT WALKED LEISURELY along a well-worn trail near the edge of Tlingit longhouses and residences in the late evening's dusky light. Loud conversations and laughter from villagers and the *Eclipse* crew accompanied aromas from fish smokehouses and spruce and fir boughs. Light glacial breezes passed over assorted wildflowers to greet the two men as they reached a rocky clearing dotted with red and yellow lichens. Beside the forest's edge on the far side of the meadow, a small, ornate funerary box stood aloft on four ten-foot poles. It was adorned with interlocking painted bird designs in red and black, designs Hall found to be both interesting and appealing.

As the two men continued along the trail, Hall looked farther out upon the island's mountainous interior. Several waterfalls tumbled down raw granite peaks thousands of feet in elevation, while a yellow moon, now receding from its previous fullness, hovered close to Venus and a few bright stars. *Eclipse* rested at anchor on the calm, flat sea just off the village point.

"A most peaceful scene, Mr. Hall, wouldn't you agree? I believe our captain made the right choice in coming here."

"Indeed sir, calm beauties all around us at rest. It reminds me of tucking my young, mischievous nieces into bed back in New Hampshire. God knows I love those little troublemakers."

Micah chuckled as he set his musket down and lit his tobacco pipe.

"Ah yes, playful rascals and a good woman at your side. They make all the privations and toils of life bearable."

Hall pulled out his log to write, catching the sweet, pleasant smell of Micah's pipe tobacco.

Little Grace and Margaret always at play. The little victories and subtle glories in life, clever reminders of light playing tricks on the darkness.

Hall leaned against a rock, staring at *Eclipse* and the heavens.

"Sir, Micah if I may, tell me about Alamea and the other islanders."

Triplett was caught off guard and surprised at the informal question.

"Micah is fine. Well, Joshua, what exactly would you like to know about—

"Everything."

"Very well. Aolani, Liko, Alamea, and Kekoa are—

"Alamea first."

"Alamea, Captain Fletcher's wahine."

"I'm well aware of that. What I'm interested in is her personal history, along with her brother, Liko, and cousin, Aolani."

"Yes, of course. The three of them were once members of the O'ahu ali'i, the island's noble families. Most of their ali'i relatives were killed during the 1795 invasion by King Kamehameha. The few high ranking O'ahu ali'i who survived fled to Kaua'i, still independent under another king named Kaumuali'i. Many of the lower ranking ali'i did not have an opportunity to escape to Kaua'i and were killed for having resisted the invasion. Alamea, Aolani, and Liko might have suffered the same fate had it not been for a kind ali'i man from Mau'i, Koloa, allied with Kamehameha, who declared his *hanai* over the three O'ahu youngsters."

"Hanai?"

"Oh, sorry, the word refers to a tradition among the ali'i to adopt children of others and raise them as their own. Kamehameha's O'ahu Kuhina Isaac Davis . . ."

"Ah yes, how could I forget? The marooned Welshman, Kamehameha's governor for the island."

"Yes, well, Davis, acting on Kamehameha's orders, accepted the hanai, but stripped all surviving O'ahu ali'i of their titles and made them commoners, maka'ainana in the Hawaiian tongue. Kekoa was always one of the maka'ainana, though, and was never among the ali'i. Anyway, the O'ahu commoners are under strict kapu imposed by the Hawai'i and Mau'i kahunas who arrived after the conquest."

"I see, so this explains why the common people frequently wish to sign on to work on our vessels."

"Yes. Alamea desires a return to ali'i status, and she hopes Captain Fletcher can assist her in this ambition."

Triplett paused a few moments, looking out over the water as the reflection of the moonlight caused tidal ripples to sparkle as they lapped at the shoreline.

"To be completely honest, I don't know if her feelings for the captain are genuine or more of convenience."

"And what of the captain toward her? You have my strictest confidence, Micah, sir, I give you my word."

Micah bit his lower lip as he broke eye contact for a moment. Sipping from his personal flask of whiskey and inhaling from his pipe once more, he looked around first before continuing in a whisper.

"There's no doubt the captain is very interested in Alamea's adoptive Mau'i ali'i father, Koloa, as a means to valuable sandalwood. As you know Joshua, the Hawaiian trees grow more lucrative in the China trade every year with the Fijian and Solomon Islands sandalwood groves nearly exhausted. Regarding his personal feelings towards Alamea, I'm not sure, but there's been recent strain. Be advised not to respond to any advances from Alamea. The captain has a short fuse and our entire voyage would descend into—"

"I'm not stepping into that volcanic stew. Thank you, sir."

Micah glanced at *Eclipse* with unease as he breathed in the aromas of forest and sea. Within moments, a repetitive raven's call echoed through the woods, deflecting off trees in multiple directions like a painting in sound. Footsteps and conversations in heavily accented English drifted up the trail. Two Tlingit boys around nine or ten years of age accompanied Tom.

Tom spoke slowly to the boys as he guided them towards Micah and Joshua.

"Yel, however, helped people in many ways without tricking or scaring them. He taught them how to construct boats, and inspired virtues for living an enriched life guided by principles of truth, honesty, generosity, and brotherhood. There are other stories for these events of long ago. Perhaps I will tell you more when the time arrives."

The boys were excited to meet the sailors. One boy, wearing brass earrings and a woolen cloak with black and red sea animal images, boasted, "Mr. Joshua, Mr. Micah, we can speak your Boston men's tongue! We have met many sailors, and have teachers like Tom in the village! We have practiced many stories!"

The other boy, dressed in sailor's clothing obtained in trade, and wearing a circular wide-brimmed, finely woven spruce root hat in black-lined block images of red and green marine animals, added, "We Tlingits call Raven Yel. Yel is at the center of many of our stories from long ago. Would you two care to hear one?"

Tom grinned as a raven glided over the nearby woods before disappearing below a large fir, catching the eyes of the three men and two boys.

Micah was eager to flush his uncomfortable conversation with Hall from his mind.

"That would be splendid, young men."

Tom looked intently upon the woods and leaned against a large granite boulder, ready to assist and coach as the boy with the earrings commenced with the story.

"Long, long ago, all of the animals, fish, trees, and people lived in darkness as there was no sun, only an eternal night with no moon or stars. Yel learned of a clan leader and his splendid daughter. She possessed the sun, moon, and stars in special carved cedar boxes."

The boy paused, and the other boy with the root hat and sailor's clothing eagerly took over.

"The clan guarded her and the boxes very closely, and Yel knew he had to trick the villagers to get near the boxes, so he flew upon a tall tree beside their house and turned himself into a hemlock needle and fell into the daughter's drinking cup. When she filled it with water, she drank the needle, and Yel transformed himself into her baby son. Her father loved the grandchild and gave him anything he asked."

The two boys both started to speak simultaneously, and frowned at each other, so Tom raised his hand to continue the next part of the story as a truce.

"The stars, moon, and the sun remained in the beautiful cedar boxes, which sat on the wooden floor of the house. The grandchild, who was actually Yel, began crying and demanded to play with the box holding the moon and stars. The grandfather obliged, and as soon as he had the stars and moon, Yel tossed them up through the house's smoke hole. They instantly scattered across the sky, and although the grandfather was angry, he adored his grandson too much to punish him."

The boy with the earrings seized the initiative when Tom paused, determined to impress the Boston men with his story skills.

"The little grandson began crying for the box containing the sun. At first the grandfather refused to hand over the box, but his little grandson kept crying and acted like he was sick. Finally, the grandfather gave him the box holding the sun. After playing with the box, Yel turned himself back into a bird and flew up through the smoke hole with the box."

Not to be outdone, the other boy seized the moment to finish the tale. He removed his hat and spoke with firm resolve.

"Once he was far away from the village, Yel heard people speaking in the darkness and approached them, asking the people, 'Who are you? Would you like to have light?' The people mocked Yel, saying no one had the power to give light. To show them he was telling the truth, Yel opened the cedar box and let sunlight out. The people were terrified, and they fled to every corner of the world. This is why there are people everywhere, not just in our homeland, Lingit aani, but also Boston, London, and everywhere else."

Joshua grinned.

"That was a grand story, gentlemen."

Micah studied a small dark shape on his hand, a mosquito. Smashing the insect, a small bit of blood splashed across his left hand.

"And what about these blood sucking creatures, Tom? What do your legends say about them?"

"It's said that people long ago caught a terrible giant, a cannibal named Gutikl. They burned him. But afterwards, the ashes turned into mosquitoes who love blood no less than their fearsome ancestor. They remind us that life is not easy."

"Ah, a very clever explanation," Joshua replied. "Tell me more stories. They remind me of some old sailors."

Tom admired Joshua's interest in the legends. The *Eclipse* officer reminded him of an old Wampanoag he and Thaddeus had met on Cape Cod in 1798. The elderly man eagerly listened to the boys' Tlingit stories, but soon insisted Yel was, in fact, the hero Gluskap, since Gluskap had no beginning and was always there, and had arrived from across the ocean to name stars, slay monsters, and trick dangerous animals.

Tom nervously rolled his lips inward.

"Certainly, sir, but I wanted to bring to your attention some rumors that might assist the captain in enlisting help from the Kuiu men for our journey to meet Captain Coe."

Micah sighed.

"More mischief to mix in with Captain Fletcher's schemes."

Joshua scratched the back of his neck, disappointed he would have to wait for more stories.

"Very well, go on Tom."

"Thaddeus and I overheard some talk about a plot coming together among various clans to attack the Russians at *Gajaa Heen*, the location of their Saint Michael colony on Sitka Island. The attack is still being planned and is several weeks away. Many of the clans here at Kuiu expressed a desire to aid in the assault, as family members and relatives have been insulted on many occasions by the Russians. A prominent leader from this island, along with his wife and children, were murdered by a Russian-Aleut hunting party last year. If I heard it correctly, the party was led by a Russian named Urbanov. As you know, the Russians steal pelts from our clans on a regular basis without any compensation. They even seized a great shaman, Wolf-Weasel, as a prisoner for a short time."

Joshua put his hands in his pockets as he turned back toward the village.

"Yes, I've heard all about Alexander Baranov, the Russian-American Company, and the frequent flotillas of Aleutian and Kodiak hunters in the straits from Mr. Perkins and our crew. How does this matter pertain to us getting cooperation from the Kuiu men?"

"Well, sirs, Thaddeus is informing the captain on this matter right now, but I was thinking we may offer some assistance to the Kuiu clans in coordinating and supporting their attack. Thaddeus is hesitant, but I support my clan relatives and wish to fight with them."

A chill raced through Joshua as the three men rose and walked the trail to the village. Micah recited stories of violent skirmishes and lost sailors from past voyages. Joshua didn't like Micah's tales and stressed the desperate need to avoid such encounters.

The woods remained silent as the three men and two boys approached a fish smoker beside the water. The boy wearing the sailor's clothes spoke.

"Hear the silence? Raven has been listening to our stories. Perhaps he's planning some things for us."

Musket shots from deep in the woods shattered the quiet. A ball tore through a branch just above the group and barely missed Tom's head, while another shot struck a tree sapling inches from Joshua.

"Move! Someone's sniping us!" Joshua screamed as the three men grabbed their muskets and the two boys and sprinted into a patch of thick woods. Another shot sent scraps of bark into Micah's face.

"Shit!" Triplett shouted. "Must be at least two or three of 'em!"

Tom spotted a large moss-covered fir log and within seconds the small group dove for cover as two more musket balls sent bark, moss, and dirt into the air.

"Tom, these woods are on a small peninsula, right?" Joshua asked between heavy breaths as the three loaded their muskets.

"Aye, sir, there's a small cove a few hundred yards north."

Another shot ripped into the log mere inches above them.

"Tom," Micah paused as more bark and dirt rained on them, "on my signal, run with the boys back to the village for help. Joshua and I will lay cover fire for you. Has to be now, while we still know the general area of the snipers' nest."

"Aye, sir."

"Micah, sir, after Tom departs, I can flank the snipers in a wide arc through the woods. You can remain here and keep up fire. Here's some extra powder and shot, I'll call out for you later."

"Permission granted. Now, on my mark, five, four, three, two, one."

Tom rose and sprinted towards the village with the boys as Joshua and Micah rose above the log and fired shots in the snipers' direction. The tactic worked as Tom and the boys disappeared into the forest's darkness after one sniper shot missed the three by a few feet. Joshua reloaded and fired again after another shot hit a tree a few feet above him.

"On my mark, Joshua." Micah ordered as Hall reloaded in under a minute.

"Mark, five, four, three, two, one."

Both men fired at the snipers, and in an instant Joshua sprinted towards the cove. Micah ducked behind the log again to reload as Hall disappeared into the woods.

NINETEEN

JOSHUA SPRINTED LIKE THE WIND FOR OVER A MINUTE before his burning lungs demanded a reprieve. Sweat poured over dirt covering his neck and face as he moved behind a centuries-old Sitka Spruce. His heart pounding, Joshua listened for any hint of the snipers. A raven cried out a rapid repetitive call in the vicinity of the snipers' nest, which Hall estimated to be around fifty to seventy-five yards away. He closed his mouth and forced himself to breathe through his nose for better listening. The faintest hint of footsteps reached his ears. The raven cried out again from the same vicinity and Joshua crouched to continue his wide flanking arc towards the cove. Within a couple of minutes, he spotted the ocean and a large vessel, its masts distinguishable between the tall spruces and firs at the forest's edge.

Centurion, shit! Billy Lee!

The footsteps grew more audible and after another minute passed, Hall spotted three armed sailors, among them Billy Lee. Hall took aim and fired, killing one man. Lee and the other sailor dove for cover while Hall reloaded behind a spruce tree.

"Micah! Now!" Joshua screamed.

A musket ball smashed into the spruce tree. Hall kept his cover, but could hear Lee and the other man moving through the brush in front of him. Hall crouched and sprinted as a shot rang out. Joshua felt the ball pass within an inch of his head, and he turned to see the two snipers advancing on his position while ducking for cover every few seconds. Hall pivoted behind a small fir and returned fire. Lee's sailor fell from a shot to the chest and bled out on the forest floor.

"Micah! I'm over here!" Joshua screamed again.

"Almost there!" Joshua heard faintly.

Lee charged at Hall with a large knife, enraged. Joshua frantically tried to reload his musket, but he dropped his powder.

"Shit!" Hall muttered as he pulled his knife to engage Lee. The South Carolinian lunged and slashed Joshua's shirt with his knife tip but failed to wound Hall. Joshua struggled to keep balance as Lee attacked again and violently drove Hall to the ground. The air smashed out of his lungs, Hall dropped his knife and couldn't breathe. Dirty sweat dripped off both their faces, and Lee lifted his eight-inch blade to stab Hall in the chest. Thunderous crackling of gun and cannon fire erupted in the nearby cove, causing Lee to pause for an instant and glance at his ship. Still unable to breathe, Hall fought to grab his attacker, but he was too late as Lee turned to Hall and positioned his knife a second time over Joshua's heart.

A musket shot tore through the air. Lee spat blood and collapsed as the knife fell from his hand.

"Goddammit!" Micah Triplett screamed as he ran with his musket to Hall amid sustained musket and cannon fire in the cove. "Are you hurt?!"

"I, I . . ." Joshua replied as he struggled to regain normal breathing.

"Lee's dead! I got him!"

"You saved . . . my life, Micah, I . . . thank you." Joshua strained.

"Thank God! Here, let me help you. Hear all that down there? Our crew and several village clansmen are engaging *Centurion*!"

Joshua stood with Micah's assistance as the roar of battle intensified below them, and the two men made their way to the forest edge to see the cove in full view. Tlingit war canoes were beached nearby and Hall and Triplett could see their shipmates and clan fighters maintain an almost continuous barrage of fire on the ship.

A massive blast and fireball exploded on *Centurion*'s deck. Hall and Triplett looked on in horror as the entire vessel and several crew members were consumed in the ensuing inferno. Three sailors being burnt alive fell into the sea as they helplessly flailed their arms in the air.

"Jesus Christ!" Micah blurted. "A powder magazine must've been hit!"

The two watched the ship's burning masts crack and fall into the sea, with pieces of burning sail carried into the air like hovering angels of death.

"Madness! What a fucking waste! And for what?! So Billy could get revenge for Jonathan's antics on Mas a Tierra?" Joshua stated in disgust. "Let's head down to the canoes, sir."

"SIRS! YOU'RE SAFE, THANK GOD!" Tom cried out in relief as he saw Micah and Joshua emerge from the woods.

"And you as well." Joshua replied as he observed the *Eclipse* crew and dozens of Tlingit fighters load weapons and a few surviving boxes of *Centurion* provisions and pelts into canoes. "Where's the cap?"

Tom pointed to a clump of trees just above the tidal zone, a few dozen paces beyond the canoes. Hall and Triplett walked over rocks and seaweed, stopping every few moments to offer thanks to others.

Thaddeus approached and asked, "Sirs, have you seen Billy Lee? Cap wants to know."

"Yes, Micah killed him in the forest. He saved my life."

"Good. Cap's behind those trees." Thaddeus replied with some hesitation.

After another minute of walking, Hall and Triplett arrived and were shocked to see Captain Fletcher and a Tlingit man torturing two captured *Centurion* sailors. Tied to the trees, the two men had small knife cuts and burns all over their naked bodies. Fletcher turned to address his two officers.

"Seen Billy Lee? These two bastards won't tell us."

"Lee's dead, captain. Micah shot him and saved my life. What the hell are you doing to these two men? They're prisoners now! Untie them and let 'em go under guard!"

"Glad to hear that bastard Billy Lee got what he deserved!" Fletcher growled, ignoring Hall's demands.

"Captain, those men! Untie them now!" Hall repeated.

"We're not in Massachusetts anymore, Mr. Hall. A different law prevails here. Mr. Triplett, you can attest to that."

Hesitant, Triplett looked down at the dried seaweed under his feet before nodding to Hall and turning in the other direction to walk away. The Tlingit man beside Fletcher proceeded to disembowel and kill one sailor. Hideous screams filled the air as Fletcher slashed the other *Centurion* sailor across the chest with a knife, deliberately prolonging the man's agony before he killed him with a slash to the throat. Fletcher walked past Hall.

"Mind your place, Mr. Hall! Meet at the village, we have much business before us."

TWENTY

JOSHUA HALL WATCHED THE TLINGITS PERFORM near the village's ceremonial longhouse hearth, mesmerized. The theatrical setting rested in a large rectangular pit dozens of feet wide and three feet below the longhouse's cedar plank floors. Behind the performance space a massive wall carving ten feet high and twenty feet across depicted a supernatural eagle figure in deep black, red, and green hues. Joshua noted the creature's multiple sets of eyes and wings, locked together in impressively intricate circular and rectangular patterns. Thick interior posts on either side of the wall carving offered fierce humanlike faces bearing teeth in ferocious silence. Eagle faces with carved protruding beaks and deep set, black rotund eyes rested just above them, stretching completely around the entire four-foot thick posts. Fifteen feet above Hall were large crossbeams holding racks of dried fish below giant vaulted ceilings over twenty-five feet high, where sunlight from the ceiling's several foot-wide smoke square morphed with flickering firelight.

Accompanied by a steady rhythmic drum beat and songs from seated singers, a Tlingit dancer wore a wooden frontlet hat with the Eagle totem crest while spreading his feather-costumed arms. Attached over the frontlet were signs of wealth: brilliant white eagle down, ermine furs, reflective copper plates, and iridescent abalone shell inlays. Hall was especially struck by the dancer's use of an eagle mask concealing his head and face. Two small human faces were carved into the forehead of the larger red eagle head.

The stunning stagecraft honored the coming of age of twelve-year-old twin boys, who, having received new ear piercings and hand tattoos of eagles, sat next to their proud parents and other prestigious guests. The two boys' clan kin were adorned in ceremonial frontlet hats and dark black cloaks holding woven images of the Eagle crest outlined with shiny mother-of-pearl buttons.

Hall quietly opened his log to pen a short observation.

Initiation ceremony for two Kuiu Tlingit boys' coming of age. Eagle totem house. Appears to unite the past and future into a transformative journey.

A stack of several gifts stood off to the side, and included thick elk-hide vests and two new muskets for the boys' parents, courtesy of *Eclipse*. Aside from Kekoa and Liko on board ship to keep watch, the entire *Eclipse* crew, including the sullen Peter Lansing, sat in a semi-circle on log benches elaborately carved with raven and eagle images on the ends. Next to Hall was Micah Triplett, his arm around Aolani's waist, while Thaddeus sat behind Triplett and Hall. On the other side of the longhouse was Captain Fletcher and Alamea. Discreetly sipping from a flask of whiskey every few moments, Fletcher, glassy eyed, grinned and occasionally tried to whisper in Alamea's ear or kiss her, drunk and oblivious to the cold look she gave him as she pulled away.

Hall noticed two young women and a small boy not more than five or six years old periodically enter the far side of the longhouse, away from the ceremonial area, placing food and utensils in various locations to prepare a ceremonial feast. Quietly moving in and out every few minutes, Hall wondered if the three Indians were Tlingits based on their appearance. He leaned toward Thaddeus, curious.

"Thaddeus, do you know the identity of those Indians on the far side of the longhouse? I'm guessing they're slaves."

"You're correct, sir. I actually spoke briefly with one of the women earlier today. The three were taken in a raid by several Haida war canoes over a year ago, faraway in Puget Sound. They are Salish. Apparently, the three are from the same village, but are unrelated to each other. She told me their small village was destroyed and those who survived fled in many directions. Raids on the tribes far to the south are not uncommon since it makes escape virtually impossible for captured slaves. No need to worry about them now, sir, slaves are never killed in these callings to honor children."

"When are they killed?"

"A funeral for a high-ranking person, a clan victory in war, or something similar. On rare occasions they're freed."

"I see."

Hall looked at the small Salish boy. The handsome child caught sight of Hall, despite the low light and theatrics in the longhouse, and managed a smile. A moment later, one of the slave women placed her hand on the boy's back, urging him to resume work. Before he turned to continue the boy grinned as Hall raised his left hand and waved. Hall's reason battled with his emotions, but empathy proved more powerful as he continued to watch the boy.

Aolani was surprised and pleased with Hall's interest in the Salish boy.

"Joshua. *Maika'i makua keiki kane!*"

Triplett sat up in confusion. With a puzzled expression, he glanced at Hall and roughly translated Aolani's Hawaiian expression.

"'A good father to the young boy?' What? What is this?"

"Sir, I should have recalled O'ahu women's talents of observation. It's my intention to free that Salish youngster over there, and perhaps the two women if we're lucky. That little one has his whole life ahead of him and deserves to see the world. He has the look of a fine sailor."

Micah grew alarmed.

"Joshua! This is not the place or time for that sort of thing!"

Concerned after hearing the exchange, Thaddeus added, "Sir, Mr. Triplett is right. An attempt to negotiate for the boy's freedom will, at the very least, cause severe complications, and—

Joshua interrupted.

"Thank you for your advice, but I've made up my mind. The boy is leaving with us on *Eclipse*."

TWENTY-ONE

A N ICY BREEZE SWEPT OVER THE VILLAGE to remind the *Eclipse* crew of winter's slow surrender at high latitude.

Negotiations grew delicate as the hours left to rendezvous with *Jackal* slipped away. Peter Lansing reminded Fletcher of the time left, only to be shouted away.

"Go wipe King George's hind quarters, or 'arse' as you Englishmen say. These are my negotiations, not yours, Mr. Lansing. Captain Coe will know to remain if we are delayed!"

The captain issued new orders as evening began. Only Tom could accompany Fletcher inside the Eagle Crest home for negotiations. Adding to Hall's dismay, Tom entertained the idea of training with the Kuiu men for war against the Russians.

"We need your intellect, not your fighting prowess, Tom," Joshua pleaded, but he recognized a few years in Boston with the Perkins family were no match for the young Tlingit man's passionate loyalty to kin and fierce love of land.

"Tom will always remain a Tlingit, as will I, but Tom is still negotiating his own journey between our worlds. He just needs time," Thaddeus remarked to Hall.

FLETCHER REMAINED UNAWARE OF HALL'S PLAN to offer payment for the Salish boy. Hall would only act after the captain had finalized his agreement with the Kuiu clans, so as not to disrupt any negotiations. Triplett and Thaddeus kept quiet on the matter, although Triplett still advised Hall against the move, arguing the boy would be a burden on the ship and Hall's responsibilities. Thaddeus warned of complications in trying to purchase the boy, particularly the strong possibility of exorbitant demands. Aolani kept quiet about Joshua's plan, with one exception: she told her cousin Alamea. Throughout the day, Hall noticed the two Hawaiian women speaking discretely with one another. Alamea frequently glanced at Hall, smiling with what seemed like admiration.

Captain Fletcher and Tom continued their talks with the clans' leadership. The rest of the crew relaxed by a large campfire at the opposite end of the village among the common people. The *Eclipse* crew mingled with dozens of individuals to share stories and trade small objects, with Thaddeus occasionally translating some of the villagers' conversations about fishing, hunting, clan politics, or gossip about relatives and friends. People of all ages, ranging from elderly individuals to small children playing with dogs and wooden toys, sat or loitered in the large grassy spaces around the fire.

A few commoners from clans holding the Wolf, Sea Lion, and Frog Totems prepared to speak. Hall was intrigued by the great deference and attention given to each speaker. One story by a young man around twenty-five years of age particularly captured the crew's attention. As he spoke, the man held a small pole that presented a foot-long carved wooden totemic frog in a sitting position with wide open eyes painted in green, red, white, and black. Thaddeus translated as the sky began to fade into a darker shade of blue above low rolling clouds. Glacial breezes from the island's interior sent embers spiraling into the air amid popping and hissing fir boughs in the fire. All activity halted as the young man spoke, with mothers admonishing small children who ran, shouted, or misbehaved.

"I remember when the Russians first arrived in our lands a few years ago and built their colony with the permission of our Sitka clan leader Skaultlelt. Baranov promised us many goods for our otter pelts and other furs. Instead, they have only stolen from us these last three years. Our sea otters have been taken by their Aleut slaves, who would all be killed by us were it not for Baranov's armed escort ships. Some of our slave women have been taken for wives by Baranov's men without permission. The Russians have no sense of honor or justice. Many are criminals who have defiled the Frog totem and the honor of our clans. Baranov's managers Kuskov and Medvednikov issue apologies, but nothing else is done. It is time for their contemptuous riffraff to go back home! If they refuse, we shall kill them and restore our property and honor!"

A huge cheer erupted. As the minutes passed, people of various clans and social ranks recited more stories of outrages and insults. As an older man finished a story about getting shot at by a Russian fur hunting party the previous year, three Tlingit canoes appeared in the distance below the increasing cloud cover, their occupants paddling in perfect synchronization to one canoe's steady drum cadence. The campfire orations ended as men, women, and children all rushed to shore to observe, with a few of the Kuiu men and women holding muskets for security. Hall, Triplett, and a few other *Eclipse* crew members grabbed their side arms as a precaution.

As the large war canoes came ashore, Hall was struck by the impressive woolen cloaks, rain hats, and copper and shell jewelry that ornamented the men and a few women. He noted one of the canoes was mostly empty with only three men when it could easily hold up to twenty or more. As formalities began, and small gifts of food were exchanged, Triplett, Hall, and Thaddeus inched closer over the small rocks of the shoreline to listen. Thaddeus translated for his officers, but his expression soon turned to concern.

"They are from Tlingit villages of the Taku River kwaan, which is quite distant from here, a journey of several days by canoe. A distinguished clan leader unexpectedly died just a few days ago, and they do not have enough slaves for the funerary calling now being planned."

"Why would slaves be needed at a funeral?"

Thaddeus measured the puzzled look on Joshua's face.

"Sir, the clan elite sponsoring the funeral at Taku desire slaves as they are symbols of great wealth. By giving them away to guests, freeing them, or killing them, the sponsors enjoy great prestige and honor."

Joshua's eyes widened. He bit his lower lip and motioned for Thaddeus to continue.

"Sir, the Taku men claim their slaves fled to a Russian ship in the straits last fall, and that some drowned in the attempt. They are here to purchase any available slaves for handsome prices, and to make invitations for select clan relatives here at Kuiu. The deceased leader's clan totem is—

Thaddeus hesitated as Joshua pressed the teenager.

"Go on, tell us. Micah and I need to know now."

"Sirs, the deceased Taku elder is of the Eagle Totem and the Raven Mother Lineage, the same as much of the clan leadership in this Kuiu village like those two twin boys and their relatives at the recent calling. It's thus a near certainty the clan leaders here at Kuiu will not only be invited to the funerary calling at Taku, they will almost certainly agree to give their Salish slaves for the ceremony."

Joshua struggled to process Thaddeus' words. Micah, empathetic, gently placed a hand on Joshua's shoulder and leaned into him.

"Joshua, your desire to free that young boy is noble and you're a good man for wanting to do it. You must realize there's at least several hundred slaves just on this section of the coast, perhaps more. And as I told you before, it's very unwise to interfere in the clans' personal business, especially when it comes to their ceremonies. We are foreigners among them. Trying to free that boy might also jeopardize—

Hall snapped at the first mate.

"Jeopardize what, sir? Securing some extra otter pelts? I will gladly give up part of my payment share at the end of the voyage if that's your concern. We're talking about the lives of an innocent boy and two young women."

"Joshua, you're letting your emotions overwhelm your logic and your duties as second officer on this ship," Triplett countered. "By trying to free that boy and the women, our entire crew and vessel is put at risk. If you insist on continuing I'll have no choice but to inform the captain. The circumstances have changed. Thaddeus, do you have anything to add for Mr. Hall?"

Thaddeus was unsure how to answer and hesitated, not wanting to be caught between the two officers and the growing conflict.

"Mr. Hall, sir, you would be wise to heed Mr. Triplett's advice. There's great risk in trying to negotiate the freedom of these particular slaves, as a funerary calling involves the prestige and honor of clan leaders. Perhaps there'll be a less volatile set of circumstances in the future where you could free a different slave."

By the time Hall crafted a rebuttal to his counterparts, an even larger crowd of Kuiu villagers descended around the shoreline of the Taku canoes. Not far behind them were Kuiu clan leaders, Tom, and Captain Fletcher. All seemed satisfied with the negotiation's outcome, and within moments younger clansmen shouted a trade agreement was reached with Captain Fletcher. Joshua remained focused on the young Salish boy as Triplett, Thaddeus, and several other crew members gathered to hear the details of Captain Fletcher's grand bargain.

Alamea eased through the crowd to stand beside Joshua. He sensed her silent support and empathy for the situation with the Salish boy as he admired her extraordinary beauty in the firelight.

TWENTY-TWO

Tom stood by the captain before the large gathering of villagers and *Eclipse* crew members, all watching and listening as the Kuiu clan leaders acknowledged the arrival of the Taku guests and their desire to buy slaves. After several minutes of ceremonial oratory reciting the glorious deeds of the deceased Taku leader and his clan, the Kuiu father of the twin boys announced his agreement with Captain Fletcher. Tom translated the speech for the *Eclipse* crew with each momentary pause.

"Villagers of Kuiu *kwaan*, we trade all eight hundred of our sea otter pelts and other furs to Captain Fletcher. Five of our best fighting men will accompany Captain Fletcher to the Stikine kwaan as protection against possible treachery from a King George ship and men of the Raven's Bones Totem. In exchange, Captain Fletcher gives us over one thousand yards of high quality blue and red cloth, fifty brass and copper tools, ten new muskets with ample powder and shot, and two small brass cannons. After their return from Stikine, Captain Fletcher and his men will provide assistance in driving the Russians from our land!"

After several moments of cheering and shouts of approval, Captain Fletcher spoke to the scores of villagers and the *Eclipse* crew. Hall and Alamea walked to the edge of the group to listen. As the captain spoke in broken Tlingit to offer thanks to the Kuiu clans, it soon became apparent to Hall and others that Fletcher was drunk. Joshua immediately made his way to Triplett and Thaddeus.

"Sir, it appears that our captain was a bit over indulgent with his whiskey during negotiations. In my opinion, the agreement just announced is far too generous. Our vessel is giving away too much to these Kuiu men. The Perkins contract states if you and I both object to a trade agreement, the captain must allow an opportunity for debate and reconsideration. That he negotiated while intoxicated strengthens our position. Are you with me?"

Rolling his lips inward in a pained expression, Triplett despised the developing dilemma as concern washed over him like an oncoming tide. With Thaddeus, Alamea, Aolani, and Hall staring at him, Triplett shook his head, flipping a small gray beach rock with his foot.

"I see what you want, Joshua. You wish my support in demanding the captain request the release of those slaves as part of the agreement. With all respect, you're risking far too much. And I . . ."

Aolani grabbed Triplett's hands and spoke forcefully in Hawaiian. Alamea nodded in agreement and added a few phrases in her native language to support her cousin. Triplett responded, likewise in Hawaiian, in a pained but determined effort to discourage them. Hall needed no translation as he felt the words' power and saw the two women nod in victory as Micah succumbed to their pressure.

"Alright, Mr. Hall, let's go speak with the cap. I must warn you though, if the Kuiu or Taku men threaten to break the agreement, or hint at violence, then that must be the end of this risky intervention."

Aolani embraced and kissed Micah, whispering words into his ear. Joshua observed Triplett's tension ease to the point where he even betrayed a half grin.

"Thank you, Micah, sir, rest assured, I'll not soon forget this."

FINISHING HIS BRIEF THANKS TO THE GATHERING on the beach, Captain Fletcher shouted orders to crew members on board *Eclipse* to begin loading the small launch boats with the various trade items and row them ashore as villagers brought out pelts from their homes. Believing their main business with Fletcher concluded, the Kuiu leaders spoke with the visiting Taku dignitaries about prices for the Salish slaves. Within a few moments, the two Salish women and small boy appeared and the pace of conversation among the parties accelerated as the slaves stood in silence watching the negotiations. Fletcher looked with satisfaction at his crew's efficiency in loading several skiffs and rowing them ashore. He turned to greet his two officers, oblivious to the serious expressions on their faces as the whiskey flowed through him.

"Mr. Triplett, Mr. Hall, look there at our marvelous ship. I bet Mr. Folger and Mr. Clark could organize and pack items on skiffs in their sleep.

Nothing finer than an experienced crew, unlike the green hands I some-times had on my voyages in the '90s. Liko and Kekoa are just as good as any New England mariner. Look at them move, it's almost like they have wings. What a bloody shame their islands have already come under a few pestilences from the outside. I mean, goddamn, Captain Cook only stum-bled upon them in '78."

Triplett folded his arms together as he looked over the bustling scene.

"A shame indeed, captain. As you may recollect, the same misfortune hit this part of the American coast according to Thaddeus and Tom. Their clan histories reveal a terrible epidemic sometime in the '70s, perhaps brought by a Spanish vessel. The symptoms Tom and Thaddeus described indicate a type of pox. It carried off up to a third of all the people living on these shores, at least that's what Tom's grandfather told him."

"Aye, terrible, just terrible. And yet, for whatever reason, God wills it." Fletcher sighed.

Hall's patience slipped at Fletcher's remark.

"With respect, captain, in my view, God had nothing to do with it. There are evil forces in the world, and when they strike, we must confront and combat them when possible, even if our efforts are belated and our means limited and small."

Fletcher responded with sarcasm and a touch of anger.

"I see, my second officer is not only a merchant seaman, but a secret missionary as well, I never would've guessed. What are your views on this subject, Mr. Triplett? And why the look of trepidation? We've just secured ourselves a healthy profit."

"Captain, Mr. Hall and I respectfully urge you to reconsider the agree-ment made with the Kuiu clans. We feel you've been overly generous with our trade items, and we humbly request—"

"What the bloody hell are you talking about?! Are you insane?! To re-voke this agreement would permanently damage our relations with the Kuiu villagers and wreck our profits so far! I am captain and supercargo of *Eclipse*."

"Captain, Mr. Triplett and I have the right under the Perkins Company contract to urge your reconsideration of a trade agreement if we both feel it's disadvantageous. We simply request—"

"Well you might as well save your breath because I'm not reconsider-ing anything! The agreement is made and I'll be damned to go back on it!"

"Sir, Mr. Triplett and I know you've been drinking, and we will duly report that to Mr. Perkins in Boston if you refuse to reconsider."

Enraged, Fletcher took out his whiskey flask and threw it on the ground at Triplett's feet.

"So now I have two goddamned Puritans as officers! William Bradford and Jonathan Winthrop back from the grave to lecture me on a few sips of whiskey? Have you lost your bloody minds?"

Within moments, the *Eclipse* crew's rapid pace on board ship and in the skiff boats slowed to almost a standstill. Kuiu and Taku dignitaries halted their discussions for the two Salish women and the boy. Fletcher sensed an overshadowing burden of eyes and ears upon him, including Alamea, who stared at him like a judge pondering the guilt or innocence of a defendant. Aside from the gentle lapping of the sea on the beach, an occasional mew gull's cries, and a dog barking in the distance, all was silent as fate collapsed in on the captain for a brief moment. Fletcher deliberately lowered his voice and slowed his speech.

"Alright gentlemen, what is this 'request' of yours? I hope it's reasonable, for all our sake."

Fletcher motioned to everyone to recommence the delivery and exchange of merchandise for the otter pelts.

Hall volunteered to speak first as the sounds of conversations and working resumed, much to Triplett's relief.

"Captain, Mr. Triplett and I agree we should not rescind any of the items promised here to the Kuiu men. That would be bad diplomacy, and thus, bad for business. However, we feel that due to the very generous volume of goods agreed to, additional compensation from the Kuiu men should be requested."

"Mr. Hall, the Kuiu men have promised us all of their otter pelts and other furs, there is nothing else to request."

"Captain, we have a different compensation in mind, specifically those three Salish Indian slaves over there. Alamea, Aolani and I can look after the boy, and we can drop the two women off to a vessel heading south to Puget Sound, or perhaps at the Russian-American Company settlement on Kodiak Island."

Fletcher, incredulous, struggled for a moment to respond. Alamea stared at Fletcher as she stood just a few feet behind Hall.

"Jonathan, no boy, no *ai*!"

The captain's expression turned to flustered consternation as he argued in Hawaiian with Alamea, demanding she reconsider her ultimatum.

Triplett grinned and placed his hand on Hall's back to urge him away.

"We have our captain now, Mr. Hall. Alamea's telling him no more sex for the voyage if we leave the slaves here, particularly the boy. My concerns from this moment forward are the Taku men bargaining for the slaves. They won't take kindly to our request to take possession. We need our crew to proceed with the transaction as quickly as possible and be armed and ready for any contingency that may arise here."

"Agreed, sir."

"I'll order the crew to accelerate the transaction of goods and furs on the skiffs without drawing too much attention, plus report the volumes to the captain as soon as I have the estimates."

"Thank you, Micah, sir. Captain Fletcher, Tom, Thaddeus, and I can negotiate the release of the boy and two women."

"Aye, Joshua. God be with you."

TWENTY-THREE

T OM AND THADDEUS SAT BESIDE FLETCHER AND HALL on a carved
spruce bench in the Kuiu village's main residence of the Eagle totem.
Just a few feet across from them, beside the home's fire hearth, were five
Taku men and one woman armed with knives and muskets, their long coal
black hair in feather-adorned buns, and noses and ears pierced with large
brass rings. Adjacent to them were seven Kuiu men holding new muskets
acquired from *Eclipse*, including the Eagle House's owner and father of the
twin boys. The Tlingit dignitaries seemed anxious to conclude the meeting and move on to other matters and spoke only a few minutes. Thaddeus
agreed to provide the translation with Tom's consent.

"Sirs, the Kuiu men of the Eagle totem have already been invited to the
funerary calling at the Taku kwaan, and the three Salish slaves are promised as gifts to their Taku kin. There's nothing to negotiate here because
this involves ceremony and honor. The Kuiu and Taku men hope you understand this is an entirely separate matter from the current business arrangement with *Eclipse*."

Fletcher, calm and composed, addressed the Kuiu and Taku dignitaries.

"I have a proposal. In exchange for the slave boy, I will offer additional
assistance to the clans' efforts to rid your lands of the Russians, who steal
so many of your otters."

Joshua scratched the back of his neck, alarmed with Fletcher's new offer while a Taku man spoke to his Kuiu hosts.

"This Boston captain and his second mate are quite the bold ones
facing us well-armed Tlingits here in this room, all for the sake of some

slaves. Their vessel and crew could indeed help us in driving out Baranov's vagabonds and thieves. But some of these Boston men over the years have proven themselves to be not much better than the Russians. Many lie and steal, and have no honor."

Another Taku man spoke.

"We are not engaging in trade here! We are inviting guests and collecting properties, including that slave boy, to honor our deceased father! Besides, these Boston foreigners cannot be trusted!"

Two Taku men nodded, followed by most of the Kuiu men. Fletcher slowly stood and handed some small brass trinkets to both the Kuiu and Taku parties.

"Please accept these gifts as appreciation for your time and consideration in this matter. I am departing to oversee the conclusion of our transactions with our gracious Kuiu hosts and prepare our vessel for departure. Mr. Hall, I leave you here with Tom and Thaddeus if you wish to conduct any further discussions on your own behalf, but I'll require your assistance within the half hour."

The Taku woman stood to scold her male counterparts after Fletcher exited.

"You fools! We can always get slaves at other villages! You did not even allow the captain a chance to elaborate and specify his offer! Let us listen to this officer here."

His mind racing for a proper response, Hall forced himself to speak slowly and deliberately in order to buy a few extra moments.

"My desire here is to obtain the boy and the two women if possible, with an honorable agreement if you are willing to engage with me. I cannot negotiate on behalf of the captain and our vessel, but I can offer you some of my own personal property. This may include my sidearm here, in addition to some fine red cloth. I can also trade you an exceptional spyglass in my pack that allows you to see things from a great distance."

The Taku woman was envious of the offer, in addition to other Taku men whom Tom identified as the woman's brothers. Arguments broke out among the Taku men and spread to some of the Kuiu men, leading the Kuiu house owner to step into the bickering and appeal for calm.

"Mr. Hall," Thaddeus blurted, "I strongly advise you to reconsider your offer! Many Taku leaders see this as a matter of honor and not business. As you see, some of the Kuiu men agree with them. Please, sir, if you don't break off your effort here you may be risking lives!"

"Thaddeus . . ."

Before Hall could finish the Taku woman's brothers raced outside to get the slave boy. Taku men opposed to the trade pursued them. The woman ignored the men and turned to Joshua.

"Officer Joshua, I accept your offer in exchange for the slave boy. The slave women, however, will remain with us for the journey back to our kwaan."

As Thaddeus and a few Kuiu men exited the house, Tom grabbed Hall's arm and spoke emphatically.

"Sir, if you are going to rescue that slave boy, it has to be now. I'll help you, but it can't wait."

Hall handed over his sidearm, spyglass, and red cloth to the Taku woman as she began to argue with the Kuiu house owner, who complained she was disrupting his business with Fletcher. The one Taku man remaining by the woman's side tried to mediate between the two, but unsuccessfully. Within a few moments all were outside the house, arguing. On the beach next to *Eclipse*, the movement of goods, pelts, and people accelerated.

Micah Triplett ran to Hall and Tom.

"Nearly all of the merchandise has been unloaded off *Eclipse*, but our skiffs still need to get the remaining one hundred pelts on board. What the hell is going on? The captain told me the deal for the slaves failed. Why are those Taku men arguing over the Salish boy?"

"I've traded for him. We have to move, now!"

Hall and Triplett rushed toward the boy, who was beginning to cry amid the shouting of four Taku men holding him and pulling in separate directions. Hall raised his voice.

"I'll tell you the details later, sir, right now we have to get the boy and the remaining pelts on board and leave. Inform the cap we must make sail within the next few minutes."

"You were able to make a deal for that boy?!"

"Yes, now move and get Thaddeus on board. Tom will assist me in getting the boy."

"Joshua, those men are well armed, it's too dangerous, you'll—"

"Damn it, Micah, sir! Lead or get out of the way! Tom, come with me!"

Joshua and Tom approached the arguing men and the crying boy. One of the Salish women dropped some *Eclipse* merchandise she was ordered to carry into the village and ran over to get the boy, only to be shoved to the ground by one of the Taku men. The woman jumped to her feet and began exchanging blows with the man. Several Kuiu men closed in on the scuffle in an attempt to quell the trouble, while the Taku woman held up the objects Hall had given to her. She shouted in vain for the fighting to end, while the boy cried out for the Salish woman. The slave fought her way back to the boy, only to be stabbed by one of the Taku men. She fell to the ground, screaming in agony. Tom and Joshua forced their way into the circle with Hall grabbing the boy as Tom shouted in Tlingit.

"The boy is ours! We traded with the noblewoman fairly, now let him go!"

A tugging match ensued with threats of force shouted by all parties. A Taku man pulled out and pointed a large knife at Tom.

"He's our property and you're disgracing our deceased father, now let go of him!"

Seeing their fellow crew members in danger after just coming ashore in their skiff, Lavelle Clark, David Woods, and Liko raced toward the confrontation. Fletcher, in another skiff making its way to shore, screamed out orders, but was unheard amidst the shouting on shore. The remaining *Eclipse* crew hurriedly pulled up rigging and prepared sails on orders shouted from Triplett, who was still in a pelt-loaded skiff approaching the ship. Instead of handing up the pelt bales to the crew, Triplett rowed back to shore after the crew heard his orders. To the shock and horror of Triplett and several other crew members, Captain Fletcher, after reaching the beach, ran to the remaining bales of pelts, loading them on his skiff instead of intervening in the altercation involving his crew. Gasping for air from the effort, Fletcher shouted at Hall.

"Get out of there now! Leave the boy and get the remaining fur bales on the skiffs! We need to evacuate immediately!"

A gunshot rang out. The Taku man wielding the knife fell to the ground, shot by Tom after lunging at Hall and the boy. Amidst the confusion, the boy's hysterical screaming, and the moans of the mortally wounded Taku man, Liko, Clark, and Woods managed to muscle their way out of the scuffle with the frightened boy. Tom and Hall joined them as they ran for the skiff. Hall saw Triplett toss his skiff's nearest fur bales overboard for better speed over the water and to make room for at least one crew member and the boy. Fletcher did nothing to ready his skiff, instead, he yelled for two sailors to grab the remaining fur bales. Woods obliged him with one bale after diving into the small boat. The skiff immediately pulled away from shore towards *Eclipse*. Two Taku men chased Hall's party with knives drawn, while another began loading his musket. Liko ignored Fletcher's shouts to grab the remaining fur bales and instead leapt into Triplett's skiff, spinning around to receive the hysterical boy from Hall.

Clark jumped into the remaining skiff, watching aghast as a musket ball hit the water mere inches away as Hall and Tom scrambled aboard. Moments later, in his haste to escape, Triplett smashed his skiff into a rock outcropping twenty feet from shore. An excellent swimmer, Liko grabbed the young boy and jumped into the ocean, struggling against the cold and an incoming tide while holding the terrified boy on his side as Hall, Tom and Clark turned their skiff to retrieve Triplett.

David Woods lifted fur bales on board *Eclipse* on captain's orders. Alamea screamed at Fletcher with fury and desperation as he climbed the starboard side netting to board.

"What are you doing?! You can't let this happen! Liko and the boy need your help. *Now!*"

Fletcher angrily shoved Alamea aside as he climbed on deck.

"Out of my way, goddamn it! Harper, Folger, lay down cover fire for our men! Lansing, throw a line to the skiff still out there! Thaddeus, Kekoa, finish making sail and get us the hell out of here!"

Aolani, terrified of the gunfire, huddled below the helm.

"Alamea, no!" she screamed as Alamea dove into the water.

Fletcher spun around to hear a splash in the ocean just below the port side. Alamea frantically swam towards Liko and the boy, reaching them after a few strong stokes. She grabbed Liko and the boy, helping them swim to the ship, reaching it just as the skiff holding Triplett, Hall, Tom, and Clark was able to secure the line thrown by Lansing. With the anchor lifted and the sails catching the breeze in the bay, Fletcher climbed back down the ship's side netting, tying an additional line and throwing it to Alamea and Liko, who still held the boy. Anchoring himself into the netting, Fletcher pulled on the line to help retrieve the two exhausted Hawaiians and the terrified Salish boy as gunshots rang out and musket balls struck the sea around them.

Clawing his way up to the deck, Liko collapsed for several moments from exhaustion, while Alamea and Aolani grabbed blankets for the traumatized boy as he gagged up seawater. Clark's skiff approached the port side, where Fletcher remained to assist the last crew members on board. After tying the skiff, Fletcher, Clark, Tom, Triplett, and Hall climbed on deck as the shocked *Eclipse* crew grew quiet. All eyes rested on Alamea, who glared defiantly at Captain Fletcher as she held the weeping, shivering boy tightly against her chest.

TWENTY-FOUR

J OSHUA HALL AWOKE FROM A FITFUL, DREAMLESS SLEEP to the sound of a strong gale. His hammock rocked in uneven bursts as *Eclipse* battled eastward through cold, subarctic air flooding over the coastal mountains from the continent's interior. Exhausted, Hall embraced the warmth of his two wool blankets as if his modest cabin was a wooden womb within the sheltering mother of *Eclipse*. Pulling out his log, he penned a few lines.

> *Tormented over the chaos caused by freeing the Salish Indian boy. Not sure of larger impact of this rescue on success of voyage and finding Elias, will have to answer to Perkins over this event if failure becomes our companion. Fletcher and Alamea at breaking point, creating much uncertainty and tension for crew.*

After sensing the ship dip into a deep trough after cresting a large wave, Hall began to overhear faint conversations from neighboring cabins in the momentary silence that followed. Much of the dialogue was lost to the tempest outside, with spoken words like drowning sailors struggling for breath between large waves. Still, Hall discerned a few bits of conversation while the ship navigated the trough below the wind.

He listened as Micah Triplett reported to Captain Fletcher in his cabin that winds, like the currents, were contrary, and constant tacking across the wide strait was unavoidable. The crew was doing its best under difficult circumstances to get the ship to the rendezvous island where *Jackal* would be waiting. Yes, the captain grants permission for some crew members to come below deck and rest, including Mr. Triplett. Fletcher himself will be going above to take command, and Hall should be awake in another hour or two. If, by chance, Aolani or Alamea, who are sleeping in Triplett's cabin with the boy, awake before Triplett falls asleep, Triplett is to send them above to speak with the captain.

After Fletcher climbed above deck, Hall heard only silence for several minutes, but low voices could soon be heard. The conversation's rapid pace indicated it had been ongoing and only recently evolved from whispers forever lost to Hall. A mix of mostly Hawaiian with a bit of English flowed from Triplett's cabin. Understanding limited words and phrases of Hawaiian, Hall only detected the names mentioned, "Jonathan," "Joshua," and "Kanoa." Alamea stated one phrase repeatedly throughout the conversation, "*a'ohe hou* Jonathan."

Repeating the phrase in a whisper to himself, as he recalled his time on O'ahu, Hall remembered the meaning, "No more."

AFTER SEVERAL HOURS OF LABORIOUS SAILING on alternating port and starboard tacks into the easterly winds, *Eclipse* reached a more sheltered area of the strait where the winds receded and the rains gradually transformed into low, thick mist embracing dark forested coastlines of large islands. Salty marine aromas and scents of spruce and fir wafted over the vessel, only to be temporarily washed away in rain showers that soaked sails, rigging, and protective clothing. The rain created a cold, damp chill throughout the ship as the crew complained for warmer and drier weather.

Above deck near the ship's bow, Fletcher argued with Alamea. Hall watched the captain hold up his arms, pleading his innocence against her scornful indictment. After a brief and unsuccessful mediation attempt by Triplett, Fletcher stepped on the ladder to descend below deck with the pain of rejection. Aolani and Thaddeus took the Salish boy to the stern of the ship, near the helm, where Hall periodically gave orders to the crew on navigation. The boy smiled as he approached Hall. Aolani knelt down beside the boy whispering encouragement into his ear. After several moments the boy spoke in a rehearsed, heavily accented English.

"Hello, sir, Mr. Joshua, my new name is Kanoa, 'the free one.' Miss Alamea gave me the name. I thank you for saving me."

Hall knelt down to be level with the boy and shook his hand.

"You're very welcome, young man. I'm pleased to have you on board."

Thaddeus spoke to the boy in a slow, basic Tlingit to translate Hall's response, and added a few additional questions to which the boy responded, punctuated with long pauses, in Tlingit with encouragement from Thaddeus and Aolani. As the boy explained tidbits of his life to Thaddeus, Hall admired the boy's improvised, but effective sailor's clothing and jacket the Hawaiians had cut and tailored from donated crew clothing. A dark wool cap and blue jacket accentuated the boy's handsome, chestnut brown eyes and long black hair, while a small Hawaiian turtle necklace draped about the boy's neck, a gift from Alamea.

Thaddeus translated the boy's responses.

"Kanoa believes he is six years old, and he remembers very little about his kidnapping from Puget Sound, except his village was burned to the ground and all were killed or captured. The Salish woman stabbed during the fight with the Taku men had drawn close to him, like an adoptive mother. He said the other Salish woman only recently arrived, and he did not know her, but what's interesting is she was delivered and sold by another ship of white men. Unfortunately, he doesn't know what ship or captain, which is not surprising given Kanoa's age and lack of English skills. Based on what Kanoa has told me about his own kidnappers, I'm guessing they were probably Haidas who later sold them to a clan house at the Kuiu kwaan. This would not be unusual."

A peculiar mix of empathy, pride, and determination swelled within Hall. Was he more like an older brother to the boy, or a father?

"Thank you, Thaddeus," Hall replied. "The Perkins Company informed us there are a few despicable captains who sometimes engage in slaving for the sake of advantages in trade. At least we've rescued this little one. It appears he has no home to return to, perhaps he's destined for O'ahu or Boston. Let's focus on having him learn English and the Hawaiian tongue as well. I'll teach him a few things on sailing when opportunities arise."

"Agreed, sir."

The boy made his way from the helm to the stern of the ship, followed by an overly-protective Alamea. Benjamin Harper, Lavelle Clark, Liko, Kekoa, and Nathaniel Folger gathered around the boy, joking and playing with him. Harper lifted Kanoa onto his shoulders to the boy's immense delight, and pointed at a passing pod of orcas in the distance.

"Mr. Hall, you and Kanoa remind me of my family, as my pap stole us away to Boston from the Chesapeake plantations back in '91."

"I'd heard this about you, Mr. Harper, but never learned the details. Exactly how did your father manage that accomplishment? That's quite a feat."

"My pap was hired out many times as a sailor with coastal southern traders for wages, which of course were later taken by our owner. Well, turns out on his fifth voyage there was a Nantucket Quaker on board traveling from Baltimore to Charleston and back to talk whale oil prices with customers. He secretly taught my pap some reading and writing when opportunities arose and wrote a letter to our owner requesting my pap's services on his ship in a few months. He promised high wages, triple the going rate at the time, the only condition being that I accompany him for training as a sailor. Well, our owner agreed, never realizing it was from a Quaker captain! We were lucky since my mama had been sold a few years earlier, so it was just the two of us! I'll never forget gettin' on board out on the Chesapeake under those giant white sails. They were like clouds against the big blue above, carrying us away to our liberty northward. So, you see, sir, the ocean was our means of escape, our pathway to freedom."

Nathaniel Folger pulled tobacco from his shirt pocket and grinned.

"From tobacco planting and picking to otter pelt trading. Here, Ben, have one of my smokes!"

Harper accepted the tobacco, thanking Folger. Laughter broke out among the crew, forcing a smile upon Alamea's previously stern expression in the wake of her bitter argument with Fletcher. Hall again relished in Alamea's beauty. Her graceful presence and manner only added to an overpowering, if not disquieting attraction that he was beginning to realize could never be defeated, only contained, though for how long he was uncertain. Resting her right hand on Kanoa's upper back and taking Hall's right forearm gently into her left, she spoke to the crew with gratitude and clarity.

"Joshua, you are a good and brave man for freeing little Kanoa. The rest of you are courageous as well. You have spirits rooted in the soils of the heart. You are not pathetic, wandering apparitions of men like some of the sailors who visit Hawai'i and this great northeastern shore of our ocean. Captain Jonathan, I am afraid, is now more of a ghost than a man."

Joshua felt his heart pound, not only at her touch, but also the realization that Alamea was selecting him. He wasn't certain if it were a choice of convenience or if there was more, and he labored, perhaps in vain, to secure wild and frightful passions within a box of reason.

ECLIPSE MOVED SLOWLY OVER THE MIST-SHROUDED SEA towards the small island in the distance. Identified by Peter Lansing as the rendezvous point with *Jackal*, the heavily wooded island appeared to be deserted. Captain Fletcher was taking no chances, however, having ordered up boarding nets with all hands armed and ready. Lansing, Triplett, and Hall stood next to Fletcher as the ship drew closer to the island, the swirling mists now revealing, for the moment, no ships, but instead two small fishing canoes with four unarmed Tlingit men. A temporary camp appeared on shore, where two Tlingit women tended fires and fish smokers next to a rack of freshly caught halibut.

"Lansing! Where the bloody hell is your goddamned *Jackal* ship?" Captain Fletcher yelled. "Yes, we're over a day late, but your captain should've had the basic sense to stay and wait. Coe can't be such a fool as to take on the Raven's Bones men by himself."

The Englishman was dismissive, his demeanor angry as he stood tense and rigid.

"You just answered your own question, captain. I warned you about being late to this rendezvous, but you wouldn't listen to me when we went over the charts. I suggest we—"

"Alright, shut your smart mouth! Mr. Triplett, Mr. Hall, I suppose the two of you recommend asking these Indians if they've seen *Jackal*?"

Hall weighed in first.

"Aye, captain. I also advise we drop anchor here and weigh our options, acquire some fresh fish, and allow our crew some much deserved rest after a difficult sail."

"I agree with Mr. Hall, sir, even if it's only for a few hours. Then we can be on our way again towards whatever destination we choose," Triplett added.

Fletcher frowned, perplexed with his first mate's answer.

"'Whatever destination,' Mr. Triplett? Now what do you mean by that? We're going to get our stolen pelts back from those insidious Raven's Bones men, whether Mr. Coe joins us or not."

Hall's exasperation eroded his patience, like a storm surge battering a sea wall.

"Sir, Mr. Triplett and I urge you to reconsider this whole scheme of sailing over to the Tlingit Raven's Bones village near the Stikine River to reclaim those pelts by force. The risks far outweigh the possible rewards, particularly since we don't have the Kuiu men with us, and—"

Fletcher shouted as he glared at Hall.

"Tom! Thaddeus! I require your services!"

The two Tlingit teenagers hurried to the captain, wondering what had triggered his latest outburst.

"Whether we locate Captain Coe and his vessel or not, we *will*, gentlemen, be heading over to that Stikine River village. And we *will* fight, if necessary, to recover this vessel's stolen property. I'll be damned if anyone on this lawless, unforgiving coast—insolent savages, conniving Englishmen, even a stubborn O'ahu wench—dares to stop me."

TWENTY-FIVE

ANCHORED THIRTY YARDS OFF THE FISHING CAMP'S SHORE, Hall, Fletcher, Lansing, Tom, and Thaddeus disembarked from *Eclipse* and rowed a skiff to the small island to offer a few small gifts in exchange for information from the four fishermen and two women. One of the Tlingit men spoke with Tom, his tone polite.

"I see you are of the Sea Lion crest, young man. These waters are owned by our totem crest, so feel free to drop some lines in as there are plenty of halibut."

Tom, wearing a new Tlingit rain hat, nodded in appreciation and accepted the offer.

"Thank you, I'll take you up on your offer as our crew could use some fresh fish. We're very tired since our ship passed through gales and rains further west, down the strait. We hope you enjoy these yards of cloth and copper utensils. We wish to inquire of you regarding an important matter. Have you by chance encountered a King George vessel named *Jackal*? An Englishman named Ian Coe is captain, and the crew is small."

Another fisherman responded as he untangled a net.

"Yes, we saw that ship two days ago, it was anchored not far from where your ship is now. Coe and one of his crew spoke broken Tlingit, but we understood each other enough to get by. We noticed he had some Haidas on board, but they never left the ship to come speak with us and mostly kept out of sight. That English captain kept asking us about other ships in the area, including your vessel, and villages that might be open to trading pelts. We told him that a great funerary calling was going to take place at Taku kwaan, and they would most likely offer many pelts for fine goods."

"Did he go there, to the Taku villages?" Tom asked.

Another fisherman spoke as he baited several large hooks carved from bone.

"Yes, at least that's where he told us he was taking his ship. What really convinced that King George captain to travel to Taku was when we mentioned many Stikine River villagers planned to head north to Taku, particularly the wealthy clan houses of the Raven's Bones totem crest. That really caught his attention."

Peter Lansing's eyes widened.

"Did Captain Coe indicate he would be returning to this island? Or did he leave instructions for us to meet him at Taku or Stikine?"

The fishermen looked at each other with puzzled looks before one of the Tlingit women interjected in English, to the surprise of the shore party.

"I can answer that question. I know what that King George captain said."

The woman became silent after her statement.

"And?" Fletcher and Lansing blurted out simultaneously.

"For ten more yards of fine red cloth, I will tell you."

Shaking his head, Fletcher bit his tongue and signaled to the ship to bring another skiff over with the requested merchandise. Once the woman had the cloth and secured it in her possessions box, she proceeded to speak.

"My village in the Henya kwaan had many Boston and King George ships visit over the years. One of my sons has been to Canton and the South Seas on a King George ship. He taught me much of your tongue. I now understand English fairly well."

Fletcher stared at the sky for a few moments, his patience clearly exhausted.

"Yes, ma'am, go on now and tell us, you've received your payment."

"Coe stated he would first proceed towards Taku kwaan to intercept and attack the Raven's Bones canoes heading north to reclaim some stolen furs. Afterwards, he would head south to Stikine and seize any remaining pelts from the Raven's Bones clan houses at their village. He boasted that his ship had Haida warriors on board and they would make quick work of the Raven's Bones men and any others who resisted them. He also said your vessel, *Eclipse*, was entitled to half the pelts stolen by some Raven's Bones men a few years ago. He instructed me to tell you to meet his vessel near the Stikine village. This now ends what I know."

Peter Lansing grinned.

"Ha! You see, Captain Fletcher, your fears have been misguided all this time! Captain Coe is honorable in his agreements! Your vessel doesn't even have to perform any of the unpleasant business of fighting the Raven's Bones men!"

"We'll see about that," Fletcher retorted. "Never underestimate these Tlingit clans, Mr. Lansing. They're well-armed and protect their property and homes fiercely. Nonetheless, gentlemen, we'll proceed to Stikine with our boarding nets and arms at the ready."

Hall remained skeptical and warned Fletcher and the shore party.

"Captain, we have no idea where *Jackal* or the Raven's Bones fighting men will be when we arrive at Stikine, nor do we know the exact location of the stolen pelts. The risks are still too great in my opinion."

Fletcher strutted toward the skiff, angry, without looking at Hall. His resentment was building toward his second mate.

"Which is why we'll head to Stikine, Mr. Hall. To gain more intelligence on this situation. And if Captain Coe proves himself dishonorable, I'll personally sell Mr. Lansing as a slave to the highest bidder among these clans. We'll take precautionary measures and assess our options at Stikine. Now, we have no time for fishing for halibut. Tom, prepare the skiff, we depart immediately."

AFTER THE SHORE PARTY WAS BACK ON BOARD and *Eclipse* pulled anchor and set sail in the light winds, the four Tlingit men resumed their halibut fishing around the small island. A solitary raven hopped along shore uttering low-pitched calls over the green sea. The two women watched the Boston brig slip into low set clouds, slowly sailing eastward into the increasingly narrow strait towards the Stikine River.

On board ship, Joshua Hall looked back upon the fading shore of the island with unease, noticing for a few fleeting moments a great blue heron fending off a glaucous-winged gull over a small fish just off the beach.

Thaddeus stood beside Hall.

"Sir, I see you're anxious."

"Unfortunately, yes," Joshua mumbled. "But don't worry about me."

Thaddeus looked back at the small island and its patch of rocky shore near the spot where the Tlingit fishermen had returned to their endeavors.

"Did you see that blue heron battling the gull a moment ago? The animals can tell us many things about ourselves, such as sea captains trying to outwit each other."

"I suppose you have a story to tell me Thaddeus? I would like to hear one. Tom and two boys told me one not long ago about Yel."

"Yes. This story also involves Raven."

Sipping a mug of hot tea, Hall remained silent, but nodded slightly for Thaddeus to proceed. Thaddeus grinned and began the story.

Raven was hungry and walked along a beach. The sea teemed with herring, but he was too lazy and didn't want to work for his food. He had to think of a way to get the fish.

Raven looked around and saw a heron standing in the ocean, fishing, while nearby a gull swallowed a fat herring he had just caught. Raven thought to himself, 'I must have that herring or I will starve.' So, he walked up to Heron and spoke to him and then went over to speak to Gull.

Returning to Heron, Raven said to him, 'I did not want to tell you this, because it's none of my business, but I feel that I must since I am your friend. You saw me speaking with Gull over there a moment ago, right? He said that you are stupid, ugly, and that all of your ancestors were wretched slaves.' Heron looked over at Gull, but did not say anything.

After a few moments, Raven walked back to Gull and spoke with him again, saying, 'You saw me talking to Heron just now? I regret to say this very much, but he called you several bad names and insulted your ancestors.' Gull said nothing but looked over at Heron.

Raven walked back again to Heron and told him, 'I think I should warn you. Gull just told me that he is coming over here to fight you. I advise you to kick him hard in the chest if he carries out his threat, as this is the only way to beat him.' Heron looked over at Gull who seemed agitated.

Raven went back to speak with Gull and told him Heron was angry and wanted to fight him. Raven told Gull how he should use his strong chest if Heron tried to kick him. At that moment, Heron shifted his feet because the other was getting tired.

'See!' shouted Raven to Gull. 'He is preparing to come over and fight you! You should attack him now, while you still have a chance! Remember to use your chest as a shield!'

Grateful for the warnings from their friend Raven, Gull and Heron began to fight each another. Heron kicked at Gull and Gull used his chest just as Raven had told him. When Heron's foot struck him, the hard blow made the herring come out of Gull's stomach. Raven caught it before it hit the water and flew away, laughing at the two birds. Heron and Gull realized they had been tricked by Raven and ceased their combat.

Raven flew away looking for his next meal as he was still hungry.

Hall laughed and smiled in appreciation as he took another large sip of tea. The rocky beach disappeared behind thick sheets of rain, and the gull and heron were no longer visible. A faint solitary call of a raven reached the two men, only to vanish into the familiar sounds of winds and wake.

TWENTY-SIX

LAVELLE CLARK PULLED HIS WEIGHTED DEPTH MEASURING LINE amidst small pieces of glacial ice floating in the strait.

"Five fathoms captain! The measurement matches your charts, sir. We must be near the Stikine!"

"Very well, Mr. Clark!"

Fletcher looked at his ship's underfilled sails and spoke as Hall and Triplett stood by the helm.

"Now if this pitiful wind would pick up, this damned fog might lift. This country seems to be stuck in autumn for nearly the entire year, and—"

David Woods pointed to the south, interrupting.

"Sir, a pod of otters off the starboard bow! Lavelle, grab my musket!"

Hall ran to view the sea otters along with a few other sailors, curious as to why Triplett and Fletcher failed to follow him. Within moments, he stood a few feet from Woods and Clark as they took aim at the floating mammals, fired, and missed. As soon as the musket balls hit the ocean the five otters instantly dove below the surface and disappeared.

Fletcher bellowed laughter.

"You boys won't see them again anytime soon! When they resurface it will be far away from us, closer to the large glacial ice. And that is why we New Englanders must acquire our otter pelts by other means. Only the natives of these lands know how to catch the creatures. Old man Baranov and his Russians are wise to use Aleutian Islanders in their fur company. The Aleuts are masters of the sea hunt."

Triplett added to Fletcher's comments as Hall and some of the crew returned to the stern of the ship.

"They are indeed, as are the Kodiak Islanders. I even hear Baranov and a small number of Russians have learned the skills as well. I remember once, on my last voyage, watching two Aleutian one-man hunting boats, *baidarkas* as they are called. The Aleut men, with great stealth and the element of surprise, speared the animals from a distance. Flotation devices made of sea mammal intestines were used to further exhaust the animals after they dove underwater. When the otters surfaced the men finished them off, with only a tiny spear point in the pelt. I wouldn't be surprised if this otter pelt trade diminishes a few years from now. The Tlingit and Haida clans take an enormous number themselves, and now Baranov's Aleuts are here in these seas as well. I'm glad I'm not an otter!"

After a few bits of fleeting laughter from crew members over the folly of Woods and Clark, Fletcher took advantage of the gathering and called together his crew.

"Men, although we have slight winds and much fog around us, I've decided to push on to the Stikine village, where houses of the Tlingit Raven's Bones men reside. At stake are several hundred pelts, pelts that will provide income to feed, shelter, and clothe your families back home. We may encounter *Jackal* and simply acquire our share of pelts, but do not stake your hopes on this, as you well know the harder pathways tend to prevail over the easy ones in our profession as seamen. We've taken precautions with our boarding nets, and each sailor on board is to be equipped with side arms, while others will man our cannons. My orders are to be obeyed instantly and without question during our encounter ahead."

Alamea glared at Fletcher defiantly from the opposite side of the ship, holding Kanoa at her side.

"Why have you ignored the words of Joshua and Micah? You betrayed my heart, Jonathan. I *will not* allow you to betray the families of these men by getting them killed over some pelts!"

The captain exploded into a scalding rage.

"Get below deck, you damned insolent bitch, and take that bastard boy with you before I throw both of you overboard! It is you, Alamea, not I, who has hindered our chances of a profitable voyage thus far! And you will address me as captain from now on, or I'll lock you and that boy below!"

Micah Triplett and Nathaniel Folger rushed to Alamea and Kanoa to take them below deck as Liko and Kekoa climbed down from nearby rigging to confront Fletcher. Hall and the remaining sailors formed a wall to separate the infuriated men from each other.

"You touch Alamea and I will kill you myself, you damned coward!" Liko shouted.

Kekoa immediately turned from Fletcher to grab Liko, knowing threats against the captain were punishable by severe lashings, cut rations, and lengthy confinement in the ship's smallest cabin.

Triplett tried to diffuse the situation.

"Enough! All of you! I demand order! Now! Lansing, Woods, Kekoa, escort Liko below deck! Mr. Hall, Mr. Clark, Tom, Thaddeus, assist me in calming the captain!"

Ignoring Triplett, Liko and Fletcher broke free from the men trying to restrain them, with Fletcher pulling out a knife and holding it to Liko's face.

"Threaten me again Liko and you're a dead man!"

A musket shot and the smell of gunpowder consumed the deck. Aolani peered out of a partially opened hatch and held a small hand musket that shook violently in her trembling hands. Tears streamed down her face as she put the gun down and wept hysterically. Shouts of "Aolani! Aolani!" shot through open hatches from below deck as Fletcher laid down his knife and slowly backed away, holding his hands in the air to indicate a truce. Silence shrouded the group for several moments. The sounds of the ship moving through the water, accompanied by periodic bumps of small chunks of ice against the stout oak hull, were all that remained.

TWENTY-SEVEN

*E*CLIPSE CRAWLED OVER THE SILENT SEA, approaching the Stikine village that rested behind the fog. Hall prayed the fragile truce negotiated by Triplett and himself would hold, lest an all-out mutiny transpire. In exchange for Captain Fletcher's pledge to drop all threats of punishment against Liko and Alamea, the crew promised their full support to carry on with the business concerning *Jackal* and the Raven's Bones men. Liko apologized to Fletcher and recanted his threat as part of the bargain, although Hall knew Liko would closely watch the captain for the rest of the voyage. Hall secretly pledged to the Hawaiian men that he would personally intervene to protect Alamea from the captain should Fletcher go back on his word.

All was quiet in the small village, with no one visible on shore despite *Eclipse* being less than fifty yards from the beach. On Fletcher's orders, Thaddeus and Tom shouted to the village asking for a meeting with clan leaders willing to discuss an exchange of furs, and if anyone had seen *Jackal*. After a few moments of silence, a middle-aged woman emerged from a longhouse near the shore.

"No, we have not seen the vessel you speak of. Most of our village traveled north for a Taku funerary calling, including all of our clans' nobility and most of our common folk. There are only a few of us here of the Drifted Ashore and Raven's Bones Houses, and most of our pelts went north to Taku."

Twenty people emerged from the homes and longhouses over the next few minutes, most of them middle aged and elderly women, with a few old men and children. The woods beyond the edge of the village were almost entirely hidden by fog. Micah Triplett labored to suppress his fear.

"Captain, this could be a malicious trap. I can't see any young men on shore, only kids and older people. We don't know who might be hiding in the village or those woods. Remember, sir, we can always wait this out or return in more favorable conditions."

Fletcher fought to contain his temper and respond in an even tone.

"I'm well aware of the risks, Mr. Triplett, which is why we'll proceed with extreme caution. You and I will lead a well-armed shore excursion, while Mr. Hall will be in command of the ship's defenses should any treachery arise. Tom! Mr. Lansing! Mr. Woods! Liko! Prepare a skiff and assemble your weapons, we're going ashore."

Fletcher rubbed the back of his neck, adding, "These damned insolent natives only appreciate bold action, and we must seize the initiative for ourselves."

Seeing there was no changing the captain's mind, Hall ordered the remaining crew to man the ship's defenses, with Aolani, Alamea, and Kanoa to go below deck.

"I will remain here with my musket, Joshua," Alamea retorted, "Aolani will take Kanoa below deck. Don't ask me to leave again. I am *wahine ka'ua*. Battle woman."

Hall's admiration for her courage outweighed his annoyance with her for defying his order.

"Very well, Alamea, you can take a position by the mast."

Hall turned to the rest of the crew.

"There is to be no firing of any weapon unless I give the command. Should I fall, Mr. Folger will be in command followed by Mr. Clark."

THE SKIFF REACHED THE SHORE WHERE TOM addressed the small gathering of villagers.

"Captain Jonathan Fletcher of Boston requests a search of your village. We're looking for some pelts stolen from our vessel. In exchange for your cooperation, he offers you some fine gifts of brass and cloth. You will only receive them, however, once the furs are shown to us."

The middle-aged Tlingit woman who first spoke to *Eclipse* responded with resigned indifference.

"Very well, we are poorly armed and few in number, while you are strong and powerful. I will lead you to the bales of pelts, follow me."

Triplett's concerns tumbled closer to panic, for apathy and submission was not the Tlingit way.

"Sir, this is all too easy, there's something wrong here."

"Settle your nerves, Mr. Triplett. Tom, Lansing, come with me. Liko, Mr. Woods, stand guard over this group of people."

The shore party arrived at a small house bearing the Raven's Bones totem crest, where the woman pointed Fletcher to a few bales of pelts hidden below several large chests.

Fletcher frowned, disappointed with what he saw.

"Damn, only about a fifth of the stolen pelts are here. Coe must have intercepted the rest somewhere between this village and Taku."

"Captain Fletcher, there's no need for alarm, Captain Coe will honor his agreement," Lansing replied, his voice calm.

"He better," Fletcher warned, "because if he betrays me I'll have your hide, boy."

Triplett's anxiety surged with each moment, for he felt betrayal was at hand.

"Sir, I recommend we load these pelts on to the skiffs immediately, leave our gifts, and be on our way. Perhaps you and Tom can search the remaining houses here while Liko, Mr. Lansing and I load these bales."

"Agreed, Mr. Triplett."

Several minutes passed without incident as the three men carried the bales of pelts from the home near the edge of the woods to the skiff. Tom and Fletcher soon returned to announce there were no other pelts in the village.

Lansing, grimacing, scanned the woods before turning to Fletcher.

"Captain, there are just two bales left at the house, would you mind if I relieve myself in the woods? That pork stew from last evening has gotten the better of me, I'm afraid."

"Very well, Mr. Lansing, but make it fast. I'm not going to wait an eternity as we have our business nearly concluded."

As Lansing disappeared into the forest, David Woods and Liko carried the remaining bales to the skiff. Most were loaded and rowed to *Eclipse* just a few dozen yards from shore.

"Now was that so dreadful gentlemen?" Fletcher shouted smugly to the ship.

PACING THE SEAWEED STREWN TIDAL ZONE, Triplett barely contained his panic in the shadow of Fletcher's overconfidence.

"Tom has already distributed the brass trinkets and red cloth to the villagers. Where the fuck is Lansing?" Triplett hissed.

"Relieving himself of Mr. Clark's cooking from last night."

Fletcher remained calm and confident, pleased with the ease with which he'd obtained the pelts.

Within moments a middle-aged man approached Tom, Triplett, and Fletcher, waving his arms as if performing for a large audience in a theater. Liko had just returned to shore with the skiff as the man began shouting in Tlingit.

"Young man, I see you are of the Sea Lion totem crest! You may be a Tlingit, but you are still a foreigner here amongst our people of the Raven's Bones and Drifted Ashore Houses! You tread on our clan properties, along with your captain and the others!"

Fletcher instinctively pulled a sidearm and aimed at the man, followed by Triplett and Tom. The man shifted to a voice barely above a whisper as he addressed the shore party, while Liko pulled the skiff onto the beach.

"That was for show in case the King George men and their Haida allies are watching us right now from the woods. I must warn you, the King George captain kidnapped three of our clan nobility, taking them as hostages, and burned our canoes when we were traveling north to Taku. He also seized nearly all of our furs and only brought a few of us back here to our village, threatening to kill us and the hostages if we spoke of this to you. The other villagers were let off at another Stikine kwaan village south of here. The King George captain intends to ambush you! Please, captain, our clan houses will trade you the other pelts if you help us free our kin!"

After Tom furiously translated for Fletcher, Triplett, and Liko, Fletcher gave no orders, instead, he sprinted towards the woods.

"Lansing, get your miserable fucking hide back out here!"

A volley of musket fire opened up from the forest in flashes of red, piercing the dense, low mist. Within moments, six Haida fighters streamed out of the woods, screaming war cries and accompanied by Peter Lansing and two other *Jackal* sailors. The scene momentarily stunned Captain Fletcher, despite the shots tearing past his head and body.

"Fuck! Liko's been shot!" Triplett shouted.

Fletcher sprinted back toward the shoreline as Triplett and Tom struggled to lift Liko's large, motionless body into the skiff. Cover fire rang out from *Eclipse,* which cut down two Haidas and slowed the other attackers, who cautiously advanced while repeatedly loading and firing their muskets. Fletcher glanced back as he got closer to the skiff, seeing Peter

Lansing grin at him before firing his musket. The shot hit Fletcher in the left forearm, knocking him to the ground. His rage overwhelming his pain and fear, Fletcher turned and fired his sidearm without aiming as he scrambled to his feet towards the skiff.

"You goddamn son of a bitch! I'm going to kill you Lansing! You hear me you bastard! I'll string you up alive and skin your balls!"

Tom, still struggling with Triplett to get Liko's body into the skiff, shouted at Fletcher.

"Captain, please, we must get into the skiff!"

A moment later shouts arose from *Eclipse,* filling the air.

"Canoes! Canoes! There! They're firing on us!"

On board *Eclipse,* Joshua Hall furiously screamed orders as the crew scrambled to fight off the attackers from both land and sea.

"Harper, Kekoa, Folger, keep up the cover fire for our shore party! Alamea, Thaddeus, Clark, follow me to starboard, we must engage the canoes!"

As gunfire roared on deck and on shore, Thaddeus recognized the attacking canoes.

"Mr. Hall, those are the Haida men! And look, there's white men with them too!"

"Keep up your fire!" Hall shouted.

To Hall's amazement, Clark, Alamea and Thaddeus all proved to be deadly shots, killing and wounding several Haida men in the attacking canoes. Hall fired a brass cannon at one of the four canoes, sinking it instantly and forcing one of the other canoes to disengage from the attack and retrieve survivors floundering in the water. Thaddeus dropped his musket after his powder misfired.

"Fuck! A flash in the pan!"

Thaddeus pulled a sling of dressed moose skin and hurled a small iron spike at tremendous velocity. The hull of an enemy canoe cracked open from the spike's impact, forcing the remaining two canoes to take on the occupants and withdraw back into the fog.

Hall heard Nathaniel Folger yell above the noise.

"Look, there's a ship off our port side! We're saved!"

Hall raced to the port side of *Eclipse* with Folger to see a vessel emerging several dozen yards distant in the murky fog.

"Everyone, keep your fire up towards the shore! Train the cannon fire on the area just below the woods! I'll see what this is about."

Folger grew confused as the ship approached.

"Sir, why aren't they firing in support of us? Wait, is that *Jackal*?"

Without warning, musket rounds fired from the approaching ship, hitting Folger's left arm and lower abdomen. The sailor fell to the deck, screaming in pain. Hall took cover as musket balls and small cannon fire hammered *Eclipse*, damaging some of the ship's hull and rigging.

Lavelle Clark shouted above the battle as he reloaded his musket.

"Folger was right, it's the damned *Jackal*! They've betrayed us!"

Hall saw Alamea and Clark race to return fire with two blunderbusses that scattered shot over a wide area. Ben Harper hurried to position a brass cannon as Hall struggled to move the wounded Folger to a more protected area on deck.

Kekoa screamed as tears flowed down his cheeks.

"Mr. Hall! Captain Fletcher, Tom, and Mr. Triplett are still shouting at each other on shore! They can't get Liko into the boat!"

"LIKO IS DEAD! THERE'S NOTHING WE CAN DO FOR HIM! Now grab those last two bales and row for your lives men!" Fletcher demanded, gripping his wounded forearm.

"Do as the captain commands, Tom! We must evacuate now! He's dead!" Triplett ordered.

With musket balls tearing through the sand and seaweed around them, the men reluctantly grabbed the remaining bales and then pulled away from shore.

"Lord forgive us! Please guard Liko's soul!" Tom muttered between heavy breaths as he and Micah rowed toward *Eclipse*.

Triplett, his lungs on fire from furious rowing, said nothing. Holding his wounded forearm and lying beside the fur bales, Captain Fletcher watched as tears flowed down his first officer's face. Remaining silent amidst his two crew members' labored breathing, Fletcher held pressure on his wound as he looked down, his face red with rage as he listened to taunts shouted from Peter Lansing and the others on shore.

The skiff reached *Eclipse* under a deafening roar of musket and cannon fire as the crew continued their assault on *Jackal*. Fletcher and Triplett noticed Hall's tactics in concentrating fire upon the vulnerable areas of the smaller vessel were proving effective. For a few moments Hall and the rest of the crew caught sight of Captain Ian Coe, who stared angrily at Hall before ordering his crew to disengage from *Eclipse* to the southwest. Within less than a minute, all fire ended as *Jackal* vanished behind the low-lying fog. As Fletcher, Tom and Triplett climbed aboard carrying the last two bales of pelts, they heard Nathaniel Folger moaning, though his agony was subsequently drowned out as Aolani and Alamea wailed inconsolably over Liko's death.

With the ship damaged and still in danger of another attack, Fletcher ordered *Eclipse* to depart northwest towards the evening subarctic sun, its faint reddish hues nearly obscured by the deep green of forest and sea.

TWENTY-EIGHT

JOSHUA HALL EMERGED FROM BELOW DECK to issue a report to Fletcher on the status of Nathaniel Folger. Walking across the midsection of the ship through the mist, Hall noticed Fletcher glance toward him. The captain instinctively knew his weakened authority and Hall's strength.

"Mr. Hall, you performed well in defending our ship and crew. You have my gratitude."

"Thank you, sir. Mr. Triplett and the rest of the crew also deserve thanks for their perseverance during our misfortune several hours ago. We'll report Captain Coe's barbarism to the next vessel we encounter. That fiend's responsible for the death of Liko and possibly Nate, who I'm sorry to say, captain, is in very bad condition. He may yet pull through, however."

"Save him, Mr. Hall, whatever it takes. He's our best carpenter and boatswain, and we sorely need his skills now, given the damage to our rigging and hull." Fletcher shook his head and stared out to sea, adding, "And yes, that son of a bitch, Coe, and his rabble will get what they deserve, a voyage with Captain Lucifer to an eternal fiery hell."

Sipping whiskey, Fletcher scrutinized the bandage Hall had placed on his wounded forearm before glancing across the deck to see Alamea walk hand in hand with Kanoa. A feeling of hopelessness overtook the captain.

"Love leads to passion, and passion leads to blindness, a blindness that locks a tormenting night around one's heart. One searches for a key to unlock the boxed darkness, but one cannot always find one, at least not right away."

Sighing, Fletcher continued, nodding in Alamea's direction.

"That wild soul over there has blinded me. The success of this voyage is the only key I have left. Please see to it that it's not lost."

A moment of silence passed between the two men. Hall mustered all of his patience and empathy to restrain his anger at Fletcher's decisions.

"Captain, you should go below and rest. Mr. Triplett and I recommend we find a secluded area to make landfall and tend to Mr. Folger, gather fresh food and water, and make repairs to the ship. Tom and Thaddeus informed us there are medicinal plants on shore that could possibly aid Mr. Folger as well as yourself."

Triplett appeared from below deck.

"Captain, our charts for this particular area of the straits are deficient, particularly on depth measurements, however, Mr. Hall and I feel it imperative to stop soon given the frequent fogs and lack of strong winds. Tom and Thaddeus can assist us in finding a good hiding place somewhere among the many islands along this stretch of the Inland Passage. After regaining our strength and making repairs, we could sail for the open sea and link up with friendly vessels off the coast for assistance to find and capture Coe and his crew," Triplett added.

Fletcher walked to a small bench in the rear center of the ship and took a seat. The sails snapped in the light winds, but otherwise there was silence as Fletcher considered his options.

"Gentlemen, you offer sound advice. However, we must push on to the open sea. This weather has to change soon. *Jackal* and her vile riffraff could stumble upon us, and many of the clans in these central straits have caused trouble for certain vessels. Mr. Triplett, you may recall the story of the *Jenny* in 1800, for it was around this very strait that Captain Bowers lost some of his men to Tlingit slavers. Remember our meeting with him at the tavern last year? And then there's the disappearance of Elias and *Panther*. No, I don't want to risk a landing given our condition. We can make repairs here on the sea. Better that than to risk slavery or death."

Hall rubbed his forehead in frustration as he composed a rebuttal.

"Points taken, captain. However, with due respect, I must disagree with you on the level of damages to our vessel. The rudder suffered a hit from a small cannonball, and although it's still working it might break at any moment. Our headsail's rigging is also severely damaged, plus our aft mast's upper spar. We must put ashore at the earliest safe location."

Triplett sensed Hall's refusal to back down. Perhaps Fletcher would be open to reason if both officers stood firmly in opposition.

"I concur with Mr. Hall, sir. And there are many shoals around these straits, captain, which combined with the fog elevates our risk of going aground. You saw the damage we inflicted on *Jackal*. Coe's out there licking his wounds as well."

Fletcher, irritated and exhausted from his injury, doggedly held to his position to the surprise and disappointment of Triplett and Hall.

"I'm going below, gentlemen, to recuperate. My order stands. We press on to the coast and leave the straits for now. The crew will make repairs as best they can. *Eclipse* is a tough old bitch. We'll join other vessels at the coast because I'll be damned if we let that infernal bastard Coe get away with his crimes. And I'm personally going to crucify that rotten scoundrel, Lansing. May God rest Liko's soul."

FACING THE EAST, KEKOA CHANTED a melancholic refrain in Hawaiian as Alamea, Kanoa, and Aolani stood silently nearby. Triplett translated for Hall and the other crew members gathered to remember their fallen crewmate.

> *Left in the misty air*
> *Are the bones of the traveler*
> *My body lies sleepless*
> *My eyes strain into the distance*
> *Like a chilling fog is my bitter grief*

Kekoa, holding Liko's favorite tapa cloth shirt and pants, handed them to Alamea. Whispering in Hawaiian for her lost brother as she looked to the sky, she soon bowed her head and after a few moments threw the islander clothing into the sea. At her request, the entire crew turned to the west before returning to their duties. Wiping her tears away, Alamea rested her hands on Kanoa as she stood behind him. She looked at Joshua, and hung a small cloth sling over Kanoa's shoulder with a few of Liko's koa wood carvings and his Haida pipe from Kaigani.

"Joshua, Kanoa now has Liko's mana. We must see to it that he grows into a brave and strong man, with kindness and a gentle heart. Like Liko, he must never fear chasing the stars over the horizon."

TWENTY-NINE

Hours passed as *Eclipse* sailed onward through the mists to the northwest. The crew improvised repairs to the rigging and rudder, aided by barely perceptible winds and their slow-moving ship. As Hall oversaw the repairs to the aft mast's upper spar, David Woods and Lavelle Clark shouted out depth measurements once every few minutes. The fathoms measured were slowly shrinking in number, but still provided safe depths well below the ship's keel. Triplett ordered continual port and starboard tacks to find deeper water.

"We are fighting an incoming tide," Triplett remarked to Hall. "The wind's not strong enough yet, and we can't see a goddamn thing beyond fifty yards."

While he shared Triplett's frustration, Hall remained calm, letting the silence settle over them for some time.

"Patience, sir. Let us focus on what we can see, measure, and hear."

Hall called for Tom and Thaddeus as he looked over the charts once again.

"Tom, Thaddeus, what's your best guess on our location?"

"Sir, Tom and I have only been through this particular area twice, and in canoes, when we were much younger. There are many small uninhabited islands around here, but unfortunately underwater shoals as well as strong currents and tides accompany them."

Tom pointed to the chart as he smoked a small tobacco pipe.

"Sirs, my best guess is we're near this small cluster of islands, in the territory of the Kake kwaan villages. If we can make our way past these channels here, we'll soon be out into the main strait leading to the coast and the Sitka kwaan. Sirs, if you don't mind my asking, why would the captain insist on making for the coast in this fog and unfavorable wind and tide? Surely, we can find a safe anchorage around here. There's nothing other than infrequently visited fishing camps on these small islands."

"Perhaps he thought the weather would improve in our favor," Triplett remarked. "However, the real reason is *Jackal*, plus the danger of encountering a large Tlingit canoe flotilla that might enslave us."

Escaping the unpleasant direction of the conversation, Hall shouted to the crew above deck.

"Crew members who have been awake over twenty-four hours may go below to rest. For those of you who have not, or wish to remain above deck, extra rations of coffee."

MORE HOURS PASSED AS *ECLIPSE* BARELY MOVED over the gray green sea in the foggy dampness. Joshua Hall, Lavelle Clark, Aolani, and Thaddeus played with Kanoa, whose antics lightened the otherwise dreary surroundings. They sipped coffee and waited, hoping for more favorable winds.

"Aolani," Hall asked, "you seem quite skilled there with Kanoa. Do you have any children back on O'ahu?"

"No, sir. But as a young girl on O'ahu, I spent many days tending my four younger brothers. Young Kanoa reminds me of them. When I was eleven, I went to live with my cousin Alamea on my uncle's lands. That's when the invasion happened and our ali'i lost everything. Micah and I will marry once this voyage ends, and we intend to live on Kaua'i. Or perhaps Martha's Vineyard or Boston, we shall see."

"And Clark, what about you, what place do you call home in Rhode Island?" Hall continued.

"I'm actually a Newport man, first went to sea when I was thirteen. Joined the U.S. Navy in '98 and saw action against the French during the Atlantic Quasi War aboard the *U.S.S. Constitution*. We made those bloody Jacobins pay for their treacheries against our merchant ships. Not too much different from our fight against *Jackal*. Now that Jefferson's in charge, we'll probably be fighting the Brits again, or maybe those Mohammed pirate nests in the Mediterranean."

Clark continued as he exhaled smoke from his tobacco. "Thaddeus, you're quite the scholar, what's that new book now entertaining your thoughts?"

"Ancient Rome, a book about their stories and history. I'm intrigued with Romulus and Remus, the twin sons of Mars, and how they were raised by a wolf and went on to lead their Roman clan houses to greatness. It reminds me of our clan stories, especially Bear Mother and her two twin sons."

Hall, excited by the prospect of another story, urged Thaddeus to continue, as did Clark and Aolani. Thaddeus began the story and paused to speak in Tlingit every few moments for Kanoa after using English.

> *Long ago, Bear Mother strengthened our people's bloodlines and gave our clans powerful new skills and knowledge. She actually was a human who was seduced by a Bear Prince, who first appeared to her as a handsome young man when she was out picking berries. When she later discovered he was a grizzly bear, it was too late, they had long been married and she had given birth to two male bear twins. She was sometimes unhappy with her husband, but the Bear Prince had special powers over her so that she still loved him.*
>
> *Bear Mother's older human brothers went out looking for her, but were unsuccessful. Then her younger brother went searching for her with a trusted dog. When Bear Mother saw the dog, she threw a snowball out of the cave she lived in, and the dog smelled the snowball and began barking. The younger brother and his hunting party approached and discovered the cave where his older sister and her bear family resided. The Bear Prince, realizing he was doomed, called out his two young bear twins and sang a song that passed on his special powers to them. He then changed the twin cubs into young human boys, and ordered the Bear Mother's brother to kill him. Bear Mother was sad, but ordered her brother to carry out her husband's wishes.*
>
> *After singing for her deceased husband, the Bear People came to take and care for the body while Bear Mother returned with her twin sons and brother to her village. The bear twins grew up as human beings and became great hunters and leaders, renowned throughout all the kwaans.*

Young Kanoa clapped his hands and shouted in Tlingit.

"Good story, Thaddeus, good story!"

Aolani whispered in the boy's ear, and Kanoa looked at Clark and Hall and spoke in English.

"I like this Bear Mother story, don't you?"

"A fine tale, Mr. Kanoa," Clark replied.

"Agreed," Hall added, "a wonderful story Thaddeus, as well as an apt comparison, I might add. Well done."

Several moments passed amidst the relative quiet of the gentle breaking of water against the hull before Hall broke the silence.

"Listen, are those canoe paddles striking the water?"

Heavy breathing and splashing grew louder with each passing second. David Woods shouted from high on the aft mast as he repaired rigging.

"Look, a swimmin' beh! Over deh!"

"Well I'll be damned! Look, sir! A bear, and a grizzly no less! It must be swimming between islands!" Clark exclaimed in amazement.

Kanoa squealed with delight and began laughing as the bear came into view. Hall lifted the six-year-old onto his shoulders while Clark, Aolani, and Thaddeus climbed up on the railings for a better look. With broad, strong paddles, the bear briefly looked up at the ship as it swam by snorting from its nostrils. After several moments the bear vanished into the fog off the port bow of the ship, its splashing slowly fading away.

Woods laughed.

"That beh moved through the wada faster than our ship!"

"Unfortunately, you're correct, Mr. Woods!" Hall shouted as all looked at Thaddeus. "Quite remarkable! Your timing is impeccable!"

Alarm seeped into Thaddeus's voice.

"Sir, that bear indicates land nearby. Perhaps I should resume taking depth measurements?"

Hall opened his mouth to reply, but stopped himself as he picked up a faint trembling sound in the distance. Holding his hand up to Thaddeus as a sign to wait and listen, Hall shouted above to Woods and Kekoa.

"Gentlemen, do you see or hear anything unusual up there?!"

"No! But let's be silent for a bit! Deh might be somethin' up ahead!" Woods replied.

The sound increased in volume as moments passed. Nothing could be seen in the dense fog.

"Breakers, sir! It's surf hitting rocks!" Thaddeus shouted.

Woods descended the aft mast in panic.

"Deh are waves breaking into foam in the distance, sir, I can see 'em now!"

"Make that depth measurement!" Hall screamed.

Within a minute Thaddeus completed his depth measurement. Horror washed over his face.

"Sir, just under three fathoms! We're almost at keel depth!"

Hall frantically yelled orders as the crew rushed to their stations in an effort to avoid the forthcoming disaster.

"Gentlemen, come about in the opposite direction, on a port tack! Aolani, run below and wake Micah, the cap, and the others!"

Additional crew members arrived on deck and frantically pulled on rigging to try and catch every last bit of the breeze in the fully unfurled sails. *Eclipse* was locked in a battle with an incoming tide. Above deck, Captain Fletcher ran to the helm, yelling at Clark to pull the wheel as far as it would go to the right to assist the ship on her port tack. Without warning, groans from straining wood erupted across the decks, followed by a loud crashing snap. Micah Triplett raced above deck to the stern of the ship. He saw part of the rudder broken under the strain of entangled seaweed and the stresses of tide and wind battling each other.

"Captain! Our rudder! Part of it's broken off under the pressure of the tack!"

Thaddeus shouted, "Captain, we are below two fathoms, at keel depth!"

With adrenaline overwhelming whatever fatigue he had been sleeping off, Fletcher screamed orders, but it was too late. One large crash was followed by another as the ship vibrated and strained against the rocky bottom. Small waves hitting the shore were now fully visible, and Hall, up in the rigging assisting other sailors with the tack, could see *Eclipse* had just passed a rocky promontory before entering a tidal zone, explaining why the light surf had not been fully audible until it was too late. From below deck, Alamea rose up through a hatch.

"Our hull is breached! There's seawater leaking in from two separate areas!"

Just two dozen yards from the beach, *Eclipse* came to rest amid several large rocks, with small waves pounding against the stern and starboard side of the ship. Fletcher barked orders to stop the strain on the ship.

"Furl the sails quickly! Triplett, Harper, Clark, get below to man the pumps! Repair the hull breaches as best you can!"

Fletcher cursed his predicament amid the maelstrom of frantic crew members.

"Fuck! Goddamn my luck! This damned fog is like a diseased whore's affliction!"

Hall feverishly furled a sail as a beach appeared just off the ship's port side. A large, solitary brown bear moved off the boulders, shaking seawater off its fur. The powerful animal sniffed the air and appeared to glance at *Eclipse* before meandering over stones and sand into the dark shadows of the forest.

THIRTY

B LOOD SPOTTED THE FAINT TRAIL, still warm under forest mist. Tom and Joshua gripped their muskets as lungs and legs labored over the small island's ridge. A raven's deep rolling call announced the young men's descent towards the sea.

Tom grabbed Joshua's shoulder.

"Sir, Raven delivers a curfew. We must turn back soon, with or without the deer."

Joshua barely contained his impatience amid panted breaths.

"Nate needs fresh provisions to survive his battle wound. Fishing's poor on our side of the island, and our crew's exhausted. We push on."

Tom wiped sweat from his brow. The fog momentarily broke a few paces away.

"Poles, sir. Raven's Bones totem crest. We are trespassers."

The two froze. Joshua studied the carved nightmarish animal faces in faded red and black.

"Could you reason with these clan men?"

"Sir, my house totem is Sea Lion. I'm just as much an intruder here as you. We risk torture, slavery, and perhaps death if we continue further."

Incessant drips of water fell on the men's neck-to-knees elk hide armor and ball and flint pouches. Joshua shook his head.

"Nate's life, our crew . . ."

Joshua failed to finish the sentence as fog obscured the totem poles. The raven's low-pitched cadence fell silent. Tom fastened his musket behind his back and unsheathed a double-bladed Tlingit dagger from his waist.

"With permission, sir, I'll get the deer undetected. He's likely bled out by now and can't be far."

"We stay together, Tom."

"With respect, sir, if Raven's Bones men are by the sea, at least one of us must remain hidden to withdraw and warn the crew."

Joshua removed his woolen blue cap and pressed out moisture. A pained sigh followed.

"Alright, agreed. No more than fifteen minutes. Password is eclipse. And stick to this game trail, no exceptions."

"Eclipse, yes. Thank you, sir. Just a few minutes."

"Godspeed, Tom."

Tom whispered in Tlingit as he disappeared into a white wall of fog.

"Great Sea Lion House hunter, *L'eixi*, guide me and grant success. Let my feet be silent in the presence of enemies."

JOSHUA RESTED BESIDE A GIANT FIR. Several minutes passed as a slight sea breeze unveiled more totem poles standing like ship masts beside full sails. His mind faded into an abyss of fatigue. *Captain Fletcher. Goddamn his decisions. Hang on Nate. Please, Tom. I'm endangering the entire crew. Hurry, Tom. Elias, where are you? Exhaustion makes cowards of us all.*

Joshua closed his eyes. *Eclipse* appeared, her crew assuming animated faces of totemic animals and supernatural beings. A beautiful and terrifying cacophony of animal cries and distorted human voices engulfed the ship. Joshua fell into the tempest of sound. Nate appeared below him for an instant, drowned. He vanished into darkness.

A MUFFLED GUNSHOT.

Startled awake, Joshua reached for his musket and dagger as he crouched and moved into the mists.

"Tom."

The fog swirled between the sea and forest. He was alone in the silence. His unsheathed dagger and clenched musket provided little comfort as he strained again into the unknown.

"Tom, Tom."

A sudden crash broke several paces away. A jay streaked overhead in a flash of blue, shrieking a shrill warning.

"Goddamn it! Tom!"

Joshua held out his dagger, his arm coiled for action. An outline appeared.

Joshua lunged. His dagger penetrated the deer's neck, killing the weakened animal. He dragged the deer a few feet off the game trail and remained still, catching his breath, but heard bleated animal cries and heavy bursts of snapping limbs and branches in the near distance.

Joshua crouched low after loading his musket and cautiously moved over the descending game trail. The smell of the sea grew stronger.

TOM DROPPED TO THE WET, MOSSY GROUND beside a small hemlock. In mere seconds, a brown bear cub sprinted to within inches of his face. The small animal's hoarse calls and curious, playful eyes locked on Tom as thick saliva flowed from its mouth.

"Little one, I don't know what you're asking of me! Move on now!"

The cub sprinted past Tom, surprised by his outburst. Within seconds, the mother bear emerged from behind two ancient spruces, growling, stomping her front legs, and huffing displeasure at his presence. The enormous size and strength of the bear froze Tom on the ground. His musket would do no good this close to the bear. The mother charged at Tom, snorting angrily, but did not strike him. His heart exploded in primal fear as he curled in submission.

"Great Bear Mother, spare my crew! We bring no harm to your child! Protect us!"

An almost interminable moment passed as the bear's heated breath fell upon his head and neck. Overwhelmed, Tom placed his fate within the mother's power.

The cub cried out from the beach below and the mother tore through the forest downhill into the tidal zone. Urgent voices shouted and filled the air. Canoes hastily scraped over rocks. Paddles slapped water.

Tom remained still over the next several moments. The noises soon vanished into a hidden songbird's melodic call and the soft sounds of buzzing insects. The fog was lifting. Tom saw Joshua descend the game trail, smiling with relief.

"Tom, you're safe! Praise God! I have the deer back by the trail."

"And I had a bear cub and his mother, sir. She sprinted down to the beach, saving us from a few Raven's Bones men. One of them shot at me earlier, but missed. The great bear mother chased them away. I heard their canoes leave. Some English may have been spoken, but I'm not sure. They're gone now."

Joshua fought his emotions, thankful all was not lost. He stared into the mists and spotted the faint outline of a small ship for a few fleeting seconds.

Panther?!

"Come, Tom, we have no time to lose. We need to depart back to our side of the island."

"Aye, sir. I'll carry the deer first."

THIRTY-ONE

Tom and Joshua pushed hard through the woods over the game trail, exchanging the deer carcass every fifteen minutes to rest each man's back. Over two hours passed.

"Sir, my muscles and joints ache. Can we take a few minutes for water and rest?"

"Yes. Fifteen minutes. My shoulders and back feel like a giant burning ember as well."

The two men faced each other a few feet apart, resting against moss shrouded trees. Joshua pulled out his leather-bound log from his elk hide waist pack. He asked Tom a question as he glanced over a recent entry.

"Ground Devil's Club root as a poultice for wounds. Bull kelp tea for strengthening one's body. These will help Nate, right?"

"They will, sir. The poultice reduces pain and swelling. The kelp tea provides good energy and health."

Tom shut his eyes.

"If you'll indulge me, sir. A few minutes for a nap?"

"Yes, go ahead Tom."

Joshua flipped a page in his log. The previous day's entry glared up at him.

> Run aground in heavy fog on an unknown island. Starboard hull damaged. Danger of attack from hostiles or slavers hangs over us like the Sword of Damocles.

Joshua jumped several more pages back in time. A letter from his older sister, Laura, fell out. He opened it and read the words for the first time in months.

October 9, 1801

> *My dearest brother, thank you for your visit last week. I know your spirit still cries out in pain over Anne, but remember, as I have learned, a heart that is broken is a heart that is open, open to traveling vast distances and striving through storms to reach the far glorious shores in life. And remember your own words, brother: "We cannot control the winds and tides, but we can adjust our sails and helm."*
>
> *You are a man of the sea now, Joshua, in ways even you perhaps do not fully understand yet. Never forget that, my brother.*

Hall looked into the forest canopy as a pair of glaucous-winged gulls cried out and passed overhead. Closing his eyes, Joshua indulged memories of the red and gold autumn New Hampshire woods, where he played with his two nieces and offered comfort to Laura after her husband's death at sea. His sister was stoic and subtly directed the conversation away from her own heartache to address his troubles—their brother Elias, a long voyage with an unfamiliar captain and crew, and the lingering pain of breaking off relations with his sweetheart, Anne. His time at sea had proven too much for the relationship. He fell overboard into regret, drowning in dark emotions.

Joshua desperately yearned for his sister's wise counsel and the simple joys of his nieces. A rare courageous soul, Laura never seemed to surrender to emotional fatigue. She called upon resolution in difficulty, defiance in defeat.

"Tom. Time's up, off we go. Nate and the crew need us."

Tom slowly shook off his slumber as Joshua penned a new entry in his log.

> *Back away. Alamea's too dangerous. Hold fast to responsibilities. Stay anchored in duty and honor.*

THE UNMISTAKABLE SCENTS OF SALT AND seaweed guided Tom and Joshua to the beach. The silence that embraced the men for most of their time away from camp was shattered by axes swinging into the flesh of a cedar tree not more than a quarter mile distant. Shouts in Hawaiian and English periodically echoed through the woods as the two came upon Kekoa, Ben Harper, and Lavelle Clark, all shirtless as they worked to cut planks from a recently felled medium-sized cedar, their muscular, tattooed bodies sweating profusely from the exertion despite the cool mists. Clark spotted Hall emerging from the woods with the deer over his back.

"Glad to have you back, sir. That's a fine deer. Mr. Folger will certainly appreciate the fresh food."

Hall spoke between heavy breaths.

"What's his condition?"

The men glanced at each other, their faces somber, as if each man were willing the others to volunteer an answer to Hall.

Clark finally cleared his throat and replied, "Nate's still in bad shape I'm afraid, sir. His wounds are not healing very well, and his will to keep going seems diminished. Thaddeus is treating him with local plants, which have helped a bit. In fact, I think they're the main reason he's still hanging on. Captain Fletcher's been at Folger's side nearly the entire time, urging him to fight on. I know they'll appreciate some venison. Hopefully, it'll give Nate the strength he needs."

Hall mustered every bit of confidence he could for the crew members.

"Very well, I'm on my way to him now. That cedar will provide some excellent planks to repair our rudder and some of the damaged areas of the hull and masts. Keep up the fine work, gentlemen."

Kekoa stared at the ground, frustrated.

"Sir, Mr. Folger is our best carpenter. What if he—"

Hall interrupted.

"Gentlemen, I'm going to make sure Mr. Folger remains with us in this world, we need to encourage him. The rest of us will carry on with repairs as best we can. Now, I'm off to help prepare some venison, you're welcome to join us once Mr. Folger has his fill."

After Hall and Tom vanished behind the trees, the three crew members took a rest, drinking some water and having a modest snack of salmonberries. Kekoa seethed over Liko's death as he sat with the others.

"If Captain Fletcher leads us astray into disaster again, I'll support taking the ship from him and making Joshua or Micah the new captain."

Harper and Clark nodded as a raven's call sounded a short distance away.

THIRTY-TWO

HALL SAT NEXT TO THE LARGE campfire where Nathaniel Folger, grimacing in pain, labored to eat a meal of freshly cooked venison with greens and berries. His back was partially upright against a large driftwood log as he lay under a heavy wool blanket, his brow soaked with perspiration. A few feet away, Micah Triplett wrote in his log while Captain Fletcher sketched out measurements and methods needed for repairing the various damages to the ship. Muskets, charts, and cooking utensils lay strewn about the campfire area. Kanoa, Aolani, and Alamea periodically returned from the nearby woods with new supplies of plants and berries for Folger and the rest of the crew, having been taught by Thaddeus what was edible and medicinal, as well as what plants to avoid. Thaddeus, meanwhile, busied himself preparing the remaining venison. Just yards off the beach, Ben Harper and David Woods worked from a skiff on damages to the ship's hull above the high tide waterline.

Captain Fletcher, looking up from his sketches for a few moments, broke the relative quiet of the crackling fire and subdued conversations of crew members around the beach and woods.

"Mr. Triplett, Mr. Hall. We have a range of rather unattractive options at the present time. Mr. Folger is in no condition to perform his boatswain duties, so the rest of us will have to work on the ship's hull repairs with each low tide. Needless to say, gentlemen, the longer we remain here on this island with our ship being repaired, the more likely we are to be discovered by hostile clans and enslaved or killed."

Hall spoke as he stared at *Eclipse*.

"Captain, Mr. Triplett, perhaps some of the crew could take a skiff out into the straits once the fog clears? We might be able to find an American or British vessel that could assist us. I may have spotted one on the other side of the island for a moment, but I was exhausted."

Fletcher rubbed the back of his neck in frustration, both at the conversation as well as his efforts to calculate the needed repairs for *Eclipse*.

"Too risky," Triplett offered. "*Jackal* could still be out there, and a skiff would be easily overwhelmed by a Tlingit canoe party. Given the state of our vessel right now, we can't afford to lose any more crew members."

Fletcher glanced at both men, though this time he was more reflective. He smoked a Haida pipe carved in the shape of a small raven head.

"We'll remain here for now and repair our ship as fast as we can. Mr. Hall, it was mentioned you and Tom traveled for well over four hours in pursuit of the deer. Apparently, this island is large enough to support us with fresh provisions for the time being. Once *Eclipse* is seaworthy and the weather clears, we'll make haste to enter the straits. Unfortunately, due to our limited tools, the nature of the tides here, and the ship's damages, only part of the crew will be able to work on repairing the hull at any given time. Crew members not engaged directly in repairs will scout out more of this island while also gathering more provisions as needed."

Hall spoke, his arms crossed over his chest.

"Agreed, cap. Of course, I'll also tend to Mr. Folger as his condition evolves."

HOURS PASSED AS HALL DOZED AND WAITED for Folger to regain some strength. One musket ball was removed the previous day by Hall, but a second ball still lodged in his lower abdomen required a more difficult surgery. His training as a medical apprentice on previous voyages would now be sorely tested.

Folger spoke to Hall, his voice weak, while the others gathered by the campfire.

"Mr. Hall, sir, I'm ready for you to remove the ball. I just want to be over it."

Fletcher interjected some humor, to the surprise of Hall, Triplett, and the other crew members in the vicinity.

"Nathaniel, you're ordered to stay alive. You need to get permission from me if you intend to die."

Folger managed a smile as the others chuckled around their wounded colleague, knowing the upcoming surgery would be brutal. Hall looked directly into Folger's eyes and placed his hand briefly on the sailor's shoulder.

"Nate, I'll do my very best, you have my word. The captain, Mr. Triplett, Tom, and Thaddeus will hold you down after you have some whiskey. May God be with you. And with me."

Folger gulped a copious quantity of whiskey while Hall boiled the surgical instruments nearby. When everything was ready, Nate put a smooth wooden stick in his mouth for the pain. Hall took a swig of whiskey to calm his nerves before making an incision on Folger's left lower abdomen.

Folger bit hard into the wood piece in his mouth as he tried to control his screams. Hall realized he had no choice but to cut deeply into muscle tissue to retrieve the musket ball. After two agonizing minutes, Hall dropped the small projectile into a cup and immediately began sewing the wound as Triplett poured whiskey over the stitches. Once the last stitch was sewn, Hall wiped the sweat from Folger's face and neck.

"Are we finished, Mr. Hall?" Folger asked in a weak, raspy voice after removing his mouthpiece.

"Indeed, we are, Nate. You're one of the bravest sailors I've ever met. Your job is to rest, and to eat and drink when you can."

"Aye, sir. Thank you."

As Folger closed his eyes to rest and the crew complimented Hall on his work, Joshua was overcome with fatigue. As the thanks and congratulations from various crewmembers subsided he reclined by the campfire, needing to rest. Hall's bones were no different than the beach's driftwood and pebbles, and his fatigued muscles felt like immovable sand. Only half awake, Joshua saw Kanoa standing over him, grinning. Mustering a smile, Hall rolled over a bit under his wool blanket, only to feel the young Salish boy crawl under beside him, followed by Alamea on the other side of the boy.

HALL AWOKE FROM A LENGTHY NAP to the sea breaking gently on the rocks. A light breeze filled the air as sunlight danced nimbly upon his face through openings in the forest. The dampness and fog had disappeared like ghosts, and the light and warmth seemed like an army lifting a prolonged siege on the *Eclipse* crew. Kanoa still rested beside him, but Hall soon heard Alamea arguing with Fletcher.

Micah Triplett tapped Hall's shoulder as he motioned towards the couple.

"Well, it's not like we haven't heard that before. Coffee?"

"Yes, that would be delightful, thank you, sir."

Triplett sat next to Aolani, who rested her head on his shoulder as the two relaxed, their blanket pulled around them. Hall remained silent as he drank his coffee.

Triplett held a satisfied grin as he looked at the second mate.

"You did it, Joshua. Nate appears to be on the mend. His complexion is much improved from that ghastly skin tone he had yesterday. That fresh venison and your deft hands did the trick, I believe."

"Give thanks first to the Almighty above, Mr. Triplett. We're going to need His services no doubt for the remainder of our voyage."

THE MORNING HOURS PASSED INTO EARLY AFTERNOON, and Captain Fletcher and the crew worked fixed schedules and established rotational groups for repairing the ship, keeping watch and procuring food. Amid the crew's shouts and conversations, Folger sat by the campfire, his eyes closed to soak in the sunlight on his face. He grinned as if he were relishing one last fleeting moment of glory before opening his eyes and looking at the fire. His right hand moved to grip his left hip as a slight grimace of pain washed across his face.

Hall walked up the beach to check on Folger, having finished a four-hour work detail on *Eclipse*. His next task was to fish the island's main stream several hundred yards away in the woods for salmon and trout. As Hall approached, Folger forced a smile.

"Mr. Hall, sir, I see you have your fishing gear with you."

"Indeed Mr. Folger, with a few additions and alterations by Tom and Thaddeus. We'll see how this old Yankee fishing pole holds up in these waters. Those two are fishing just off the beach for halibut. They indicated there may be good opportunities in the deep pools as one climbs in elevation along the stream. That's where I'm headed, but first I wanted to check on you."

"Oh, other than some fatigue and modest pain around the wound, I'm fine. You know, sir, the crew is truly blessed to have you on this voyage. You deserve to be a captain sometime soon. I'd sail with you anywhere."

"Thank you, Nate. I'll see if I can bring you back a fine trout. You just rest, my friend."

"Sir, I need to join you on your walk. I'm convinced what I need now is a good stirring of my muscles, heart, and lungs. I've been idle long enough and need to move. They need my skills out there on the ship."

"Absolutely not, you're still recovering. You'll stay here, that's an order."

"Look sir, Tom carved me a fine walking stick with his Sea Lion totem on the top, although he still needs to finish it. I can do this sir, just give me a chance."

Shaking his head and moving his hand through his hair, Hall relented.

"Alright Nate, you can join me, but on one condition. The moment the pain becomes too severe, you're to sit down and rest and return here to the beach as soon as you're able. Or, some of the crew can come assist you."

"Agreed. Thank you, sir. God knows I must get up and about."

Hall knew Folger was risking his health and possibly his life, but he sensed Folger's weakened spirit from the hardships and traumas of the last several days. Hall never forgot Folger already suffered from the recent deaths of his wife and father. Perhaps a short hike to the stream would restore some emotional vigor.

The two men slowly made their way into the woods towards the stream. Hall was alarmed, but not surprised at Folger's very slow pace and severe limp favoring his left side. Folger brushed off Hall's verbal concerns as they walked up the incline from the beach below. The roar of the stream, not more than fifteen yards across, made speaking difficult once the two men reached a small game trail beside the rushing waters. They remained silent for several minutes as they walked upstream, though Folger eventually motioned to Hall that he had reached his limit. Heavily relying on his walking stick, Folger marveled at the scene before him as he sat beside the stream, pain painted across his face. Unusually bright sunlight bathed a crystal-clear pool, fed by a small waterfall that passed under a large fir log covered in moss. The light and shade around the pool glistened and danced off one another in what seemed like a dream, causing Folger to almost completely forget about Hall. After a few minutes of uneventful fishing, Hall shouted to Folger that he was departing further upstream in search of more pools. Joshua looked back for an instant to see the wounded sailor smile and salute in acknowledgement. He continued upward along the stream, still uneasy about his decision to allow Folger off the beach.

Folger leaned back against the edge of a spruce log beside the small waterfall and pool. Closing his eyes momentarily, he whispered to himself.

"Alone at last. Take me home."

The loss of his wife and father imposed its vice grip of sorrow. His mind, body, and spirit fatigued beyond anything he experienced before, his wounds screaming in pain, Folger opened his senses to everything around him. Sounds of the stream and songbirds above became accentuated, the sharp smells of moss and evergreens more acute. Light and shade increased their frantic movement over the water. Seduced by the primal force flowing all around him, Folger felt his sense of linear time fading into a ceaseless, cyclical rhythm. The clear pool beckoned like a mother welcoming a long-lost child as faint voices of loved ones called upon him. Struggling to his feet, he peacefully limped into the water.

A river otter appeared at the center of the pool. The small mammal stared intently at Folger, who, locked in a hypnotic state, surrendered to a soothing energy emanating from the riverine creature. A vibrant collage of color, light, and darkness enveloped Folger as he slid underwater, where he felt himself sinking into the seemingly bottomless pool, drifting deeper into a faint void of cold aquatic blue. He observed the otter gently moving through the water above him on the stream's surface, in possession of a potent and terrifying wildness that vanquished all memories and dreams. Folger vanished, and the stream's pulsating waters continued on to the sea.

THIRTY-THREE

AFTER TREKKING FOR AN ADDITIONAL THIRTY MINUTES upstream, Joshua came to rest by an even larger pool and waterfall. Sweating profusely in the unusually warm temperatures, Hall set down his fishing gear, knife, and musket before stripping and jumping in, unable to resist the cold, clear water. Several dozen feet across, the pool allowed Hall to swim on his back and soak in the rare sunlight beaming over the stream's path between the forest's towering evergreens. The sparkling water and brilliant blue sky invigorated Hall's spirit. Energy flowed through his veins like a thunderstorm's first raindrops falling over a parched landscape. Swimming on his back and breathing deeply, he thought of home back in New England, of relaxing by a small lake in early summer with Anne and finding her irresistibly beautiful. He would cross all the world's oceans for her crystal blue eyes, porcelain skin, and superior intelligence. A memory of Anne letting down her long hair and laughing infectiously forced Joshua to grin. The past, alive again with joy, locked in a duel with the sorrow of the present. With Anne at his side, life would be vast, boundless, with possibilities beyond his wildest comprehension.

Hall dove deep underwater trying to cleanse his mind of Anne's memory, swimming through the waterfall's thundering, oxygenated roar beneath the surface and emerging on its far side underneath a large granite overhang. Climbing a few feet onto a small patch of moss and sand strewn with pebbles and driftwood polished by the stream's ceaseless forces, Hall leaned against a rock wall. Naked and shivering, the air gradually warmed him after a few minutes. Hall allowed himself to rest in the shelter of sound beside the tumbling waters. The roaring soon lulled him to sleep. In his dreams Anne and the small lake faded away to a vision of shade and light under a great Hawaiian Koa tree, of warm sands, breaking surf, and white seabirds floating effortlessly on soft trade winds above an endless blue ocean.

HALL AWOKE A FEW HOURS LATER, his eyes fixating on the back side of the waterfall a dozen or so feet away from his small sandy outcrop. He remained still and quiet to reengage his mind to his surroundings, only to see after a few moments a blurred image of a human figure through the waterfall, standing on the far side of the pool near his clothing and gear. A chill raced up Hall's spine and his heart pounded furiously as he jumped to his feet. Hall cursed for allowing himself into such a vulnerable position. The figure dove into the pool and swam underwater towards the waterfall. There was no escape route for Hall. He could only wait to see who emerged from the water, and possibly fight for his life.

As the figure swam through the turbulence below the waterfall, Hall realized it was a woman with long black hair. Within moments, Alamea emerged naked from the pool, her curved figure moving over the small boulders to the sandy outcrop where Hall stood. Her breasts swayed gently as she looked up at Joshua with a beguiling grin. Climbing the last few feet to him, Alamea breathed heavily with a slight shiver as the cold water dripped from her body. For a moment, the two stood facing each other in silence, inches apart, staring into each other's eyes as if entranced. Alamea moved closer and put her hand over Joshua's heart as she looked up at him, her smile transforming into an expression of longing.

Desire overpowered Joshua, utterly obliterating moral fortifications he thought were strong. Cares and burdens vanished as he locked his arms around Alamea in an unconditional embrace, releasing a hurricane of passions he knew his heart would forever pursue. Alamea moved her hands over his lean, muscular body carved over years at sea, as Joshua eagerly explored her soft curves and smooth skin with firm grasps alternating with gentle caresses. She stared into his eyes with ferocious intensity.

ALAMEA LAUGHED AT JOSHUA'S STORIES of his boyhood years in New England as they watched two river otters emerge and play in the pool below. Sitting upright on a patch of moss, Joshua held her from behind as he rested his chin on her shoulder, grinning and laughing in a manner that only lovers can. Alamea leaned her head back on his shoulder, staring into his eyes, willing him to lower any remaining emotional walls.

"Tell me more about Anne, Joshua, and what Boston women are like."

Hall paused a few moments, looking up as a few puffy clouds lazily drifted eastward towards the continent across the blue sky. A blue-winged kingfisher darted over the pool past hovering dragonflies, announcing its presence with punctuated shrill cries as the river otters continued their play in the clear water of the pool. As he spoke to Alamea, he felt an immense burden being lifted off his spirit, pleasantly surprising him.

"Anne, yes, I loved her. She'll always have a piece of my heart. But now, I have you, my dear. You've strengthened what remains of my heart beyond measure, as does Kanoa."

Alamea smiled and ran her fingers through Hall's hair before pulling him to her and kissing him.

"You saved him, and you love him just as I love him," she spoke, her voice soft. "And he will be our son, always, wherever we may go in this world. Now, tell me more about the Boston women. Our Hawai'i men go to sea all the time, as do many of our women. I don't understand why the Boston women won't do the same."

Hall breathed in the deep, sweet air, while gently tightening his embrace around Alamea, savoring her naked body against his. He was silent for a few moments, having to force his thoughts back to her question.

"New England men travel on long voyages, some in search of pelts, some for whales, and others for trade. The women almost always remain at home, it's just expected of them, the exception being the occasional wife of a ship's officer. Voyages sometimes last two, three, even four years. Many of us, including myself, have sailed around the entire world and its great oceans, the Atlantic, the Pacific, the Indian. New England is a long, long journey from your islands, and the voyage is often difficult and dangerous. A good number of sailors never return home, such as my brother-in-law, who died at sea. If I'd married Anne, she would've endured long separations, and the possibility that I might never return."

"I see, so she could have traveled with you on your voyages. That is why you still have some bitterness left in you over her."

"Not exactly, I was actually somewhat nervous over the idea of her accompanying me on overseas voyages."

Hall stroked her hair as they held each other, a far off look in his eyes.

"In Hawai'i, our women sail just as well as the men, so there's no reason why they cannot learn. Boston women should travel more with their men and children, as should the King George women. If they did this, it would perhaps restrain the wickedness that is seen among some of their sailors, such as with Jonathan, the rotten scoundrel. But I'm glad you said no to Anne, because I will sail with you wherever you want to go, Joshua. I would like to visit all of these places you have told me about, especially Boston and New Hampshire, and talk to the women there and teach them how to sail. Young Kanoa should see these places and become familiar with them as well."

Hall kissed Alamea on her temple, feeling her warm breath on his skin.

"Indeed, we will, my lovely Alamea. I must say though, of all the places I've seen, your islands are the fairest and loveliest of all."

"Oh Joshua, with you at my side we can look forward to honor, rank, and many children in addition to little Kanoa. The ali'i seek English-speaking men who can serve as advisors."

The two lay on the moss in another passionate interlude, soaking in the glorious ecstasy of the moment. Joshua fought back warnings that echoed in his mind, scratching and clawing against the emotions surging within him. Was Alamea only interested in him to promote her ali'i status, or did she really love him? Fletcher was another concern.

"But I must learn Hawaiian, and we have to finish this voyage with Captain Fletcher. How will we act around the crew?"

Alamea replied without hesitation in a firm, yet understanding tone.

"You will learn Hawaiian quickly, Joshua, you're smart and resourceful, and I will teach you. And I'm done with Jonathan Fletcher and his lies and schemes. It's my fault that I did not earlier recognize the deep wickedness within his shallow heart. He is a disgrace. Kekoa will protect me if—

"As will I."

As tears glistened in Alamea's eyes, she continued, her voice tinged with anger at thoughts of Fletcher's part in Liko's death.

"Joshua, I must tell you, some of the men confided in me that they wish to see you or Micah as captain. Kekoa, Lavelle, Ben, and perhaps Micah will support you if you decide to remove Jonathan from command. They don't want any more men to suffer the fates of Nathaniel and my poor brother, Liko, and—

Hall gently placed his fingers on her lips and embraced Alamea ever more tightly as he closed his eyes to speak, sensing now was not the time to worry over the inevitable difficulties ahead.

"My beautiful Alamea, let us not trouble ourselves with those matters now. We'll reach the shores we seek."

Her eyes closed, Alamea sighed deeply.

"A great typhoon awaits us though, and we must cross through it. We must, Joshua."

THIRTY-FOUR

Alamea and Joshua reached the last hundred yards of woods beside the beach as the deep blue hues of early evening above the top of the forest turned to gray. The aberrant warm sunshine had slowly retreated before the returning cool overcast typical of the southern Alaskan coast. Hall noted Nathaniel Folger was no longer by the stream, but had no concern, reasoning the ship's carpenter and boatswain had simply meandered back to camp. As the smells of campfire smoke, seaweed, and salty air began filtering through the woods, Hall and Alamea became aware of distant voices emanating from the direction of the beach. The two stopped and waited in silence, staring at each other with expressions of concern, listening intently.

"Boats! Baidarkas! Captain Fletcher, come quickly! They are Russians!"

"Joshua, listen. That's Micah, if I'm not mistaken."

Hall grabbed her hand.

"Let's go! Hurry!"

They sprinted the remaining distance over the small game trail as ferns and other small vegetation snapped against their ankles and calves. Shouts and loud conversations continued to pour from the beach, including unfamiliar voices with strange accents and words. Breathing heavily, Hall and Alamea reached the edge of the woods with their weapons drawn. They immediately saw the *Eclipse* crew gathering from several directions as Captain Fletcher, Micah, Tom, and Thaddeus all shouted a chaotic brew of English and broken Russian to two kayak-like Aleutian *baidarkas*, which contained one man and one woman each. Floating in a stationary position a few dozen yards from shore, the men and women were no older than their early twenties, unarmed for the moment, and clearly exhausted.

Hall and Alamea walked hurriedly towards the beach. Fletcher glanced over at the two emerging from the woods with an angry scowl, but remained silent as he turned again to listen to Thaddeus and Tom translate the Russian phrases. The *Eclipse* crew grew calmer and eventually lowered their weapons, realizing the new arrivals weren't a threat. Triplett rushed to meet Hall and Alamea who were approaching the crew gathered on the beach. A puzzled look clouded Triplett's face as he gaped at Hall, shocked over his unanticipated arrival with Alamea. Hall spoke before Triplett could form his question.

"Sir, my apologies for my late return. Who are those four individuals in the *baidarkas*?"

"Russian-American Company fugitives. Have you two lost your minds? Did you think the captain would overlook your simultaneous absence? And then you return together! By the way, where the hell is Folger? No one has seen him since he walked into the woods with you, Joshua, many hours ago. Alamea, have you seen him?"

Alamea's expression morphed from surprise to growing concern.

"No, I haven't seen Nathaniel. I'm sure he's close by somewhere."

Hall stared at the beach.

"Damn it!"

He placed his hand on Alamea's shoulder.

"You didn't see Nathaniel on your walk up the game trail beside the stream?"

"No, I didn't see him at all. Wasn't he supposed to stay here on the beach anyway to rest his wounds? What's going on?"

Hall looked to the mostly overcast sky as frustration overcame him. He stuck his elbows out, his fingers interlocked over his head as he grappled with worry over Nate.

"We need to initiate a search immediately as soon as Captain Fletcher makes a decision concerning these visitors. I fear something dreadful has happened, as Nate insisted on following me into the woods for exercise and to relax by the stream. I should've ordered him to stay here on the beach, despite his protests. He stopped to rest after only about twenty minutes of walking, and I left him there after he assured me he'd be fine. I fear I've failed him."

Triplett's shock gave way to concern.

"Here now, I would've allowed Nate the same thing, had it been me. We'll mount a search, and he shouldn't be too far. Tom and Thaddeus can help us once they're done assisting the cap."

Thaddeus walked over to Triplett, Hall, and Alamea, while Tom remained with Captain Fletcher and the other crew as discussions continued with the four strangers floating just off the beach.

"Thaddeus, do tell us now, who are those four people in the baidarkas? Are they Russians?" Alamea asked before Thaddeus could speak.

"Sirs, Alamea. Yes, they are indeed from the Saint Michael settlement on Sitka Island, but they are now fugitives, having fled the oppressive discipline imposed by Baranov's men. The man in the second baidarka is their leader, Nikolai Karaulov. He's a Creole, of mixed Russian-Aleut blood. His wife Tanya is a Kodiak Islander, an Alutiiq woman. The other man is Sergei Popov, a Russian from Siberia, and the woman with him is his female companion Alina, an escaped Tlingit slave, apparently of low birth as I've discerned from her vocabulary. All four of them are about our age. They said they cheered, as if God had saved them, when they saw the small American flag on the stern of *Eclipse*. All four of them pledge to assist us in any way they can in exchange for their eventual safe passage from this coast. Captain Fletcher promises them our help for their labor on board our vessel."

"Thank you, Thaddeus, for the report," Hall replied before continuing. "Have you seen Mr. Folger at all in the nearby woods? He's missing and Mr. Triplett and I will momentarily be organizing a search party."

"No, sir, I'm afraid I haven't seen Nate."

The group watched Captain Fletcher and the other crew members assist the exhausted Russian-American Company fugitives ashore with their small, Aleutian-built boats. Ben Harper, Kekoa, and David Woods built a new separate campfire and temporary lean-to shelter, while Lavelle Clark and Aolani prepared a meal of rice, beans, and venison, accompanied with a small amount of whiskey for each person. The weary runaways managed smiles as Kanoa handed them their plates of food. After wolfing down their dinner, Sergei, Alina, and Tanya repeatedly thanked their hosts for the meal before falling asleep underneath the lean-to. Nikolai Karaulov remained awake, sipping a cup of tea and talking with Tom and Fletcher in broken English and Russian beside the campfire.

Hall, Triplett, Thaddeus, and Alamea approached and soon sat opposite Captain Fletcher, Tom, and Karaulov as a light breeze bent the orange flames, the firelight casting a light reddish glow over Captain Fletcher's face. He struggled to contain the seething rage within him as he glared at Hall and Alamea. Jealousy washed over him, though for the moment duty to *Eclipse* demanded he address his crew.

"Mr. Karaulov's narrative has been quite useful in informing my future plans. After fleeing Saint Michael two days ago, his party tried to reach a small King George ship in the straits near Sitka Island. Nikolai's description of the vessel matches *Jackal*. He also spotted other ships from a distance."

Triplett put his hands in his pockets, nervous and irritated. Joshua glanced at Karaulov, asking, "Tom, has Nikolai heard of Elias Hall or his ship *Panther*?"

"No, he hasn't." Fletcher hissed. He stared at Tom and Nikolai like a hawk and folded his arms.

Triplett jumped in to speak during a moment of pause, despite recognizing the captain's desire to continue. Fletcher, raising his eyebrows, stared first at Triplett before turning his eyes on Joshua as he listened to the proposal.

"As you are well aware, captain, Mr. Folger has still not returned from the woods. Mr. Hall and I request a few men to immediately commence a search of the surrounding woods before the sun becomes more obscured by the clouds and terrain."

"I'll help you!" Tom volunteered instantly, tired of bridging communication between Karaulov and Fletcher. "Cousin Thaddeus, your Russian is a bit better than mine, come take my place next to Nikolai."

Fletcher spat and folded his arms.

"Thaddeus, Captain Tom orders you to take his place here beside Mr. Karaulov, as he has to initiate a search to remedy Mr. Hall's irresponsible actions regarding our wounded boatswain Nate Folger."

Awkward silence followed, and Tom and Thaddeus stared at their officers before moving to switch places.

"Captain, I accept full responsibility for Mr. Folger, and I can explain what—

Fletcher interrupted Hall.

"I am not interested in hearing excuses from my second officer. It's quite clear to me what happened. You exercised poor judgment with an injured crew member, and I expect nothing less than his safe return. Otherwise, I will have to consider stripping you of your officer privileges."

Infuriated, Alamea pointed at Fletcher as she spoke.

"You're a damned hypocrite! Liko is dead because of you, Jonathan! You! And the only reason Nathaniel was wounded was because of your own disastrous decisions! Joshua saved his life, and has been proven right every time in his advice against your rash commands!"

Karaulov looked on, concerned, needing no knowledge of English to understand what was being said as Sergei, Alina, and Tanya awoke, hearing the commotion, before lying back down to sleep. Crew members scattered around the beach moved towards Fletcher's campfire, weary from working on *Eclipse* and unsure and confused over what to make of this latest episode of escalating tensions between the officers. To everyone's surprise, Fletcher remained calm as he tightly clasped his hands together.

"Alamea my dear," Fletcher began, struggling to keep his tone even. "Your continued insolence does not surprise me in the least. But I forgive you, as you are partially correct. I am indeed responsible for Liko's death and Mr. Folger's severe injuries. However, that does not excuse Mr. Hall's actions."

Fletcher paused for a brief moment to reconsider the trajectory of his comments as he glanced at the concerned faces of his crew members, all of whom had gathered within a few feet of the campfire. Several loud sparks shot off the top flame breaking the uneasy silence. A crew's disappointment and frustration, if allowed to fester, would evolve into more dangerous consequences for a captain. As Fletcher silently renegotiated his words, ever conscious of the dire need to appear appreciative and empathetic, he noticed Alamea grasping Hall's right forearm with both her hands, while Kanoa, on the verge of tears, clung to her. Nearly overcome by bitterness, Fletcher called upon all of his inner strength to suppress his anger. He spoke calmly while making eye contact with all the crew to indicate he was concluding his remarks.

"Crew of *Eclipse*, you have already sacrificed much on this voyage, and yet, you have persevered, and I thank all of you. I do not need to tell you that misfortune has been our unwelcome companion thus far, but I am convinced the worst difficulties are behind us. We have opportunities before us that present favorable balances for us with much reduced risks. One of our new guests, Mr. Popov, is a skilled carpenter and will surely speed the completion of the ship's repairs tomorrow. As I know you're all very tired, I'm granting a few hours extra rest to everyone once our immediate tasks for this evening are completed, excepting our standard rotational night watch. Tom, Mr. Hall, Mr. Triplett, and Mr. Clark will embark now as a search party for Mr. Folger. Kekoa, Mr. Harper, and Mr. Woods will join me on board for more repairs while Thaddeus, Aolani, and Alamea will oversee our beach camp and keep watch."

"And then what?" Alamea retorted scornfully. "Are we off to get more of our crew killed for a few pelts?"

Fletcher stared coldly at the young Hawaiian woman.

"Charming to the last, with your beauty still wondrous to me, my darling."

Fletcher turned to the entire crew.

"My orders for our departure and future endeavors will be announced tomorrow evening. That is all."

The captain turned and walked to the edge of the low tide as the crew stared at one another with weary disengagement. As the sailors dispersed to commence their ordered tasks, Nikolai Karaulov rested under the lean-to shelter beside his wife Tanya. The light breeze, crackling campfire, and perpetual sounds of the ocean sent him into a deep sleep. His friend Emelian Taradanov appeared before him in a dream, pleading with Nikolai not to abandon the company settlement at St. Michael.

The risks are too great Nikolai! Elias Hall and his fanatics lurk in the shadows. His ally, the demon shaman Wolf-Weasel, curses us, and you will drown in the straits and lose your soul.

Emelian morphed into Nikolai's Aleutian grandmother telling stories and singing ballads of a homeland he would never see again, a haunted archipelago of windswept, treeless islands standing in eternal stoicism against violent tempests.

THIRTY-FIVE

T HE SEARCH PARTY GATHERED AT THE SMALL POOL where Joshua last saw Nathaniel Folger. As they examined Folger's clothes and belongings left beside the stream in the creeping dusk of late evening, Tom spotted a river otter on the opposite bank. The small animal dove underwater after staring at the young Tlingit man. Triplett noticed Tom become tense, even frightened as the otter did not resurface.

"Tom, what's the matter? Why are you so concerned with that river otter? He probably just swam downstream or something."

Hall and Clark broke their concentration from Folger's scattered belongings to look at Tom, who was visibly shaken. Hall placed his hand on Tom's shoulder, reassuring him.

"Tom, what's troubling you? We'll appreciate anything you can tell us, you have my word."

Borrowing a Hawaiian word, Hall added after a prolonged pause, "There is no *kapu* here."

Tom replied after a moment of hesitation, his voice breaking.

"Nate has drowned, I fear. If so, he may be forever lost to the Land Otter People, the Kushtakas. An Otter Man has horrific power to charm and enslave weakened, dispirited people. I pray that Jesus above was able to catch Nathaniel's soul before the Kushtaka got his chance."

As Tom stared down, trembling, Clark chuckled and shook his head in disbelief.

"What fairy tale nonsense is this? My goodness."

Triplett angrily grabbed Clark by the collar.

"You just deviated from your superior officer's statement to Tom. Shut your trap from now on during this search, unless Mr. Hall or I ask you something, is that clear?"

Clark stood silent, confused and agitated. Hall was pleased with Triplett's decisiveness.

"Are we clear, Mr. Clark?" Triplett demanded.

"Yes," Clark finally muttered, his mouth agape as he glanced at the other three men before looking down in disbelief.

"Very well then," Hall followed, "I already wandered the game trail upstream for at least a mile as I was returning to the beach, and saw no sign of Mr. Folger. If Nathaniel drowned, his body will be downstream, otherwise he has to be in the surrounding woods somewhere. Perhaps he is delirious from his injuries, having left his clothes and belongings here. This island is not too terribly large, so we should find him eventually."

Triplett and Clark began their search downstream, while Hall and Tom crossed over the stream on a moss strewn log to search the woods. The two search teams agreed to rendezvous in two hours.

ENTERING THE WOODS ON THE FAR SIDE OF THE STREAM, Hall marveled at Tom's abilities to stay on increasingly faint game trails through the dense green vegetation. They called out Nathaniel's name every few moments, hoping for a response.

"Well, with all our noise, the bears should leave us alone," Joshua remarked.

"Yes, noise," Tom responded. "My previous silence caught the attention of a brown bear mother and her cub. The mother thought my life was worth sparing. Always respect them. The brown bears will take pity on you for humbling yourself before them. I've done it many times."

Joshua shuddered as he rechecked his musket.

"Good for you Tom. Now keep talking."

AN HOUR PASSED, AND THE DUSKY LIGHT FADED under the towering trees and overcast sky. Having reached the far side of the island and the forest's end at a small cliff, Tom and Joshua turned back towards the stream, continuing a zigzag pattern. Hall noticed Tom was still upset about sighting the river otter. The teenager's voice betrayed a slight fatalism as they continued to shout Folger's name. With his prior optimism fading into despair, Joshua found himself fighting back emotions as the harsh reality of Folger's disappearance became clearer. When the two sighted Triplett and Clark waiting by the stream without Folger, Hall could no longer deny the pain of the sailor's loss. Determined to uphold a brave front for his men, Hall blinked back tears as he clung to his musket amid the sound of the rushing water.

"Perhaps a brief prayer is in order gentlemen. I thought a bit of *Psalm 69* would be appropriate," Micah Triplett said after several moments of silence.

The other three men nodded in agreement before Triplett recited the prayer for Nathaniel Folger's suspected drowning.

> *Save me, O God; for the waters are come in unto my soul. I sink in deep mire, where there is no standing: I am come into deep waters, where the floods overflow me. I am weary of crying: my throat is dried: mine eyes fail while I wait for my God.*
>
> *Deliver me out of the mire, and let me not sink: let me be delivered from them that hate me, and out of the deep waters. Let not the waterflood overflow me, neither let the deep swallow me up, and let not the pit shut her mouth upon me. Hear me, O Lord; for thy loving kindness is good: turn unto me according to the multitude of thy tender mercies.*

After several moments of reflection, Clark spoke to break the solemn silence among the four men.

"I know I'm breaking your order by speaking first, sirs, but I want to say how terribly sorry I am for everything. Nate was a good man who happened to fall upon great misfortune. Mr. Hall, sir, it's not your fault that he disappeared, any man would have respected his wish to get off that miserable beach and move around, God knows all of our spirits need some rejuvenation."

Hall nodded as Clark and Tom turned and walked slowly back toward camp in silence. Hall looked at the stream and ambled over to the spot where he last saw Nathaniel Folger. Micah watched him, restless, since he knew Fletcher would be suspicious if the two officers remained away from camp for too long.

"Joshua, some of the crew support removing Captain Fletcher from command. Can I count on you?" Micah whispered, using the sound of the rushing stream to shield his voice.

Hall picked up a small rock and threw it in the stream before turning to Triplett.

"Sir, I think we should . . ."

Within moments, Jonathan Fletcher stepped out onto the trail from the woods several yards away. He charged and grabbed Hall's shirt and pushed him against a large moss-covered spruce.

"You son of a bitch, Hall! You take my woman and think I would just let it go?! Fuck you!"

Hall pushed Fletcher off and raised his fists.

"Just try me Jonathan, go ahead," Joshua spat. "And Alamea's not your woman anymore! She made that decision, not me!"

Fletcher tried to rush Hall, but Triplett intervened between the two men, shouting, "Stop! Goddamn it!"

Fletcher pivoted away from Hall and violently shoved Micah aside. Falling hard on his shoulder, Triplett grimaced in pain, but jumped to his feet and tackled Fletcher.

"Fuck you, Jonathan!" Micah screamed in fury as he raised a fist to strike the captain. Joshua threw a bear hug around Triplett just as Tom and Lavelle Clark arrived after sprinting to intervene and put a halt to the fighting.

"Shit! What the hell, sirs?!" Clark shouted in bewilderment as he aided Tom in restraining the captain.

Within moments, Kekoa, Ben Harper, and David Woods could be heard shouting and running through the woods to the stream. Joshua released Micah after he gave assurances under panted breaths he was done fighting. Clark and Tom let go of Fletcher, wherein the captain began brushing dirt from himself as he gulped air.

"Captain," Joshua spoke as he stared at Fletcher. "There are no court-rooms, barristers, or marshals on this unforgiving coast. We either work together or perish. You know this as well as I do."

A loud raven's call echoed through the woods. Fletcher spat on the ground and angrily stared at Hall before turning and stalking back towards the beach.

THIRTY-SIX

NIKOLAI KARAULOV'S PARTY AS WELL AS the officers and crew of
Eclipse labored intensively in the mid-afternoon warmth, processing
lumber from the woods and making feverish repairs onboard ship under
a sky alternating between clouds and sun. Having moved up orders to the
crew after breakfast, several hours earlier than planned, Captain Fletcher
declared a new urgency to get *Eclipse* sailing again. Hall chipped away bark
from freshly felled logs with his hatchet, his mind repeating the captain's
words from earlier in the day.

*Mr. Karaulov spotted Jackal near Sitka Island, who we will
engage with assistance from other vessels. We must act now to reach the
island, gentlemen, to correct the injustices inflicted by Captain Ian Coe on
our vessel and win the many hundreds of pelts that are rightfully ours. I
promise to you that thousands more can be won elsewhere on this coast,
but only if discipline prevails onboard ship.*

Sweat dripped off Hall's brow as he paused to catch his breath. He
recalled how Fletcher's masterful verbal cadences and body movements
intoxicated the crew's minds, for he had the ability to draw men under
his control.

*We mourn the losses of Liko and Nathaniel, and I swear before
you today as your captain, that I will protect each of you as best I
can. Remember, slavery, great suffering, even death awaits those
foolish ones who would engage in sloth and sedition in these
merciless wilds. Let none of us forget the consequences for willful delin-
quencies. Our collective security and prosperity rests within our ship's
order, the sanctity of which I intend to uphold for the inevitable glory of us
all, whatever the cost.*

Hall flung his hatchet down into the wood, hostile, as he centered his mind on what happened in the moments afterward. David Woods had begun applauding loudly, followed by Benjamin Harper, Tom, and even Lavelle Clark, as if previous concerns evaporated from their minds. As Thaddeus translated for Karaulov's party, they too began clapping enthusiastically to avoid displeasing the man who represented their best chance at freedom. Micah Triplett, observing the crew and the captain, lightly applauded as he glanced at Joshua to silently communicate his duress. Aolani and Kekoa, dispirited and resigned, simply turned aside to their assigned tasks. Alamea moved to stand beside Joshua, her eyes watering in a blend of empathy with Hall, but also defiance towards Fletcher. As the crew dispersed, Fletcher walked to his second officer after noticing his lack of support.

Mr. Hall, fear not, you are not alone in your dissent towards my command. Your little wahine whore is by your side to support you.

Joshua pulled his hatchet from the wood, the sweat dripping down his face, his chest heaving as a breeze fluttered his dirty linen shirt. Staring over the crew's work on ship and shore, his hatchet fell upon the spruce log with ever more velocity and power as he remembered Fletcher's jabbing, accusatory finger pointed in his face.

There will be no more dissent from my authority, Mr. Hall, no more interferences with my personal affairs. This is your fair warning. From now on, I expect nothing less than your finest example as an officer in upholding discipline and order.

Hall refused to be intimidated.

Captain, regarding your plans, there are . . .

Fletcher fired back, furious at Hall's dissent.

No 'Yes, sir', Mr. Hall? Did you not hear what I just said to you?

Joshua cast his mind to Micah Triplett's hasty intervention in an effort to diffuse the situation.

Jonathan, let me explain to you what has happened . . .

'Jonathan'? Fletcher responded incredulously. *'Jonathan', Mr. Triplett? No 'captain'? No 'sir'?*

Fletcher raised his eyebrows and rubbed his chin in condescension as he contemplated his next move.

I expect Eclipse to be seaworthy this evening. The crew is executing their orders now and requires your assistance. We move forward in unified purpose. That is all, thank you.

Joshua set his hatchet down, drank from his water flask, and lifted some processed lumber over his shoulder as he walked the few dozen yards to the beach. The smell of supper being prepared on board ship floated over the rocks and sand as Hall watched the high tide return. Before him rested the repaired *Eclipse*, her last damaged timbers nearly all refitted and caulked, her torn sails mended and rigged, her rudder realigned and reinforced. Exchanging a brief wave with Alamea and Kanoa as they collected small utensils and cleaned laundry from the beach, Joshua launched a small skiff filled with fresh lumber towards *Eclipse*. Upon arrival Kekoa, Lavelle Clark, and David Woods pulled the lumber off the skiff with Hall's assistance. Joshua placed his hand on the side of the stout New England brig, closed his eyes for a moment, and, in unease, sensed dangerous human frailties residing within her.

THIRTY-SEVEN

*E*CLIPSE CRUISED OVER WHITECAPS across THE wide strait, heading on a northwest tack into strong headwinds and occasional bursts of light rainfall. Their *baidarka* boats and weapons stowed below for security, Nikolai Karaulov and his three companions were allowed above deck as there were no other ships or canoes sighted in the wide strait. Sergei Popov, grasping Alina's hand, looked over the green sea as he spoke to Karaulov.

"Northward again, back to Baranov's rabid dogs and the savage Koloshi racing like devils over these Hades waters. You won't see me at heaven's gate if they lay a finger on my precious Alina. I'll kill the lot of 'em if they try to take our freedom away. The two Koloshi boys better mind their own business as well, especially the one called 'Tom.' The bastard's thrown dirty looks my way and spoke down to Alina. He thinks he's Tsar and Alina some miserable serf."

Alina smiled and wrapped her arms around Sergei. She fastened her eyes on the young Russian as he held her bottom and kissed her deeply.

Karaulov spoke, irritated with Sergei's insolence.

"You need to hold your temper and your tongue, Sergei Ivanovich. These Americans have been generous and promise us safe passage south once their business is concluded. We must remain patient and composed. The captain and his officers are resentful of each other, and we don't need to inflame them anymore on our part. Fletcher told us to keep quiet over what I told him about Elias Hall, or he'll kick us off this ship. All of us need to keep our mouths shut when the Kolosh boys are nearby, mind you, they speak decent Russian. And don't forget the second mate is Elias's brother, so think before you open that foul mouth of yours."

Popov pulled Alina into a protective embrace as she leaned into him. Her arms rested around his waist as her fiercely protective stare lingered on Sergei.

"Yes, Nikolai Mikhailovich, I know," Popov replied. "But that Tom needs to get off his high horse. And Fletcher reminds me a bit of the head guard when I was a prisoner in Irkutsk, a low living son of a bitch who exploded his wrath on you at any time. He beat me many times, like I was the worst kind of criminal, even though all I had ever done was steal some bread. Well, Pavel and I killed that bastard when we escaped. He bled and screamed like a stuck pig. The dirty tyrant had it coming. Pavel deserved to be free, only to come out here to toil for Baranov for almost nothing and end up a slave under the savage Koloshi."

"Pavel fought to rescue me, and you and Nikolai carried me to freedom. Once a slave, but now free! I have my whole life ahead of me with you! If anyone tries to harm my Sergei I will kill them!" Alina added.

Tanya fidgeted nervously, not liking the strain between the two. Her loyalty and support were for her husband, Nikolai.

"You heard Nikolai, now keep your mouth closed you foolhardy Kolosh girl, or none of us will ever escape this wicked coast!"

"Everyone shut up!" Nikolai snarled, his patience all but gone. He closed his eyes and raised his chin, exasperated.

"Just shut up and be thankful for your food and passage on this ship. Now drink your tea and keep to yourself. Volunteer to help the crew in their various labors here on deck and keep quiet. If the officers ask us something, I will do the talking."

HOURS MELTED AWAY WITH NO SIGN OF ANOTHER VESSEL or canoes as *Eclipse* continued to sail northward on alternating port and starboard tacks in the miles-wide strait. Nikolai, Tanya, Sergei, and Alina all assisted crew members on deck with small tasks, eager to please Fletcher, Hall, and Triplett, who held the Russian fugitives' fates in their hands. To Nikolai's relief, Sergei worked quietly and performed well in his carpentry on deck. Alina and Tanya assisted the Hawaiian sailors with sewing and mending sails, while Nikolai caulked a few remaining damaged spots on the ship's railings. Walking over to inspect Sergei's repairs on a few deck planks, Captain Fletcher nodded in appreciation, using the few words of Russian he knew.

"Very good, thank you."

Sergei smiled in appreciation, using the English he picked up from visiting American and British ships at Kodiak and Saint Michael.

"You are welcome, captain, thank you."

Alina was tired and held out her hand to Sergei with a teasing smile, speaking in Russian.

"Come rest with me, my love."

Fletcher waved over Tom to interpret. Although Alina motioned with hand signs to Fletcher that she was going below deck, Sergei spoke in Russian to Fletcher, assuming Tom could hear him.

"Captain, my woman Alina is going below for a rest. With your permission, I'd like to join her as I've completed the deck repairs and am a bit tired myself."

Instead of translating, Tom spoke in Tlingit to Alina.

"Where do you think you're going, slave woman? There are weapons below deck and you need to get permission from the captain first."

Incensed, Alina shot back without hesitation.

"Who the fuck are you to give me commands?! I'm no longer a slave of your clan houses and can do as I please! Now translate for Sergei, he's asking the captain permission!"

Infuriated, Tom moved towards her as she descended the ladder, yelling in Tlingit.

"Stop climbing down that ladder and get your ass back up here, you insolent bitch!"

Not needing a translation, Sergei instinctively placed himself between the two and shoved Tom slightly backward as a warning, while a confused Fletcher proceeded to separate the two young men. Karaulov, Triplett, and Hall all dropped their various tasks and rushed to the group as Fletcher yelled for Thaddeus to translate the angry words.

Sergei yelled in Russian at Tom, who tried to lunge at both Sergei and Alina, barely restrained by Fletcher.

"Leave Alina alone, you Kolosh dog!"

"Goddamn it, Tom, settle down!"

Fletcher yelled in English while Karaulov threw himself in front of Sergei and Alina and stared at them in disbelief.

"Did you not hear anything I said earlier?! You are damned fools, both of you!"

Tom, consumed by rage, switched to a broken Russian and shouted at Sergei and Nikolai.

"We of *Eclipse* are to aid the clans in destroying your Saint Michael colony! Your riffraff scum will no longer steal our property and insult our clans' honor!"

Sergei, Nikolai, and Alina froze, unable to believe what they were hearing. Karaulov, flustered and searching for a response, looked at Fletcher and Thaddeus and spoke slowly in Russian.

"We are to go back to Mikhailovsky colony? It is to be destroyed?"

Tanya screamed, silencing everyone momentarily as she wept hysterically and shrieked in Russian.

"My younger sister and her two daughters are still at Mikhailovsky! They will be killed or taken as slaves by the Koloshi! We must warn them! Please Captain Fletcher, we must return and save them!"

Thaddeus furiously translated for Fletcher, Hall, and Triplett, which other crew members could not help but overhear. Triplett and Hall were stunned. After the frantic breakout from the Kuiu village and the fight with *Jackal*, the two junior officers assumed Fletcher would avoid more trouble. Even more alarming, the captain had told Tom of his plans, but failed to share the information with Triplett and Hall.

Lavelle Clark stared at the sky, exasperated, before looking at Fletcher.

"We're getting involved in an attack on the Russians at Sitka Island? Captain, what the hell is going on? For Christ's sake, we can't be caught in another fight!"

Fletcher, Woods, and Tom pulled knives and side arms. The captain spoke without hesitation.

"Mr. Woods, put Mr. Clark in shackles and take him below. For his defiance, he will be locked in the designated cabin until further notice."

Fletcher continued, staring directly at Ben Harper and Thaddeus.

"Mr. Harper and Thaddeus, you will come here now and join us."

Harper, nervous and torn between loyalty to the captain and his good relations with Hall and Triplett, slowly walked to Fletcher's group while averting eye contact with the two officers. Hall couldn't help but notice the sailor's dour facial expression and drooped shoulders. By the time Harper reached Fletcher's group, Kekoa had rappelled down the aft mast to join Hall, Triplett, and Alamea, who also pulled side arms. Only Aolani remained unarmed as she held Kanoa. Sergei pulled a hidden knife and grabbed Alina to stand with Hall's group, while Nikolai and Tanya, who was weeping bitterly, reluctantly moved over to join Fletcher's side. Woods emerged from below deck and rejoined Fletcher.

Thaddeus stood alone in the middle, the pressure on him unbearable.

Shaking visibly, with tears welling in his eyes, the seventeen-year-old Tlingit spoke with trepidation.

"Please, sirs, don't make me choose sides here, I'm loyal to all of you. We all have our faults and mistakes on this voyage, but we do not need to have trouble like this, it will only end in ruin. I beg you, think of your families back home. Think of all those who have put their trust in us and the honor of our voyage. This is our world here, *Eclipse*, she is all we have."

Triplett turned to Captain Fletcher. The first officer appeared defiant, but his breaking voice betrayed his true feelings.

"Captain, your plan to involve us in the attack at Saint Michael will lead to ruin and cause many deaths. Under the authority invested in me by the Perkins Company and the law of the sea, I am placing this ship under my command with Mr. Hall in turn as first officer. Now put down your weapons. Tom, Harper, Clark, Woods, you will not be detained below if you swear allegiance to our command. This is my only warning."

Fletcher responded in a deadly tone, his face crimson with rage.

"Damn you, you just sealed your fate, boy. I'll have your hide nailed to the mast."

Disaster opened its jaws around the entire crew.

Remember Elias. Don't give up.

"Wait."

Hall set down his weapons and walked into the middle of the deck between the two groups to join Thaddeus, who also had set down his sidearm and knife. Putting his hand on the young Tlingit's shoulder and whispering in his ear to translate for him for Karaulov's party, Hall spoke without hesitation.

"We're apparently locked in a destructive standoff, so I offer a way out. Tanya mentioned she has a sister and nieces at Saint Michael. Captain Fletcher, I volunteer to lead a party from Sitka Island's eastern shore over the mountains to accompany the Tlingit fighters in the rear, since the attack is apparently going to occur regardless of our actions. We'll help negotiate the release of Tanya's relatives and any other prisoners, as well as make an accounting of the number of pelts so *Eclipse* receives her fair share. Then we'll rendezvous with you on the western shore of the island not far from Saint Michael. In return you must pledge not to punish Mr. Triplett and the others with him, including Mr. Clark."

Dumbfounded, Fletcher began chuckling softly as he lowered his weapons and grinned.

"You have a bold streak, Mr. Hall. I now see why Thomas Perkins hired you. Your instincts serve you well."

Fletcher paused and pulled a Hawaiian necklace out from under his shirt given to him by Alamea on O'ahu. He ripped it off and threw it to Hall.

"The moon deity, Lona."

Fletcher stared for a moment at Alamea, a dozen feet away.

"She passed over my burning heart, blocking all of its light. The goddess now passes to you, but beware Joshua, beware of her power."

Holding the necklace in his hand, Joshua sighed and shook his head, annoyed.

"Captain, your answer to my proposal?"

"Agreed," Fletcher snapped, "and you and the Triplett rabble can redeem some honor on this ship if you execute this plan successfully. Continue our northward tacks until we reach the eastern shore of Sitka Island. If Elias Hall lives, he will be there."

THIRTY-EIGHT

Eastern shore of Sitka Island, June 1802

ECLIPSE SAILED NORTH, NO LONGER HAVING to conduct tacks as the wind shifted and blew in from the south. Periodic heavy drizzle blanketed areas of the strait as the brisk southerlies nimbly carried the vessels over the strait's whitecaps and tidal chop. The southern tip of Sitka Island soon appeared in the far distance behind a swirl of clouds. Jonathan Fletcher smoked tobacco as he gazed upon the island that would largely determine the success or failure of his voyage. Elias Hall and thousands of pelts were within his grasp. All that was needed was finding *Panther* and a Tlingit victory over the Russians. Then he would deal with *Jackal*.

With his fortune secured, he would never have to return to this dreary, dangerous coast again. Fletcher grinned as tobacco smoke exited his nostrils. His confidence surged, for he was on the far side of the world and would do as he pleased, no laws, no courts, no authority to answer to except himself. God, he reasoned, ignored this coast as He passed over high above. Men like him were anointed to forge discipline and decide what was to be done in places such as this one. Besides, this ocean was too vast, its spaces too distant and far apart for memories to remain.

AN EARLY SUPPER WAS PREPARED FOR THE CREW. Recently released from his locked cabin, Lavelle Clark handed Joshua Hall, Alamea, and Kanoa plates of rice and salted fish. Anger and disappointment consumed Clark, and Hall knew that he felt betrayed.

"I am sorry, Lavelle, for the unfortunate turn of events," Hall sympathized, "I'll do my utmost to make sure you remain safe."

"Fletcher should not be in command of this ship, that's all I'm going to say for now," Clark replied. "His constant scheming is going to get more of us killed, and—

"That will be all, Mr. Clark," Hall replied as he began eating his meal.

Sitting in a secluded area by the bow, Alamea pleaded with Joshua to reconsider the shore party scheme and keep alive the idea of removing Fletcher from command.

"Sitka will be too dangerous, and I fear you may be killed. I know we may find your brother Elias, but please, Joshua, think of Kanoa, think of me and the future. You promised you would teach him how to be a sailor on the great ocean, *Moana*."

Wearing the *Lona* necklace beneath his linen shirt, Hall replied with empathy and reassurance as he set his food aside and took Kanoa's hand to guide him onto his lap.

"I remember an old islander refrain Liko told me a few days out of O'ahu. He said it could be used for courage in storms and the unknown. 'Mine is the migrating bird winging afar over remote oceans, ever pointing out the sea road of the black bird—the dark cloud in the sky of night. It is the road of the winds coursed by the Sea Kings to unknown lands.'"

Alamea smiled as tears rolled down her cheeks. She embraced Joshua and Kanoa.

"My glorious men, Joshua and Kanoa, you are my heart, my hope, my moon and stars in the heavens above."

"CANOES! THERE, OFF THE PORT BOW IN THE FAR DISTANCE!" Tom shouted as he spotted Tlingit canoes painted with deep red eyes and black wings of Raven and Eagle, a stark contrast to the cloudy drizzles and deep green of Sitka Island's southeastern shore. Crew members ended card games over coffee and whiskey rations, tobacco, and laundered socks and shirts, while Thaddeus concluded a discussion with Captain Fletcher over a chart of Sitka Island after reviewing clan politics and good trails over the island's mountainous interior. Boarding nets were raised and weapons checked as precautions over the next few minutes.

"Mr. Woods, turn the helm to the canoes." Fletcher barked. "We'll have a look. The stars and stripes are flying high, there should be no mistaking us for the Russians."

"Aye, cap."

Joshua Hall approached from midship.

"Captain, with permission, if Elias is indeed here, I would like to speak with him first, in private."

Fletcher stared at the island shore without glancing at Hall.

"Permission granted."

"Thank you, sir."

"And one more thing. You and Mr. Triplett are only officers on a probational basis. And Mr. Hall, I haven't forgotten your actions regarding the O'ahu wench or your associations with Triplett's mutinous rabble. My overlooking of these transgressions will only become more fixed once you successfully execute our plans on Sitka. Is that understood?"

"Understood, sir."

Hall turned to walk back across the deck towards the bow when Fletcher added a postscript to his remarks.

"Keep that bastard boy and insolent bitch of yours out of my way on deck as well Mr. Hall, otherwise they'll be locked below."

Hall turned back to face Fletcher.

"Alamea and Kanoa are God's children, the same as you and me, no more, no less. A higher authority governs us all, even in these remote corners of the world. Whether you want to admit to that or not is entirely up to you."

Hall turned and walked towards the bow. Fletcher remained silent as he lit a fresh patch of tobacco in his pipe. Exhaling voluminously as he watched Hall rejoin Alamea, Kanoa, and Triplett on the other side of the ship, Fletcher felt the southerly winds swirl around him and carry the tobacco smoke into his face. He looked up to avoid the smoke and rub his eyes, and noticed a crescent diurnal moon momentarily emerge from behind several thick clouds, only to disappear again behind the deep gray of the horizon.

Several minutes passed before a starboard tack led *Eclipse* towards a narrow cove entrance. After coming about into the new tack towards the island, *Eclipse* entered a narrow passage between wooded hills, one of which was fortified by the Tlingits. David Woods shouted as he stood in amazement.

"Would ya look at that! That tout up deh must be a hundred feet around or so, and twenty feet high! And all those brass swivel cannons mounted up deh, my goodness!"

As *Eclipse* fully rounded the narrow point guarding the large cove, the crew was astonished again as nearly fifty war canoes appeared, scattered along the cove's shorelines where dozens of campfires lit the woods and small meadows.

Micah Triplett held his hand on his head, stunned.

"Must be four or five hundred fighting men here."

"And from many clan houses, given the totem crests on shore." Thaddeus added as he held his spyglass steady.

Joshua lowered his spyglass, his eyes shedding slight tears.

"There's *Panther*, moored to another smaller schooner. Can't make the name out."

Tom put his left foot on the railing as he held his spyglass steady.

"A few canoes with about two dozen men are leaving shore, cap! They all appear to be Tlingits, and armed!"

"No white men that I can see." Fletcher added as half the crew peered through spyglasses. "Everyone, hold your weapons at the ready. Trouble is unlikely, but we take no chances. No one fires unless I give the command."

"Goddamnit Elias, where are you?" Joshua blurted as several anxious moments passed.

Gulls and terns cried out overhead, while faint raven calls echoed from shore. Pungent scents of fir, spruce, and campfire smoke mixed with the smell of the sea. Two canoes stopped paddling about forty yards from *Eclipse* while the third continued onward at a reduced speed. A man dressed in a Tlingit rain hat and red and black woolen cloak rose to stand in the front of the large war canoe.

"Steady, everyone, steady!" Fletcher shouted as he held his musket tight.

Within seconds the canoe turned parallel to *Eclipse,* ten yards away, and was brought to a halt by its six paddlers. Joshua stood at the port railing with Alamea and Thaddeus at his side. The man who stood in the canoe removed his hat and cloak, revealing ragged blue sailor linens and long brown hair that fell over his shoulders to his lower back. A necklace of carved shells and wooden pieces complemented a nose ring and neck tattoos of suns and stars. Bird tattoos adorned his hands and lower arms.

Joshua leaned over the railing between heavy breaths.

"Elias."

"Joshua, I dreamed of you many times crossing over to my world. You always arrived as a bird. A Hawaiian noddy, a young albatross, a raven. Clever, resilient creatures. We meet again, brother."

THIRTY-NINE

E LIAS EXHALED PIPE SMOKE THROUGH HIS NOSE and grinned at his brother. His wide open green eyes burned a hole through Joshua as the two sat below an ancient Sitka spruce. Around them were two dozen teenagers and young adults of various ethnicities, evenly split between men and women. Like Elias, most were dressed in a peculiar mix of Northwest Coast, Polynesian, and European clothing, and had ample tattoos and jewelry. All held muskets and carried attached knives, and Joshua noted they obeyed Elias's orders without question. Steam from nearby hot springs floated over small but well-built cedar planked Tlingit homes a few paces away. *Eclipse*, about a hundred yards distant, remained visible through the woods.

"Do tell me, Joshua, how are Tom and Thaddeus holding up under Jonathan Fletcher? I'm surprised they haven't bolted ship yet."

"You tutored them well back in Boston, Elias. They're excellent sailors and scholars, and have fight in them. They've helped to save *Eclipse* more than once."

"I look forward to speaking with those two again. Last time was in late '99, when my crew and I left Boston on *Panther*. It wouldn't surprise me if at least one of them decides to remain here in his homeland."

"You may be right, Elias. If I had to guess, it would be Tom."

Elias nodded and smoked his pipe. A pair of ravens cried out to each other from the deep woods.

"You'll have to join me later in the hot springs, Joshua. Cleans one's spirit."

Joshua nodded as Elias continued.

"We were once slaves, but no more thanks to our efforts against the Russians and other unwanted foreigners. The clan houses amnestied us after we fulfilled a prophecy of their great shaman, Wolf-Weasel."

Joshua gazed up into the ancient spruce for a moment.

"I'm grateful you're alive, Elias. You'll have to tell me what happened here with yourself and these people."

Pausing for a moment, Joshua looked away to the cove through the woods. The two masts of *Eclipse* became visible through the trees under a mixture of sunlight and shade from passing clouds.

Just do it now.

He turned again to face Elias.

"I'm here to bring you home."

Elias folded his arms, looked up and laughed. The others soon followed. Joshua guessed some were original *Panther* crew, and perhaps sailors who deserted from another ship. A few were no doubt fugitives from the Russian colonies and former Tlingit slaves. After several moments, Elias held his hand up and the others fell silent. Joshua, uneasy, took a deep breath and only moved his eyes.

"Home." Elias pronounced with a touch of bitterness. "And what is 'home'? Governments, gods, laws, prejudices. And fathers who dictate to their sons."

Joshua surrendered to silence for the moment. The Hall brothers gazed over the sea and distant mist-shrouded mountains covered in glaciers. The indomitable wildness cast a hypnosis. Joshua thought of the moment Kanoa's eyes met his for the first time in the village longhouse.

Elias picked up a small rock and threw it into the flat sea as he spoke.

"I often go back into the heart of who we were as small children. A divinity reigned within us. Remember? Like the glory of autumn woods, the purity of winter skies. The time before the assassin of innocence."

He's gone mad.

"And who might that be?"

"Father, of course."

"Oh come on now Elias, you were always his favorite."

Elias scoffed.

"He gave up on me not long after mother died. Sent me out on those apprenticeships. He turned his ambitions on you."

Joshua rubbed his forehead.

"Nonsense. He never lost faith in you. He wants you back for God's sakes."

Elias sat rigid.

"He'll never see me again."

"Parents have frailties and flaws. Father is no different. We're men who should recognize this fact."

Elias stood and smiled.

"You're just an errand boy doing the bidding of father and Thomas Perkins. And you know that."

"Fuck you."

"You'll learn in time only an eyelash stands between us brother. We have a common destiny."

Joshua spat and shook his head. Elias exhaled pipe smoke, and waved his left hand around to acknowledge his followers.

"Father is dead to me. This is my family now. They've placed their will in my leadership, for freedom, in an eden of our choosing. It may be here, the South Seas, Alta California, or some other shore."

"I see."

Elias is under one of his manic delusions. Or is this him now?

"You can join us too, Joshua. And your crew as well. I leave that to you, brother."

A few more quiet moments passed until a raven's call filled the woods. He watched as Elias and his followers walked into the collage of firelight and shadows at the forest edge.

FORTY

ALAMEA AND KANOA LEANED ON JOSHUA after he climbed back aboard *Eclipse*, clasping his hands as they looked at Elias Hall's sailors work on *Panther* and their newly named second ship, *Icarus*. Micah Triplett and Aolani held hands by the port railing next to Joshua as a lone bald eagle soared high above the masts of *Eclipse*.

"So, Joshua," Micah asked as he sipped tea, "how did Elias get his hands on that small schooner, *Icarus*?"

"Seized it from the Russians in the straits, sir. He's acted as a sort of privateer for the clan houses."

"Why so melancholic, Joshua? We've found your brother and the surviving *Panther* crew against all odds. Boss Perkins and your father will be pleased."

"I may not be able to get him back to New England. Elias has wild mood swings, and he's in one of his manias. They can last for long periods of time."

Micah nodded and rubbed the back of his neck.

"Well, he's gone native in his appearance. Did Elias and the cap get along on shore?"

"Yes, our vessels are to provide weapons and tactical support to the clans. There are about a thousand clan fighters combined here and on Sitka Island's western shore. In return for our support, *Eclipse* is to receive a quarter of all pelts at St. Michael after the Russians are driven out of these lands."

Alamea watched several canoes and skiffs launch from shore for

Eclipse, *Panther*, and *Icarus*, to begin exchanging supplies and weapons. She thought of Liko as she spoke.

"And what of the treacherous Englishman Coe, Joshua, did Elias or the others sight *Jackal*?"

"Unfortunately, no. That slithering serpent may have already made his way to O'ahu or Canton. If he's still on this coast we'll find him."

Heavy gray mists hovered above the thick woods and mountains as Captain Fletcher arrived in a skiff from *Panther* with a few Tlingit men.

"Mr. Triplett, Mr. Hall, prepare the shore party."

Tom, Thaddeus, Sergei Popov, and Nikolai Karaulov lowered weapons and supplies into the skiff. After completing their task, they started to climb into the skiff with Triplett and Hall.

Alina ran to Sergei, embracing him desperately before pleading with Captain Fletcher and the Tlingit men on board.

"Let me go with him! I will fight and die if needed!"

Alamea was already clinging to Joshua, tears flowing from her eyes, as Kanoa cried piteously.

"Let me accompany Joshua and these men, I can carry supplies and fight as well!"

Fletcher, intrigued by the proposals, remained silent for a moment as he rubbed his whiskers in contemplation. He relished having uncontested power, especially over Alamea. His chance to decide was soon lost, however, as the clan men responded directly to Fletcher through Tom and Thaddeus.

"No, no women. They will slow your shore party, and thus our fighters crossing over the mountains. If you want your share of the Russians' pelts, and Aleut prisoners for ransom to Baranov, these two women must remain on board."

"Agreed, the women will remain on board." Fletcher ordered.

Throwing a defiant look at Fletcher, Alamea remained locked to Joshua.

"Please come back to me, Joshua, when we rendezvous with you two days from now. Remember Kanoa and I always walk with you wherever you may be."

She rested her palm on his chest.

"Our hearts beat with yours."

"And mine with yours." Fighting back tears, Hall added, "Let us carry on now."

After ending his embrace with Aolani, Triplett spoke to the women in a final effort to comfort them.

"Remember our shore party is to only remain in the rear and observe. Our task is to simply acquire our pelt share and Tanya's relatives. We'll practice the utmost caution."

"Alright," Fletcher interjected hastily. "Enough with all this sentimental rubbish. Everyone in the shore party into the skiff, Elias Hall is already ashore and is waiting for us to finalize our arrangements with the clans. Mr. Clark, you're in command here onboard while I'm meeting with Elias and the others. You and the crew are to assist the Sitka men in loading the designated canoes on board and preparing deck spaces for the dozen clan men accompanying us around the island. I will return in the morning."

"Aye, sir," Clark responded, as Woods, Harper, and Kekoa began assisting several high-ranking clan leaders aboard. Despite whale oil lubricant applied to winches attached to the ship's side rigging, several loud ear-piercing squeaks shot out across the deck as the first canoes were lifted aboard. In the ensuing commotion, Alamea and Kanoa hurried to the ship's stern for a final wave goodbye to Joshua, who raised his hand and smiled as the skiff glided over the calm green waters towards the shore. Alina came alongside them, placing her hand on Kanoa's shoulder as she stood in solidarity with Alamea.

TWO EIGHT-FOOT BONFIRES DEFIED THE DARK OVERCAST and steady drizzle of late evening, illuminating not only the four hundred men gathered under the flames' deep red glow, but also *Panther, Icarus,* and *Eclipse,* anchored dozens of yards from the beach. Wooden and hide armor, battle collars and helmets, and knives and muskets lay strewn near the edge of the forest's darkness, barely visible, an ominous reminder of the conflict to come on the other side of the island. Jonathan Fletcher and Elias Hall smoked and sipped whiskey as Tlingit dancers, wearing woolen cloaks and wooden helmets carved with totemic animals, moved in rhythmic, hypnotic circles to several drums hitting the same precise cadence. Tom, wearing a blue and green helmet carved in the image of a fierce Sea Lion with human qualities, was among the dancers. A protruding nose, angry black oval eyes, and real sea lion whiskers complemented an intimidating grin filled with small, carved white teeth. Except for his chin, Tom's face was obscured by the helmet.

Sitting on the opposite side of the bonfire from Fletcher and Elias Hall was the rest of the *Eclipse* shore party. Mesmerized, Joshua Hall sketched the scene before him in his private log, unaware of the nervous whispers between Sergei Popov and Nikolai Karaulov a few yards away. Thaddeus, tapping Hall on the shoulder, relayed the two Russians' concerns.

"Sirs, Popov and Karaulov are worried that some of these Tlingit fighters will simply kill them at some point during the next two days, even though they're with us. Popov in particular is very anxious."

Micah Triplett, sitting next to Hall, reassured the two Russian fugitives.

"The clan leaders recognize you are no longer with Baranov's company. They know you're with us, and consider you to be 'Boston men' under Fletcher's authority."

Karaulov worked hard to suppress his fear.

"It's not the elite Koloshi we are concerned over, rather, it's some of these lower-ranking Koloshi men who harbor lingering resentments. We've learned from hard experience not to trust them. Two common men from the Sitka villages have hurled insults at us, and one of them even threatened to slit my throat."

"Just stay close to Mr. Triplett and myself," Joshua replied after Thaddeus's translation, "and use common sense. We fully intend to get off this island the minute our duties are concluded. Remember, we're only here to observe and acquire the women and pelts already agreed to by the clans' leadership. We have fulfilled our end of the agreement by providing weapons, tactical advice, and transportation for the clan elite aboard the vessels."

Karaulov stared into the fire and wrapped his arms around his knees.

"We'll indeed remain close to you, Joshua and Micah, but please remember that Sergei and I have lived on these unforgiving shores for three years. Koloshi people never forget insults and injustices towards their kin, and unexpected hostilities and misfortunes can arise. Young Thaddeus here is an exception, though. He's calm, reflective, and engaged with your Boston men's ideas and beliefs."

Hall nodded in agreement, appreciating the Russian's kind words.

"Thaddeus is indeed an asset for all of us, as is Tom. Stay focused on the task at hand, gentlemen. Get some rest. We have a long, arduous trek before us tomorrow. Is there anything else?"

Karaulov gazed at the flickering orange and red hues across spruce trees surrounding the camp. He glanced at Popov before looking back at Hall and Triplett.

"No, Mr. Hall, there's nothing else but our sincerest desire to earn our freedom."

Joshua nodded as Elias walked around the bonfire to join him. His long hair now tied in a bundle behind his head, Elias had also removed his nose ring and wore a woolen blue sailor's sweater. He sat next to Joshua, his legs crossed. A reflection of the orange bonfire a few yards away danced in his deep set green eyes as he held a small book in his hands.

"Hello again, brother."

"Elias."

"You know, Joshua, I've reflected on our talk today. Quite a bit, actually. Perhaps I'll visit New England for a short time. I would like to see sister Laura again, and little Grace and Maggie."

Joshua sat up from his reclined position, his eyes wide open as Elias continued.

"Young innocence always resides within us. We just have to open the boxes around our hearts. Unleash the light, the potential of our souls."

"Can you do that for father?"

Elias lit more tobacco in his pipe. His voice soured.

"I have a world to forge, and I've no use for old and tired ways. Father's dead to me, I've told you that."

Damn it Joshua, just get Elias home, the rest will take care of itself.

"Alright. We'll leave him out of your return to Boston. I'll take you straight to Laura, Grace, and Margaret in New Hampshire."

"A time of my own choosing. Or perhaps you and Laura will decide to join me someday."

"Very well, Elias."

Joshua closed his eyes for a moment.

Patience. Don't force things with Elias.

"Here, brother." Elias tore a page from his small book and handed it to Joshua. "I've memorized this for all time, from William Blake's *The First Book of Urizen*. Professor I apprenticed with in Boston passed it to me. The world I left behind is lost to me, gone. Do not forget that Joshua."

Elias smiled, and walked into the dark woods towards the hot springs. Joshua was tempted to follow him, but chose to remain by the fire. Fletcher left and followed Elias moments later. Joshua looked at the poem.

And their children wept, & built
Tombs in the desolate places,
And form'd laws of prudence, and called them
The eternal laws of God

Joshua's eyes watered. He longed for the advice and counsel of his older sister Laura in this moment, but that was impossible now. He rubbed his forehead and looked down, whispering to himself, "Elias walks on the edge of an abyss. Please, God, let me help him."

AN EARLY MORNING CHILL GREETED JOSHUA HALL as he awoke to gull cries, campfire smoke, and roasting fish. While the rain had subsided, heavy clouds blanketed much of the bay and nearby mountains. Dozens of Tlingit men were already moving about their small camps preparing wooden-framed packs for the journey over to Sitka Island's western shore, while others continued to eat meals of cooked fish over mixed greens. A few dozen yards away, Fletcher spoke with Tom as the two sipped coffee. After noticing Hall sit up and rub his eyes, Fletcher approached, his swagger boasting confidence.

"Mr. Hall, you awake to a most important day of our voyage. Might I recommend those hot springs just a half mile or so through those woods in that direction? Quite refreshing, I admit, my spirits are invigorated once more. I'm to depart in the skiff back to *Eclipse*. As we've discussed, we'll rendezvous with your shore party after Saint Michael is destroyed tomorrow. Two thousand pelts is our share. And Karaulov will identify the woman and two girls to be brought on board our vessel. Your party is not to engage in any fighting. Elias and his vessels will be accompanying us around the north end of Sitka. Any questions?"

"Yes, cap. If you don't mind my asking, what did Elias say to you last night about his plans?"

Fletcher rubbed his hands together and frowned.

"Your brother is a romantic, a wild man, but just civilized and ambitious enough to see our plans through. Whether he returns to Boston with us or not concerns me very little at this point, Mr. Hall."

"But cap, sir, I've some worries over him. He may try something extreme and . . ."

Fletcher spat and rubbed the back of his neck, impatient.

"Your concerns will center on our task at hand. That will be all."

"Captain, sir, please hear me out. Elias could . . ."

"That will be all! Goddamnit, man!"

Joshua put his hands in his pockets and looked down in resignation. He allowed his anger and frustration with Fletcher to drift away with the calls of a few gulls circling overhead.

"Very well, captain."

The captain remained silent, pulling out his pipe and lighting some tobacco. Staring at Hall, Fletcher exhaled smoke toward the sky and turned toward the beach.

Looking eastward across the bay, Hall observed the rising sun's deep orange light penetrate the receding mist hovering around the three ships. As Fletcher rowed the skiff over the flat surface to *Eclipse,* an unexpected shiver raced through Hall's veins.

The sea was blood red.

FORTY-ONE

WESTERN SHORE OF SITKA ISLAND, JUNE 1802

WOLF-WEASEL SAT UPON A ROUND, MOSSY BOULDER at the forest's edge, just out of sight from the meadow and narrow beach below. His long, uncombed hair shrouded his arms and legs, while an owl bone charm rested in his nasal septum against a face blackened by charcoal. A necklace of fox and wolverine teeth complemented wrist and ankle bracelets of ivory. Painted wolf and weasel faces covered his skin leggings, fringed with puffin beaks, and a headdress of white ermine and black wolf fur flowed over his back below a crown of mountain goat horns.

A slight breeze whispered his chants and calls to the far ends of Sitka Island, to Wolf-Weasel's *yek*, his spirit helpers. His friendly yek, black wolf, weasel, kingfisher, and heron, soon arrived beside him, for Wolf-Weasel faithfully held to fasting and drank purgative Devil's Club juice. Other powerful, more dangerous yek required additional risks and sacrifices. Their aid would ensure victory over the Russians and their Aleut slaves.

Clan fighters from throughout *Lingit Aani* gathered below in the meadow poised for battle, awaiting Wolf-Weasel for wisdom and power. Wolf-Weasel's calls into the forest grew louder and more fearful. He held fast to his bundle of bear claws, sea lion whiskers, and land otter tongue, urgently pleading his respect and humility.

Escorted by his friendly yek, Wolf-Weasel entered *The Other*, a space of unknown distances and dimensions, devoid of linear time, where life, death, darkness, and light freely mixed in potent concoctions. Raven called to Wolf-Weasel from behind a frightful collage of swirling stars and earthly settings of mountains, forest, and sea.

Bull Sea Lion Man, Land Otter Girl, and Angry Brown Bear Mother join you now, Wolf-Weasel. Be mindful and respectful of them, for their powers can leave you at any moment and hide away in hidden spaces.

Wolf-Weasel rose from his meditation and stepped off the boulder, his hair covering his back and the ground beside his feet. A cedar mask carved in the combined features of wolf and weasel hid his face. Painted black, the mask held a long, protruding nose and wide grin with several white teeth. White oval eyes and locks of weasel and wolf fur straddled the top fringes.

As he emerged from the forest, Wolf-Weasel pulled a black woolen cloak over his back and shoulders with sewn, red mother-of-pearl kingfisher and heron heads facing one another. The fighters, below in the meadow, halted their preparations for battle and became silent as Wolf-Weasel walked towards them. On the long shore beside the meadow, dozens of giant cedar war canoes lay motionless. Their sides painted with red-and-black lined depictions of marine animals, the largest images rested on the bows of the canoes and arched upward as tall as a man.

Wolf-Weasel danced and shouted into the meadow, alternating every few seconds between slow stomping and crouches to sudden sprints and jumps. He returned to the mossy boulder, and within moments, sprinted into the meadow behind a new mask, weaving between clan fighters in fluid movements like an animal gliding through the sea. Wide white beady eyes rested below a dark brow. Whiskers protruded up from thick brown lips surrounding tightly packed teeth. Wolf-Weasel turned sharply, screaming mixed cries of a man and a bull sea lion as he approached the forest's edge. He turned to face the meadow, his upper body swaying in fluid gyrating movements. Astonished clan fighters observed proud Bull Sea Lion Man for a brief moment before he vanished into the woods.

Soon the air around the forest edge became distorted, like a reflection of trees in a gently lapping pool of water. Land Otter Girl stood at the forest's edge, casting wild and volatile powers over the meadow. Her upper lip, caught under a rotund nose, rested below round, absorbing eyes that penetrated all before her. The adolescent held out her arms protruding from her furry brown chest and shrieked a melancholic cry for a lost love. Terrified clan fighters, their limbs slightly numb, listened as the sound transformed into a muffled underwater-like shrill. Land Otter Girl bolted in a hunched position to the center of the gathered men. Gasps filled the air as clan fighters observed her head and body grow more disproportionately elongated. Land Otter Girl stood fully upright and turned her head in a fluid motion from side to side. She released another piercing scream, her small sharp teeth fully visible as she darted back into the woods and vanished.

Angry Brown Bear Mother paced back and forth beside the meadow's edge, stout and strong. Lifting her nose, she stomped her legs as saliva dripped from her enormous mouth. She charged the clan fighters below. All knelt before her power, asking for forgiveness, but also strength and courage. Unsatisfied, Angry Brown Bear Mother growled at a few men and feigned attack as she continued treading among them. She roared in furious passion and stood on her hind legs before dropping to race back into the woods. All remained silent for several moments as a low heavy mist slowly rolled in from the sea.

A raven cried out from a giant spruce and Wolf-Weasel emerged from behind the trees sweating profusely. Utterly exhausted and barely able to stand, he had no masks and no woolen cloak. Wolf-Weasel's face was fully visible without charcoal and his shaman attire no longer ornamented him. Only his smothering black hair obscured his body. Between heavy breaths, Wolf-Weasel shouted to the hundreds of clan men and women.

"Raven announces his curfew for this shore. Prepare for battle, as I, Wolf-Weasel, have held counsel with my yek. The beings of forest and sea proclaim your coming victory over the Russian invaders and their Aleut slaves! Onward now, heed Raven's call! Take to your canoes and triumph will be ours!"

A feverish commotion erupted all across the meadow and beach as battle cries mimicking totemic animals filled the air. Hundreds of men and a few women began fitting wooden war collars and helmets over body armor. Wolf-Weasel, mustering what faint strength he had left, walked among clan fighters who held a variety of totemic crests. He paused to watch a Sea Lion man pull on hide shoes and leggings along with thick upper body elk hide armor. Within moments, the clan fighter placed wooden slat armor tied with deer sinew over his upper body that stretched to his thighs. Matching red and brown faces in morphed, lined renditions of humans and sea lions marked the center of lower and upper armor slats.

After fitting his armor, the man attached a copper dagger to his chest with an intricate wooden handle carved in the image of a raven's head with an abalone shell inlay. He slung a musket over his back with a leather strap and picked up deerskin pouches of powder, flint, and musket balls. At his side rested a war club with a foot-long handle and an end piece embedded with sea lion teeth.

The high-born man spoke to a lower-ranking clan member beside him.

"You, man of Grandmother Sea Lion House, assist me with my battle collar and helmet."

Without speaking, the younger man assisted in fitting a steam-bent, spruce wood battle collar piece over the high-born man's face. Fitting his nose into a carved indent, with slight eyeholes on the collar top, the man held the collar in place with a mouth piece as his younger comrade tied deer sinew at the back of his neck over heavy elk hide. Sea shells embedded in the front of the collar accentuated a carved creature's oval mouth and two small round nostrils. Additional white and red animal faces with deep set green eyes were carved around the collar's entire circumference.

Lastly, the Sea Lion clan fighter lifted his battle helmet, carved from spruce burl, onto his head. Crafted in the shape of a Bull Sea Lion, with the animal's whiskers fastened on top, the deep blue helmet hid the man's face except for his eyes, visible only in the narrow space between the front of the collar and helmet. With his armor in place, the proud Sea Lion fighter made his way to a war canoe on the beach.

Willing himself on despite crippling fatigue and sweat flowing off his body, Wolf-Weasel walked to the sea's edge beside the canoes amid thickening sea mist. All around him, fully adorned fighters moved like a myriad of supernatural beings into dozens of canoes, glorious and terrifying.

"We honor you, Wolf-Weasel!" shouted a tall, muscular man from under his ebony and white Orca helmet, which in turn held a carved Raven head looking skyward. Two other men, wearing helmets and collars depicting Owl and Black Bear totem crests, strode with confidence as they moved past Wolf-Weasel into their canoes with spears and double-bladed daggers.

"Our clans are united, Wolf-Weasel, remember this moment for all of us," they said.

Wolf-Weasel grinned despite his exhaustion.

"The forest and sea beings keep all stories past and stories to come. Honor and hold them always in the spaces of your heart, and you shall possess great power," he replied.

Like opened, narrow boxes, the war canoes filled with fighters from many kwaans. Wolf-Weasel remained on shore and prepared to enter the forest once again to rest and replenish his powers. As the canoes launched and paddles began striking the ocean, the thick, hovering mist shrouded the helmeted, armored fighters and the great canoes. The fantastic beings faded into hidden spaces beside forest and sea, poised to unleash a terrible but magnificent force.

FORTY-TWO

Emelian Taradanov laughed with his wife, Marpha, as he set small pieces of freshly cut firewood in the small cart beside him. It was an easy day to laugh for the young couple since the sun had finally come out after dreary days of rain and mist. A soft, pleasant breeze from Sitka Sound gently blew over the meadows and young spruce stands surrounding Fort Mikhailovsky, just over a hundred yards distant. Marpha had reminded him of his first attempt to paddle a baidarka and hunt with her brother in the Aleutians, four years earlier, when he had been only fifteen. Instead of moving straight forward in pursuit of the seabirds bobbing on the surface, the brown-haired Siberian had gone in circles after getting pushed by a slight incoming tide. Chuckling some more as he set down his hatchet for a brief rest, Emelian reminded Marpha that he was now fast approaching the skill level of her brother and other Aleut male kin. After all, he reminded her, he had grown up in a log cabin in the wilds of eastern Siberia, surrounded by immense forests, a place where the ocean was several hundred miles distant.

Sitting down next to her husband and offering him some berries from her basket, Marpha was pleased he'd been granted fort duty and not out on yet another dangerous hunting flotilla in the straits.

"Let the company officers take the lead this time, the two Ivans, Kuskov and Urbanov," she said. "Still, I hope Kuskov returns without misfortunes. Kuskov is a good man. He listens to our concerns and doesn't carry his pride everywhere he goes like Medvednikov and these other arrogant subordinates doing Mr. Baranov's bidding. I wish Kuskov were in charge here."

His presence always reminds me of our wedding back on Kodiak. Even though he's not a priest Kuskov presided over our ceremony with dignity, don't you agree, Emelian?"

"He did indeed my lovely one."

Emelian smiled, kissing the top of her head and stretching his legs as he embraced her.

"Now, let us rest a bit and enjoy our quiet. I want to take advantage of our little Alexei being watched over by the other women in the fort. Don't bring up the company, Medvednikov, or any of the others, either. I'm tired of worrying about all their unfortunate decisions. Plus, I'm getting another headache. Now hold me, I wish to daydream pleasant thoughts."

"Our blessed Alexei, I can't believe he's already three years old," Marpha said as she rested her head on Emelian's chest and closed her eyes.

Emelian held Marpha, stroking her black hair and lean, toned body. He tried to relax and focus his mind on returning to Kodiak soon, where his wife and child would be safe, but his concerns refused to surrender their grip on his thoughts. Fort Mikhailovsky's commanding officer, Vasili Medvednikov, arrogantly dismissed Emelian's points about many of the Koloshi becoming more abrasive and aggressive. The Indians thought Mikhailovsky was to be temporary, not a fort, but a business establishment to compete with the growing number of Boston and King George ships. Mikhailovsky was to offer attractive trade volumes to the clans, but Baranov's promises soon evaporated. The Frog Totem Koloshi, led by Skaultlelt's nephew, Katlian, were particularly belligerent. One could not blame them though, Emelian reasoned, as some of their clan kin had been insulted, even killed by some of the employees sent over by Baranov. There were too many misfits and criminals from the dregs of Siberia, the recruiting grounds for company agents. Medvednikov foolishly refused to apologize or make payments to the Koloshi, actions Ivan Kuskov practiced. Even Alexander Baranov, during his rare visits to Mikhailovsky, would pay the clans for any insults and crimes, including the Koloshi slave women who fled into the fort. Emelian pleaded with Medvednikov to pay the local Koloshi after Karaulov's hooligans fled with their women and shot their way through the straits, but not Medvednikov, for he was in charge and would not listen. Only a few dozen able-bodied men remained at the fort.

To make matters worse, Ivan Urbanov's hunting party of nearly two hundred men was overdue by three days and the situation was dangerous. Rumors abounded of a night ambush on Urbanov's party by hundreds of

Koloshi fighters on the other side of Sitka Island. Emelian was convinced that, if true, it involved the Koloshi sorcerer Wolf-Weasel. Vagabonds and pirates from Elias Hall's crew, he suspected, could also be involved.

What could he do? Emelian was a lowly employee of the Russian-American Company, not an officer, and only half Russian as his mother was an aboriginal Siberian. His wife Marpha was a full-blooded Aleut from the central part of the Aleutian archipelago. Yet, even with a laborer's status, he spoke several languages fluently and others somewhat proficiently, including his native Russian, Kamchadal, the language of his mother, the Aleutian tongue of his wife, and the Alutiiq dialect spoken on Kodiak Island. He even picked up some of the Kolosh tongue and a little English from the sea captains and sailors doing business with the company. Kuskov had recognized Emelian's language talents and ability to survive in the wilderness, and put in a word for him at Kodiak, but so far there was no news from Baranov's desk. Still, Emelian felt that somehow he was the future of the company. He figured it had to be only a matter of time before he was promoted. This stretch of the coast was starkly different from the pacified Aleutians and Kodiak, and the company needed men like him. The Koloshi were formidable people who loved their land and kin. Now they were filled with anger and well-armed with cannons and muskets from the Boston and King George men, not to mention their well-made elk hide armor.

"Emelian, what troubles you?"

Marpha knew her husband too well not to know his state of mind.

"Oh, I'm debating when we should bring a sibling into the world for our Alexei."

She grinned as she moved her fingers through Emelian's thick brown hair.

"There is something you're still not telling me, but I'll not insist upon it now. Let us be still."

The two continued their embrace as they drifted off to sleep nestled amidst thick, tall grass at the edge of the forest. Hours passed before a raven flew above the couple in bright sunshine. The bird's unblinking gaze captured the Russian settlement in its last proud moments beside Sitka Sound's glorious islands and magnificent snow-capped peaks in the far distance.

MARPHA AND EMELIAN AWOKE TO AN EAR-SHATTERING MAELSTROM of screaming and musket fire. Instinctively grabbing their knives and guns and hiding behind a cluster of spruce saplings and fireweed for cover, the young couple watched in shock as giant flames shot up from Mikhailovsky's blacksmith shop, barn, sheds, bathhouse, and barracks. For a brief instant, Emelian spotted two white men in sailor clothing and a few Koloshi women sprint away from the buildings into the green blackness of the forest. Several dozen company men, women, and children rushed out of the buildings to escape the growing flames as hundreds of Koloshi fighters emerged from the forest, adorned in wooden and leather armor and terrifying battle collars and helmets. The clan fighters sprinted from the woods and shrieked hideous and terrifying battle cries of their totemic animals. Stunned, Emelian saw hundreds more Koloshi attackers arrive in dozens of large canoes on the beach. They unleashed a thundering fire from their muskets and small cannons and set fire to the company shipyard before charging into the settlement.

Marpha, horrified and frightened, struggled to comprehend what she was witnessing. Her voice broke several times in panic.

"Emelian! Who are all those monsters and witches?! Has hell opened up to swallow Mikhailovsky?! Oh Jesus, please help us!"

"They are Koloshi fighters! I've seen them before in their war attire! Those collars and helmets hide their faces and make them look like wild animals and demons! Oh dear God, please help our men down there!"

Emelian watched helplessly as clan fighters swarmed in like an army of ferocious supernatural beings. A cannon shot fired inside the barracks, killing a few Koloshi fighters, but the flames soon forced the last defenders outside. Horror encompassed Emelian as fifty company men rushed to defend their wives and children being seized as captives. With only knives and hatchets, the Kodiak Islanders and Russians bravely threw themselves into the Koloshi fighters, only to be cut down in ferocious hand-to-hand combat from the attackers' double-bladed copper knives and blunt wooden clubs with pummels carved in the form of animal heads. One Kolosh fighter, wearing a blue helmet with a carved sea lion head, killed Emelian's Russian friend Zakhar Lebedev by driving a fifteen-inch jade spike through his skull. One by one, the desperate defenders fell before the overwhelming onslaught by land and sea, their bodies decapitated and their heads lifted on spears. Emelian spotted the manager, Vasili Medvednikov, as he was fatally stabbed through the neck by another Kolosh attacker with a copper-tipped spear. Musket balls proved useless against the attackers' thick multi-layered hide armor, reinforced with attached wooden slats. Marpha shrieked as several Koloshi fighters grabbed women and children as prisoners, including her son Alexei, and moved towards the woods.

With unrestrained fury Marpha tried to sprint towards the scene. Emelian grabbed her with all his might and covered her mouth as he forced her back into cover to avoid detection.

"We must remain here, Marpha. The Koloshi will kill us if we try to rescue Alexei now!"

Marpha desperately struggled to break free of her husband's grip as Emelian pleaded with her.

"Please, my love! Stop fighting me, we must wait! The Koloshi will hold Alexei and the other children for ransom!"

"Or as slaves, to perhaps be killed later!"

Marpha cried piteously as she sank to the ground, submitting to her husband's grasp.

His wife's tears pouring forth, Emelian continued in the most comforting voice he could muster while combating his own grief.

"Alexei being a hostage or slave buys time for all of us. You know that both of us, and likely our boy as well, would be killed if we rushed in there."

He paused for a moment, his arms still locked around his wife.

"We *will* get our Alexei back, Marpha, I swear this to you before God."

Observing the carnage, Emelian watched in horror as the fort's walls collapsed, burnt to the ground, revealing dozens of bodies strewn about the area. At the edge of the forest several Koloshi divided up captured women and children, while others grabbed equipment, weapons and pelts from the destroyed settlement.

Emelian spotted Alexei screaming in terror as he was taken by two men and handed over to a Kolosh woman near the woods. Almost overwhelmed by the powerful instinct to race in and save him, even if suicidal, Emelian fought back the urge as tears streamed down his face.

A burst of gunfire broke on the far side of the beach, dozens of yards away from the nearest Koloshi canoes. A company man took an Aleutian baidarka and furiously paddled away towards the north while being shot at by two Koloshi women guarding the perimeter of the canoes. Emelian instantly recognized the woolen cap and shirt of the man, thinking to himself, *That's Abram Plotnikov! He's trying to escape! Please God, help that man!*

As Plotnikov vanished around a small point with a Kolosh canoe in pursuit, Emelian's attention again riveted to the edge of the woods. What he saw shocked him. Several white men were freely mingling and speaking with the Indians, pointing to and discussing the prisoners, while a few others assisted in removing the six thousand pelts from Mikhailovsky's warehouse, which had been intentionally left alone by the Koloshi. Emelian recognized three American sailors, among them men who had been hired on by the company not long ago after jumping ship from *Jenny*.

"Spies! Those bastards betrayed us!" Emelian whispered out loud, his grief overcome for a moment by a burning desire for revenge against the American sailors. Emelian vowed he would kill every last one of them. As he raised his head for a better view, his jaw dropped in utter disbelief. There stood his former friend Nikolai Karaulov, the fugitive company man, pointing and nodding to a woman and two girls, completely at ease among the Koloshi and white men. Emelian's mind raced to make sense of what he was witnessing as he held his wife.

"Come on, we must move into the woods now and shadow the Koloshi to find out where they are taking Alexei and the others."

The couple crawled away through the thick grass into the woods. Marpha felt a fire burning within her, ready to do battle with her sorrow. She slung her musket over her shoulder and followed her husband through the thick evergreens. As her tears slowed, she wiped her face with one hand as the other gripped the knife strapped on her side.

FORTY-THREE

EMELIAN AND MARPHA TARADANOV HID BESIDE an ancient Sitka Spruce log just a mile into the woods from the destroyed Mikhailovsky colony. Clutching their muskets, and watching and listening intently for any sign of their son, Alexei, Emelian and Marpha silently prayed with their small Orthodox crucifix necklaces. Koloshi voices, with an occasional English voice, could be heard in the distance despite noisy raven calls and the slow drip of moisture all around them from the ancient trees. Sweat poured down Emelian's forehead and neck, his heart beating wildly. The next several minutes would likely decide the fate of his family and whether he would ever see his son again. If caught, he and Marpha would be made slaves and likely killed at one of the Koloshi's ceremonial callings.

Marpha's eyes locked on a clump of ferns two dozen yards away as she grabbed Emelian's left forearm. She pointed to vegetation being disturbed. Breathing ever more rapidly, Marpha pulled out a knife, ready to attack the unknown animal or person. Emelian grasped his knife, crouching behind the surrounding ferns and fallen trees. Adrenaline surged through him as he raised his knife for a possible attack. A frightened Kodiak woman suddenly appeared. Exhaling deeply, Emelian instantly recognized the woman from his time inside Mikhailovsky's barracks. With tears of relief, the woman motioned for her six-year-old son to join her. Emelian remembered the boy's father was one of the men who left with Urbanov's party and had not returned.

As the three cautiously moved to join Marpha, Emelian noted from her hand signals that a strange man was getting dangerously close to their hiding place. Emelian peeked above the log where an odd sight confronted him. A young Kolosh man dressed in a mix of sailor's clothes and Tlingit upper body armor walked alone while holding a new American musket in his hands. The quiet of the forest was broken by a loud call in English from a white man a few dozen yards in the rear.

"Tom, don't stray too far, I need your help back at the camp soon to help with negotiations over all these pelts. Mr. Hall is tending to wounded men, and Thaddeus is too busy translating for him and the other sailors."

"Yes, Mr. Triplett, sir, I'll be there in a few minutes, I just want to make sure there are no more of Baranov's rats lurking about."

Marpha, stunned, whispered to Emelian and the Kodiak woman.

"That Kolosh speaks the Boston men's tongue!"

Emelian concentrated hard on the English words, trying to remember the bits he learned from visiting ships over the years. The word "negotiations" he remembered, something like "working towards an agreement." A word Baranov and Kuskov used quite a bit in their dealings with the English-speaking sea captains. Emelian thought to himself, *Hostages! Yes, negotiations for pelts and hostages! That must be it!*

"Emelian."

Marpha whispered, breaking his concentration. He noticed her gripping her knife even tighter as she coiled, ready to spring. Gesturing, Emelian indicated he would take care of the approaching Kolosh man if he got too close. As sounds of small branches and twigs breaking under the man's feet grew more pronounced, another shout in English echoed through the woods from the same white man in the distance, who was now apparently walking back in the direction of a Kolosh encampment in the woods near Mikhailovsky's ruins.

"Bradley, bring some of your *Jenny* men over to this area, I need Tom back at the main camp. The clan leaders want any Russians hiding out there accounted for and taken prisoner. Do not harm them."

The words too distant and faint to discern, Emelian's sole focus rested on the young man a few yards away. The Kolosh had thick elk hide armor on his chest and back, painted with frightfully lined animal heads, but no war collar and helmet. Most of the area around his neck seemed exposed. Behind the ancient spruce log, Marpha and the Kodiak woman rested their hands on the frightened boy's shoulders while holding their index fingers to their lips to signal quiet. Marpha looked on with concern, though, as the small boy was terrified, his lower lip quivering as tears welled in his eyes. The man came closer, to within a few feet of their hiding place. Some distant voices chattering in English could be heard approaching. Sweat poured off Emelian, his heart pounding as the Kolosh man now reached the log's opposite side and prepared to climb over its centuries-old trunk. Gripping his knife tightly, Emelian looked into the eyes of Marpha for one last moment, inhaling a deep breath from the moist forest air.

He sprung up from his hiding place and grabbed the Kolosh man's hide armor. Emelian pulled the man over the enormous trunk and stabbed him in his upper left shoulder, inches away from the neck. As the man crashed into their hiding place, Marpha held her knife, ready to finish him with a fatal stab in the neck. The Kodiak woman reached to try and put her hand over the man's mouth to prevent him from screaming.

The six-year-old boy cried out in horror, catching his mother off guard for an instant. Instead of placing her hand over the man's mouth, she instinctively pivoted back to her son. The Kolosh man's agonizing shriek obliterated the quiet of the woods. Within moments, shouts in English filled the woods and gunfire erupted. As musket balls raced overhead, Emelian held the Kolosh man down and screamed at the two women to take the boy and flee south through the forest.

"Get out of here, now! Move!"

Emelian spoke too late. Surrendering to her emotions, Marpha pulled the musket from her shoulder and returned fire in the direction of the shouting English voices. Emelian instinctively pulled away from the wounded Kolosh man and joined his wife in firing into the woods.

"Marpha, get out of here!"

Tears streaming down her face, she shouted angrily while firing one more round.

"You dogs! I want my son back!"

Grabbing her musket, Emelian swung her around in the direction of the fleeing Kodiak woman and boy.

"We'll get Alexei back, but now is not the time. Now run, I'll catch up to you!"

Weeping, Marpha obeyed her husband and ran to join the other two. Emelian turned back to the wounded man whose blood now soaked part of his body armor. The Kolosh had pulled a knife to defend himself despite remaining on the ground. He shouted again in English as he stared at Emelian with an expression that fluctuated wildly between anger and fear.

"Mr. Bradley, help me! I'm over here, behind a large fallen spruce trunk!"

Emelian realized his position was compromised. There was no need now to finish off this Kolosh who couldn't be more than seventeen or eighteen. Better to fall back into the woods and lay down fire to buy time for Marpha and the others to escape. As he turned and ran, Emelian heard a musket ball race just a few feet from his head. Watching it sink into the bark of a nearby fir, Emelian pivoted back around for a moment and saw a sailor several dozens of yards away reloading and preparing to take aim. Breathing furiously, Emelian turned again to run over the ferns and wooden debris in the direction of Marpha and the others, only to hear another shot race by, this time mere inches away from his upper body. Ducking behind a young cedar, Emelian knew it was too close for guns. He pulled his knife as he heard the sailor fast approaching.

"Bradley, wait! Where are you going! Tom needs our help here!" another sailor in the distance shouted.

Despite Emelian's concealment behind the cedar, *Jenny* sailor Peter Bradley converged on his position and vaulted upon him. Struggling wildly with Bradley's knife-wielding arm for several seconds, Emelian thrust his elbow into the attacker's face, stunning him and causing the sailor to lose balance and some of his grip on his knife. As Bradley desperately tried to regain his footing and lunge back into an offensive position, Emelian swung his knife around and slashed Bradley under the chin, severing an artery. With blood pouring out of his neck, Bradley fell back upon the cedar, gasping for breath and staring at Emelian with blank eyes before succumbing to death.

Emelian took the musket, powder, balls, knife, and a flint stone from the dead sailor, whose unseeing eyes remained open. Securing the items in his small waist pack and backpack, Emelian stared momentarily at the deceased sailor before turning to run. Revenge turned to empathy.

Why did you have to chase after me? You could be alive to enjoy a wife and child as I do! God had another purpose for you.

A scream in English sounded in the woods.

"Mr. Triplett, get Mr. Hall up here right away! Tom's been stabbed, we need your help! Come quickly! Bradley, where the hell are you?! Bradley! Goddamn it, Peter, get your ass back here now!"

As the shouting in English intensified, Emelian sprinted over fallen limbs and small boulders. Reaching Marpha and the others after several minutes, he embraced her for a brief moment before hoisting the boy onto his shoulders.

"Come now, I know of a place where we can hide and rest, where there are plenty of berries and fish to eat. Let us hurry now and be brave," he cooed to the child.

FORTY-FOUR

S MALL, TEMPORARY SHELTERS AND CAMPFIRES dotted the meadows and tree clusters above the smoldering ruins of Fort St. Michael, some with wounded clan fighters being treated by their comrades and a small number of shamans. The *Eclipse* sailors rested at a site under two giant fir trees, their shady branches reaching over the edge of a long narrow meadow dotted with bright red fireweed and wild roses. Joshua Hall labored over the stab wound on Tom's shoulder. He realized Tom would have bled out had it not been for the heroic actions of Micah Triplett and two *Jenny* sailors. The men had kept pressure on the wound while carrying Tom to camp.

Triplett spoke as he watched Joshua's skilled hands work on Tom.

"We found Peter Bradley's body in the woods not far from where Tom was stabbed. Most likely it was the same attacker, who obviously has some good fighting skills."

"Mr. Hall, there are still Russians lurking about, and they know American sailors assisted the Tlingit attack," a *Jenny* sailor, Owen Thompson, added.

Hall looked up and frowned.

"That's the least of my concerns right now."

Thaddeus arrived from a large gathering of clan leaders arguing over pelt volumes to get a report on his cousin. Seeing Tom writhe in pain as Hall cleaned the wound, Thaddeus fought back grief and labored to maintain his composure. Assisting Hall with a Devil's Club poultice, Thaddeus spoke to Tom in Tlingit.

"Cousin, there is a shaman nearby, the famous Wolf-Weasel of Yakutat kwaan. He is very tired right now, but he nonetheless offers assistance if you wish. What should I tell him?"

"No, let Mr. Hall treat me first. I'll beat this soon, and when I do, I'm going back to find every last one of those damned Russian dogs."

"Quiet," Hall interrupted, "I want quiet, both of you. Your only concern Tom is to rest and remain here in a stationary position beside the fire. Drink plenty of water. Eat some food when you have the strength. All of this is an order from me, do you understand?"

Tom sighed, closing his eyes.

"Aye, sir."

"Very well then. Mr. Thompson, stay beside Tom in case he needs water or something else. My order of no talking covers you as well."

"Aye, Mr. Hall," Thompson replied, as Hall, Thaddeus, and Triplett walked a short distance away to sit and discuss the rendezvous with *Eclipse*.

"Well, Thaddeus," Hall inquired, "what can you tell us about the clan leaders arguing about the pelts and furs? I'm assuming the two large stacks beside them are now property of *Eclipse*?"

"You're correct, sir, but I've overheard some alarming rumors regarding Mr. Popov and Mr. Karaulov."

Hall grew impatient, wanting and needing answers.

"We already explained at length the status of those two. They fled the Russian-American Company and are now with us. What's the problem now?"

Triplett rubbed his chin, his posture tense.

"Thaddeus told me that some men from the Frog totem clan houses suspect Sergei Popov is the one who murdered a prestigious man who owned many slaves. Apparently, the man—"

"Kaklen," Thaddeus indicated.

Triplett continued, "Thank you, Thaddeus. Yes, apparently Kaklen tried to recapture the slave woman Sergei took with him. Alina, if you remember, on board *Eclipse*. Well, rumors hold that Sergei shot and killed Kaklen during the pursuit. And Karaulov was there when it happened."

Thaddeus anxiously glanced at Karaulov and Popov, several dozen yards away, eating and speaking around a small campfire with Karaulov's rescued sister-in-law and two nieces.

"Sirs, please remember that if members of the Frog totem clan houses recognize Sergei and Nikolai, they will demand at minimum apologies and ample material compensation, or perhaps the two men themselves."

Triplett gazed over the sprawling camp towards the sea before turning to Hall and Thaddeus.

"Let us remain silent on this matter for now. We must focus on the rendezvous so we can all get the hell out of here."

"Aye, sir." Hall and Thaddeus replied simultaneously.

Hall watched as more Aleutian, Kodiak, and Creole women and children were brought in from the woods by Tlingit fighters. Thaddeus looked with pride upon the fighters' indomitable presence.

"Our warriors are like the ancient Greek soldiers described in Homer's *Iliad*. Wouldn't you say so, sirs?"

Triplett sat with his legs bent and his knees near his chin, nervously rubbing the back of his neck.

"They remind me of Japanese samurai from a few sketches in the East India Society Museum in Salem, from Captain Samuel Hill of Boston."

Hall observed the scene around him. The intimidating war helmets painted and carved in the images of various creatures and supernatural beings were awe inspiring. Over the next several minutes Joshua sketched some of the fighters in his log, adding a caption below his drawings.

These people, their spirit, their land, will never be conquered.

GUNFIRE ERUPTED ACROSS SITKA SOUND IN CELEBRATION as *Eclipse*, *Panther*, and *Icarus* emerged from behind a mountainous point to the north. Small cannon shots from both ships as well as on shore added to the feverish excitement. As the ships moved closer and prepared to anchor, most of the over one thousand Tlingits converged on the beach holding up muskets and other weapons in triumph. Captains Jonathan Fletcher and Elias Hall lifted their hats and waved in recognition as the crews scurried about decks and rigging to prepare for the rendezvous. Drums beat as canoes with several clan dignitaries paddled out to greet and climb aboard the American ships, while Micah Triplett and Thaddeus joined the large crowd on the beach. Triplett spotted Aolani on board and his heart quickened.

"So far so good, Thaddeus. It looks like we'll all get out of here soon."

Thaddeus, still visibly shaken, remained silent as he glanced at Joshua Hall beside Tom at the forest's edge. Thaddeus saw a few men of the Sitka Frog Totem Houses continue to talk among themselves in low voices, occasionally animated with hand and arm movements. The men stared at Karaulov's party every few moments, whom he noticed were aware of the attention. The conversation among the Sitka men grew more heated, with two of the men pointing to the ships while another two continued to vigorously challenge them. The three surviving *Jenny* sailors soon joined the discussion with the Sitka men.

Breathing heavily, his heart racing, Thaddeus debated with himself over whether to intervene when Triplett grabbed his shoulder in excitement.

"Look, Thaddeus, the clans are delivering the pelt shares as promised, it should be just a matter of minutes before the skiffs are launched to retrieve our shore party. I just hope Tom will be strong enough to be moved, he seems pretty weak right now."

"The skiffs can't get here soon enough, that's all I can say."

Thaddeus glanced at the Sitka men, then stared at the ground, emotionally drained from the pressures of the past several days.

Please Tom, I need your help now more than ever.

FORTY-FIVE

CAPTAINS JONATHAN FLETCHER AND ELIAS HALL GREETED the Tlingit dignitaries with sweet rice dishes and tobacco and whiskey. Large war canoes brought out the promised fur bales to the ships as Fletcher noticed Tom and Joshua at the edge of the woods away from the main gathering on the beach. Fletcher called over Lavelle Clark and Ben Harper, who were busy loading pelts from the canoes onto the ship.

"It appears Tom is incapacitated in some way, perhaps wounded in the fighting. I want you two to prepare the skiff for launch to get him and the others once the crew finishes loading our pelt share."

"Aye sir."

Clark lifted more fur bales, while Harper approached Fletcher.

"Captain, the crew can finish loading those last two canoes worth of fur bales. I'd be happy to go ashore now with the skiff if you'd like." Fletcher shot Harper an irritated glance.

"Mr. Harper, you heard my order, now finish the job with the fur bales. We'll get our shore party back on board soon enough."

Puzzled, Harper assisted David Woods, Lavelle Clark, and Kekoa while Fletcher watched Elias Hall's young crew rapidly load the last of their pelt share on board *Panther* and *Icarus*. Elias paced back and forth by the bales over the next several minutes, taking notes on quantity while his crew presented food and gifts to the six clan leaders on board. Envious of the speed and efficiency of the *Panther* and *Icarus* crews, Fletcher yelled in a slight mocking tone to his sailors.

"Get that last canoe load of pelts on board gentlemen. Elias's crew has already beaten you."

Fletcher shouted to Elias on *Panther*.

"You run a disciplined crew, Elias. So, will we see you back in Boston, or are you still going to pursue those wild schemes of yours in the South Seas? You don't want to be on Boss Perkins' bad side. He'll want his ship back."

Elias turned to look at Fletcher across the dozen yards of sea separating the vessels. Fletcher grew unsettled as Elias held a manic grin and stared, unblinking.

"You and Perkins can keep your shallow world of lies, Jonathan. My followers and I will be up in a sunlight of glory."

Euphoria seized Elias. He grabbed his musket and shouted to his crew of young men and women.

"Now!"

In an instant, Elias and his two dozen sailors pulled out concealed weapons and took the six clan leaders still aboard his ships hostage. He screamed to shore in Tlingit.

"Deliver to me one thousand more pelts, or I will kill these clan leaders and dump their bodies at sea!"

Stunned silence descended over the beach among the hundreds on shore. Shocked, and staring in disbelief, Fletcher screamed at Elias.

"What the fuck are you doing?! You crazy son of a bitch, this wasn't part of our plan!"

The nine Tlingit clan leaders on board *Eclipse* soon panicked and raced over to the ship's starboard side, attempting an escape in a canoe still moored to the ship with a few fur bales.

"Goddamnit! Don't just stand there, seize those men!" Fletcher yelled at his flustered crew.

Although five Tlingit men jumped overboard and swam to the beach, the four others were captured at gunpoint by Woods, Clark, and Harper.

On shore, several Tlingit men grabbed Micah Triplett and Thaddeus and held sidearms to their heads, while at the edge of the woods the three *Jenny* sailors and five Sitka Tlingit men of the Frog Totem sprinted with weapons drawn towards Karaulov, Popov, Joshua Hall, and Tom. Popov instinctively pulled a musket and shot *Jenny* sailor Owen Thompson before being tackled by Karaulov and Hall, who realized they were no match for the onrushing group, let alone the thousand Tlingit fighters on shore. The *Eclipse* shore party dropped their weapons. They were now prisoners in a high stakes negotiation.

Seizing Popov, one of the Sitka men shouted, "Hah! We have you now, Kaklen's murderer! We will redeem his honor soon enough!"

The two surviving *Jenny* sailors stood guard over Tom, while the Sitka men marched Karaulov and his female relatives, Popov, and Hall towards the edge of the beach to link up with the group of Tlingits holding Thaddeus and Triplett.

On board *Eclipse,* Karaulov's wife Tanya screamed in terror at what had befallen her family and the rest of the *Eclipse* shore party. Fletcher shouted to Alamea and Alina.

"Shut that woman up! Now!"

Glaring at Fletcher, the two women hurried to Tanya to comfort her. Alamea glanced at Kekoa as she and Alina embraced Tanya, who was crying hysterically. Aolani rushed below deck with Kanoa, while Fletcher raged at Elias.

"You insane fool! Look at what you've done! You've endangered my crew!"

Elias laughed.

"Spare me the hollow concerns over your crew, Jonathan. Your first priority is stuffing pelts aboard your ship, why don't you just admit it now? You knew the risks involved in putting your crew ashore, and now they're paying the price for your recklessness."

"I swear before everyone here I will skin your balls and have you strung up and burned at the stake by these savages!"

Elias laughed again with a crazed grin, his mania all consuming.

"Elias, listen to me!" Joshua pleaded from shore. "It's not too late to stop this madness! Let me reason with you!"

"Too late, brother! My world cannot wait any longer!"

Elias turned to address Fletcher.

"Run along now Jonathan. Give my regards to the Perkins brothers!"

Fletcher, red-faced with fury, ran to the railing and pulled a sidearm to shoot Elias, but was confronted by *Panther* sailors who aimed their muskets at him from across the narrow strip of water separating the vessels. Holstering his weapon, Fletcher backed away, his anger seething.

Elias turned his attention to shore and screamed in Tlingit.

"My one thousand pelts! Now! Or I kill these men of yours at sea by drowning, where their souls will be taken by the Land Otter People!"

As the Tlingits began delivering the ransom to *Panther* and *Icarus,* Elias released two Tlingit clan leaders, shouting to shore the others would be let go once all pelts were aboard.

Fletcher shouted to *Panther* in one last desperate plea.

"Alright Elias, damn it, I take back my threats. Let's be rational about all this. Just help me get my crew back."

Elias ignored Fletcher and instead barked orders to his crew to prepare sails as the last two hundred ransom pelts were delivered in long war canoes. Positioning the remaining Tlingit captives at the side of *Panther* and *Icarus* as the last ransom bales were handed up to his sailors, Elias released one more hostage, but ordered his crew to pull the remaining four hostages back on deck as he shouted an order to set sail. Their hands and feet tied together, there was nothing the Tlingit men could do to escape.

Seeing Elias betray them a second time, several Tlingits on shore opened fire on *Panther* and *Icarus*, but within moments the ships caught the steady breezes of Sitka Sound and fell out of musket and cannon range. On the deck of *Eclipse,* Kekoa and Clark signaled to Alamea and Alina. Within moments, Clark tackled David Woods and disarmed him. Ben Harper and Kekoa raced over with two side arms to continue guarding the Tlingit hostages, while Alamea and Alina rushed Captain Fletcher, pulling out concealed sidearm muskets and aiming them directly at his head.

Alamea screamed wildly at Fletcher.

"Drop your gun, now! Or I swear I'll blow your head off!"

"Alamea, think about what you're doing here! Have you lost your mind? Jesus Christ! You're putting all of us in danger!"

"Drop your weapon! Now! Or I *will* shoot you dead!"

Fletcher stared at Alamea in utter shock. He set his musket on deck while continuing to plead with his ex-lover.

"Alamea, darling, listen to me. I promise to—

"Shut your mouth now! Not one more word! Now, kick the musket away and get on your knees with your hands on your head! Alina, tie him!"

Fletcher reluctantly complied. After completing her task, Alina resumed pointing her musket at Fletcher's head. Alamea moved over to the side of the ship and shouted at Thaddeus to translate.

"Thaddeus! Tell the clan leaders on shore I am prepared to make an immediate agreement. In exchange for the release of the entire *Eclipse* shore party, I will release all of their men and give them Jonathan Fletcher as well. Five hundred pelts from our vessel will also be delivered to them as goodwill from us, in light of the despicable crimes committed by Captain Elias."

Fletcher could not believe his ears. A flustered panic gripped him.

"What?! This is outrageous! Alamea, damn it, listen to me, we can—

Alamea screamed in unbridled rage.

"You! You are the reason we are in this situation! And now you will pay the price for your recklessness! Kekoa, if Jonathan says one more word knock him out!"

Fletcher spat on the deck toward Alamea in anger and disgust, remaining silent on his knees.

On shore, Thaddeus listened to the gathering of clan leaders as they discussed Alamea's proposal, but Hall took him by the forearm.

"Thaddeus, I have to remain with Tom here on shore, he's still in a condition where he can't be moved without great risk to his life. Tell the clan leaders. Tom and I will have to rendezvous with *Eclipse* at a later time, whether it's here on Sitka Sound or another place. Micah will be the new *Eclipse* captain for now."

"Sir, you don't have to do this, I can stay with Tom, just tell me what I should do. The rest of the crew needs you on board."

Joshua looked at *Eclipse*. Alamea was staring directly at him and fighting back tears as she waved and smiled. Hall grinned and waved back, then tipped his wool cap in admiration of her heroism before turning back to Thaddeus.

"Your bravery matches your sharp wits, my friend. I must decline your offer, however, as Tom needs my fullest attention and the crew needs your talents. Now, please tell the clan leaders, that's an order."

Thaddeus looked around, searching for an answer.

"Very well, sir. God bless you. God bless Tom. Just remember one thing."

"Certainly."

"Don't let him wander off into the woods again. There are dangers that sometimes cannot be seen or anticipated. And make sure he wears that cross Mr. Perkins gave him."

Puzzled slightly at the request, Hall replied after a prolonged pause.

"Of course, Thaddeus, I'll take good care of your cousin. He'll make it. Tom's a strong fellow in more ways than one."

"Thank you, sir."

Thaddeus walked over to where there were discussions underway among the clan leaders and began speaking to them. Hall noticed the pace and demeanor of the discussion become more relaxed and focused as the minutes passed.

One of the primary leaders of the attack on the Russians, Katlian of the Frog Totem and Sitka kwaan, told Thaddeus of the final decision. His long black hair tied in a bundle, his muscular body bulging beneath his battle armor, Katlian exuded authority and strength. He stood beside Thaddeus as the teenager spoke to Alamea and the rest of the *Eclipse* crew on ship and shore.

"Alamea, Katlian and the clans' leadership accept your offer with one condition. The Russian Sergei Popov will remain with the Sitka Frog Totem leaders, as he is responsible for the death of an important man named Kaklen. He will not be harmed for now, but rather will face judgment at the great victory calling to be held in the Tlingit Chilkat kwaan to the north five days from now. As a guarantee of this pledge, and the safety of Mr. Hall, who will be staying here to watch over Tom, Tanak-ku of the Frog Totem will remain on board *Eclipse*. The Frog Totem men wish to hear the counsel of 'Mother,' who holds the totem of *Yachte*, the Great Bear Constellation, regarding Popov and the many events that have unfolded over these last few days. She is *Aankaawu*, master of the ranking house of the highest clan. Mother's clan house is the North Star, the same as mine, Alamea. I think I can help save Mr. Popov if we rendezvous there."

"Joshua!"

Alamea cried out as Hall raised his hand and nodded to reassure her that he would be fine. Alamea called over Alina, who already knew from Thaddeus's mention of Sergei that her lover was to remain on shore. Upset, she called out hysterically to Sergei.

"I will join you, I will never leave your side!"

"No! Stay on the ship, Alina! We'll be together again, I swear it! Officer Joshua will be staying here on shore to help the Kolosh boy Tom, so I won't be alone! It's alright, don't worry my love."

Overwhelmed with adrenaline and emotion, Alina was escorted away by Lavelle Clark, her cries filling the deck of *Eclipse* as she went below. Alamea, barely able to contain her own emotions over Joshua, pronounced her agreement with Katlian.

A simultaneous exchange of pelts and hostages, including Jonathan Fletcher, were rowed between ship and shore. Hall made his way to the edge of the beach.

"Alamea, my fierce one! My heart is with you and Kanoa!"

Captain Micah Triplett saluted and called out to Hall on shore.

"See you at the Chilkat kwaan in five days, First Officer Hall!"

"Aye, Captain Triplett! Fair winds to you!"

A moment later Hall watched Jonathan Fletcher arrive on the beach in a skiff, dejected, his eyes like a convict arriving at prison for the first time. Joshua turned to look out to sea. *Panther* and *Icarus* had passed the last islets of Sitka Sound, and were now specks on the horizon.

I've not seen the last of Elias. I know this in my bones.

FORTY-SIX

Emelian Taradanov stared into the small campfire as he ate the last bits of fish caught in a nearby stream. The mother and young son from Kodiak Island lay asleep, while Marpha rested on her back and stared up at the large rock overhang. The four had trekked south through the forest for several hours along Sitka Island's western shore. It was almost a miracle, Emelian reflected, that no Koloshi war parties had discovered them during their exhausting hike through the thick woods. The salvation of his small group now rested in reaching a Russian, British, or American ship, but so far, he hadn't seen any. A Russian ship was highly unlikely as Alexander Baranov only had a few at his disposal, with most at Kodiak and the Aleutians. Emelian had the skills to fish and hunt for his small party, so they could survive indefinitely in the forest, but for how long they would have to wait for rescue, he couldn't say.

"Is there a chance that perhaps one of the fur hunting parties might appear along the shore? Urbanov's party had lots of men. Surely, they must be looking around these waters for survivors? They were only on the other side of the island." Marpha asked.

Emelian sighed heavily and shook his head.

"Unfortunately, they were probably attacked as well. The Koloshi are very skilled in planning and coordinating ambushes. Urbanov's men, if any survived, are probably heading north to Yakutat to find Ivan Kuskov's party."

"What about Kuskov and his men, wouldn't they come south to investigate and search for survivors? They would use one of the company ships at Yakutat and rescue us."

"That's a longshot, at best. Kuskov knows the strength of the Koloshi, and he's probably focused on reinforcing our Yakutat settlement and getting to Kodiak to inform Baranov of our catastrophe. Even Baranov most likely won't do anything, at least for now, as he has very few men and ships to spare. No, our best chance is getting to an English or American vessel."

Deeper gloom settled over Marpha.

"How will those foreigners treat us if we come across one of their ships? I've never met them up close. Most of the captains and crews are civilized, right?"

"Yes, they are not like the Koloshi in how they live. Most are men of good Christian morals, although a rotten few have been corrupted by an insatiable lust for profit. There are evil men to be sure, but not more than any other group of people I would imagine."

"Remember those American deserters who hired on with the company at Mikhailovsky? You saw them with the Koloshi!"

"Yes, that's true. We'll just have to take what God gives us, if we are blessed enough to even sight a ship. Make sure you keep watch when it's my turn to sleep."

Marpha nodded to her husband. Turning onto her side, she looked over at the sleeping mother and young son, Timofei. Marpha choked back sobs.

Oh God, please watch over our Alexei. There must be Koloshi mothers who will care for him.

EMELIAN SLEPT DEEPLY, LOST IN A DREAM. He soared as a raven over a vast expanse of deep green woods. In the distance stood giant granite spires covered with slender ribbons of silver waterfalls tumbling into an ice-strewn bay. A pod of orcas appeared below, spouting every few moments on the sea surface as if guiding him towards a place in the distance. Sea lions barked cries from scattered islets as a cold wind lifted him higher within view of stars of late dusk. His eyes locked on the Great Dipper and North Star, their magnetism drawing him further into the bosom of the mountains. Below, several ships rested at anchor beside a great Koloshi village, their sterns bearing English names. He dove towards them, accelerating ever faster, desperately trying to understand the letters. A great eagle raced towards him. Emelian fell towards one of the ships, sensing danger and fear. The eagle screamed as it raced past him, and Emelian spun wildly out of control as he began hearing his son Alexei's voice cry out not in terror, but in joy.

Papa, papa! Here I am! Near the animals of sea and land! I am under the Great Dipper, in the House of the North Star! Do you not see? Mother is beside me!

"MAMA! A WHITE BIRD IS UPON THE OCEAN! LOOK MAMA!"

Emelian awoke suddenly to Timofei's voice. The Kodiak boy shouted and pointed towards the sea at the edge of the woods a dozen yards away. Rubbing his eyes and desperately trying to shake his mind from the dream, Emelian saw both women asleep.

"Damn it, Marpha, you were on watch."

Emelian trotted over to the boy. Placing his hand on Timofei's shoulder, Emelian saw white sails a few miles to the southwest, a schooner a mere mile offshore heading towards his party's hiding place. His heart raced. Emelian dashed over to the campfire and added prepared loads of brush and sticks.

"Marpha! Vera! Wake up, gather your things! A ship approaches from the south! Hurry, we must climb down to the beach!"

The boy threw his arms around Emelian's shoulders as the group made their way over loose boulders and gravel to the wet, rocky, seaweed-strewn beach thirty feet below. Their campfire, which soon grew to several feet tall, billowed large clouds of smoke from above their heads. Shouting and waving clothing, Emelian and his party watched the small ship for what seemed like a few interminable minutes before her sails began fluttering in the steady westerly breezes. The ship slowly turned towards the island.

Emelian shouted wildly.

"She's tacking! She's coming towards us! Look!"

Emelian strained his eyes to see how many sailors were aboard, and if the vessel's name was visible on the port and starboard bow. Within a few minutes he could see the ship was even smaller than he had first thought, and its crew only numbered four sailors.

One man on deck shouted in English.

"Hello there! We'll prepare our skiff in a moment to come fetch you!"

Marpha looked on in excitement.

"It's a King George ship! I recognize the accent, even though I can't speak their tongue."

The ship came within a few dozen yards of shore. Emelian concentrated on the letters as they slowly became visible, having learned to read some limited English as a part-time clerk in Baranov's Kodiak office. Straining his mind to switch from Cyrillic letters to a more unfamiliar alphabet,

Emelian spoke to himself out loud as the ship's name became more visible. "Jo . . . Jaa . . . Jookale . . . Joocal . . . Jac . . . koll . . . Jackal. The ship's name is *Jackal*, Marpha, Vera! No need to worry, these England men are quite civilized, they will help us."

FORTY-SEVEN

Captain Ian Coe welcomed the small refugee group on board and immediately offered food, drink, and new clothes. With immense gratitude and thanks, Vera, Marpha, and Emelian went below deck and changed into clean sailor's clothes, while Peter Lansing cut up clean sail fabric and stitched together an improvised outfit for Timofei. The survivors soon emerged back on deck to warm cups of tea with drops of honey. To Emelian's surprise, Captain Coe spoke some Russian, although it was mostly broken. It was clear, though, that the Englishman wanted to know why they were out alone and in need of rescue, and if anything had happened at Mikhailovsky. Mustering his very best English, Emelian replied with a heavy reliance on hand gestures and signs.

"Mikhailovsky no more, many deaths, fire, savage Americans attack us. Indians, we name them Koloshi. Koloshi get muskets and help from civilized Americans."

Captain Coe unrolled a map before his guests. Pointing to charts of Sitka Island and other islands to the north, Coe switched to English and spoke slowly and methodically, pausing occasionally to use drawings and his limited Russian if something wasn't clear to Emelian. Lansing poured more tea and honey and listened intently as Coe asked another question.

"Can you recall any names of the American ships or sailors?"

"Yes. A few sailors from vessel *Jenny*. I kill one, Peter. He attack."

Lansing's jaw dropped.

"John Crocker, he didn't mention any deserters to us! He was on his way back to O'ahu and perhaps other islands for more sailors and supplies.

Peter Bradley, I've heard that name. A violent troublemaker according to many seamen."

Coe rubbed his chin, intrigued with Taradanov.

"Interesting. It appears Captain Crocker gave up on finding them and chose to withhold this information from us. Mr. Taradanov, are there any more names you recall?"

Emelian paused for a few moments. His mind raced to remember other details of the attack. Marpha interjected in Russian.

"Emelian, remember the Kolosh boy who spoke like the Boston men? The *Jenny* sailors called out his name I think, but I can't remember it."

"*Da!*" Emelian shouted in his native language before switching to English with excitement.

"Yes! I remember name of Kolosh Indian boy in big trees by Mikhailovsky. Tom. His words English."

Lansing scratched his forehead in disbelief.

"*Eclipse*, that miserable bastard Jonathan Fletcher! I'll be damned."

Emelian noticed that Coe kept calm, despite his first mate's response. The English captain's eyes never betrayed his thoughts as he sipped from his mug of tea. After a few moments, he continued in a calm, slow voice.

"Mr. Taradanov, how many of your countrymen did the Koloshi capture as prisoners?"

Pausing as he whispered his English numbers, Emelian replied, "Over twenty, all women and children. More hide in big trees, but with Koloshi Indians, I think now. I see one Russian man, Abram Plotnikov, run north in baidarka, chased by well-armed Koloshi women. Only man I see."

"And fur hunting parties in the straits? Kuskov? Urbanov? Kochesov?" Lansing asked Emelian.

"If not dead from Koloshi, they journey to Kodiak, talk with Baranov. Kuskov welcome *Jackal*, talk money, otter skins for you at Kodiak."

His chin in his right index finger and thumb, Coe nodded slowly.

"*Spaceba,* Mr. Taradanov. Drink as much honey and tea as you wish, *minya droog.*"

Coe turned to Lansing.

"My friend here, that is, Mr. Emelian Taradanov. Treat him, the women, and the child as my personal guests."

"Aye, sir."

"Wait, Mr. Lansing."

Coe pondered another order for a few moments before speaking.

"On second thought, have Mr. Chadwick and Mr. Morris set a new northerly course for Cross Sound and the Icy Strait, the villages of the Chilkat kwaan will be our next business arena. We might acquire for ourselves some more Russian refugees to take to Kodiak for a handsome reward from Mr. Baranov. And, perhaps, we may come across some additional otter pelts in the process, free of charge."

Lansing froze, shocked at his captain's order.

"Captain, with all respect, we know the clans are well armed and will fight dearly to protect their property and kin. We are few in number and more vulnerable in the narrow straits and bays. Why not stick to the coast as we make our way over to Kodiak? That would give us a good probability of encountering this Abram Plotnikov and Ivan Kuskov's hunting party, and Baranov would surely pay us handsomely in pelts for their safe transport given the attack on Mikhailovsky. Our information regarding American involvement would also fetch us additional rewards."

"Excellent points, Mr. Lansing, and I fully intend to capitalize on all of them. But Mr. Taradanov's information has presented some fleeting yet lucrative opportunities we can seize upon."

"Captain, I fear we may be grasping for our ruin."

Coe chuckled. He admired and appreciated his first officer's bold willingness to challenge him. In his view, Lansing's ability to wrestle with competing ideas and weigh their dangers and possibilities reflected a superior intellect. The Bristol man also willingly accepted danger and fought well when asked. Lansing's temperament, however, was often defensive and controlled. No, Coe told himself, he must pursue bold initiatives on this wild shore.

"Fear. He sometimes makes friends with Caution and Moderation, and later laughs at them when they cannot find Success and Freedom. And now, Fear wants to make you his associate, Mr. Lansing. Banish that imposter from your mind."

Deep in his heart, buried under his ambitions, fear stood firm. Coe knew if he failed his crew's lives would be cast aside, forever adrift upon the ocean.

FORTY-EIGHT

DEJECTED AND MISERABLE, JONATHAN FLETCHER RESTED beside the *Eclipse* crew's campfire as two well-armed Tlingit men stood near-by on guard. The fireweed and wild roses blew in gusty breezes as mew gulls circled effortlessly above the beach and meadow. Two blue herons patiently straddled the shoreline, catching a small fish every few minutes. Fletcher remained silent, occasionally staring through the flames towards Joshua Hall, Sergei Popov, and Tom. He looked down while moving his fingers through his hair in exasperation, his mind racing from anger to frustration to bitter reflections on recent events. Hall moved to break the tension as Tom slept beside him.

"Tom was stabbed by a Russian not too far into the woods. It occurred after the main attack was over. His wound would have killed most men, but Tom is fighting hard despite his weakened condition. We were fortunate our shore party was able to stop the bleeding not long after the fight."

Fletcher stared at Tom as he spoke, his eyes weary.

"Tom's a stout fellow, tough as anyone as I've ever met, he'll pull through."

A few moments of silence passed as Fletcher glanced at Hall.

"Your lunatic brother, I'm going to catch that devil and make fish bait out of him. Or maybe hand him over to the clans, where they can work their imaginative and ingenious tortures upon him. We'll pursue Elias to the ends of the earth if need be, you have my word on that."

Popov looked at Fletcher with anger in his eyes.

"Mr. Triplett is captain of *Eclipse* now. And if you harm Alina, or Joshua's woman, I kill you."

His face red with rage, Fletcher wanted to lash out at Popov, but Hall stared down the former captain.

"Mr. Triplett and I are in command of *Eclipse*, Jonathan, as your reckless actions have led to the deaths and sufferings of many people and a near total loss of the voyage's directive. However, I will see to it that you, along with Elias, will receive a fair trial in O'ahu or Canton among other American seamen, and—

Fletcher screamed in anger and lunged at Hall, who grabbed him by the arm and threw him on his side. Popov lunged at Fletcher and smashed his right fist into Fletcher's face, breaking his nose. Stunned, Fletcher fell backward with blood flowing freely down his chin and neck.

"We Siberians know how to fight. I kill you next time."

Fletcher tried to stop his bleeding with a small cloth.

"You filthy Russian! I'll slit your throat, and—

One of the Tlingit guards approached and knocked Fletcher unconscious with a blow to the head. The two surviving *Jenny* sailors, several dozen yards away at a separate campfire, were digging graves for their deceased crew members Thompson and Bradley when they paused to shout at Popov.

"Hey, Russian, you're a dead man!"

Popov stared at the American sailors with a crazed grin and raised eyebrows, relishing the moment.

"Why don't you come and get me right now?! I kill you both, maybe slit your throats! Bash your skulls in! Or do you prefer another way to die?!"

Trepidation fell over the adolescent *Jenny* sailors as Hall intervened.

"Alright, that's enough! Hawkins, Smith, mind your own business, you hear me?! This is your only warning."

Tom awoke to the loud commotion, but was still too weak to sit up and move around. Upon seeing him wake, two Tlingit dignitaries approached and began addressing Hall in Tlingit. Tom, sipping water as he listened, translated the minutes-long message to Hall and Popov.

"Tomorrow we'll be departing in canoes to the north end of Sitka Island, and from there, proceed through Cross Sound and Icy Strait to the Chilkat kwaan where we will rendezvous with *Eclipse* and perhaps another friendly Boston ship or two. The journey will take two or three days. As was agreed upon, negotiations on prisoners and pelts will be finalized there after the conclusion of a great victory calling. A woman of the Great Bear, or Big Dipper totem, resides at the main village. Her name is 'Great Bear Mother,' but she's more commonly known as just 'Mother.' Her family lineage resides in the House of the North Star, the same as Thaddeus. Many Tlingits respect her as a wise old leader, including clans that do not share her totem."

Tom paused to drink water, then continued.

"I've met her, Mr. Hall, she's a good matriarch who makes just decisions and brings great honor to her clan and totem. Her position is *Aankaawu Shaawat*, Master Woman."

"What about sea captains?" Joshua inquired. "Will she be fair to the Boston ships?"

Tom winced in pain as he spoke.

"Yes, she sees white people as her children. And she recognizes, like children everywhere, some behave badly while others act respectfully, such as you, Mr. Hall. In her view, Boston and King George men all belong to the Guski kwaan, the villages of the 'cloud-face' people. The Big Dipper of course is far above the clouds, higher up in the heavens, thus she is your 'Mother.'"

Intrigued with the young man's descriptions, Hall grinned and placed his hand on Tom's shoulder while holding a cup of water for him to drink.

"Try to eat a bit and drink more water, you've been sweating profusely under this fever. And rest, that's an order."

"Aye, sir."

"And, I do look forward to meeting 'Mother,' this honorable woman you describe. My first concern, though, is your health."

Hall wiped some more sweat from Tom's brow as he nodded and remained silent. For a few minutes Joshua looked upon the scattered encampment of hundreds of Tlingit men and women busily preparing canoes and meals.

"Like 'Mother,' you bring honor to us as well, sir." Tom said as he gazed at Hall with pride.

MIDNIGHT PASSED, AND THE EARLY MORNING'S dusky summer light assumed a grayish color between the overcast and campfire smoke hovering over the meadow. Tom rose in a feverish sweat, jolted out of chaotic dreams of strange creatures and frightful human figures, all of whom pleaded distress from behind shadows as if they were drowning. Looking around the encampment, he noticed everyone sleeping amid unusually dark black and gray hues. The forest appeared darker and in different shapes than what he remembered. He looked to one side and saw Hall and Popov asleep next to fading embers. Tom noticed his cross necklace, the one Mr. Perkins had given him back in Boston, lying on the ground. He reached to grasp the Christian symbol, but heard a voice from the woods cry out in English.

"Tom, I'm over here! Help me, please!"

Adrenaline raced over his spine and pulsated through his veins.

Nate? Mr. Folger? Tom thought to himself. Confused, his mouth agape, Tom yelled back.

"Mr. Folger! Could that be you? We thought you were dead!"

Tom looked back at Hall and Popov, both still asleep. The other men sleeping in the distance also did not stir. Breathing rapidly and sweating profusely, Tom's adrenaline carried him to his feet as he walked into the woods.

The voice cried out again.

"Tom, I need your help, over here!"

Tom picked up his pace, passing several ancient spruce trees.

"Nate! Where are you?! Stay where you are, I'm coming to help you!"

"I'm over here!"

"Just stay where you are!"

Tom moved faster through the woods as anticipation and adrenaline overwhelmed his body's cries of fatigue and pain. He grasped the bark of a particularly large fir as he maneuvered around a fallen log. A voice in Tlingit barely above a whisper spoke to Tom.

"Beware of Kushtaka. Heed my warning, Sea Lion brother."

Startled, Tom spun around in the dark forest and shouted in Tlingit.

"Who's there?! Show yourself!"

Only silence greeted Tom, who drew his knife, breathed harder, and sweated more profusely.

"Nate," Tom shouted again. "Please, where are you?!"

Semi-delirious with fever, Tom strained to remain upright as fear and exhaustion began to press downward on his adrenaline-fueled courage, his heavy breathing the only sound for several moments. Tom felt his neck for his cross necklace, but realized he left it back at camp. Holding his knife as his arm shook, a shadowy figure slowly emerged from the dark green woods. Tom watched Nathaniel Folger appear with a relaxed, serene look upon his face. His unblinking eyes locked on Tom.

"Tom, my good man, I'm so glad to see you once again. You've always been a helpful one. There are others requiring assistance, come with me now."

Tom instinctively knew something was wrong, but before him was Nathaniel Folger, seemingly back from the dead. Fatigued, Tom struggled to make sense of his experience.

"Nate, we all thought you were dead, drowned in that river. How did you make it to this island? Who are these other people?"

"There is a beautiful village ahead for weary, conflicted souls such as ours. Just stay with me, Tom, all will be answered soon enough."

"No! Stop! I will not travel to your village! You are not Nathaniel! He is with Jesus!"

Tom backed off, holding his knife as he willed his numbing legs to keep moving away from the imposter before him. Folger screamed in a high-pitched shrill that was not human. Within moments, several creatures in the shapes of men appeared from the shadows, their faces that of the River Otter, some with arms emerging out of chests covered in brown fur.

Tom shouted defiantly at the creatures in Tlingit.

"Move away now, you will not have my soul! I will resist and fight! You will not enslave me for your village of the dead!"

The Land Otter men stared at Tom through the dark green hues of the woods, their large, wild eyes possessing a crushing omnipotence of terrifying primitive energies. Tom called upon all of his will to resist a chaotic clash of powers emanating from the creatures. He backed away further and eventually turned to run despite the almost unbearable numbness gripping his legs.

Nathaniel Folger's voice echoed through the woods once again.

"Tom, please come back! I need help! Please, my soul has been enslaved! You must return!"

Tom wept freely as he refused to heed the call, stumbling over logs and rocks until he emerged from the woods at the encampment. Collapsing, Tom fell into ruthless collisions of color and sound. He heard feral animal cries and violent storms, and the rushing of rivers and crashing waves. He saw brilliantly colored auroras and solar eclipses, as well as ferocious clashes between death and birth, dark and light. Tom screamed wildly with all the resistance his will could muster, terrified yet determined.

TOM AWOKE TO MORNING. ABOVE HIM SUNLIGHT PEEKED through the trees as sounds of songbirds and soft conversations passed over him. Campfire smoke and the scent of coffee filled the air.

"Glad you could join us, Tom."

Joshua handed a cup of coffee to Tom along with his cross necklace.

"You look much better now, like you've passed through the worst of your affliction."

Tom fastened the cross around his neck and sipped his coffee.

"Indeed, sir, I have passed through a terrible tempest, but I'm back on shore now."

"Well done sailor."

FORTY-NINE

Two giant war canoe flotillas moved along the northern shore of Sitka kwaan. Tom rested as Joshua paddled.

"Just about another hour or so, sir, and we'll be upon Cross Sound and Icy Strait, the waters of the Tlingit Huna kwaan and its villages of the 'People from the Direction of the North Wind.'"

"Aptly named, as this northerly breeze is making us earn every yard. These canoes cut through the whitecaps quite well though," Hall replied between heavy breaths.

Tom looked around at the two flotillas. Each contained about one hundred canoes and stretched over several hundred yards, with just a few dozen yards separating the large groups from each other. The lead flotilla included canoes holding Tom and Joshua, Jonathan Fletcher, Sergei Popov, and the two *Jenny* sailors. The flotilla immediately behind them contained several canoes of fur bales and a few Russian-American Company prisoners from the destroyed Saint Michael colony, each having several Tlingit men on either side as a deterrent to escape. Prisoners, otter pelts and other loot seized after the attack filled every spare bit of space, to be traded or distributed at the Chilkat kwaan's great victory calling.

While nearly all of the canoe occupants paddled, a few well-armed Tlingit fighters watched for any possible dangers appearing from the shore or the sea. Each flotilla was prepared to assist the other one in the event of an attack. Despite the strength and firepower of the flotillas, Tom knew from his sailing experience that a large, well-armed vessel could wreak havoc on low-lying canoes, no matter how skilled and brave the occupants. Still, the odds of an attack were very low.

He rested against a soft bale of otter pelts and watched thousands of murres, terns, gulls, and puffins swim, hover, dive and dart along the sea surface. A few miles ahead stood several clusters of islets, shrouded in thick noisy seabird colonies of white and black, punctuated occasionally with the dog-like calls of sea lions. Tom closed his eyes, smiled, and listened to the wind and small waves breaking against the canoes.

TOM AWOKE TO SHOUTS IN TLINGIT FROM SEVERAL CANOES at the head of his flotilla. Joshua yelled into the wind.

"Tom, look over there, from behind that large islet we just passed, it's a small ship, a schooner."

The two observed the full sails bearing downwind on the flotilla with most of the pelts and the Russian prisoners. Within moments, Tom and Joshua recognized it was *Jackal*.

As Tlingit canoe leaders in Hall's flotilla began shouting orders to turn around to assist the rear flotilla, a small cannon boom echoed across the sea along with musket fire. Hall watched in utter astonishment as five sailors laid down withering fire on two canoes, killing or wounding several Tlingit men, with one canoe sinking from a direct hit by the ship's cannon. Other canoes in the vicinity returned fire, hitting two *Jackal* sailors. Mortally wounded, one sailor fell overboard and vanished under the sea, while the other dropped his musket and fell on the deck, screaming and writhing in pain from a stomach wound. Ignoring his wounded sailor, Captain Coe pressed his attack. A woman ran to take the helm as Coe and the other two sailors raced over to the ship's side netting to grab floating fur bales. With the wind at their backs, *Jackal* easily outran pursuing canoes as the ship rammed two others holding a few Russian-American Company prisoners. As the canoes broke apart and the occupants began struggling in the water, *Jackal* made a sharp turn back into the wind, her sails fluttering wildly in the breeze as the hull slowed its pace through the water to a crawl. Dozens of yards away Hall and Tom heard Fletcher scream with all his might.

"Ian, you devil! We'll get your miserable hide!"

Coe and his crew reached to assist company prisoners from the water. The English captain shouted, "Lansing! Once we pull up those young Kodiak lads and Aleut wench, execute an immediate port tack so we get downwind again and escape from the canoes!"

"Aye, sir! What about Chadwick there?! He's shot in his abdomen!"

"I'll get to him once we escape. Now grab those prisoners there in the water before those canoes close on us!"

Emelian Taradanov raced to grab two small Kodiak boys out of the water, while Lansing and Coe pulled an Aleut woman from the choppy sea. A struggling Tlingit man tried to grab onto Lansing, but was struck in the face by Coe and fell back into the water, breathless, as other Tlingit men swam over to the fast approaching canoes. More shots rang through the air, ripping holes in the schooner's sails and mast. As Lansing tried to help the Aleut woman below deck, he slipped and twisted his ankle. Shrieking in pain, he struggled to get back on his feet. Coe turned to Emelian, yelling orders.

"Tell your wife to pull the helm right, on a port tack!"

Emelian screamed the order in Russian to Marpha, who immediately tried to turn the helm to execute Coe's orders. The ship resisted, however, as the main sail still fluttered wildly and the vessel's starboard hull caught increasing winds blowing from the north, causing resistance against the rudder. Emelian and Captain Coe frantically pulled on the mainsail's low-lying boom to help reduce pressure on the helm and assist the ship in turning into the new tack. In what seemed like an eternity for Coe, wind, slowly, but steadily, began filling the mainsail and the ship gradually heeled to its right side into the desired tack. For a few moments, it appeared *Jackal* would escape.

A sickening groan soon filled the deck for several seconds. Like a tall tree cut in a forest, the main mast snapped and came crashing down onto the deck, killing the wounded sailor, Chadwick, and crippling the vessel, preventing its attempt to flee.

"Jesus Christ! Please, no!"

Coe screamed in horror, his scheme failed. As Tlingit canoes caught up to the ship and surrounded it, muskets drawn, Fletcher shouted in delight.

"Hah! You bastard, Ian, you're done for now! As well as you, Lansing, you fool! Both of you just signed your execution orders!"

Several Tlingit men stormed aboard the crippled vessel, weapons drawn, as Coe, Lansing, Emelian, Marpha, and the others all threw up their hands in surrender. Infuriated by the drowning death of one of his clan members, one young Tlingit man knocked Coe unconscious with the end of his musket as a trickle of blood streamed from the captain's forehead and face. Peter Lansing, terrified, visibly shook as he and the *Jackal* prisoners were thrown roughly into surrounding canoes. The Kodiak boy,

Timofei, wept loudly as his mother tried to comfort him amid the terrible scene. Emelian and Marpha sat stoically together in a separate canoe, watching over a dozen Tlingit men offload several bales of pelts, copper and brass tools, cloth, food, and other items of value from the English ship into dozens of canoes. After several minutes, the men climbed back into their canoes and resumed paddling to the north. The ship was left to drift with the crushed corpse of the sailor, Chadwick, on deck. Peter Lansing glanced back one last time at *Jackal* as winds and currents pushed the schooner southward towards the rocky islets and their thousands of seabirds and hundreds of sea lions, her haunted memories to be scattered upon their shores for eternity.

FIFTY

D AMP, HEAVY MIST ENVELOPED THE TWO CANOE FLOTILLAS resting on shore beside the Icy Strait, guests of a Huna kwaan village and its clan houses of the Shark, Brown Bear, Moon, and Marten totems. Tom pointed to the north.

"Soon we'll be turning north again, sir, up Chilkat Sound, Lynn Canal as sailors call it, through the waters of the Auk kwaan to the Chilkat kwaan and Mother's village."

Joshua Hall looked out on the soaring mountains and distant glaciers. Every few moments, a humpback whale pod spouted on the surface, while lines of black cormorants flew just above the small waves and whitecaps.

"And *Eclipse*. Hopefully another vessel such as *Otter* or *Grace* arrives as well. At least we know Captains Henry Hamby and Caleb Evans are civilized, and not cut from the same cloth as Coe and Elias. God knows our voyage has endured more than its share of misfortunes."

Tom was still weak, but ate smoked salmon, his appetite gradually returning.

"The clans won't tolerate any disruptions of the great victory calling hosted by the Chilkat kwaan. If Elias shows his wicked face at Mother's village, he will sorely regret it."

Hall drank from his water flask and ate a piece of venison jerky, taking his time with his words.

"Yes, he would suffer the same fate as Ian Coe and Peter Lansing. Jonathan doesn't have it much better, being watched and followed wherever he walks. I hope he's learned reckless actions have consequences. He'll have a lot of explaining to do once he returns to Boston."

"If he returns."

"What?"

"Mother may decide that he deserves to be enslaved, or perhaps killed to honor the clan fighters who fell in battle fighting the Russians. Remember sir, Jonathan and everyone else trading here are subject to the laws of the clans, even if they ignore or refuse to recognize this fact. When Thaddeus and I lived in Massachusetts, we were bound to follow its customs and laws."

"Fair and just points. Jonathan will win his freedom back only when he commits himself to order and reverence."

Tom nodded as he rolled some tobacco and lit it for himself and Hall. Gray mist hovered over the green sea as a pod of orcas surfaced.

"Ah, the wolves of the sea," Hall marveled as he rose to his feet. "They might be after that whale pod in the far distance. What a magnificent sight. And look, there are youngsters among them."

"The darkfish people have arrived from their undersea kwaan and are on their way to Mother's village. They heard us speak, and acknowledge us. This is a blessing since they bring gifts of great strength and wisdom, and their hearts are boundless."

Alexei Taradanov shouted from the middle of the canoe.

"Look mama! Look papa! More blackfish, over there! They have their little ones with them!"

Emelian and Marpha were joyous and hopeful, despite being prisoners of the clans. Their young son Alexei was back in their arms. The clan leaders had allowed them to paddle together in the same canoe after discovering they were a family and lowly employees, not officers, of the Russian-American Company, having only been picked up by Ian Coe's vessel. The Kodiak woman, Vera, and her son, Timofei, were also allowed to remain with Emelian's family.

The two great flotillas made their way north through Chilkat Sound and its patches of ice from surrounding glaciers. Emelian reflected upon his visit to the Chilkat kwaan three years previous. He had accompanied an expedition led by Alexander Baranov through the various northern kwaans to win permission to build Fort Mikhailovsky. Baranov had focused his attentions on a middle-aged Tlingit woman holding the totem of the Great Dipper, as she was held in highest regard by other clans. She was fair and just, and acted like a mother would to her children. She gave her permission to Baranov on the condition the Mikhailovsky colony would respect clan laws and trade high volumes of goods for pelts, all promises later broken.

Emelian pondered the events that brought the attack about as he paddled vigorously in tandem with other company prisoners. Perhaps this sealed his fate as well as that of his family, Emelian thought, for they were Russians in the eyes of the clans and might be enslaved or killed for that reason alone. In his heart, Emelian hoped for a better outcome though. Surely God's wisdom and justice was among these people since they shared hopes and dreams for their own children, just as he and Marpha did for Alexei.

Joshua Hall stared in awe at the massive glaciers and towering waterfalls tumbling from the Chilkat Mountains into the sound. Along the shore, several totem poles held various clan stories, full of intricate painted animal carvings set in a myriad of colors. Beside them lay a few wooden touts, fortresses built with slender removable ladders in preparation for a possible Russian retaliatory attack. Just a few hundred yards in the distance stood Mother's village beside a thick forest and nearby river, where hundreds of men, women, and children lined the shore to welcome the great canoe flotillas. At anchor rested *Eclipse*, to Hall's immense relief, in addition to the American ships *Otter*, Captain Henry Hamby, and *Grace*, Captain Caleb Evans.

Micah Triplett soon came into view on shore, grinning and raising his hat in salute as Aolani stood at his side. Alamea and Kanoa soon joined them, waving and jumping as Hall's canoe became visible from shore. Drums beat in identical cadences from both the shore and a few of the canoes, while some of the Tlingits broke into song as the first canoes arrived on the beach. As the first fighters stepped ashore with prisoners, several village men and women fired muskets into the air in celebration. Jonathan Fletcher, Ian Coe, Sergei Popov, and Peter Lansing, their hands tied, were hustled away to a nearby house. Emelian Taradanov and the other female and child prisoners were allowed to walk freely about the village.

Hall's canoe pushed onto shore and he ran to Alamea and Kanoa, embracing them as tears streamed down Alamea's face. Hall lifted Kanoa up as Alamea clung to Joshua. His weary eyes shed tears as he was overcome with joy.

FIFTY-ONE

Emelian Taradanov and his family rested under a large fir tree at the edge of the village and its sliver of ocean. Although they enjoyed a respite and were allowed to eat from the village's dried fish stores, Emelian was informed they would be expected to work by cleaning homes and hauling rubbish in preparation for the victory calling. As Alexei played beside them with a wooden toy given to him by a Kolosh woman, Marpha grew increasingly anxious.

"What do you think the Koloshi will do with us? Do these good Boston captains have any say over us?"

Emelian sighed before responding, his weary mind trying to find the right combination of words that would not alarm his wife, yet offer a dose of realism.

"No one knows what will happen, of course, but I sincerely believe the Boston officers will argue for us in their talks with the Koloshi. I've met one of the Boston captains, Henry Hamby, his vessel *Otter* visited Mikhailovsky two years ago. He struck me as a fair person. I don't know about the other Boston ships there, *Eclipse* and *Grace*, but I think our chances are good we will be taken to Kodiak as the Boston men know Baranov will pay good rewards to them. There is also a Kolosh woman in this village, 'Mother,' who makes many important decisions. I haven't seen her yet, but she—"

Emelian froze and put his hands over his face. Alarmed, Marpha grabbed his arm.

"Husband, what is it? What's the matter? Tell me, please."

"Down by that longhouse with the Sea Lion totem, it's that Kolosh boy I stabbed in the woods near Mikhailovsky. He must have been in the other flotilla. There, you see, he's with one of the Boston officers from *Eclipse*."

"He appears well, other than walking more slowly than the others and having a sling over his shoulder. Emelian, if he sees you what will happen?"

"I don't want to think about that. Just keep an eye out and avoid him if possible. Perhaps we can make arrangements to get on one of the Boston ships, but I don't think the Koloshi leaders would allow that. We are too valuable as prisoners when negotiations begin a few days from now."

"A few days? What can we do? He will eventually see us!"

Marpha began shaking as Emelian held her. He watched the young Kolosh man enter the longhouse with the officer. Over the next few minutes, a few additional wounded Koloshi men from the fighting at Mikhailovsky entered the longhouse, accompanied by two more Boston officers and several clan leaders.

Emelian used the calmest voice he could muster.

"He hasn't seen me yet, and we need to stay away from him as much as possible. We can survive Marpha, we just have to be smart and put our trust in God."

Taking deep breaths, Marpha remained silent and nodded in agreement. Their son, Alexei, ran toward the longhouse to play with a Kolosh boy similar in age and his small brown puppy. Seeing her son just a few feet from the longhouse entrance, Marpha panicked and ran to retrieve him as Emelian tried to stop his wife.

"Marpha! Wait! He's just playing! Don't draw attention to ourselves!"

It was too late. After enduring the trauma of being separated from her child, Marpha's motherly instincts caused her to chase after her son.

"Alexei! Come to me at once!"

A tall Kolosh man in his early twenties emerged from the longhouse with a puzzled look as he observed Marpha approach and take Alexei by the arm. Marpha looked in fear at the young man who had shoulder-length black hair and two long knives attached to his waist. She noted his tattoos of the Sea Lion totem crest on his hands, and his fine woolen garments, indicative of high social rank. Ear pendants made of brass and a finely carved shell nose piece added to the man's fierce appearance.

Emelian walked away with his woolen cap pulled low over his face. The Kolosh man shouted in heavily accented Russian.

"You there, come here at once!"

Emelian halted. He was unarmed, his wife and child were now mere feet from the longhouse, and escape was impossible. He had no choice but to comply and walk the few dozen yards towards the man. Emelian's thoughts focused on what he would say to save his wife and child, as his fate, he reasoned, was likely sealed. He was to be made a slave or killed.

"Mama?" Alexei asked as Marpha fell to her knees and held him. The young Kolosh boy handed the puppy to Marpha, which proceeded to lick Marpha's face. Alexei laughed and the Kolosh boy grinned. Her eyes bloodshot, Marpha looked at her husband, distressed by the turn of events as he complied with the man's order to enter the longhouse.

Emelian walked with the young man past slave quarters near the entrance to the longhouse's far side, where several wounded Tlingit fighters were treated by a few Boston men and traditional Tlingit healers beside a fire hearth. Racks of dried fish and seaweed hung from the ceilings, while private sleeping quarters behind interior walls lined some of the sides of the house. Colored images of Sea Lion and Wolf totemic symbols adorned the walls, posts, and benches, while pungent smoke from the hearth filled the air.

Tom spoke with Joshua Hall in muted tones as he watched a Russian Creole man approach with the Chilkat Sea Lion house owner. His shirt off, Tom sat upright against the wall as Hall cleaned and dressed his stab wound once again, while an old Tlingit woman tattooed Tom's left hand with the Sea Lion totem crest. As the two men approached, Tom's heart raced, for he remembered this Russian Creole man. Tom closed his eyes and breathed deeply as he struggled to suppress his anger. Images of ancient fallen logs and shadows appeared before him, while terrifying screams echoed off trees as the sounds of gunshots and knives being unsheathed filled his ears. A River Otter Were-Man appeared before him and spoke in Nathaniel Folger's voice.

"This man who approaches you is to be our slave. He is to be killed in your honor at the great victory calling at Chilkat. His body will be thrown into the forest, where his soul will be carried to our village. He belongs to us. You belong to us, Tom."

"No! And Nathaniel lives within the freed boy Kanoa!"

Tom screamed as he grasped his cross and opened his eyes, staring wildly at the Chilkat man. Hall and the tattoo woman paused, startled and taken aback, and leaned away from Tom as the Chilkat man spoke.

"Is this the Russian dog that stabbed you back at Sitka kwaan? He has a wife and small son outside matching your descriptions."

Yes, Tom thought to himself, there was no doubt this was the man who nearly took his life in the woods of Sitka Island. Tom looked into Emelian's eyes and immediately sensed, to his surprise, a certain calmness.

Tom sat up a bit higher, turning his eyes to his Chilkat host, and spoke in Tlingit.

"No. This is not the man who stabbed me. Just let him walk about the village for now. My first mate here, Joshua Hall, and Captain Triplett, will offer many gifts to you and Great Bear Mother as payment for this man and his family. The Boston men know the thief Baranov pays well to get his people back."

The Tlingit Chilkat man raised his eyebrows, puzzled.

"Very well then."

Emelian stepped out of the longhouse, crossed himself in Orthodox tradition, and walked to Marpha. Alexei and the Kolosh boy were laughing and petting the puppy. Emelian grinned, relieved by the turn of events.

"No worry here, my love, everything is fine. You see my dear wife, trust in God and you will find freedom."

Flush with relief, Marpha embraced her husband as Alexei and his new friend played under a large tree with their four-legged companion.

FIFTY-TWO

SAILORS OF *ECLIPSE*, *OTTER*, AND *GRACE* assisted the clans in raising new giant totem poles in the Chilkat village. Among the images rested a few faces depicting Russians and some of the Boston captains and sailors. Joshua Hall pointed to one of the carved Boston captains and looked at Thaddeus.

"Well I'll be damned if that's Jonathan Fletcher amid all those faces and clan crests up there."

"You're correct, sir. That is indeed Mr. Fletcher's image. In case you didn't notice, Alamea's image is on that pole about a third of the way up."

"My goodness. Well, she deserves commemoration."

"And sir, there are plans for another pole after the victory ceremonies are concluded, and your image is to be carved on it amid many others. You see, these are the clans' stories, these poles. The good and bad of human actions are always included, because all of us face choices within our short lives here on earth, but our clan totemic crests transcend time and physical existence. They at once represent all generations across time, the past and future together. Our origins and destinies, *Kaa Shagoon* in our language."

"Immortal, like God and His Law," Hall added.

"Yes, sir, one could make that comparison, like an immortal soul in the Christian sense. Our totem crests are eternal. They provide all generations the strength to face danger and uncertainty, and to press on through the bad in reaching for what is good in human potential. Each generation honors the past and recognizes their obligations to the future."

OVER TWO HUNDRED VILLAGERS and nearly three dozen American sailors from *Eclipse*, *Otter*, and *Grace* arrived at the giant rectangular planked longhouse of the Great Bear Constellation to the melody of a clan victory song. All entered through the carved mouth of a massive bear painted in blue and yellow. Farther up the cedar totem pole at the base of the house rested carved blue, white, and red faces of wolves and ravens, surrounded by stars, sun beams, and moons. High-born clan leaders, entering first, wore woolen blankets with dazzling, interlocking design fields woven in the shape of traditional copper blades. Atop the high-born guests' heads rested circular cedar bark hats that rose in a coned shape with varying numbers of round wooden potlatch rings. Painted blue, the rings rested over interlocking colored designs of animals and supernatural beings.

After the elite followed common clan people wearing interlaced hide clothing with less elaborately sewn animal designs. Most wore simple caps of spruce root embroidered with grass that imitated Boston sailors' caps. In deference to their hosts, the Americans entered last. Hall noticed over a dozen village slaves near the inside entrance, busily organizing and setting out food while another group hurried to position gifts near the center of the longhouse.

Alamea and Hall held Kanoa's hands as they listened to Thaddeus.

"This is all preparation to hear an oration by Great Bear Mother of the North Star House. You probably noticed the prisoners, Jonathan, Sergei Popov, Ian Coe, and Peter Lansing, are being kept under heavy guard at the other side of the village."

Hall looked at Alamea before turning to Thaddeus.

"What can we expect Mother to say about those men? Will she make any decisions here?"

"I'm not sure, sir. She probably won't make any decisions right away."

Micah Triplett, a few feet behind Hall, Alamea, and Thaddeus, offered his insights.

"We need to be patient with the clan leaders, and work closely with Captains Hamby and Evans. Anything could happen. Mother and the other clan elite may decide to free them, hand them over to us, enslave them, or kill them."

Hall was alarmed, but before he could press Triplett and Thaddeus for more insight, a loud drum beat broke the silence. Dancers moved in slow circular motions wearing red and black cloaks. Slaves positioned two stacks of gifts a few yards from the longhouse hearth. Boxes of various sizes held fine copper and steel blades, tailored hide clothing, fishing equipment, and goods from the American ships, including mirrors, colored clothing and fabrics, mother-of-pearl buttons, and muskets. Thaddeus noted to Joshua a few muskets were decorated with painted line images of supernatural beings.

Commoners and sailors sat on the floor, while the clan elite and the American officers rested on carved cedar plank benches and chairs. A small wooden platform with a large, finely carved chair was fixed near the hearth fire that warmed the longhouse against the damp overcast day outside. About two dozen high-born Tlingit children, ranging in age from four to fifteen years, gathered around the hearth and chair, awaiting the arrival of Great Bear Mother. All had black and red woolen cloaks with mother-of-pearl designs of totemic animals. Older children wore round spruce bark hats decorated with red and black-lined creatures.

Within moments, the drum ceased and the dancers sat down. A Tlingit woman around fifty years in age emerged from behind a small interior wooden wall at the far end of the longhouse. Arriving at the hearth and her chair, the children around her all remained silent and well behaved, their eyes focused on the two hundred plus guests. Hall, Alamea, Triplett, and other sailors from the American ships knew this was Great Bear Mother. All were mesmerized by the clan matriarch's appearance, which included a circular wooden labret in her lower lip extending three inches, shark's teeth pendants hanging from her ears, a necklace holding a totemic symbol of the Great Bear Constellation made of polished and carved bone, and ivory bracelets on her ankles and wrists. Atop her head rested a circular spruce bark hat of brilliant lined facial images of red wolves, blue bears, and white stars, with six potlatch rings on the coned top. A woolen cloak presented dyed colored symbols of the Great Bear and her mother's lineage, the Wolf. Her piercing dark eyes and posture exuded dignity and strength throughout the longhouse, which was completely silent in anticipation of her oration. Thaddeus prepared to translate for Joshua Hall, Micah Triplett, and Alamea, though he waited several moments until Great Bear Mother finished her opening greeting.

"Thank you for coming. I am very pleased to see you all. It is good to look upon your faces."

After a long pause, Mother continued. She raised her hands in one grand acknowledgement of all gathered. Joshua Hall recognized why this woman held such power and influence. Her confident voice never betrayed a hint of hesitation, and was pleasant to the ear in its cadence and accents.

"It warms my heart that all my children are here. Our clans welcome the Boston ships *Eclipse*, *Otter*, and *Grace*, and their captains, Micah, Henry, and Caleb. We also greet those among us from Hawai'i, a land, I hear, with no winter."

She paused again and moved her head about to look upon everyone.

"We are here to honor those who have fallen in battle, to celebrate our victory over the Russians at Sitka kwaan!"

A loud cheer and shouts of approval filled the longhouse for several moments until Mother motioned for silence.

"The Russians overstayed their welcome. They turned from being our guests to insulting us. They have taken our slave women without payments, they hunt our sea animals without permission, and they have murdered some of our clan brothers and sisters. And to redeem the honor of our kin, we shed their blood as demanded by our laws. If that contemptible dog Alexander Baranov dares to return to our clan houses with his Aleutian and Kodiak slaves, we will be ready!"

More shouts of approval echoed off the longhouse walls before Mother turned towards the gathered sailors.

"We thank our Boston friends for trading their muskets and cannons to us. You are here to trade, not steal, like the Russians."

Tlingit villagers nodded in agreement. Mother then addressed the captains.

"I am curious about your Boston women. Many of you are honorable men like Captain Cook, the first cloud face man I ever met many years ago. Other captains are no better than the Russians. They take and steal from us like naughty children, with lies and deceit."

Pausing for a brief moment, she continued her inquiry of the New Englanders.

"Are your Boston women not offended with these men?"

Mother motioned for the officers to answer, with Thaddeus interpreting. Captain Caleb Evans of *Grace* rose to speak.

"Yes, Great Bear Mother, our Boston women are deeply offended when they hear of their men's misdeeds."

Joshua Hall stood.

"We share their offense. Wicked men from the Boston and King George ships dishonor us all."

Captain Henry Hamby of *Otter*, along with Captain Triplett, also rose to repeat similar sentiments to Mother and the great gathering in the long-house. Mother turned to Thaddeus and requested he rise and speak about his years in Boston with his cousin Tom. Thaddeus acknowledged her with a nearly imperceptible nod.

"Mother, the distant, wild shores of New England hold many cloud face people and much feverish activity, and Boston and its surrounding villages stand as the greatest kwaan. The Boston men hold the Eagle as their totem crest. Some come from prestigious families who own many great ships that travel across their ocean, the Atlantic, bringing many goods and slaves to the kwaans of the cloud face people. Mother, all of their kwaans worship one God, and the Boston women are strong in honoring Him, as are many men such as Micah, Joshua, Caleb, and Henry."

Mother, nodding in approval, motioned for Thaddeus to continue. Thaddeus was somewhat nervous since everyone's eyes were riveted on him. He took a deep breath before continuing.

"I learned of the great deeds of the clans of the Boston kwaan. They fought the King George men many years ago in a great clan war among the cloud face people. The King George men committed many insults, thefts, and murders, in violation of established laws and customs among all cloud face people. A clan leader named George Washington, from the Virginia kwaan far to the south of Boston, upheld the honor of the Eagle totem crest and defeated the much stronger King George men."

Mother, excited with Thaddeus' oration, motioned for him to continue though she asked a question before he could speak.

"Child of the Great Bear totem, of the House of the North Star, will you return to the faraway kwaans of the cloud face people, or are you to remain here among us?"

Thaddeus responded confidently after a moment of silence.

"Great Bear Mother, the world is very large with many lands and kwaans, each having their own laws and customs. My desire for more knowledge and learning reaches as high as the mountain peaks. I am like a hungry wolverine who climbs ever higher in search of nourishment, and so it is my intention to travel once more on the Boston men's ships. I have seen many places such as China, Hawai'i, and the London kwaan of the King George men, Mother. And, I have learned to speak, read, and write in their tongue. Their 'books' as they call them, possess great knowledge and wisdom. My Sea Lion cousin and I can teach you if you wish."

"Ah! I would like that very much my child! You honor us all!"

Tom walked in through the main entrance, clearly on the mend from his shoulder wound, smiling at his cousin before turning his glance to the *Eclipse* crew, and finally, Mother.

"Our brave Sea Lion child has grown stronger! Let us dance, let us feast, let us sing!" Mother pronounced.

FIFTY-THREE

JOSHUA HALL, MICAH TRIPLETT, HENRY HAMBY, and Caleb Evans sat alone together, naked and sweating profusely inside a village sweat lodge. Each man pondered the unfolding decisions of clan leaders, including Great Bear Mother. It had been a day since her oration, and already there was word from Thaddeus and Tom that at least two prisoners were to be killed at a ceremony honoring a prestigious Tlingit man who died from battle wounds at Sitka Island. Thaddeus confirmed one of the prisoners was a Russian-American Company flotilla leader, Vasili Kochesov, captured in the straits.

Captain Evans whispered in the scalded air.

"Kochesov, I know about that man. Full-blooded Kodiak Islander. Poor fellow, there's no saving him. He killed many Tlingits with his marksman skills. The clans who fought the Russians over the years call him Gidak."

Captain Hamby poured more water over the heated rocks, unleashing hot steam that raised the temperature to the absolute limit of the men's tolerance.

"That will be enough, Henry, thank you." Evans whispered.

"Yes, quite enough," Triplett followed. "I'm keeping three Baranov people on board *Eclipse*, Nikolai and Tanya Karaulov, plus a former Tlingit slave, Alina, the female acquaintance of Sergei Popov, one of the prisoners held onshore. Perhaps we can convince the clans to let the others go."

Hall leaned his head back against the cedar planks of the lodge, his eyes closed as he spoke.

"Coe, Lansing, Fletcher, and the Russian-American Company men may all be in imminent danger of death. Of course, Kochesov is already a dead man."

Hamby spoke as he wiped sweat and struggled to endure the heat.

"One company man is Emelian Taradanov, I met him a few times over the years when I visited Mikhailovsky and Kodiak. Russian father and Siberian Native mother. Kamchadal, I believe. Taradanov's a sharp fellow who speaks some limited English and Tlingit, even though he's not an officer. The man has a wife and a small son, and I know Baranov favors him for possible promotion, at least that's what the old Russian told me a few months ago. The man should be saved if we can help, God willing."

Triplett leaned forward from his cedar plank bench, his upper body bent over as he looked down.

"I propose we offer a handsome payment for all the men, and the women and children as well. It is our duty, gentlemen. Of course, all of us will lose some of our profits, but the clans by all indications will be giving us a handsome share of pelts. As despicable as their recent actions are, Coe, Lansing, and Fletcher should stand trial back home, or at the very least face a tribunal of several sea officers such as ourselves in Honolulu, Canton, Valparaiso, or another port."

"Or Van Diemen's Land," Evans interjected. "Yes, Tasmania, Coe and Lansing would fit in nicely with all those convicts. Or maybe dump them at Juan Fernandez. As for Jonathan, well, I think Thomas Perkins would lynch him on the Boston wharf rather than serve as a witness in a trial."

The men chuckled before going silent again for several moments. Henry Hamby swiped more sweat from his brow with a thick cotton cloth. The twenty-two-year-old captain from Cape Cod opened his eyes briefly amid the scalding steam to look at the others, whose eyes remained shut.

"I agree, gentlemen. The three of us will offer an equal share of goods from our ships. One must remember the clans' laws prevail here. For example, we could offer them everything we have for the five men and the others, and yet, Mother and the Tlingit elite might still refuse."

Hall wiped sweat from his brow.

"But we must still try. I'll speak with Tom and Thaddeus."

Evans asked, "When is the funeral procession to take place?"

"Tonight," Hamby replied, "and we can expect no negotiations over furs and trading until after ceremonies are completed."

Evans folded his arms and sighed.

"So, Joshua, any ideas on where Elias may be going with his band of lunatics?"

"After he sells his pelts at Canton for goods for his utopian schemes, it's anyone's guess as to where he'll end up. He mentioned California or the South Seas. My instincts haunt me though. He may yet still be on this coast."

Triplett wiped more sweat from his brow.

"With respect Joshua, your brother Elias has several thousand pelts on *Panther* and *Icarus*, wealth he could use to start his own small country. There's no chance he would risk staying on this coast."

Henry Hamby nodded as he rested his hands on top of his thinning black hair.

"I am truly sorry for your loss, Joshua."

Triplett and Evans nodded in empathy. The *Eclipse* captain wiped his upper legs with a cloth as he spoke.

"We stand with you Joshua, you did your best. If you wish, I'll help you write your report for Thomas Perkins when we're back home."

"Thank you, sir."

Joshua exhaled and leaned over. The bitter salty sweat rolled over his face like a torrent.

FIFTY-FOUR

Emelian Taradanov busily cleaned a house inhabited by clan members holding the Sockeye Salmon totem. Marpha prepared a meal of halibut steaks and various greens as instructed by the owner, a middle-aged Kolosh man. As Emelian swept and looked out of the home's main entrance with his son at his side, he noticed dozens of villagers emerge from several different homes to join a growing procession headed in the direction of Sockeye Salmon House and the thick woods nearby. At the head of the procession were four muscular Koloshi men holding up the dressed body of a Kolosh fighter who had recently died from his injuries. At the rear of the procession, Emelian noticed, walked the American prisoner from *Eclipse*, the two English prisoners, the company fugitive Sergei Popov, and Vasili Kochesov, all with their hands tied and under heavy guard. Emelian grew nervous. Was he to be in the procession as well, to be possibly killed at the funeral pyre?

Marpha saw her husband's concern and paused from her food preparations.

"Emelian, what is the matter? Do the Sockeye clan people approach now?"

"No, but there is something big happening, apparently a funerary procession, but I don't know who it's for. I can't identify the deceased man."

"Oh God, don't the Koloshi do awful things to their slaves at their heathen ceremonies?"

Emelian labored to maintain a calm demeanor.

"Yes, love. Remember, we're not slaves, we're prisoners. And, I might add, prisoners most likely to be freed by the American captains and taken to Kodiak, to home."

Marpha left her work site and walked over to the house entrance to catch sight of the procession. Straining her eyes to see who was at the rear of the procession, she suddenly gasped at the sight of tied and heavily guarded men.

"Those poor men! Vasili Kochesov is among them! And there's Captain Coe and Mr. Lansing, our rescuers! What is to become of them? Tell me the truth, Emelian!"

"It doesn't concern us now, let us keep quiet and maintain a low profile. Go back to preparing the meal."

"Tell me!"

Emelian looked down in annoyance for a few moments.

"Alright, damn it, since you stubbornly insist, I will tell you! The Koloshi usually kill at least two of them and burn the bodies on the funeral pyre, to accompany the deceased in the afterlife. I have heard from others the Koloshi sometimes set slaves free at their rituals, but it is uncommon."

"Please Jesus, watch over them! Can't we do anything?! What about the Boston captains, can't they intervene?"

"They already have. I overheard that the captains offered many fine goods from their ships in exchange for the men, but the Kolosh woman Great Bear Mother and other clan leaders refused. Apparently, the issue was non-negotiable, at least for now. Perhaps some of the men are to be slaves of the clans for all time."

A shrill, high-pitched voice shouted in Kolosh from the rear entrance of the house.

"What are you doing? Get back to work, now!"

Marpha, Emelian, and Alexei were startled as the teenage daughter of the house owner appeared behind them at the opposite door. Marpha looked down and hurried back to the house hearth to continue meal preparations. The adolescent Kolosh girl was still incensed, however.

"You call this a meal? I told you to add more wood to the fire! And you forgot to add those smaller greens to the meat, they are not separate! Father will be angry now!"

The girl threw a few of the stems and leaves over Marpha's head in frustration.

Marpha, who learned conversational Kolosh over several days, exploded in anger, and before Emelian could intervene to try and maintain calm, Marpha fired back at the girl.

"We are not your slaves, you foolish girl! My family is assisting your home as a courtesy while we wait to leave with the Boston men in a few days!"

The Kolosh girl laughed derisively in smug satisfaction.

"Hah! Not anymore! Our clan elders have decided you Kodiak mice are to be slaves!"

Within moments the girl's father walked in the same door with several finely carved items, including a small box with various delicacies.

"Silence daughter! Move on now and get the other gifts, the funerary procession is already nearing the woods! You there, Emelian Taradanov, assist me now with these gifts. I am a guest at the pyre, and you are to accompany me."

Marpha began to panic as Emelian felt his heart pounding. Alexei began to cry. As the daughter returned from her room with a few additional gifts for Emelian to carry, her father scolded her again.

"Now listen! You will assist this Aleut woman in preparing the meal. Some relatives of ours from the Auk kwaan will be feasting here once ceremonies have concluded. You will also comfort the small boy and be polite to the woman. I do not want to hear of any undignified rudeness when I return."

Emelian's mind raced in circles as he addressed the man.

"Salmon House owner, with respect, I wish to ask our status as prisoners. Are we—"

"Enough talking, all of you. Emelian Taradanov, carry these gifts with me. We walk in silence now to the funerary pyre."

FIFTY-FIVE

EMELIAN LOOKED BACK THROUGH THE THICK GREEN WOODS toward the village, where he spotted Alexei and Marpha standing outside the Sockeye Salmon House. He noticed the two Koloshi teenagers from *Eclipse* and First Mate Joshua speaking with her as she pointed towards the forest, pleading with them while Alexei remained still, clinging to his mother. Before the scene faded from view, Emelian glimpsed Joshua motion with his arms and hands in conciliatory fashion, as if to indicate there was no reason for alarm. The scene did little to calm Emelian's nerves, though, as his heart raced. In silence, Emelian labored on along the trail with the Sockeye Salmon House owner's gifts for the deceased.

After a half hour of walking, people in the procession came to a clearing of grasses, shrubs, and large boulders. Emelian, near the back of the procession just a few yards ahead of the prisoners and a slave, saw a giant red-orange flame over eight feet tall. In the background, miles away, stood a wall of granite covered in glaciers and small waterfalls, with the peaks of the Chilkat Mountains towering above low-lying narrow clouds and mist. Emelian drew closer to the fire as hundreds of crackling sparks lifted into the air. It was the deceased's body burning in the pyre.

The rear of the procession emerged from the woods, approaching the flames. Emelian set down the gifts as instructed by the Salmon House owner. Near the ceremonial area, finished cedar planks and poles for a home lay strewn about along with a few unfinished totem poles. Several wide, deep holes for house posts sprawled in a neat, rectangular pattern.

Standing to the rear of the numerous Koloshi guests, Emelian placed his hand over his Orthodox cross necklace and prayed as a Kolosh shaman chanted. The eldest son of the deceased, in his twenties, was dressed in a fine cloak, leggings, and a wide-brimmed cedar bark hat. He approached the box Emelian had carried, while trying to conceal something with his right arm. The son shifted his grip on the object, and for a split second, Emelian noticed it was a weapon, a "Slave-Killer" with an eight-inch long stone lashed to a carved wooden handle.

The shaman invoked new chants and motioned for the gifts to be deposited on the fire to accompany the deceased in the afterlife. Emelian prayed to God to save him and the five prisoners standing a few dozen yards away on the opposite side of the funerary pyre, still under heavy guard. As the minutes slowly passed, the gifts burned in the towering flames until none were left. Emelian noticed that of the five men on the other side of the pyre, only Sergei Popov and Vasili Kochesov appeared resolute. The American and two English sailors were clearly terrified. When the youngest of the three tried frantically to speak with one of the nearby clan leaders, he was immediately struck in the face. All remained silent as the shaman moved in circles around the pyre, eyeing the five men with an occasional glance towards Emelian, who now visibly displayed his cross necklace.

Emelian breathed deeply, his hammering heart gradually slowing as he prayed. Sweating from the heat of the funeral pyre, he closed his eyes with the fire's glow still penetrating his eyelids as time seemed to stand still. Placing his right hand over his cross, Emelian sensed the shaman approaching again in his direction. The shaman's chant grew more intense, and Emelian could see the man's charcoal blackened face, despite having his eyes closed. A raven's deep-throated clicking call sounded in Emelian's ears, and within moments, the shaman's face transformed into the deep black eyes and feathers of a raven. The inquisitive, penetrating gaze of the bird communicated its wisdom.

Emelian gasped and opened his eyes. The shaman stood by Vasili Kochesov and looked at the deceased's son a few feet away. Kochesov taunted his tormenters with contempt.

"I, Gidak, will stalk and snipe you all in the next world. And I will never relent."

The shaman sliced Kochesov's face and chest with shells.

"You die now, Gidak."

Kochesov suppressed his screams, defiant to the end. The young Kolosh man pulled his Slave-Killer weapon and smashed it into Kochesov's skull, killing him instantly. Two Koloshi commoners rushed over to throw the body into the fire.

Captain Coe screamed in a flustered mix of Kolosh and English.

"No! No! I'm an Englishman, damn it! King George's ships will punish all of you! Please! Lansing, Fletcher, Popov, help me! Stop! Please!"

Emelian watched in horror as the son smashed Coe in the head with the Slave-Killer. Within moments, the same commoners lifted the sea captain's body into the flames. Emelian glanced at the three remaining prisoners. The younger Englishman broke down completely and openly wept, while the American had a dazed look of disbelief. Only Sergei Popov remained unchanged in his blank stare.

The two Koloshi commoners looked at the shaman, who only nodded, before seizing Peter Lansing and walking him to one of the deep foundation holes for what would become the son's new home. Emelian watched several more Koloshi commoners lift a large cedar log, apparently to place in the hole. Lansing fought to break free of his captors' grip, but to no avail as he screamed in wild panic. The deceased's son arrived, and with the aid of two commoners, pushed Lansing into the eight-foot hole. Trying to claw his way out like a frightened animal, and shrieking in terror, Lansing felt a shower of earth fall over him. The shower soon turned into a torrent, and Lansing's last horrific scream was silenced as Koloshi commoners positioned the cedar log into the hole with the cascading dirt. As the funeral pyre receded in size, Emelian, Fletcher, and Popov were led away with the procession into the woods towards the village, enveloped in silence as demanded by the Koloshi.

Popov, the crazy bastard!

Emelian reflected on how the young Russian did not even demonstrate the slightest fear or emotion during the whole ordeal. The unpredictable young man just might provide the means to escape this place, Emelian reasoned, if the Boston men failed to win the Taradanov family's release. Emelian knew Popov's woman, Alina, was on board *Eclipse* from his talk with Joshua Hall the preceding day. There would be no stopping Popov, Emelian reasoned. He would find a way with that lunatic, for nothing less than the love and freedom of his wife and son were at stake.

FIFTY-SIX

Alamea held Joshua under their blankets on the deck of *Eclipse*, gazing up at the faint light of Venus, along with a few other bright planets and stars able to emerge in the brief dusky summer night of the southern Alaskan coast. Joshua spoke softly to her as she moved her hand over his chest and abdomen.

"The clan elders will meet tomorrow with the captains to discuss final arrangements on business and the fates of the prisoners. If all goes well, we should be able to depart for Kodiak the following day with the Russian prisoners, that is, if we have any. I'm worried, though. These clans seem insistent on keeping many of the prisoners here, including several women and children. At least this is what Thaddeus is reporting."

"'Mother' and some of the other clan leaders know you're a good man, Joshua. I saw it in her eyes when you spoke to her at length yesterday. She knows the captains are honest, decent men as well, unlike Jonathan and Ian Coe. What happened to Coe is awful, but he put himself in a position to reap those terrible consequences. Now, let us relax for a bit."

"And Elias. I want the captains to search for him, but they refuse. He's somewhere on . . ."

"Elias made his choice, Joshua."

Joshua tried to continue speaking, but Alamea had already moved her hand further down Joshua's abdomen and positioned herself on top of him under the blankets. As she moved in rhythmic ecstasy over him, Hall felt his cares and the day's stress melt away amid Alamea's heavy breathing and soft moans.

EMELIAN'S MIND RACED BETWEEN NIGHTMARES IN A FITFUL SLEEP. He awoke beside his sleeping wife and son, amid tall grasses and wildflowers next to Sockeye Salmon House. Venus glowed over the snowy Chilkat Mountains, and faint perfumed aromas from the meadow mingled with the more familiar scents of hearth smoke and the salty ocean. The calm, beautiful setting helped settle his nerves. This land could inflict terrifying fear and cruelty, he reflected, but it could also inspire deep courage and nobility.

Emelian moved over a few feet to sit against the home's cedar plank walls. Pulling out a small stash of tobacco given to him by the *Jackal* sailors, he filled and lit his Kolosh-made pipe, pondering his options amid fluid uncertainties. He had heard more disturbing rumors from some of the Aleutian and Kodiak women. All prisoners would be kept as permanent slaves among the Koloshi at the Chilkat village and elsewhere. The Boston men also seemed intent on leaving soon. Perhaps he, Marpha, and Alexei could sneak on to one of the vessels somehow? Or, Popov might be able to help him steal a canoe. How though? The Koloshi posted guards along the beach day and night. The wild man, Popov, would need to kill the guards silently. Alina could fight, Emelian remembered, and she knew how to use a knife and fire a musket, but she was on board *Eclipse*. The Boston sailor, Fletcher, might help too, for he was a desperate man. They would have to steal two canoes and several weapons to have a chance. It had to be a collective effort.

His train of thought was broken when a slight bump on the wall and several giggles and moans filtered from the house. It was the owner with two of his wives. Emelian closed his eyes and inhaled deeply from his pipe, annoyed at the disruption. As the minutes passed, the moans grew louder and were accompanied by the sound of limbs bumping the wall. In disgust, Emelian rose to look around for a new spot to rest several yards away. As he stood up and scanned the meadow around him, two loud moans and a third scream of pleasure filled Emelian's ears. Shaking his head, he stared at Venus and began walking away, but soon heard the low, contented voices of the husband and two wives behind the wall. Silently moving back to the wall, Emelian could clearly hear the conversation. He focused his mind on picking up the Koloshi words as the Sockeye Salmon House owner spoke.

"Great Bear Mother has advised all clan nobles to keep the Aleut and Kodiak people as slaves, to serve as guarantees against future retaliation from Baranov and his miserable Kodiak wretches."

"And so, husband, what have you decided on the Kodiak family out-side?" one wife asked.

"We own them now. I have decided. They are to be treated well and not killed, mind you, as healthy slaves will ultimately fetch our Salmon House lineage added wealth from another clan house, or from Baranov if the damnable Russians return. At the very least, the slaves outside will be a valuable dowry when our eldest takes a husband in another year or two."

"And good riddance to that spoiled brat, as her mouth never ceases moving in spewing complaints and insults. A strong and wise husband will serve her well," the second wife vented.

"Yes, I agree," he replied. "Now, let us sleep. We are to make final ar-rangements with the Boston men tomorrow and see them on their way. I want to have a rested mind."

"Oh husband, please get me many rolls of the Boston ships' red cloth," one wife replied.

"And don't forget the mirror, remember, you promised me the large one Captain Hamby has on his ship," the second wife added.

"Yes, I haven't forgotten," the husband answered in an irritated tone as Emelian heard him shift, apparently tired of his wives' demands.

"Wives, you have closed your eyes, now close your mouths as well."

SERGEI POPOV AWOKE TO THE UNPLEASANT sensation of a large pebble hit-ting his upper back. Bleary eyed and half asleep, he rolled over to see Emelian Taradanov several yards away, hiding behind a pair of young spruce trees to stay out of sight of two Koloshi guards pacing the nearby beach.

"What the hell do you want, Taradanov? Just leave me alone."

"Listen to me, we are to be slaves of the Koloshi indefinitely, I over-heard it from the Salmon House owner himself. They are not going to ransom us to the Boston men. And not only that, the Boston ships will be departing tomorrow sometime."

Popov remained silent for a few moments, rubbing his eyes to buy an additional moment to clear his mind. He scratched the back of his neck with his right hand and sighed deeply.

"Fuck."

"Listen, we must do something now if you want to see your woman, Alina, again. Our only chance to save ourselves and our families is to stow-away on one of the ships, or steal some canoes and get the hell out of here."

"Alright, we'll do something, but it means dispatching the two Koloshi guards over there. I'm not leaving without Alina. She's on *Eclipse*."

"Is there any way we can stowaway on board that ship? What's the captain like? I've only met the first mate, Hall, and just for a brief time."

Popov rubbed the side of his neck, frowning.

"The captain is Micah Triplett, and his first mate is Joshua Hall. He already has Nikolai Karaulov and his wife on board. I don't know if they would hide us, though, as the Koloshi will discover it was us who dispatched the guards. And, it would be against the Boston men's self-interest to shelter us. These particular officers seem fair on the surface, but one can never trust these men, these so-called 'civilized' Americans."

Popov paused to spit, then continued.

"The Koloshi would refuse to give the captains their promised pelts if they protected us, the murderers of their kin. I know we're deep in their territory, but the only sure way to escape is to take our chances with canoes and hide along the coast as best we can. Your woman and my woman know how to fight, so that makes four of us in case we encounter the Koloshi on our journey south."

His mouth wide open, Taradanov could not believe Popov's words.

"South? Are you out of your mind? Yakutat colony is our only realistic hope."

"Then you're on your own, Taradanov. I'd rather be a slave to the Koloshi than return to the company. We head south, or no deal. Besides, the Koloshi probably destroyed the company colony at Yakutat just as they did with Mikhailovsky."

Emelian remained silent for a few moments. He knew Popov meant every word he said, and was probably correct in his assessments. Still, the odds of survival in a long southward journey were slim. Their best hope would be to encounter a new southward-moving Boston or King George ship, which also presented very unfavorable odds. No, he would travel south only until Icy Strait, and then turn west for the gulf. If the Yakutat colony were destroyed, he, Marpha, and Alexei would head further west to the Great Sound of the Chugach people, the one the King George men called "Prince William." There Emelian and his family would encounter company hunting parties, perhaps even Ivan Kuskov or Alexander Baranov.

"Alright then, Popov, I'll meet you halfway on your proposal. We'll dispatch the Koloshi guards and take those two small canoes over there. Once we reach the Icy Strait, though, I turn west with my wife and child."

"You have a deal, Taradanov. You will need to get some guns and food for us within the next hour and meet me back here and then we'll take care of the guards. The sun rises in three hours and we require what faint darkness there is to aid our escape. And, we stop at *Eclipse* to get my woman."

"Very well, I'll do my best to get what I can, but we need to move in an hour regardless of whether I can get the guns and food."

"If you come back empty handed, we take what we need from *Eclipse*. Agreed?"

"Agreed. Say, should we bring along the Boston sailor over there? He would probably fight well, as he has nothing to lose."

Popov rubbed his fingers on his chin, moving his tongue around the inside of his mouth.

"The Boston man was once the captain of *Eclipse*, Jonathan Fletcher. He was removed from command by his officers and his former lover, a woman from Hawai'i who now has relations with the first mate. Wait! That gives me an idea, Taradanov! We'll take *Eclipse* and put Fletcher back in command. He would surely take us south to Hawai'i as a reward, or maybe the Spanish ports in California or Mexico. Yes, forget the canoes! We'll take the whole damned ship for ourselves, Taradanov, and if Fletcher should try to betray us, we'll dispatch him like those miserable Koloshi on the beach!"

Emelian was shocked at Popov's new idea and taken aback at his arrogant grin which betrayed the young man's wild streak. Bewildered, Emelian rubbed his forehead and looked down. After a few moments, he glanced at Popov. Emelian remembered his promise to himself to free his family, even if it meant harnessing Popov's lunacy. Still, he struggled in his response as he faced a terrible dilemma.

"Popov, your fantastic idea just may work, but if we fail that will surely be the end of us. And, our actions may cost the lives of many innocent crew members. Perhaps we should reconsider—"

"What the hell? It's either our hides or theirs. I've already changed my mind. I'm waking Fletcher. You can either join us or not, Taradanov, I really don't give a shit at this point."

Emelian thought of his wife and child, and closed his eyes for a moment, distressed and torn.

"Alright, alright, count me in on your plan. I'll go see what I can do on gathering some knives or guns, there were a few around Salmon House."

"That's the spirit. No need to worry, Taradanov, you have Sergei Popov on your side."

FIFTY-SEVEN

JONATHAN FLETCHER AGREED TO THE RISKY SCHEME hatched by Popov. Taradanov managed to slip stolen knives and Tlingit clothing to all three of them, although it took longer than expected. Only an hour before sunrise remained. The next task was to jump the two guards after Taradanov and his family appeared around the large rocks a hundred yards away in a canoe. After dispatching the guards and sinking their bodies into the ocean, the escape party would paddle behind *Otter* and *Grace* dressed as Tlingit men. They would then climb aboard *Eclipse* from the stern, while announcing they wished to hand over the "prisoners" Marpha and Alexei. Fletcher knew the odds of being identified by someone before they boarded were high, but it was a risk worth taking given the alternatives of slavery, humiliation, and possible death. He would be captain of his ship again.

The village slept, along with most of the ships' crews. Staring out at the vessels from beneath his wide brimmed Tlingit rain hat, Fletcher noticed only the standard, solitary crew member stood watch on board each of the three anchored ships. Good, Fletcher reasoned, the fewer pairs of eyes to possibly identify them, the better. The two Tlingit guards turned back in direction towards his small group, but were not looking at the American and Russian. Taradanov still did not emerge from behind the point.

Popov mumbled as the seconds seemed like minutes for the men.

"Cross my ass over the Styx. Come on, Taradanov. Where the fuck is he? That Aleutian bitch had better not have talked him out of our plan."

"Now would be a good time to take out those guards," Fletcher whispered.

Popov's eyes suddenly lit up.

"There, behind the point of that largest sea rock! It's Taradanov with his wife and child in the canoe."

Popov pulled his knife, and started to whisper in English until Fletcher interrupted in Russian.

"*Da vy!*"

"*Spaceba,* Jonathan, yes, 'let's go!'"

Within seconds the two men moved behind small saplings to flank the two Tlingit men, who had spotted Taradanov's canoe and were walking in its direction to investigate. Utilizing stealth, Popov approached one of the musket-toting guards after several moments, while Fletcher fell behind the other man. Holding their knives, Popov and Fletcher surprised the guards and cut their throats while holding the guards' mouths. Within a minute, the canoe arrived on shore and Emelian immediately assisted the other men in pulling the two corpses into the ocean after tying them with bags of rocks. With Marpha and Alexei seated in the middle of the small canoe, Emelian took the lead position. Popov and Fletcher, dressed in large, Tlingit woolen cloaks and rain hats to shield their faces, sat in the rear to paddle. Emelian wore a smaller Tlingit hat, as he would be the one looking up to speak in broken English while posing as a Chilkat man to the three ships' watches.

As the canoe rounded large rocks and approached the anchored *Otter* and *Grace* first, Marpha held Alexei close to her bosom. Their destinies hinged on what happened in these next few moments, and she silently said her prayers. As the weak, shady summer darkness of southern Alaska retreated around the canoe and the ships, Emelian looked once more to the towering Chilkat Mountains high above their narrow channel of ocean. Against a clear, cobalt blue sky, the sun's rays illuminated the very highest peaks and glaciers, and with the exception of Venus, all the other planets and stars had faded from view.

The armed sailor on watch aboard *Otter* shouted, "You there, state your business!"

Emelian mustered his best Kolosh accent to shout in English.

"We paddle to *Eclipse* to deliver two prisoners! Captain Micah declared gifts to our clan houses!"

"Very well then, I will convey the message to the other two vessels' watches!"

The *Otter* sailor strode over to his ship's port side to convey the message to *Grace*, who in turn shouted over to *Eclipse* dozens of yards away. As the canoe rounded past the stern of *Grace*, an icy northerly breeze blew up the narrow stretch of ocean between the mountains. Marpha looked briefly to the south, where she caught sight of what she believed was a faint cluster of grey-white sails behind the trees of a small island several miles distant.

Is that a ship?

Marpha could not stare long as the canoe now found itself a mere dozen yards from the stern of *Eclipse*. Fletcher and Popov immediately noted who was on watch— Alina and Ben Harper. Harper shouted down first.

"You state you have two prisoners to deliver for gifts distributed by the captain? Captain Triplett never mentioned such an arrangement to us."

Emelian, who had prepared for such a scenario, responded once again in his faked Kolosh accent.

"You must be mistaken. We simply wish to deliver this woman and child as promised. Great Bear Mother has ordered us, as this woman and child are also sickly and require rest."

Harper's expression grew more puzzled.

"Alina, keep watch here while I go fetch Mr. Hall. Tell them not to board until we return. Use that loaded musket of yours if needed."

Alina nodded, and proceeded to shout her newly learned English words to the canoe while firmly holding her musket.

"You there, show yourselves!"

Fletcher's grip upon his knife tightened. The plan agreed upon was to leap on to the ship in a direct frontal attack if they were discovered. Accordingly, Fletcher began to stand up in the canoe when, at the same moment, Popov jumped to his feet and threw off his hat.

"Alina! It's me, Sergei! We've escaped from the village and have come to stay now on the ship! Please, let us aboard, quickly now!"

Alina dropped her musket and cried out in joy, her passion overwhelming her reason as she climbed over the deck on to side netting to embrace her lover as Sergei also dropped his weapon in sheer exuberance.

"Bloody hell, Sergei, this wasn't the plan agreed upon you bastard! Now, out of my way! All of us have to take this ship or we're done for!" Fletcher demanded.

Alina gasped as Fletcher and Taradanov threw off their Tlingit hats and, wielding knives, lunged for the netting and began climbing. Fletcher screamed to his fellow attackers, "Come on now, forward, this is our moment!"

Sergei flew into action as he grabbed Alina's shoulder and pulled her on deck of *Eclipse*, while Fletcher rolled his body over the railing. Emelian reached out to help Marpha and young Alexei climb the ship's side netting. A shot rang out from *Grace*, striking the netting just inches from Alexei, who screamed and fell into the water. Emelian looked to see his son's eyes wide open in shock from the frigid water as he dove in after him. Marpha screamed in panic.

A loud, authoritative male voice shouted across the deck of *Eclipse*.

"Drop your weapons, now! Or we shoot!"

Fletcher spun around to see Joshua Hall, Alamea, Lavelle Clark, and Ben Harper all pointing muskets at the small band of attackers. Within seconds, Fletcher, Popov, and Alina set down their knives and placed their hands in the air. Nikolai Karaulov and his wife emerged from below deck to investigate, just as a loud splash broke over the side of the ship. Marpha dove into the sea to retrieve her son and husband.

"Help us, please!"

Emelian shouted in Russian as he desperately tried to lift Alexei up by the ship's netting. Hall sprinted over to the side and worked with Taradanov to lift the boy and Marpha from the ocean to the deck. Shaking with cold, Emelian climbed up the netting. Hall looked at Emelian, dumbfounded as he shook his head.

"Madness. This is all madness."

Hall turned to Fletcher, who was seated with the others under armed guard several yards away.

"For God's sakes, Jonathan, what were you all thinking?"

Fletcher shook his head and looked down, his two hands gripped together atop his head.

As Ben Harper escorted Emelian to the other prisoners, Hall shouted to Captain Evans aboard *Grace*.

"I thank you for your decisive action to protect our ship! We have disarmed the uninvited boarding party, which consists of Fletcher and some of the Russians. If you could send over a few men to assist us in securing *Eclipse*, it would be most appreciated."

"Certainly, Joshua," Captain Evans replied, "I'm just sorry our watch didn't detect them sooner. You probably didn't notice in the excitement over there, but two ships approach. You see those sails in the far distance? One's a brig, the other a small schooner. I just hope it's not *Panther* and *Icarus*. Probably is, though."

Hall peered through a small spyglass. His heart beat out of his chest.

"Yes, it's my brother. We need to warn the clans now, and fetch Captain Triplett and our crews from shore."

Joshua glanced at Alamea for a moment, his lips rolled inward. He looked through his spyglass again, whispering, "What do you want, Elias? What could you possibly want?"

FIFTY-EIGHT

GREAT BEAR MOTHER STOOD ON THE DECK OF *ECLIPSE*, accompanied by Thaddeus and Tom, several heavily armed Tlingit men, and the three captains and their officers who brought to bear additional firepower. The crews of *Grace* and *Otter* also held their weapons, with additional Tlingit fighters deployed on board at the request of the captains. Captain Elias Hall and his crew set *Panther* and *Icarus* at anchor several dozen yards away. All gathered could see the crew lining up thirteen Tlingit hostages on *Panther*'s deck, and it was clear some of the men had been seized in the straits, no doubt through deceit and lies. The hostages' hands and feet were tied as twelve *Panther* sailors stood guard with muskets. Another ten sailors manned small cannons on *Icarus*, ready to fire on order of Elias.

Great Bear Mother looked down in sadness and spoke softly. Thaddeus translated for Captain Triplett and the gathered officers.

"This is not good. All of the hostages are very high-ranking clan men, of houses holding totems of Great Bear Constellation, Raven's Bones, Drifted Ashore, and Sea Lion. Great Bear Mother requests your assistance, whatever that may entail. She will be grateful to all of you and can offer many rewards for a successful resolution. I might add a few of those hostages were originally taken at St. Michael, one of whom is Great Bear Mother's brother. Elias probably kidnapped the others from the Tlingit Auk and Huna kwaans to the south of us."

"Greetings, gentlemen." Elias shouted. "My apologies for interrupting the victory celebrations here at Chilkat, but I require one more business transaction before my crew heads out to sea."

Joshua responded first as he stood on the deck railings.

"Stop this madness, brother. Do you really understand what you're doing here? Let those men go and be on your way."

Elias remained still and grinned.

"Oh, I'm sorry, I can't accept that request. And mind your tone little brother, it's not conducive to good business. These men will be released once my payment is received, and as a guarantee of this pledge, I will agree to a simultaneous exchange of prisoners and merchandise aboard skiff boats. Now, my payment will consist of—"

Captain Evans shouted in a more diplomatic tone as he held out his arms.

"Elias, wait, listen to me. Our three vessels here are prepared to offer a substantial number of fur bales to you. The clan leaders here are also open to negotiations."

Elias's grin soon morphed into a frown as he folded his arms.

"You're wasting my valuable time. Here are my terms, and they are non-negotiable. I want all pelts in the village and aboard your vessels delivered to my ship, along with any Russian prisoners who wish to join my community. If the furs and the prisoners are not delivered within the hour, I sail out to sea and throw these Tlingit men overboard, where they will drown and have their souls taken by the Land Otter Men. Tell that to Great Bear Mother and the others aboard your ships. And Joshua, you will board *Panther* to travel with me."

"No!" Alamea screamed as she embraced Joshua. Kanoa started to cry, and Aolani took him below deck for the moment. Joshua did not hesitate in his response.

"No deal, Elias, not unless Alamea and Kanoa can join me."

"Very well, they can step on board *Panther* once all my demands are met."

"You're trapped in a mania, brother," Joshua shouted as he held Alamea, "it's not too late to tear it all down and walk away."

Elias ignored Joshua and shouted in Tlingit.

"Deliver my pelts and prisoners, or these men's souls are forever enslaved by the Land Otter Men!"

Several clan leaders and Great Bear Mother consulted with the officers on how to respond. Great Bear Mother spoke calmly. It was clear to the others her mind was made up.

"Captains, those men must be freed. If we cannot free them by force, our clans are prepared to pay the required ransom."

Hall asked the captains, "Well, gentlemen, any ideas? If we try to storm *Panther* and *Icarus* there will be certain bloodshed and death."

Captain Evans sighed and held his hands behind his neck.

"We can pay the ransom and then beat our way across the Pacific to intercept Elias and reclaim our stolen property. At the very least we can head back to Boston and file charges, although there's no guarantee Elias will return to New England anytime soon, if ever."

Triplett looked toward *Panther* and *Icarus* as loathing seethed through him.

"Elias is too clever for his own good, and his followers are fanatical. Unfortunately, I see no way out."

Emelian Taradanov watched the stark crisis unfold before him on the deck of *Eclipse*. Although he could not hear what was being said in the tight circle of the officers, Great Bear Mother, and the clan leadership, Emelian instinctively knew what was happening. He had been in many situations involving hostage exchanges on company hunting expeditions, and understood Elias Hall was demanding an outrageous ransom for the important clan men held on his ship. The Boston captains and the clan leaders likely realized they had no winning options, short of terrible violence and loss of life. Emelian turned to Marpha, Alina, and Sergei.

"This is our opportunity to win our freedom. Let me do the talking."

Before the other three could respond, Emelian whispered to the officers' group several yards away so as not to draw attention from Elias and his crew.

"Thaddeus, Joshua, a word with you please."

Thaddeus and Hall eased toward the prisoners, seating themselves a few feet from them, knowing full well that secrecy and deception commanded every move and word. Without making eye contact with Emelian and the others, Thaddeus whispered.

"Mr. Taradanov, you have an idea I can share with the officers?"

"Yes." Emelian answered in slow Russian. "Tell Mr. Joshua and the others that we, the company prisoners seated here, can be ransomed aboard *Panther*. We'll conceal weapons, including our women, who fight well. That Boston captain Elias will think us happy and never suspect our ambush against them. I will take him hostage. Sergei, Nikolai, Alina, and Marpha will kill or seize other *Panther* men as hostages. Tanya will stay on board *Eclipse*, she can't fight, I remember her from Mikhailovsky. After this, the Boston men and Koloshi will rush aboard to help. *Icarus* won't fire on *Panther* if their captain and other crew are alive."

Hall's eyes opened widely after Thaddeus' translation, but he soon was overcome with skepticism.

"Very risky, if you ask me. I will, however, pass this idea to the captains and clan leaders."

"Wait," Emelian demanded as his heart beat faster. "We want a guarantee of our freedom from Great Bear Mother and the other clan leaders, otherwise, no deal."

Joshua looked at the mountains as he replied.

"Of course, I should have realized."

Joshua and Thaddeus walked away while Marpha looked at Emelian with deep concern as Sergei's crazed expression returned. The stocky Russian periodically licked his lips in anticipation.

Marpha pleaded with her husband.

"This plan is too risky. Look at those ships. They have many well-armed sailors. I don't want Alexei to be an orphan."

Before Emelian could respond, Alina hastily interjected.

"Do you have a better plan, Marpha? The alternative's slavery, and a likely gruesome death sometime in the future. I'd rather die fighting with my beloved, Sergei Ivanovich."

Marpha bit her lower lip as she turned to look at Alexei, who was playing with a small canoe toy given to him by a Kolosh boy. She envied his blissful separation from the terrible crisis all around him. Marpha turned to her husband.

"All right, we shall risk everything for our freedom. I will fight with you."

FIFTY-NINE

G REAT BEAR MOTHER LISTENED INTENTLY AS Joshua Hall explained Emelian Taradanov's daring offer. All three captains agreed with Hall's assessment of the high risks, but offered support for the plan, including a pledge of armed intervention once the stealth attack went into motion. One man holding the Sea Lion totem pleaded with Great Bear Mother.

"Mother, you know these Russians and Aleuts cannot be trusted. What's to stop them from betraying us once they are on board *Panther*? The woman there, Alina, is a slave, who, along with that Russian, insulted and killed some of our kin."

"Your concern has been heard, but I have made my decision," Great Bear Mother replied.

She paused and motioned for Emelian to come to their gathering on deck. As Emelian approached and sat in silence, Great Bear Mother continued her answer to the entire group of clan leaders and captains.

"We will give this man and the other Russians their freedom if they defeat the wicked Boston child, Captain Elias, and secure the release of our clan kin."

Turning to Emelian, Great Bear Mother added, "I shall watch over your son, Alexei, and if you should betray us, I will raise him as my own child. Now, we plan and carry forward this action."

Rising to address Elias Hall a few dozen yards away, Great Bear Mother began the deception, using a defeated voice.

"We agree to your terms and will commence delivery of pelts and prisoners to your ship in skiff boats. We expect delivery of hostages to us at regular intervals."

Elias stood tall in confidence, arrogant in his reply.

"A wise decision, Great Bear Mother. Prepare the skiffs shortly and commence the exchanges. And, may I ask, what of the captains and their loads of pelt bales?"

Captain Triplett shouted with feigned resignation.

"We agree to the ransom. If you fail to release all of the men, however, there will be hell to pay."

Elias laughed smugly.

"No worries on that point, Micah, all the men will be released, as I will not be returning to this coast ever again once I demand and receive payment from Mr. Baranov at Kodiak for rescuing his people. With this, and the Canton goods purchased with the pelts, we will haul the goods my people and I need to build our beautiful vision of freedom in a place of our choosing."

Elias's crew members let out a cheer of approval.

"What you think is freedom is just greed, brother." Joshua countered in disgust.

Elias put on his Tlingit rain hat to shade his face.

"You will see, Joshua. You will see. I expect you on board within the next few minutes."

Chuckling at his victory, Elias shouted orders to some of his crew to lower skiff boats to receive the ransom. To ensure an orderly transfer of pelts, prisoners, and hostages, it was agreed three high-ranking Tlingit men would come aboard *Panther* while three *Panther* sailors would go aboard Captain Hamby's vessel *Otter*. Once transactions were completed, the men would be simultaneously returned.

As the plan went into motion, Nikolai, Emelian, Marpha, Sergei, and Alina hid multiple knives underneath their clothing while standing behind stacks of fur bales. Alamea watched Joshua and Thaddeus kneel to discuss tactics with the group. After a few moments, the Russian party entered separate skiffs and began rowing towards *Panther*.

Alamea spoke as she fought back tears.

"Please Joshua. We're so close to finally getting out of harm's way. I can't lose you now."

"I've already agreed. It's my brother, and a matter of honor. Captains Hamby and Evans have also pledged to fight should it become necessary, as have the Tlingit men who are going on board *Panther*. Taradanov's party has hidden enough knives to arm them as well."

She embraced Hall, her fear morphing into pride. Alamea's deep-set Polynesian eyes locked on Joshua, like one of her distant ancestors sighting a new island for the first time after a long voyage of exploration. Joshua sensed his spirit setting foot on a new glorious shore, and realized she truly loved him.

Closing his eyes for a few moments, Joshua shifted his thoughts back to his sister's home in New Hampshire, where he heard Grace and Margaret's laughter. The "Captain's Box" rested in his hands, unlocked and fully opened. Inside rested a small portrait sketch of Laura, Grace, and Margaret sitting together with Joshua, locks of hair from his sister and two nieces, along with various homemade woolen items for the cold latitudes. A sea turtle necklace carved from shell, once owned by the girls' father, rested atop a circular cross stitch sampler sewn by Grace and Margaret, their names in block letters at the top of the oval cloth beside *OCTOBER, 1801*. In the sampler's center, a ship in full sail glided over the ocean, surrounded by sea birds and whales. Moon cycles circled along the sampler's edges, while prominent constellations from both the northern and southern hemispheres filled the skies over the ship. Under the Great Dipper and North Star, a sailor held hands with his family.

> *Uncle Joshua*, Grace instructed, *always bring this box with you on your voyages. To keep memories of people you love and all that is curious and beautiful. Use your box for stories past and stories to come.*

Tears welled in Joshua's eyes. He knew in his heart Alamea and Kanoa stood beside him for all time in the Captain's Box.

SIXTY

Joshua boarded *Panther*, where he was promptly searched by crew members for weapons.

"Your brother's clean, cap." *Panther* sailor Seth Ayers proclaimed.

"Very well, Mr. Ayers. Keep your eyes locked on *Eclipse* as the others come aboard."

"Aye, sir."

With a smug grin, Elias fixed his manic, unblinking stare on Joshua.

"Father always favored you, Joshua. But he will no more when he learns you're with me."

Joshua spat on the deck.

"You love your insanity and the way it feels, don't you Elias?"

"Joshua, the son who followed the straight and narrow in this world of shadows and lies. Reason, tradition, faith." Elias hissed.

"That's the only oasis we have in this world, brother. Your imagined path out of it will only lead to a desert. To oblivion."

"Fuck you!"

Elias swung and hit Joshua with his fist. Joshua fell to the deck as Alamea screamed on board *Eclipse*. Joshua fought his instinct to hit back.

Alamea, Kanoa.

Joshua held his hands up and complied with the *Panther* crew as they dragged him to the main mast to sit.

Panther sailor Seth Ayers kept his eyes locked on *Eclipse* to watch for any suspicious activity. So far not much aroused concern, everything appeared to proceed as agreed upon by both sides. Fur bales were being delivered in large quantities to *Panther* and *Icarus*, and the captain was releasing one hostage for every seven to eight skiff boats full of pelts and Russian prisoners. A good, steady breeze blew in from the Chilkat Mountains, so there was ample wind to escape once the transactions were completed. Nothing seemed so unusual that he needed to sound the alarm. The three Tlingit men who boarded *Panther* were thoroughly searched and had no weapons, and the three *Panther* crew on *Otter* were treated well. The Russian-Aleut Creoles, nearly all women and children, seemed to be quite happy aboard *Panther*, eagerly anticipating their safe return to the Russian colony on Kodiak Island.

Only two skiffs of prisoners remained left to come aboard. Ayers noticed it was the two couples who had been behind fur bales with Joshua Hall. As the two skiffs tied up to the ship, the Aleutian woman and her Russian Creole husband climbed aboard and stated their names. Ayers glanced at them and they both grinned. Right behind them were a stout, muscular Russian and his Indian woman, smiling like all the other prisoners. Ayers briefly took his eyes off *Eclipse* when Sergei and Alina shouted out *Spaceba! Spaceba!*, waving in salute to the *Panther* crew.

Still, something didn't quite feel right for Ayers.

There should be another child here, yes, the small boy who had been with the Russian Creole man and his Aleutian wife. Why would this Emelian and Marpha be smiling if they were now separated from him, especially if the Indians had decided to keep the child? Well, better to error on the side of caution.

"Captain!" Ayers shouted. "Something's amiss, it may be nothing, but it needs to be checked out."

Elias walked over to Ayers in an arrogant strut.

"And what troubles you, Mr. Ayers?"

"It's the Russian prisoners, sir, none of the children brought on board appear to be the child of that Russian Creole man and his Aleut wife by the mast. Emelian and Marpha, if I remember. I am near certain of this, and yet they acted happy when they got on board."

"And how do you know this missing child belongs to them?"

"When we first arrived and demands were being made, I noticed the Aleut woman Marpha holding the boy and kissing him. The boy had to be hers, and he's not here, sir."

"Very well Mr. Ayers, a little extra caution never hurts. *Panther* men, search the Tlingit men once more, and take a look through some of those bales just brought on board!"

Two *Panther* crew members searched the three Tlingit men again and found no weapons, and moved to search the fur bales. The sailors still found no weapons. Elias nodded, put his right thumb and fingers under his chin and turned to look at the new Russian-American Company prisoners now under his authority. Three men, five women, and eight children sat beside each other on deck under the shadows cast by the stacks of fur bales taking shape in the center of the ship. Elias spoke in Russian to the men.

Kak vas zavoot?

"Sergei Popov."

"Nikolai Karaulov."

"Emelian Taradanov."

Elias stared directly into the men's eyes, remaining silent. After several moments the *Panther* captain nodded.

"Mr. Ayers, I appreciate your zealous attentions to important details. Please search these three Baranov men for weapons. Tompkins, Smith, come over here to assist Mr. Ayers."

Emelian knew the moment had arrived. Shouting "Mother!" in Russian, the agreed upon code word for attack, Emelian leapt towards Elias while pulling out a seven-inch blade from below his jacket. The two men fell to the ground, with Elias barely holding back Emelian's knife-wielding arm. As the two screamed in a life and death struggle, Sergei Popov fell upon Seth Ayers and stabbed the *Panther* sailor through the neck, killing him instantly. Popov ran and tackled Tompkins and Smith, stabbing both men wildly before they were able to pull out their own weapons. Nikolai, Marpha, and Alina drew out hidden knives and threw them to the three Tlingit men on board ship. Other Tlingit fighters climbed the netting from the sea. Musket fire exploded everywhere.

Within moments, several skiff boats from the nearby ships raced to *Panther* unopposed as *Panther* sailors rushed to subdue the attackers already on board. Marpha cut two of the Tlingit hostages free, Raven's Bones men, who ran to fight the remaining sailors on *Panther*. Seeing her husband, Emelian, almost overpowered by Elias, Marpha ran and managed to cut the *Panther* captain in the upper shoulder. Screaming in pain, Elias swung around and knocked Marpha to the deck. Emelian regained his footing and lunged with his knife at Elias, who at the last moment was able to evade the attack and tackle Emelian.

Popov dispatched Tompkins with a slash to the throat, only to be shot in the leg by Smith, who lay mortally wounded on the deck. Despite profuse bleeding from his leg, Popov crawled to reach an area where Alina pushed back the hysterical group of women and children to a safer corner on deck.

"Alina!"

Alina turned to see a *Panther* sailor running to finish off the struggling Popov with a knife. Alina screamed in panic. As Popov turned to confront his attacker in a last desperate defense, Alina threw a small knife end over end at blistering speed, lodging it in the sailor's left cheek. Popov, cursing in pain from his gunshot wound, twirled his body around to see Nikolai Karaulov kill the stricken sailor with a stab through the heart. Seeing her lover bleeding on deck, Alina raced over and pulled him closer to the area where the children lay huddled.

"Do not fire yet! Grab the skiffs and evacuate *Panther*!" Elias shouted to the *Icarus* crew after throwing Emelian aside for a moment.

Kekoa, Micah Triplett, and Ben Harper were the first sailors to climb over the railing on the deck of *Panther*. Right behind them was another group consisting of Captains Hamby and Evans, four sailors from *Otter*, and Jonathan Fletcher. Two final skiffs of sailors from *Grace* and *Eclipse* converged on *Panther* over the next several moments, along with two war canoes filled with Tlingit fighters. Elias realized *Panther* was on the verge of being overrun.

Emelian charged yet again, but Elias overpowered the Siberian, his knife just an inch from his opponent's throat.

"You fucking half-breed! I'm gonna cut you open now!"

Joshua Hall barreled in between the two men, knocking Elias off Emelian and tackling his brother near the mainsail mast. Joshua and Elias traded punches in adrenaline-fueled fury, but within seconds Elias managed to throw Joshua off balance. His back slammed against the mast, Joshua lost his breath and fell, stunned.

Elias grabbed his sidearm as blood and saliva fell from his lips.

"Damn you Joshua! You leave me with no option!"

Enraged, Jonathan Fletcher ran towards Elias as he raised his weapon at Joshua and pulled the trigger.

Fletcher gasped as blood stained his blue linen shirt, hit in the chest by Elias's shot, a few feet in front of Joshua. Fletcher fell against Elias.

Regaining his balance, but limping, Elias struggled for a few paces and crawled into a skiff from *Icarus*.

"Lay down fire on *Panther*, now!" Elias bellowed between panted breaths to the *Icarus* crew.

A female sailor from *Icarus* screamed, "But sir, some of our crew remains on *Panther*!"

"Follow my order bitch!"

For several tortuous seconds a thunderous fury of musket and small cannon fire consumed the air above *Panther*. Joshua, Emelian, and the others had no choice but to take cover. More seconds passed, and Joshua peered from behind *Panther's* cracked main mast through the smoky haze. A bloodied Elias crawled on board *Icarus* with the help of two teenage sailors.

"Fuck you, Elias." Joshua whispered to himself. He grabbed a musket and took aim at his brother on *Icarus* a few dozen yards away. Tears streamed from Joshua's bloodshot eyes. The sails of *Icarus* unfurled, catching the steady wind. Joshua loaded his musket. He had a clear line of sight on Elias.

Take it! Take the shot goddamnit!

Joshua gasped and dropped the musket without firing. He lay on his back, his right forearm over his eyes.

"Please, God, please." Joshua whispered between heavy breaths.

The combat ended seconds after *Icarus* departed out of firing range. The surviving *Panther* sailors held their arms up, their weapons seized as they surveyed the bodies of their fallen crew members. Joshua slowly regained his breath and staggered to Jonathan Fletcher, followed by Micah Triplett, who pulled off his shirt to hold pressure on Fletcher's wound. Hall knew Fletcher's wound was mortal, as the former *Eclipse* captain coughed up blood and seemed to accept his fate. Looking at Hall and Triplett with repentance, Fletcher spoke in a weak whisper between fading breaths.

"My shipwrecked soul. Please forgive . . ."

Fletcher coughed again, spitting up blood as he strained to utter words to Triplett, Hall, Nikolai, Emelian, and a middle-aged Tlingit man who joined the small group and acknowledged Fletcher's bravery in combat. Triplett noticed with alarm the man's hand tattoos and symbols on his battle dress, indicating his Raven's Bones totem crest. To Triplett's relief, Thaddeus soon joined the group.

"This crew, these people, they were my family, but I lost sight, I, I forgot . . . I let the light go out from myself," Fletcher continued.

Tears welled in Fletcher's eyes as the Raven's Bones man knelt beside him and spoke in Tlingit, with Thaddeus translating.

"Captain Jonathan Fletcher, you helped save my sons, held here on this ship by the wicked captain. Your name will live on in honored atonement within the Houses of Raven's Bones."

Fletcher nodded slightly in acknowledgement before looking at Hall. "Captain Joshua Hall . . ." Fletcher whispered.

Jonathan Fletcher took his last breath and lay motionless on the deck of *Panther*. Alamea climbed aboard from a late-arriving skiff, with Kanoa remaining on board *Eclipse* with Tanya. Alamea rushed to embrace Joshua, and after several moments she knelt beside Fletcher's body. The crowd dispersed about the ship and nearby skiffs, and she quietly bid farewell to her former lover.

"The tempest has moved on, there are no more breaking waves. Moana offers a peaceful shore with her gentle tide. Farewell, Jonathan."

A RAVEN FLEW OVER A CALM, LATE afternoon scene as dozens of mourners gathered around Jonathan Fletcher's cleaned body for burial in the ocean, sewn inside bright sails white like the clouds passing overhead. After a prolonged moment of silence, Micah Triplett and Joshua Hall looked at each other and nodded. Instinctively, Joshua closed his eyes and commenced, from memory, a solemn recitation of part of *Psalm 107*, the sailor's prayer.

> *O give thanks unto the Lord, for he is good: for his mercy endureth forever. Let the redeemed of the Lord say so, whom he hath redeemed from the hand of the enemy. And gathered them out of the lands, from the east, and from the west, from the north, and from the south.*
>
> *They that go down to the sea in ships, that do business in great waters. These see the works of the Lord, and his wonders in the deep. For he commandeth, and raiseth the stormy wind, which lifteth up the waves thereof. They mount up to the heaven, they go down again to the depths: their soul is melted because of trouble. They reel to and fro, and stagger like a drunken man, and are at their wit's end. Then they cry unto the Lord in their trouble, and he bringeth them out of their distresses. He maketh the storm a calm, so that the waves thereof are still. Then are they glad because they be quiet; so he bringeth them unto their desired haven. Amen.*

SIXTY-ONE

THE BEACH SEEMED ALIVE, BUSTLING WITH SAILORS loading skiffs with pelt bales, food, and fresh water for the four ships anchored near the village. The clan leaders and Great Bear Mother honored their agreements and made final arrangements with the captains. Russian-American Company captives, including Emelian, Marpha, and Alexei Taradanov, would be released to Captain Hamby, whose sailors would transport them aboard *Otter* to Kodiak, while some of Hamby's other sailors and the *Jenny* men would repair and deliver *Panther* to O'ahu as a gift to the Hawaiian Kingdom, in appreciation of King Kamehameha's friendship. As for the surviving *Panther* sailors, they were to become slaves of the clans. Expecting the arrival of another Perkins Company vessel at O'ahu sometime in the next several weeks, Joshua Hall, Alamea, Kanoa, Kekoa, Thaddeus, Nikolai, Tanya as well as Sergei and Alina would join Captain Evans on board *Grace* and sail to O'ahu. There they would wait for *Eclipse* to arrive under Captain Triplett. *Eclipse* would transport various clan members back to their home villages and collect more pelts before heading south to rendezvous at O'ahu with First Mate Hall and the others. Aolani, David Woods, Ben Harper, and Lavelle Clark would all remain on board *Eclipse*, except for Tom.

"Here is where I belong, at least for now," Tom told the *Eclipse* crew. "I need to regain my strength, to receive counsel from my clan brothers and sisters. I also promised to teach Mother of the world as she requested."

After he exchanged emotional farewells with each *Eclipse* crew member, Tom hesitated before addressing Hall and Triplett.

"Inform Mr. Perkins of my sincerest gratitude. It's been a privilege serving under your command, sirs."

Standing beside Hall and Triplett, Thaddeus implored Tom to reconsider.

"You can still change your mind cousin! Come with us, there's still a lot of the world out there we haven't seen, so many books to read, cities to tour, people to meet. And women, think of all the women the world has to offer, my Sea Lion cousin!"

Triplett, Thaddeus, and Hall chuckled, along with Tom. Hall, however, noticed Tom struggling to respond to Thaddeus's points, as it was obvious the young man was torn over his decision not to remain with his cousin at sea. Hall offered a way out.

"Perhaps we'll see you again sometime, Tom. You're always welcome in O'ahu and Boston, my friend."

With tears flowing down his face, Tom seized upon Hall's remark.

"Thank you, sir. And of course, you will always be an honored guest among us whenever you visit again. You'll always remain in our clan stories, as will the rest of the *Eclipse* crew."

ONE BY ONE, THE FOUR SHIPS weighed anchor and unfurled their sails. Great Bear Mother and the entire village stood along the rocky beach, singing ancient songs of joy and victory to the rhythmic cadence of their drums. White eagle feathers were tossed into the sea by the villagers as the ships began catching the icy winds, their decks lined with sailors and passengers of every kind, Russian, Aleutian, Kodiak, Tlingit, Hawaiian, and American, all shouting and raising their hats and hands in salutations of gratitude. The sights and sounds drifted over the white sails and totem poles, past the waterfalls and glaciers astride the mountain peaks, to join the great horizons stretching ever onward.

EPILOGUE

North Pacific Ocean, July 1802

Kanoa ran along the deck of *Grace*, pointing and laughing at an albatross soaring beside the last faint reddish hue of the departed sun. Soft violin music from a sailor seated beside the aft mast drifted across deck with warm Pacific trade winds. Enjoying tea with Joshua Hall and Alamea at the stern of the ship, Captain Caleb Evans watched the boy.

"That little one of yours over there is quite the feisty one. He hasn't let up playing with the crew since we departed the coast over two weeks ago. Perhaps he'll take some time to rest on the O'ahu beaches once we arrive in a few days."

"Highly doubtful," Hall laughed softly. "And I can assure you, I'll be the one sleeping on the beach."

Evans laughed loudly.

"I'll be the first to join you, Joshua! Well, I'm going below. You two enjoy yourselves up here. Mr. Weddell is quite the musician. Good evening."

Alamea smiled and spoke softly.

"Good evening, captain, *aloha*."

Joshua and Alamea walked, arms around each other, to the far railing at the stern of the ship. The warm winds, violin music, and sounds of the ship's wake weaved together an almost hypnotic ambiance. Holding his

Eclipse log, Joshua marveled at skies of limitless planets and stars before his eyes fixated on the northern horizon.

"The voyage of *Eclipse* was much like an actual eclipse in a human dimension, wouldn't you say? We were like a little wooden moon moving past a burning sun of human passions."

Alamea embraced Joshua tightly as she rested her head on his shoulder. "Yes."

Hall held her with both arms.

"Before us now are your splendid isles, and beyond them are Canton, London, Boston, great and glorious."

Kanoa brushed up against Joshua and Alamea, grabbing their legs and jumping up and down several times before laughing and running back to greet Thaddeus near the bow.

"Our little *punahele*." Alamea smiled as her black hair hovered in the wind.

"*Punahele*?"

"Our favorite, Joshua, our sacred boy."

Kanoa squealed with delight as Thaddeus presented him with a cedar wood toy box painted in black, red, and yellow with carved lined images of Raven and Wolf. Thaddeus, beaming with pride over his hand-crafted gift, spoke to Kanoa in Tlingit.

"Kanoa, this is your Sailor's Box. Use its space to keep all you love close to your heart, for stories past and stories to come."

HALL GAZED UPWARD, POINTING TO THE BIG DIPPER as he felt his sister's letter in a shirt pocket beside his heart.

"The Great Bear Constellation and North Star, forever shining above a faraway coast. A magnificent realm of nature those islands and straits, a land that embraced us in all our fears and dreams, willing us on to destinies we never thought possible."

"Like her children," Alamea replied with wonder in her expressive brown eyes, "just like her children, Joshua."

AUTHOR'S AFTERWORD

VOYAGE OF THE ECLIPSE IS A WORK OF FICTION, but the novel draws inspiration from actual historical figures and events during the turn of the nineteenth century. The 1790s and 1800s represented an apex of a vast maritime fur trade network that stretched across Alaska, Hawai'i, the Juan Fernandez Islands, China, Russia, Great Britain, and the New England states of the young American Republic. In the decades following Captain James Cook's 1778 voyage of exploration to the North Pacific for the British Royal Navy, private merchant vessels sailed to southeast Alaska and British Columbia in search of fur pelts, especially those of the North Pacific Sea Otter. Possessing the thickest and most luxurious fur in the world, these animals' pelts were literally worth their weight in gold to the maritime traders due to insatiable fur demand in China and Europe. Pelts would be traded at Canton, China, for large volumes of fine porcelains, teas, silks, spices and other luxuries to be hauled back and sold in England and the United States. Profits were immense for successful voyages, in some cases exceeding the original investment several hundred times over. The wealth produced by the maritime fur trade revitalized Boston and brought desperately needed revenues to a young country still shaking off debts from the Revolutionary War era. A historical figure mentioned in the novel is Thomas Perkins, who along with his brother, John, ran one of the most successful merchant houses in Boston. Most of the ships' crews hired by investors were young, in their teens and early twenties, including officers.

The maritime fur trade also led to an increasing American presence in the Hawaiian Islands, a convenient location for layovers, supplies, and recruiting additional sailors. Before the arrival of American missionaries in Hawai'i in the 1820s, the common people celebrated and practiced sexuality openly without much reservation. Additionally, the social and political dynamics of the islands were in flux as King Kamehameha I consolidated his power in the archipelago. Many Hawaiians recruited to work on American and British ships sailed all over the world.

Ferocious competition in the North Pacific fur trade was commonplace, and included the eastward-moving Russians, who subjugated the native Unangan people of the Aleutian Islands and the Alutiiq people of Kodiak Island with armed force and aggressive diplomacy during the middle and late 18th century. In 1799 the Russians consolidated their fur business into one administrative and economic monopoly, the Russian-American Company (RAC), managed by the historical figures Alexander Baranov and Ivan Kuskov. During the same year the RAC established a small colony on Sitka Island called Fort St. Michael, a few miles north of present-day Sitka, with permission from local Tlingits. The Tlingits realized they could make inflationary demands for each pelt they traded to American and British ships by having the Russians as local trading partners. However, poor quality trade goods and aberrant behavior by many RAC employees towards the clans rapidly wore out the company's welcome in the Tlingit homeland.

Iron and steel weapons, muskets, and small cannons traded by the English speakers made Tlingit clans militarily formidable and more than a match for the RAC. The RAC soon learned the old pattern of conquest practiced in the Aleutians and on Kodiak Island would not work in southeast Alaska with the "Koloshi," the name used by the RAC for the Tlingit and Haida people. The June, 1802, destruction of Fort St. Michael depicted in the novel is an actual historical event. It is unclear to scholars exactly how many Tlingit clans participated in the onslaught, but the attack was devastating and the Russians did not return to colonize Sitka Island until over two years later. Some documents suggest the involvement of American sailors in the attack on the side of the clans.

The Tlingits of this era were divided into clans that could be either friendly or hostile to one another depending on circumstances. Kin groups within clans, known as "Houses," identified themselves with totemic crests often consisting of variations of animals, landmarks, or constellations. A person's family lineage was determined through the mother's ancestors, and loyalty to one's kin was paramount. If a kin member's honor was insulted, or worse, immediate restitution was required. Northwest Coast

Native American societies were highly stratified, divided among clan elites, commoners, and slaves. Slaves—usually prisoners of war and their descendants—made up about one third of Tlingit society and could be killed by their owners in certain ceremonies. Some slaves were captured in distant locations such as Vancouver Island and Puget Sound, making escape virtually impossible.

As depicted by the fictional characters Tom and Thaddeus, a few clans permitted a small number of their sons to travel on American ships to New England to learn English and various business and maritime skills. These individuals would act as cultural brokers, moving between different languages and societies.

The North Pacific region in the late 18th and early 19th centuries witnessed a fluid, energetic, and sometimes tragic mixing of vastly different cultures. It was a world where young sailors carried restless ambitions and passions across great oceans to encounter ancient, socially complex societies.

ACKNOWLEDGEMENTS

MANY THANKS TO LITERARY AGENTS Mel Stinnett and Jeff Ourvan for reading early versions of this novel and providing vital editorial advice. My thanks also go out to Ray Hudson, Mary Sagal, and Sandra Hamby for their valuable editorial feedback. They all made Voyage of the Eclipse a much better story.

Although my work with them long predates the writing of this book, I would like to acknowledge my Ph.D. dissertation committee at the University of New Mexico, Margaret Connell-Szasz (chair), Rob Robbins, Joyce Szabo, and the late Ferenc Szasz, who helped guide me through my first Alaska history adventure in the late 1990s. I also thank the late Walter Soboleff, who at that time shared with me his insights on Tlingit-Russian relations. Finally, thank you to my family for their steadfast support through the long, epic voyage to publication, and to Epicenter Press.

Erik T. Hirschmann is a Professor of History at Matanuska-Susitna College, University of Alaska Anchorage, where he has taught since 2003. He holds a Ph.D. in American and U.S. West History from the University of New Mexico. Born in San Francisco, Erik grew up backpacking in the mountains of northern California and sailing on San Francisco Bay.